Don Both - MINE
Mine / Part 1
Author: Don Both
Tristan Wrangler Series... Series
©2018 Don Both.
All rights reserved!
Contact: https://www.facebook.com/DonBothAuthor/
bethy86@Hotmail.de
Cover: Babette H.
German editing: Belle Molina, Sophie Candice
German proofreading: Emma Mack, Carolin Jache
Other contributors: Babette H.
English editing, proofreading, translation:
buchuebersetzer.webs.com
Published by
A.P.P.-Publishing-House
Branch Germany
Peter Neuhäußer
Gemeindegässle 05
89150 Lachingen
ISBN epub: 978-3-96115-338-1
ISBN mobi: 978-3-96115-339-8
ISBN print: 978-3-96115-340-4

DON BOTH

MINE

Part 1

Synopsis:

Tristan Wrangler, a provocative, upscale sex club owner and stone-cold businessman who does not believe in love let alone fate. His behavior doesn't even change when Mia Angel stumbles into his life — for the second time. The past the two share changed Tristan into the dark man he is today.

Guided by absolute devotion and love for him, the young woman agrees to play a dangerous game. The new Tristan wants to break her like he was broken eight years ago when she destroyed his life.

Now, for three months, each has time to execute their plan.

His mind says, 'Slut' — his heart, 'Baby'.
Her mind says, 'Run!' — her heart, 'Fight!'
Which will prevail?

1. Emptiness

Tristan 'Sexy' Wrangler

The curvy contour of the pale back could be clearly seen through the leaping red flames. The latter cast dancing shadows onto the feminine curvaceous body, which, not without reason, had been immortalized in statues and numerous drawings since time immemorial. The splayed fingers brushing up the back of the thigh were so long they almost wrapped around the entire leg.

Slightly tormented, I closed my eyes.

The poor man in the photos, which I was currently looking at, had once been me. It was a man who would have killed for her and loved her more than life itself. A lost idiot.

Recalling her fragrant flawless skin under my hands and lips, a pained moan escaped my throat. I leaned on the table with my elbows and rested my head against my fists as I stared gloomily at the photo on my laptop.

Why did I continuously torment myself by staring every day at painful images from the past? As if it wasn't enough I couldn't forget how it felt touching her body, I had to remind myself of what I had lost forever through pictures!

Humorlessly, I laughed out loud. Why was I doing this to myself? I was actually asking.

Because I was just as addicted to the damn slut as eight years ago, she still captivated me even if only in pictures.

It was that fucking simple!

To be blunt; it didn't *seem* like an addiction, I *was* addicted. Full-blown. Back in the early days, I generally craved pussy —although it still rang true today, unfortunately, it was limited to a specific one.

And it was that one that bid farewell to my life as soon as she laughed maliciously and shoved me into the deep abyss from which I'd not crawled out of to this day.

I couldn't — didn't even want to. The darkness was exactly where I felt at home. It was a place of serenity and seclusion no other would willingly venture. All strive to walk in the light, but, reality was basically only darkness. It required luck to find a light source and if things fared well and it decided to stay, you could actually exist in the light. Well, the person I considered my sun had left me — but I already established that.

Slowly, I clicked the left mouse button and closed the picture from happier times.

As I pushed my big executive office chair back and stood up, I wondered for the thousandth time how Turkey had screwed me — Tristan Wrangler, the most popular, most feared fucker ever... Actually, it used to be me who did the dishing out, at least, since my mother took it upon herself to take her life and destroy the lives of my entire family. At the time, I had been 7-years-old, and ever since then, there was only my father and two brothers.

S*he* – Turkey – had managed to gradually pull me out of the darkness to show me the meaning behind all the fuss and brouhaha, only to ruin everything again.

It was like setting up dominos; you spend hours working on your knees to create something beautiful and unique and then, with a grin of satisfaction and a slight push of a finger, all tiles fall in on themselves.

What the hell was the purpose?

Why did she do that to me?

Exhaling deeply, I lit a joint I had recently removed from a small black box that was actually meant for cigarettes. The glass coffee table top rested upon a dark marble, meticulous copy of a female body on all fours. When I accidentally stumbled across it, I immediately bought it. The table allowed me to spread out lines on the back of a naked helpless woman without getting my ears yapped full. Perfect!

I strolled across the room and stopped next to my desk.

After I took a long soothing drag and blew smoke rings at the plate-glass that granted me a view of my empire, I felt a teeny-weeny bit better.

Not that I had ever been satisfied...in recent years.

The special emotion did not diminish, not even when I glanced out over my club that was bathed in red pulsating lights, making the entire place seem wicked. The unclothed bodies of the dancers jiggling their silicone tits in cages in every corner were seductively moving to the deep rich bass and captivating rhythms the expensive DJ was playing. The tables bordering the dance floor were occupied; some were lying or sitting naked on the comfortably padded benches giving in to their passions. Others settled for using the nude female and male staff — to blow or lick them or just fondle and fumble around a bit.

Yes, I owned an exclusive sex club. First, hygiene was emphasized and, second, not every washed-up ass received admission to just quickly hide the pickle. Granted, we did not equal Hamburg's red-light district, but I had paid thousands of dollars to have a waterfall installed on the right side of the room that ended in a large pool. Initially, it took another small fortune to keep the club open every day. Members joined for the meager annual fee of 15000 euros. Obviously, it included a confidentiality agreement because whatever happened here could not become public knowledge. In exchange, clients were allowed to completely succumb to the world of pleasure and live out whatever sick fantasies their perverted minds could create.

My club was a hit!

To ensure a boozy and profit-yielding night, the main attraction was a huge round bar with an elevated center floor. The drinks were as expensive as the ambiance; then again, the service staff was completely naked nymphs and gods.

I had two prostitutes and two male escorts permanently on staff. The rest were hired from an *escort agency* depending on need. Unlike many dives, my club offered style and class; both men *and women* were absolutely getting what they paid for.

Touching, blowing, and licking were part of the service just like wiping tables.

Anything more than that, which took place in the basement, required extra remuneration.

My subjects – who were all official sex addicts – I provided room and board. They lived on the top floor, which was where I also kept my office. The majority, more or less, joined on a voluntarily base and were committed for as long as I deemed fit. But until such time, they had to follow strict rules. Besides keeping a clean flawless appearance, as well as the obligatory full-body shave, certain fluency and intelligence played a role – nothing was more tiresome than explaining something three times to a lame brain – as well as a totally twisted personality.

Such qualifications were needed to work here.

Especially as a pain slave.

I had nothing to do with S&M scene in the old-fashioned sense; I lived humiliation and dominance on my own terms.

I had no rules to follow other than my own.

Two professionals, Lena and Garrett, were in charge of

S&M requests. They were specialists when it came to anything involving dominance and submission. Lena used to be a pain slave for the Russian mafia boss from whom I bought for a high price, but she simply was a perfectionist in what she did. Garrett, on the other hand, was acquired from a gay German politician who kept him in his basement. Since then, they have been loyal because they insisted – for whatever reason – I had saved their lives.

Then there were Mary and Georgi. She was a former mistress of an English earl, whom I won in a poker game – a sweet little blonde elf with an absolutely kinky character. Georgi, a native Russian, who had escaped from a Siberian prison to come to Germany to make a home for his wife and two children, was the remaining fourth person. Okay, he was no longer together with his wife because she divorced him after their first year here to marry an oligarch.

So much for *'til death do us part*.

Mary and Georgi were responsible for straight sex. Their last names were unknown to me, which was irrelevant in the sex industry anyway. Nobody cared about who was who or why they ended up stranded here. And many, by the way, didn't find it all that bad.

Well, whatever.

It was because of her that I strayed from the proper path society had planned for me and made money through prostitution and drug trafficking. On a side note, *she* was also to blame for me having to give up my boxing career, as well as not studying sports as planned. *Because of her,* I landed in prison and made the unpleasant acquaintance with real life.

Yes, she was responsible for everything that had happened and had done it intentionally! I was now convinced of that.

I had considered various reasons to explain her behavior, I even tried to continue believing in her love and even entertained the idea that her father, Harald Angel, had somehow messed with us by manipulating her

However, she didn't even visit me one fucking time to, perhaps, fall to her knees and beg for forgiveness! She didn't even write one *single* damn letter in all those years. And, at the hearing, she dropped the bomb.

She did not even glance, not once, at me, as if our hours-long fucking sprees all over my sanctuary and other places had never taken place... *No*...I had felt the cold the little bitch exuded. The entire time before her testimony, I did not give up hope — what an idiot. There still was time for her to come clean and perhaps save me from imprisonment — after all, she was the key witness.

Stupidly, she did not. Instead, she told one lie after another softly with her head bowed. Every damn word cut deeper into my heart, fueling my hatred for her.

Once she finished, she still did not look at me.

That was the last time I saw or heard from her, which was best — for her.

After all, given her testimony, one thing was crystal clear, she did not – ever – love me. All her sweet-talk was nothing but lies. *Tristan, I love you* — yeah, sure, hypocrite. *You are my life* — right! *Fuck me deep* — show me your innermost being so I can turn it outward and smash it!

For her sake, I did not try to find her; actually, I talked myself out of it every day, anew, because it would not have ended well for her if I had found her — which I would have in any case. Besides, I reluctantly promised Vivian Müller, my older brother's girlfriend and her former tit sister, that I would not look her up when I was in that murderous state, which I have been in for years now.

However, part of me also hoped for fate to accidentally herd her into my arms...because then...even Vivi could no longer help her.

I was lost and only she was capable of saving me. But not in the usual schmaltzy sense — it had nothing to do with damn romance. Anything that could free me from all the resentment and hatred would be my revenge on her.

Impatiently, I longed to get my hands on her...to fuck her... humiliate her...and then...completely destroy her.

Exactly in that order.

Oh, yes, love-hate relationships existed, but in my case, love no longer existed, hate dominated everything.

Mercy from the fucker in the sky if our paths ever happened to cross again.

That would be when Mia Angel had regret...like I did every minute — every damn second!

2. His Voice

Mia 'Poor' Angel

Green-brown, ice-cold diamonds glared at me. Eyes that were supposed to look at me full of love, yet instead, seemed to want to eat me alive. Eyes that once gazed at me quite passionately now flashed unbridled hatred. As so often before, I was once again trapped in the memories of the worst day of my life. The day where I betrayed and lost my true love.

Could a bad conscience make a person sick? Yes! It had to because I couldn't think of another explanation for my desolate state.

Thursday morning, I felt anything but good when I carefully slid out of bed so as not to wake up my boyfriend Francesco and tiptoed barefoot over the bleached parquet to the adjoining bathroom. I was still tired, but more depressed as was customary after a restless night of tossing and turning.

Showered. Washed hair. Brushed teeth. Dressed. Blow-dried hair. It didn't take but 20 minutes to get ready for I made it a habit to get up early enough so there was plenty of time for my morning routine. However, terrible exhaustion, my constant companion, made it hard to get out of bed even close to on time.

Finished, I looked in the mirror one final time. The rings under my dull brown eyes were the most obvious indicators that I had a health issue. Then again, it was not surprising considering I averaged maybe four hours of sleep thanks to my rest-robbing nightmares. Each night, the same agonizing memory woke me as tears ran down my cheeks.

I lay on some road in the town I grew up in, crying because I know he is gone. I wear a black hooded sweatshirt that smells of him...and then, die. On the inside. Outwardly, I am completely fine — all limbs seem intact.

Nevertheless, if you couldn't feel, you were basically already half dead. Still, there was no choice since, what seemed like an eternity ago, I had forbidden myself to show any emotions; otherwise, the pain that relentlessly raged inside might have caused my demise long ago. Now it seemed like my feelings were stuck in a bubble — even if I was happy, sad, or laughed, I only felt a smidgen of what I should have felt.

Once – a long time ago – it was different.

He had brought me to life, made me experience the most intense, most beautiful feelings, but now everything was...a mere shadow, which seemed increasingly more unrealistic the more I dwelled on it.

Who knew what would have happened to me if I hadn't had my job to keep me sane after Patrick, my uncle, had taken *charge of me* at the age of seventeen. Life with him hadn't been a lick better than *living* with my sadistic father and slob of a mother. At my uncle's, I had to cook and clean the house, just like I did at my parents. The only good thing, he wasn't a hoarder, although he was a passionate hunter.

Apart from his official job as a postman, he was also a drug mule, so he simply performed his job while raking in extra money. Of course, that didn't keep his *clients* from sitting in our living room every night, taking all kinds of shit orally or intravenously. Guess who had to clean the vomit from the toilet...certainly not Patrick.

But I did not complain for it was fair punishment for what I had done. Besides, his drug money financed my studies to become a social worker.

For as long as I could remember, I had always wanted to help people who had grown up in similar or even worse conditions than I had — be it due to a lack of money or mental illness.

I wanted to comfort people who felt alone, hurt, and humiliated. That was the reason I chose that specialty field.

When I was in my third semester, Francesco showed up at Patrick's, but he never took drugs and mainly sat there silently observing. He was calm, seemed rational, and always smiled encouragingly at me as I tended to my uncle and his friends. One day, when a *client* got handsy, he came to my rescue. Most likely, I would have been raped, but Francesco protected me.

It was strange to be defended because the relevant hero had been torn from my life.

So, it had been more out of gratitude that I acknowledged his restrained flirting. We got along quite well, although I could not fathom what such a well-mannered, wealthy man was doing in this milieu. He was Italian, a banker, from a wealthy and strict family, but he was always friendly and uncomplicated...basically, offering exactly what I needed. Nevertheless, he wasn't *exactly who I longed for* because that privilege belonged to someone — out of reach...

Francesco was simply no match for him; no one was — because only the ONE knew my innermost secrets. No one loved me with such devotion as he did nor was anyone as incredibly beautiful and appealing.

Nevertheless, Francesco also had his advantages. He was tall and quite strong — very much so. Maybe he wasn't even human, but a machine disguised in a Calvin Klein suit that drove – naturally – a bright-red Ferrari.

He kept his black hair stubble-length and had dark brown eyes. Apart from the massive muscles he schlepped around and his obsession with himself, he was absolutely average. Nevertheless, he provided me with a very special advantage. By his side, I felt protected and I needed that feeling of security in order to function reasonably at work.

Therefore, I entered into a relationship with him, albeit, not a normal one.

In fact, I was with him purely out of self-interest — being half-dead as previously mentioned. Thus, I merely used the practical part of my brain to cope somehow with life.

But, I should not have been so outgoing with Francesco because now he had finally reached the end of his patience and tried to get into my panties or, better said, into my self-applied chastity belt. Now, we had been seeing each other for over two years…and I was still unable to take the next step with him. Honestly, it was incomprehensible, even to me, for now I was 26 and the last time I had sex I was seventeen!

Nevertheless, my body was a temple that worshiped only one god, one who made me feel acceptably sacred. I could not bring myself to be intimate with someone else. When a hand touched me that wasn't his, it simply felt so odd and wrong that I started sweating, panicking, my stomach churned, and I became violently ill.

I sympathized with Stan from *South Park* because the one time I tried to prove myself, I suffered tremendously when Francesco undressed me. By the time his lips approached my genital area, I was unable to stop the nausea that rolled over me and emptied my stomach contents all over…well… Since then, Francesco and I have never tried it again and I presume he will no longer come near me. Perhaps now he no longer wants to go down on any woman, period, because the incident was quite traumatic for him.

In short, *Tristan Wrangler* spoiled me for all other males by branding me with his oh-so-personal style.

My body would only respond to that one.

Forever.

***

Once again, I spent all morning thinking about *him*.

Running late, at a quarter to seven, I headed toward the children's home where I had started working six months ago. Since I had completed my studies with top grades, during which I also completed my internship, I was guaranteed permanent employment as soon as I obtained my master's degree.

My place of work – a converted farmhouse located next to a stream a few blocks walking distance from my two-room apartment – was perfect. First, because I enjoyed running water and the noise they make...

And second, I was making money while at the same time fulfilling a dream — at least parts of it. Interacting with little ones provided me with satisfaction. And, I didn't mean conducting obligatory conversations, but when I devoted myself to a child that looked the loneliest, wrapped them in a blanket, and sat them on my lap as I told a story I spontaneously made up. I wanted the little ones to feel the warmth and closeness of another body, something those young lives had little experience with. And, if not me, who else would do it?

Then there were moments where I painted with my charges and they captured their own worlds with – colorful – cheerful – *happy* strokes! Or those moments when we frolicked in the huge garden, squirting each other with water guns, whereupon Sister Carmen, the nun who ran the children's home, reprimanded me because some of the children came down the common cold the next day.

Nevertheless or perhaps because of that, my protégés worshiped me. They were able to act like kids around me and I became one again when I was allowed to spend time with them. During those moments, my laughter almost sounded real, not empty and hollow.

I loved my job, then again, I had worked hard be able to stand here and do what fulfilled me. All that time, I had been driven by one thought, namely, that *he* would have wanted me to make the most out of my life, assuming, of course, he didn't hate me. Now, I was convinced that was the way he felt.

Mostly, I ignored the fact that he must despise me. I presumed he still wished my ruination — his last sentence to me certainly left no doubt about it. Nevertheless, as soon as he appeared in my mind, all I felt was love.

No anger, fear, or hatred. In this respect, I felt like a child for its mother. Little ones are impartial, their universe pure and they unconditionally idolize their parents, even when treated badly. Or when a mother sings off key, her offspring still believe she has the sweetest sounding voice in the whole world, the most delicate fingers, the most beautiful reassuring words...

Sighing wistfully, I continued down the gravel path running alongside the stream...shoving my hands deep into the pockets of my coat. As I rounded the bend, the morning fog lifted and I saw my favorite refuge in my new life.

Sunshine was the home's name. Besides me, three nuns, a volunteer worker, and a trainee also worked there. I was hired as a plain nurse to take care of children from the ages of three to twelve while trying to make it look like one big happy family. And I did whatever was in my power to achieve that because, honestly, I loved every single one.

But I was incredibly fond of one particular child...and thinking about him made me smile as I pulled open the misaligned squeaky garden gate and walked up to the still quiet house.

First, I would wake Robbie, a boy almost 6-years-old with big green eyes that always smiled at me. His blond, silky-soft hair lightly covered part of his forehead and every time, his broad smile warmed my broken heart as if by magic. He was beautiful with the face of a tiny angel.

However, all the other kids constantly picked on him.

He had been at the home now for 12 months, thus, he was a newcomer to the close-knit group. Besides, he stood out because he preferred painting than playing with Matchbox cars, favored using a toilet rather than peeing in the garden like the other little wannabe guys, and fancied chatting rather than letting his fist do the talking even though he was a boxing enthusiast.

Robbie was constantly harassed and ostracized simply because he behaved atypical — like me, like *he* did during his childhood. I really tried not to favor any of my charges...but...this little lost boy was my secret hero.

Therefore, I promised myself never to allow him to lose his smile or give up on being himself.

So far, he was hanging in there — and oftentimes, I wondered how he managed. An adult would have long since collapsed if they had to carry his burden. Messed up childhood, parents gone, apparently the whole world hated him... But he was a fighter and I his comrade and we fought together for his future and to keep him smiling.

Even on this misty morning, I awakened him so he could escort me to the office. It had become a habit for him to have his morning cup of cocoa, which he slurped while I told him about my daily schedule. Every morning, he told me about his dream to participate in an actual boxing match someday because he idolized Klitschko. And every time, I laughed and wiped the tears away because my chest tightened when he showed me the barrage of hooks he planned on dishing out. No wonder I felt so close to this boy with Kiwi-green eyes. From the first moment I met him, I wanted to take him home with me. Unfortunately, my chances at adopting him were limited, virtually impossible, for I was single. Francesco's help would have been essential, but then he didn't care for children — too loud and too dirty.

Regardless, I did not want to give up on the dream because Robbie had so much in common with the man I loved and always would love. My emotions for *him* were as unstoppable as the blood flowing through my veins. Being around Robbie made me feel as if I was close to *him* too, which was why there was no choice but to love the little fellow.

I understood I supported him and made his life easier for without my tenderness he might have lost himself. For a child, nothing was more important than physical contact as well as intellectual exchange with a loved one. Remember Emperor Louis IV's devastating experiment with infants, who wasted away and died simply because the nurses never talked to them and they only touched them when changing their diapers and at feeding time. All that misery just so the emperor could figure out the true language of the world.

Well? Which one was it?

Love.

***

Today I was taking a party of six for an outing in the adjacent forest. It was the peak of fall season and the landscape was bathed in various soft oranges and reds. I had to close my white coat properly as I deeply inhaled the smell of the damp forest floor we marched on.

Naturally, I wished for, as I did every moment of my life, for *him* to be here so I could hold *his* hand. As usual, my eyes, my heart, and my soul burned just thinking about him and the future we would never have.

However, the children would not allow me to give into to weakness. Watching them running ahead, tossing damp fallen leaves at each other while laughing and jumping around, even though some had experienced horrible things in the past, repeatedly showed me that you could crawl out of any hole if the will was there. A person's will was, basically, the most important drive in life and a child's was far stronger than an adult.

I grinned at Eric, my assistant, and he laughed and tossed a few leaves in my face as a thank you.

"Mia is preparing an attack! Let's throw some on her *white* coat so it has some fall color!" the traitor shouted. To make things worse, I was abruptly bombarded from all sides. I had to run away and distract them by collecting enough beautiful large red leaves to make a garland later.

Overall, I think the whole day went quite well. Considering everything, it was marvelous.

To help them fall asleep, I read the children a bedtime story, *How Findus met Petterson* — which they liked especially well and then stroked Robbie's cheek before finally starting my short journey home.

***

By the time I made it home at nine o'clock, I was exhausted and tossed my keys into the black dish that served as a key holder.

"Hey, little one!" Francesco casually skipped down the red-painted hallway dressed in a light blue shirt and designer jeans and wrapped his strong arms around my petite waist from behind. Okaaaay...

I had not expected him to *honor* me with his presence today, although lately, he was at my place frighteningly often. As always, I stiffened at his touch, but quickly forced myself to relax.

"Hey you..." I smiled shyly at him, looking into the mirror on the wall facing us and at least showed my willingness. As always, he pretended to swallow my crap and lowered his lips to my neck, yet his eyes never smiled as they stared fixedly at my reflection. He didn't seem *truly* happy often, which was sad, but then we had that in common and made pretty good companions.

"Put on something nice, today we are going out," he announced, not even bothering to first inquire *about my day* or *if I would like to shower* or *would you like a foot massage, sweetie*? His voice was a deep bass and immediately reminded me of another strong bearish man, whom I had met once... Thinking of him made me think about his brother, but I quickly suppressed the memory of beautiful eyes, velvety voice, and those absolutely skillful fingers...

We're going out? Hello? I just finished a 10-hour workday! All I wanted was to sink into a hot tub, drink a glass of ice wine, and eat a bag of gummy bears. Yes, I now could eat as much candy as I wanted because I was no longer fat like I had been during my childhood and teenage years. To be honest, I was now too skinny — totally emaciated. One hundred ten pounds at five foot three inches, there definitely was not enough meat on the bones. Another side effect of being dead on the inside was the loss of appetite.

"I'd rather cook us a nice meal," I muttered and lowered my gaze for I was never able to hold his for long. I was afraid he might become aware of my true feelings and thoughts, just like *he* used to do. God! Why was it that every minute — every *second,* I constantly compared everything and everyone to *him*?

It was a sickness, an actual curse! That story took place eight endless years ago! By now – from a rational viewpoint – I should have been over him. Regardless that I had worshiped him since the first grade like he was a teen idol, I should have forgotten his voice, his looks, his appearance, everything he said, and his damn wonderful scent a long time ago.

Every gesture, every facial expression, every peculiarity of that beautiful face haunted me. Nothing had faded, whereas the logical outcome would have been for them to fade after all this time.

I wondered if nowadays he had even more muscles than in the old days. How did he style his hair, how did he dress, how did he behave? Did he still use impertinent, crass vocabulary? Was he still so forbiddingly sexy?

Thinking about him was almost physically painful and each time a specific memory came flooding back out of nowhere, I was devastated. The worst was when I recalled the way it felt when he was inside me — on top, staring at me with dark greedy eyes, devouring me. He was familiar with every square inch of my skin and I saw in every single glance that he adored *all* of me. The movement of his strong hips against mine, sweat running over his perfect muscles, the mocking smile when he delayed my orgasm so I would lose my mind, his quiet tormented *"fuck!"* when I turned things around and drove him insane, his lips brushing over mine, his hot breath in my mouth, the two of us united, pure perfection...

It was when I had these flashbacks that my longing for him ate me up inside. Then, I experienced pulling and tugging in the place between my legs, the one I lovingly called snail — which hadn't changed. If it weren't for those memory flashes, I would have questioned whether those heated and ecstatic moments with him had actually taken place.

Francesco's voice ripped me out of my ruminations.

"Cook a nice meal? Nah, that's okay. All day long, I have felt bloated because of the bean casserole you made yesterday. I'm meeting a few...coworkers. I showed them your photo and they are really keen to meet you. Could you wear the red push-up I gave you?"

Ashamed, I lowered my head.

"You know, it so happens I don't like push-ups!" I

mumbled. Actually, I hated it when the big Italian guy wanted to dress me like a Barbie doll in a sexy mini dress and high heels just to show me off like I was the latest Ferrari he just bought with his inheritance, like only my looks were important and nothing else.

"Oh, come on, just for an hour. You never go out with me; all you do is sit in front of your stupid sketchpad." He ignored my exasperated eye roll as if my facial expressions did not exist.

"My boss is dying to meet you. I've told him so much about you. Please, baby!" he begged and gave me an almost virginal kiss on the cheek. I recoiled instantly for his lips on my skin felt unpleasant and I barely managed to suppress the urge to swipe the spot where his mouth defiled me. "You want to keep Stan, right? As you know, I only put up with that stinking mutt because of you. You might as well do something for me! That's how a relationship works, give and take." *A relationship, perhaps, but love is not involved*...I thought...

"His name isn't Stan, its Stanley! And you cannot use him to blackmail me for this is my home and I can keep as many dogs as I like, regardless if you like it or not!" I exploded like a cannon.

The muscles in my abdomen knotted, robbing me of air. I thought I might burst and smother the tasteful ambience with my scraps of skin if he continued pressing against me so close for even a second longer. When I tried to wrestle free from his grip, his demeanor instantly cooled.

"Sweetie, animals are not thinking creatures. I have no idea why you constantly make such a fuss about your old mutt!" He sounded as if he was talking to a child that had difficulty following his weighty words. The only thing missing was for him to squat so we were eye level. Hopefully, he wouldn't send me to the corner of shame!

"Of course he has feelings! Just because they differ from yours doesn't mean he doesn't have any!" I hissed. How could he say that? Stanley was my faithful companion and pillow for 10 years now! He didn't care how I looked or smelled or how I behaved; he always let me be me and stood by my side.

Francesco narrowed his eyes. We would never see eye to eye on that issue. I hated his cruel remarks, bigotry, and his ignorance toward Stanley disgusted me.

But before I could really lose it, my inner voice whispered, *he has bad fucking karma because he is a fucker, so calm down, baby... You know, his tiny cock is punishment enough!* Did I already mention that I was crazy? Mostly because I heard *voices* — angelic ones, saying dirty words. Fair enough. In fact, I only heard *one*.

Usually, it made a brief appearance when there was a chance I would explode. The voice took it with humor, it calmed and turned me on – quite obviously – and it called me Mia baby or just baby. However, I preferred, no, I loved it when it whispered Mia baby.

It sounded so...sexy!

Francesco was the complete opposite of me and *him*. I, who was proud of my open-mindedness and down-to-earth way of thinking, had hooked up with an uppity snob who disregarded all values that I held dear. He had the ability to annoy me constantly and whenever that happened, I heard my favorite voice. Another reason I was with him — pure expediency.

Overcome with guilt, I sighed because I could not be that selfish and self-absorbed, it simply wasn't me. Then again, who exactly was I, considering my ego was jaded? How could I actually have a personality?

In fact, we used each other, but unlike him, I knew it was wrong to use other people for one's own purposes. As soon as I remember that, I felt guilty and relented.

"Give me five minutes," I announced, staring calmly at the ground, *finally* managing to wiggle out of his embrace. I was facing a memorable evening: I was tired and annoyed, making the perfect companion. However, since Francesco insisted, Mia would jump whether she liked it or not. Nothing mattered anyway...because...

It seemed as if I was on starting blocks, waiting for the shot to end my miserable existence, but a small bright spot remained — it kept me alive. Subconsciously, I was searching for *him*. I saw him in strangers, constantly tapped someone's shoulder only to be infinitely disappointed when none turned out to be Tristan Wrangler...

Yes, merely stupid irrational hope kept me going.

Other than that, everything was gray and drab. The old Mia had long since perished. She died because the person she needed to exist — who provided her with air to breathe, hated her.

Besides, even if I should meet him again, what should I say to him? Would he still want contact with me? My uncle had effectively prevented me from looking for him, but even *if* I had found him, my effort would have probably been in vain. Although I had written countless letters to him, I did not trust myself to mail even one for I feared a possible reply. Besides, I was too ashamed of what I'd done, after all, I was the one who put him in prison. I completely understood why the whole Wrangler clan didn't want anything to do with me. It took a while to convince myself, but when I returned three years ago to the dinky town of my childhood, I found the house in which my entire life once lived, abandoned. It had been my one and only attempt to look them up, besides, what else could I have done?

Interview people? Internet search? Place an ad on TV? I didn't have great contacts with the authorities, someone who could locate any person's whereabouts in this world. My father might be a policeman, but after what he did, I was the last person who would go near him.

Assuming I found him — how would I go about it...

He might have a new family and was happy.

If luck was on my side and that wasn't the case (already thinking selfishly again, how quickly one forgets), I was sure he wouldn't welcome me, forgive and forget everything, and with a kiss, liberate me from my emotional paralysis like I was Snow White or Sleeping Beauty.

No — definitely not!

The horrible truth was, once he got ahold of me, he would not use his hands to caress and make me feel at ease, no, he would *kill* me...

"I won't be in prison forever...once I'm out, I'll come looking for you...and then..." his last cold words echoed in my head, causing a shiver.

The tingling I was experiencing was quite unusual. A gloomy premonition overwhelmed me.

But as quickly as fear overcame me, it vanished — for people who were dead inside didn't fear anything, certainly not death itself. Once it faded, it was replaced by what kept me in this pseudo life for the past eight years, thirty-three days, five hours and thirty minutes, namely, damn hope that I'd eventually see him again. That was it — and yet, I would be happy to finally collapse so I no longer had to play the Bavarian zombie.

Nevertheless, my dreams didn't end there.

If he would give me the opportunity to explain everything that had happened back then, maybe he would also – just maybe, for at times, just the word could provide great comfort – not only listen but actually *believe* me! Maybe – oh, God, right now, I really loved the implication – maybe I'd still get to touch him again.

At least once, then I could die — for it wasn't only my imagination that considered it to be true heaven.

I should get it.

With all the bells and whistles.

3. She's Coming Back

Tristan 'Shocked' Wrangler

The sweat running down my face and body in streams was annoying. It stung my eyes as I opened the white, code-secured door to my office.

I stumbled up the spiral staircase half-blind because I forgot to grab a towel from downstairs. The door slammed against the wall as I pushed it forcefully open, hurrying to the bright shelf that held my black towels and yanked one out of the neat stack. Relieved, I wiped the moisture from my face, carelessly tossed the cloth on my desk, and finally peeled my sticky muscle shirt off — what proved to be anything but easy. I was dancing around on the spot like a grandpa suffering from rheumatism.

Nevertheless, that was my morning routine: a few rounds of boxing to work off some tension, hanging out with the people, inhaling the odor of my gym.

It was located right in the middle of the city's poorest district, offering many kids a refuge from the cold streets. I employed two former boxers with a heart for the little guys as coaches. Boys and girls of all ages were allowed to come and learn how to defend themselves properly. We also dealt with teenagers who, like me, had a problem dealing with their aggression. That way they could work it off here before they ended up hurting someone.

I too had once been a defenseless boy, although I had dealt with it myself. That was when I headed down the wrong, the anti-social path, until *she* showed me the proper way.

At some point, I won the battle against my shirt. I walked over to the window and looked down on the huge hall. As I used another towel to dry my armpits, I noticed it was futile because the perspiration wasn't abating. Today, I spent more time training.

It was nine o'clock in the morning on the dot and so far, only three little ones had arrived. One boy was 10-year-old with an alcoholic brother and both parents unemployed. Another boy was 14-year-old and he had brought his brother along. Naturally, one of the former boxers was present. His name was Markus and he was experienced in street fighting. He even showed me a few dirty tricks I hadn't been familiar with, regardless that I had mastered all martial arts. From kickboxing to karate, Brazilian street fighting, judo, wrestling, and good old-fashioned boxing, which I stuck with because it was so honest — so straightforward.

At least at first glance. Then there was the matter of the

psyche playing a 50 percent role, not strength and agility. I was a master of my body and really loved to psych someone out, fuck with someone's brain. Yet, eye-fucking, I had given up eight years ago.

At a quarter past nine, I was expecting a group from the children's home located three blocks away. It was right along the stream that ran through the middle of town. Every morning, I jogged alongside it to warm up. I hated using fitness machines and being indoors when I could be out in fresh air. The children's home near the stream looked quite cute. It almost seemed to be out of a fairy tale with its purple shutters, ornate window ledges, colorful sprawling garden with rose vines along the fence, blooming window flower boxes, and its name, *Sunshine*, boldly spelled out in different colored letters affixed above the door arch. Every time I went by, all the windows were dark and it appeared abandoned. Thanks to the inability to sleep and a tight schedule, I usually passed it around four or five in the morning.

Anyway, a staff member from the home had called every morning for the past two weeks, annoying John, my oldest already white-haired boxing coach. So, today the little tots would get a tour, even though I usually did not offer such a program.

Again, I checked the schedule and called my older brother Phillip, who was going to interview a few people for our restaurant chain. He needed a master chef for the largest place. Yes, Phil had devoted himself to his secret passion – food – and had become a chef. And he was now pretty damn famous! Tom, my other brother, however, became a successful lawyer dealing with environmental law. Well, I had my own reputation — at least in the underworld. I made sure to stay away from the public as much as possible.

Each one of us had followed his calling. Well, it was what I told myself.

It was already ten by the time I finished the paperwork and whatever calls I had to make when someone knocked.

"Yes," I snapped and took a sip of my water.

It was Markus, my most faithful boxing gym employee, shoving his cleanly shaven head through the gap. He was in charge of showing the little shits around and had apparently finished.

"Hey, boss." He grinned in his usual somewhat bored way and entered.

"Hey, employee," I replied dryly and rose from behind my huge corner desk to stretch. My ass had fallen asleep and I was thoroughly massaging it while eyeing my employee questioningly.

"Um, that totally hot chick from the children's home would like to know if she could speak to the owner. She is absolutely thrilled with your gym and would like to send some kids here to learn self-defense. She also asked if she gets a discount for a group of 10 children." Markus rolled his eyes and I smirked.

"It seems this sexy orphanage employee is quite bold,

huh?" I grumbled and, unsuspecting, strolled over to the big plate-glass window through which I surveyed my kingdom.

Maybe I was a bit of a megalomaniac and thought of myself as God, but, then again, I had built my enterprise with my own hands...

Therefore, I kind of was God here and every now and then, cast my eyes over my entire empire; gallery, club, and gym.

"Where is she?" I searched the hall when Markus appeared next to me to help.

And then...it hit me with the force of a raging bull.

I inhaled sharply and my legs turned to jelly as my eyes latched onto an elegantly curved back partly covered by strands of curly golden brown hair. Immediately, my heart started to race and sweat once again poured over my naked torso as I braced myself with my fists against the glass to keep myself from collapsing. It had to be a hallucination. Anything else was impossible. It couldn't be *her*...not like that, without any drum roll, out of nowhere, in a totally unspectacular fashion! It didn't fit!

I simply had not imagined running into her like *that*, though, in recent years, it had been on my mind. For too long I had waited for it, preparing myself for one epic fucked-up finale. It should be the best showdown ever!

But there was no doubt, it was her, for sure, she was alive, breathing, and quite real!

I would have recognized her on the spot, anywhere...even though nowadays she was skinny and emaciated and I was only seeing her backside. She had her hands full with a couple of boys who were about to beat each other senseless.

Once again, that woman was undermining my plans. Regardless, it wouldn't stop me from getting my deserved showdown because in my head, I not only had a version of a slowly increasing drum roll that would eventually – like an orgasm – peak with an explosion; there was also that significant violin, whose strings would be only briefly and painfully plucked like in a horror movie.

Unaware, I held my breath as I watched in horror and yet, a bit fascinated when, as if on command, she turned in her tight yellow summer dress and thick brown tights.

Totally clueless.

Frowning, she rubbed her neck and her dreamy expression almost put me over the edge. However, her cheeks were sunken, her big brown eyes were missing their glow, and her usually luscious cherry- red lips were pressed together into a thin line. She eyed the hall searchingly while I could only stare at her, motionless.

The feelings I had forcefully suppressed for the past few years came rushing back so fast that I almost could not withstand them.

And the drum roll was still increasing — so far no climax in sight.

Fuck!

I used all my willpower to keep from storming down and grabbing her to…fuck her from behind in front of the innocent children. Forcefully and deep. She had that effect on me. And here, eight fucking years had passed and I was no longer a hormone-driven teenager. *Dammit, pull yourself together!*

So, I rested my forehead against the cool glass and firmly clenched my hands as the pounding in my head finally reached its peak. My breathing was laborious and I had to force myself to calm down.

Naturally, my cock woke up. It was twitching in my pants, aching for that pussy that had been created especially for it, like nothing had happened, that miserable traitor.

But I, at least the rational part, had not forgotten that I had lost my life due to that woman. She had made sure my oh-so-clearly defined future had burned to ashes and then forcefully blew them into the winds of fate.

Due to her false testimony and a couple of prior criminal charges of mine, I was put away for two years without parole.

I was thrown in with the dregs of society. It was there I made the contacts necessary for my current businesses; otherwise, they wouldn't run quite as smoothly.

In the meantime, she was successful in separating the two young brawlers and started to laugh when a blond haired boy ran up to her, smacking forcefully into her legs, his eyes so bright even I could see it. Up here, I was unable to hear what she said, but whatever it was made her giggle even more as she picked up the kid and brushed her nose over his petite one. Her expression visibly warmed...

"Fuck!" Hot tears announced themselves and I flared my nostrils. Was that her son? Immediately, my mind saw her holding our child, which could have been that boy's age, as I wrapped my arms around her waist from behind, happily nibbling her alluring neck...

As soon as I envisioned that beautiful fucking scene, I started to grow furious because all that was lost to me. *She* had deprived me of it! That damn slut down there had taken everything from me! *Everything!*

"Markus..." I snapped. He was still standing next to me, but he had known better than to disturb me. He knew how quickly I could lose my temper, which I just impressively demonstrated. An erupting Mount Etna was nothing compared to me when I was in this state.

"Yes?" Now, I was alternately clenching my hands and forcing my voice not to shake like Jell-O.

"Who. Is. That?" I managed to hiss through clenched teeth. I had no idea why I asked, I knew perfectly well... It was simply me, afraid of the inevitable consequences his reply would bring... What would happen to me now when he confirmed my personal hell had reentered my life?

"Mia Angel, Cavalli's girlfriend."

"What?" I hissed and whirled around. Wide-eyed, he backed up a step as I glared at him angrily. *That fucking prick up there! Don't tell me she has been fu...* I couldn't finish the thought without running the risk of uncontrollably puking my guts out everywhere.

"Yes, they've been together for a few years... She is the little one he's always raving about."

Of course she was. She probably mesmerized him. Ha! He was my partner in the drug business or, to be more precise, my competitor and customer... Because every now and then he hung around my club to get his juices drained, all the while he had such a woman at his side. *She was a woman*...whose last days were numbered. That much was clear.

Fate had delivered her into my waiting hands.

"Tell him to bring her along tonight," I softly ordered.

Markus gave me a look, which immediately vanished when I raised a brow. Yeah, no one wanted to fuck with me because it always ended badly for the other party. "To the gallery?"

"Yes!" I replied short of breath because right then, she was squatting down and her dress slipped up a bit. Fuck! I might have to rub one off so I didn't end up with a pecker in blood stasis. Just like in the good old days. Oh, well, there was nothing better than jerking off while reminiscing.

"Okay, boss." I was so fixated on her I didn't notice him leave. As soon as I looked at her, everything in my field of vision turned red, yet, at the same time...I felt...like screaming out of pure frustration. Oh, how I would have loved to rip my office or someone to shreds. Oh, yes, I was going to hurt someone and I already knew how...

My future target stood down there with such naturalness, including her still big, damn innocent caramel-brown eyes, as if she had never destroyed me. Her no longer quite full lips turned into a smile when her...colleague tried to pull her playfully into the boxing ring... She slapped his hands away, laughing exuberantly.

"You will stop laughing soon enough," I mumbled to myself and felt my right upper lip curl into a sneer.

Oh...I would make her pay in many ways while ensuring she ended up feeling the same way I had. I would not rest until I had ruined her happy life the way she had mine. When it came to her, I had dreamed up wonderful murderous fantasies...however, I had decided death was not good enough for her. Why should I help her find peace if I myself couldn't manage it?

Abruptly, I fantasized about her being tied up, crying, desperate, completely under my control, begging for mercy.

"Oh, fuck!" The throbbing between my legs grew unbearable. I imagined her before me, naked and beautiful, but it did not change the fact that she was...a whore, a filthy little slut...

My cock loved the images. I had to rearrange it, which only made the throbbing worse... I sighed resignedly because the children and the...she-devil started to leave.

Now I might jerk myself off, imagining it was Mia Marena Angel's hand rubbing my pecker...while visualizing how *I* would destroy and break her, just like I was broken.

Yes, revenge was a bitch. I was truly looking forward to confronting Turkey, who, obviously had turned into a devil disguised as an angel.

4. His Revenge

Mia 'Fearful' Angel

"Since when do you like art? Are you feeling okay?" I grinned as I placed my hand on Francesco's forehead to check his temperature.

"Oh, what one does for women!" Roughly, he grabbed my fingers and shot me a look because I was sliding restlessly around on the black leather seat of his Ferrari.

But I had reason to be nervous since we were going to see an exhibition by the city's most famous photographer, oh, what was I saying...in the *country*! Filled with anticipation, I could hardly sit still. My blood pressure was way beyond normal. I was familiar with a few photos and ever since, wanted to acquire one. Well, of course...my budget was not enough, but a girl could dream. Considering the world we lived in, there was no other choice!

Compared to other artists, I actually could define what I liked about his work. It was the feeling of the nitty-gritty. They emitted concise clear emotions. Last, but not least, the pictures reminded me of *him*. They were provocatively passionate and wild, but subliminally profound... To capture the refined art of eroticism required certain genius! Unfortunately, I had no idea who the aforementioned artist was or what he looked like because he kept to himself as he had an obvious dislike for the public. Who could blame him! But today, thanks to Francesco, I was going to meet him!

After a good 20 minutes, we reached the city's outskirts. The gallery was one of the last in a row of priceless mansions that bordered a forest; above its crown, you could see the rest of the vibrant city. It seemed the rich and affluent enjoyed the view because the settlement was built on a small mountain. For an art exhibition, the place was fairly secluded. Across the street from the modern house was a sizeable parking lot full of luxury cars and, like a douchebag, Francesco pulled in at an angle, taking up two spaces.

Yes, Francesco and his penis compensation – his Ferrari – were quite a team. With difficult, I bit back a snarky remark.

Today, I had made myself especially pretty. I stepped out in my white strapless cocktail dress and white coat, together with black high heels. My attention was drawn to a cherry red Audi A7, which stood out among the priceless vehicles. I was mesmerized by its beautiful elegant flowing lines. I felt like walking over to see if the hood was still warm.

"What are you doing?"

"Oh!" Confused, I stopped when Francesco's hand grasped my arm. It escaped me that I had actually moved toward the Audi.

"I think *you* might have a fever," my great companion muttered and wrapped his beefy arm around my shoulder as we started across the deserted street.

The entire front of the gallery was glass. To get to the entrance, you had to cross an extravagant park-like lawn with ornate rattan benches placed here and there. Torches lit the scenery and visitors mingled in the balmy night while enjoying a glass of champagne or some other exquisite drink.

As usual at such events, I felt completely out of place. It was Francesco's world and soon I'd be part of it. So far, I had resisted, although now I was running out of arguments. When I thought about last night alone, which I spent with boring numbers and files because I was dragged along as a charm to a business lunch, at least I knew what awaited me.

As we passed women, they stared dreamily at Francesco, which didn't bother me in the least, regardless that I was usually quite jealous. Besides, I did not love him; time had jaded me so I was no longer even interested in something like that.

I noticed a group of women in expensive designer clothes standing a bit out of the way, chattering animatedly.

"He's supposed to have a huge cock..." one woman giggled.

"... and quite adept at using it."

Instantly, I blushed.

"Oh, to land in the bed of that god — I mean just to have that view!" raved the third one. "Have you ever seen him move? What do you think? I believe he can fuck any girl to heaven!"

"I've heard he hates sex," a fourth chimed in, to which all broke out in laughter.

"What a shame," the initial woman commented before continuing her fake giggling.

Before I could suppress it, I rolled my eyes. Although I didn't like listening in on other peoples' conversation and condemning them off a phrase said in an unguarded moment, I was still constantly doing so. Nauseous, Francesco and I entered the gallery.

The pleasant fragrance struck me first. It was fruity and fresh... and...something else...sort of sweet, strong, and masculine. It hit me like a freight train and made me gasp out loud, which attracted wary looks from the people around me.

"What's wrong with you today?" Francesco hissed, obviously embarrassed.

The heavenly smell...I could barely stand it... It was so good and at the same time, triggered a piercing sensation in my heart.

Not long after, Francesco started talking to a few people he knew, so I used the opportunity to disengage from him and strolled around looking at pictures.

The photographer specialized in nudes, but not in a cheap, pornographic way. Instead, his were presentations of beautifully aesthetic images of individual body parts that he had perfectly illuminated. It was obvious he was a lover of the human anatomy.

There was an erect nipple...a sensually shaped belly button...a pair of hands holding each other...two straight noses, their tips touching...long dark hair falling over a petite, pale shoulder...a male thumb against a female mouth...a flawlessly curved waist of a woman — everything done in black and white while light and shadows artfully interacted, making each piece come alive despite lacking color. Wow!

The works of art were so beautiful tears came to my eyes when I looked at the third piece. Clearly, something had to be wrong with me. The glass of ice wine I grabbed from the passing waiter's tray did nothing to help me relax.

My neck tingled, just like this morning in the boxing gym. And so, for no apparent reason, I slowly turned around.

It was irrational or perhaps plain instinct.

In the next second, my glass shattered loudly into hundreds of shards on the expensive marble as I laid eyes on an oversized picture, which, illuminated by two spotlights, took up most of the rear red brick wall. It was so very...*disturbing*, I could barely stand it. Yet, I couldn't look away either.

Never again!

Dominating the art piece was an arched naked female back with a smooth round butt and her long moderately curly hair was roughly pulled back by a strong male hand. The big fist grasped the hair firmly.

My scalp itched.

It was a side shot of the sensually curved rear view with emphasis on the obviously domineering man-hand that controlled the pose.

My privates grew hot and tingly. I was wet like I hadn't been in years and inconspicuously rubbed my thighs together. After all, I could swear I had felt that wonderful hand. One that, though obviously rough, did everything to satisfy me.

...to satisfy me?

God! What kind of sick thoughts was my brain creating?

Madness ripped me out of my shocked frozen state. A waiter kneeled in front of me gathering up shards and Francesco was back at my side, shaking me by the arm.

The whole room had gone completely quiet. Not a soul seemed to breathe. I noticed my wet cheeks...and my trembling body... before the audio suddenly rushed back at me with full force.

"Mia! Is everything alright?" Francesco shook me roughly again and I pulled my arm away as I stumbled a step backward.

"I have to...get out of here!" I whispered. I turned around and elbowed my way through the mob of staring snobs to get outside.

My face was flushed from embarrassment as I stood in the garden and gently wiped away tears. The mascara, eye shadow, and eyeliner were smeared — which could make a woman look quite unattractive. I was glad my friend wasn't following me across the street and into the parking lot. Once out of visual range, I fished my compact out of my big white non-designer handbag and evaluated the degree of destruction while dabbing away disgusting smudges with a handkerchief.

Breathe. In and out. In and out.

What was going on? Why did I react so strongly to an ordinary photo?

I could not find a reason. All I knew was that I had to have that picture, no matter the cost, immediately so no more eyes could look at it.

Another deep breath. *Focus on your mission!*

Trembling, I headed straight back to Francesco, who was standing directly in front of the picture, making superficial charming jokes about my unladylike behavior. I simply ignored his wit and tugged on his sleeve to get his attention.

"Hey..." I whispered, interrupting his conversation with three unfamiliar women.

Reluctantly, he tore his gaze away from the blonde's unnatural breasts and turned to me. "Are you okay now?" he inquired coolly.

"Lend me..." I whispered and peeked out of the corner of my eye at the tiny price tag on the object of my desire.

"66,666 bucks!" I shouted, shocked and squinted at it again to make sure that was correct.

I was right on! 66,666 bucks. For a gigantic photo! It bordered on delusions of grandeur! The photographer had to be eccentric. Yeah, what was I saying — every genius was a bit full of themselves! I didn't think I could even borrow that much from Francesco.

"Maybe for your birthday!" he said, simply dismissing me, returning his focus to the woman.

I, however, continued staring at the absolutely overpriced piece, feverishly trying to come up with a reason for the steep price. The other photos weren't nearly as expensive and ranged from one to five thousand. There was no other piece priced as high as this one... Well, the back truly was the most magnificent form that could be found on a female and the image expressed so much empathy, together with the man's gesture... You could imagine how the naked fragile woman was pressed against the hard masculine body of the man, who, presumably, was as flawless as she...

Flawless? Well...

My gaze rested on the female butt and I was glad my hands were empty. I forced myself to keep it together and merely twitched a little when I noticed the birthmark on the woman...and was overcome with a really...astonishing...scary...horrible and downright monstrous foreboding...at the same time, goose bumps popped up all over.

Various feelings overwhelmed me and their intensity almost robbed me of my breath. Panic-stricken, I glanced around... hoping no one could tell what I was experiencing.

And, again — I ran.

I dashed to the restrooms because I had to convince myself I wasn't hallucinating. As I hurried out of the gallery, I bumped into a few guests who stared questioningly after me. Awkwardly, I stumbled down a long red velvet carpeted corridor — which appeared pretty grim, like a modern museum.

Having arrived at what looked like a pricey women's restroom, I pulled open the door. As soon as I stepped inside, closed and bolted the door, I breathed in and out deeply while brushing a loose strand out of my face. Finally, I tugged my dress up and twisted sideways to inspect my right buttock... I couldn't see anything, no matter how much I twisted and exerted myself.

"Crap!" I cursed and simply dashed out of the stall with my skirt still raised. Luckily, I was alone and quickly turned my backside to the mirror and...froze.

There it was!

Rubbing over it didn't make it go away either. It had always been there and most likely would be forever. My mole...which *he* had kissed every time since it was on my *divine ass* that he had loved so much...

"Tristan!" I bellowed painfully before my hands flew up and covered my mouth as I looked deeply into the mirror at the big shiny eyes of a confused adult woman, who instantly felt like she was 17 again and...*alive*.

"Tristan..." I whimpered against my fingers and pinched my eyes together as the impossible struck me.

The photo was of me — making him the photographer! Once again, he was presenting me to the public naked!

It couldn't be true!

And this time it wasn't to members of a small school, it was half the world!

My body started shivering abruptly as overwhelming memories flooded me.

"Oh, baby... I love those lips. They belong only to me!" his velvety voice determinedly grumbled in my ear so that I cried out in pleasure as he yanked my head back by my hair and Tristan-style, took possession of my mouth...

During that special night in our clearing...an eternity ago.

The flashback subsided...back into the deepest recesses of my mind. As usual, such severe pain coursed through me that I had to bend me forward and cradle my belly. The cramps were unbearable, I would never get used to them. Today, they were even more intense than usual. Yet, I still managed to get to the sink before throwing up.

"Crap!" I sniffled once I had emptied myself in the marble sink and quickly rinsed everything away before dabbing the sweat from my forehead.

I cursed softly as I fished for the small toothbrush and toothpaste I always carried. I hated having unclean teeth. Thankfully, no one came in to use the restroom as I repaired my desolate condition. While I was freshening up, my stomach settled as well.

Okay, Mia! Battle plan! You are no longer seventeen!

What should I do now? Was I really in *his*...yes, I shouldn't have said his name out loud, especially not twice, that would have definitely saved me from reacting so strongly...gallery? Or had someone bought the picture from him and was simply exhibiting it as his own? Would that person have *his* address and perhaps tell me? Did I even *want* to find him and did *he* even want to be found? Maybe the woman wasn't me after all. There was a chance someone else possessed a birthmark in the exact same spot, the exact same size and shape... I mean, the saying everyone had a doppelganger somewhere in the world couldn't just be made up. The figure resembled my weight eight years ago because it was anything but emaciated, yet, still beautiful...

Maybe I was imagining things...

I gradually calmed and the minty flavor in my mouth helped me think more clearly.

It's not him, it simply can't... It would be too much of a coincidence... Something like that just doesn't happen! I kept telling myself while I again checked my appearance before leaving the safety of the restroom.

"It's not him. It's not him. It's not him." Again, I had to pull myself together — really! Otherwise, I might embarrass Francesco even more and that, I didn't want.

Once again, anxious and insecure, I entered the huge

glass-enclosed room, which used an effect to make the works of art appear as if they were hovering in the black night. My body was so tense I thought I might burst, my heart fiercely beating in my chest, my stomach felt like butterflies...

As if a fog had lifted, I perceived things much more intensely, whether it was colors, or my rediscovered formerly suppressed emotions. It was overwhelming after the permanent grayness and Tristan-hunger phase. Even if simultaneously, I was dominated by fear and anticipation...

I could *feel* again!

And I was full of hope, more so than ever before. Even if he wished me dead and was the kind of man who followed through with his vows, I hoped it was him.

Because I loved him — that would never change.

A noise interrupted my thoughts. My heart raced and I had to touch my chest. A beautiful melodic laugh that sounded like the most wonderful ballad. It had a slightly hollow undertone, but the voice was still deep and yet, also soft. It could pull you under its spell, make you forget your name, and put you in a trance, just with words...and once it really talked... *Wow*!

In the next moment, I discovered *him* – *Tristan Wrangler* – and stopped again, unable to take the two remaining steps downs.

Swaying, I grabbed hold of the railing so I wouldn't lose my balance when I saw the dark wild hair that I had enjoyed running my fingers through — and which only *I* had been allowed to touch.

Like an addict, I was sucking up every single fiber of his being. Such perfection...

My memory was no longer worthy of it; the mole on that elegant neck, those broad shoulders, which had once offered me so much protection. The upright back that had never bent for anyone. Those narrow agile hips, which I used to wrap my legs around...

I swallowed.

That butt, in an expensive black suit (including cherry red tie) made you want to fall to your knees, followed by those long legs that carried him so gracefully through life. That powerful arrogant aura that constantly surrounded him. Those confident smooth movements...those beautiful hands.

Tristan Wrangler had grown up and he was – even more – amazing.

When an unplanned longing sigh escaped my mouth, he froze with a glass raised to his lips. Whatever muscles were visible, which looked bulkier than in the old days, tensed and I knew it wouldn't be long before he turned to look at me.

Instantly, I felt like running to him and snuggling against his chest, against the spot where I belonged, and at the same time, I was overpowered by incredible *fear!*

So, I did the only right thing and quickly jumped down the remaining steps to escape his line of vision. However, I forgot I was wearing high heels and naturally twisted an ankle because I wasn't used to walking in such monstrous shoes.

"Ouch!" I exclaimed as I landed on my hands and knees. So much for avoiding embarrassment. Francesco would never again take me anywhere. Never again!

Swiftly, I scrambled back up while ignoring the helping hand of a waiter who had rushed over to me. Now I really had everyone's attention and as dead silence prevailed again, I stood there blushing staring at the floor and hoping for a hole I could disappear into to open up. Unfortunately, the floor was ungracious — as was Francesco.

"Tell me something, are you drunk?" He grabbed me by the upper arm and dragged me out into the cool night.

I followed him, staggering, and forced myself not to look in *his* direction, however, I could feel his gaze burning my back and ass so that I blushed even more as my friend pulled me out into fresh air. So much for being inconspicuous — of course now *he* had also discovered me... Confident, *he* leisurely took his time looking murderously at my butt with his head tilted and his lips pursed!

"I've never seen you this out of it..." Francesco muttered angrily once we were in the parking lot.

"I... I...don't know what came over me," I stammered, without looking at him. One part of me wanted to go home – my tiresome fleeing instinct – yet another wanted to turn around and go back inside!

To him!

"Here, I've arranged a session with the photographer for you for next Friday and as a thank you, you're freaking out!" he hissed.

"You did what? I simply stared at him, stunned. "You talked to *him*?"

"Yes, of course I did. I know him!"

Tears welled up in my eyes, but I did not look away from him. "About what?"

Francesco was confused. "I told him how much you liked the photo and that I would also like to have such snapshots of you."

"What did *he* say?" I shouted somewhat hysterically for the entire parking lot to hear.

"He said your beauty is to die for. Of course, he's on board!"

Why did that sound so dirty, even if it didn't come out *his* mouth? And so...*deadly?*

Was I really stupid enough to ask myself that question? I knew perfectly well what Tristan would do to me, he'd destroy me! And now he knew my friend, probably already knew where I lived... My demise was a foregone conclusion and I had nothing better to do than to marinate and wait for the lion to pounce on me. Great!

Now, it was a matter of getting away and, ideally, leaving the country. Australia sounded good. My Internet girlfriend lived there and I was sure she would grant me asylum.

On the other hand, they would be outstanding photos. Pictures of him massacring me. Pretty bloody — but a dazzling red always looked great! It might also sell really well.

He only agreed to take shots of me because it provided him with an opportunity to enjoy his revenge. I knew how the old Tristan ticked — no scruples and ice cold to everyone who wasn't family or me. I didn't want to know what he was capable of nowadays after spending a few years in prison — *because of me!*

Now, I was panic-stricken, pulling on the door handle of the still locked car. "Come on!" I squealed into the balmy silence. Francesco stared at me in disbelief as if I was a petulant child and didn't move an inch.

"Please!"

"I'll get our jackets!" he eventually said somewhat defeated. Trembling, I stood next to the car as Francesco crossed the street and reentered the gallery, all the while, shaking his head. How adorable! Now I was all alone... in the middle of the night... in a parking lot, directly within reach! I couldn't have picked a better place to survive.

Exhausted, I rested my aching forehead against the cool metal of the vehicle and closed my eyes. In between, I banged my head against it a few times to help me think a bit clearer. He was Tristan and he would *not* destroy me — simply *because* it was him!

I could have him back in my life, could see and talk to

him, explain everything, and maybe even touch him...if only he'd give me a chance...

God, how naive was I actually?

More likely, he'd kill me — which left escape my only option... But...had I ever been able to stay away from him? Regardless of everything he had done to me? No! I was pathetic, totally obsessed, and utterly afraid...

"Afraid?" a velvety voice whispered in the dark night. I froze.

Even my heart paused briefly — perhaps a beat.

I tore open my eyes and whirled around.

There he stood...just like that...like a god.

Well, he stared at me menacingly over the roof of a car – of course his red Audi – parked two spaces over from Francesco's luxurious ride.

With the left hand in his pants pocket and something else in his other, he casually sauntered over to me. A beam of light fell on the object he was holding and it glinted dangerously! Oh, God! A knife!

Fear coursed through my body, the hair on the back of my neck stood on end. I wanted to flee, but was frozen. My last hour had struck, time was up, and I saw bits and pieces of my life flash before my eyes...while I was lost in Tristan Wrangler's penetrating stare.

I remained motionless as he walked around the Ferrari accompanied by a nerve-wracking screech that pierced the night. Shocked, I noticed the object that light had reflected off, was not a knife, but a car key, which he used to scratch the paint job of the hood and side of my friend's beloved ride. His expression was more than arrogant and openly challenging like; *you have a problem with that? Huh?*

I was relieved to see it was a key, not nearly as dangerous as a knife.

Mostly, I only marveled at his slightly illuminated wonderful face, the long lines of his neck with Adam's apple and muscle tendons that disappeared under his white shirt.

No more tie, instead, he had opened two buttons...and had the hottest body I'd ever seen... Oh, my!

"Tristan..." I don't know why I whimpered. *Fuck me? Love me? Don't harm me?* In any case, I leaned against the car behind me because my knees grew weak.

He was even more beautiful, more desirable than anything I knew or remembered... At the same time, he had a dangerous aura — something that made me want to flee again. He raised an eyebrow like a superior lion eyeing a jittery lamb. A horror flick was nothing compared to it; nobody would hear me...no one would save me.

And I would not put up a fight.

Silently, tears streamed down my cheeks, smearing my makeup beyond recognition.

"You've become so skinny, Mia Marena. You look like fucking shit! Has anyone ever told you that?" he stated provocatively and turned on the LED light on his keychain. Seemingly bored, he checked me out from top to bottom, probably to emphasize his statement... I sobbed for his words were like blows.

My heart felt as if it would burst from my chest as he closed the remaining distance. Not two steps in front of me, not even one, no, he halted right in front of me so that his scent instantly hit me full force and I could feel his body heat. His fresh male sex scent was even more pronounced than eight years ago. The same could be said for his confidence with which he confronted me.

Whimpering while making a half-assed attempt to escape the inevitable, I pressed myself closer to the smooth paint job of the car behind me and stared at him panic-stricken. I shook so violently, I feared I was making dents in the metal.

Actually, I didn't want to flee for I was still hopelessly smitten with him.

"I love you, Tristan." I desperately whispered the only words I had wanted to say all these years. Nothing else mattered to me. Only that fact had always remained the same and would never change.

Crazy! He might have become a completely different man in those eight years and here I still loved him. The feeling was obstinately anchored deep inside me and forever present.

As soon as I grew aware of it, I shook even harder and wanted to throw myself into his arms and snuggle up close to him, yet I couldn't bring myself to do it. No matter how close he was, he was still unreachably far away.

"Oh, Mia Marena, don't be ridiculous! I already told you to stick your love where the sun didn't shine," he remarked quietly. And yes, he did make that statement the last time we saw each other. His breath caressed my face; it smelled of positive memories of a better time and mint — typical.

I could only stare at the second open button and the hairy muscular chest underneath. In the old days, he had kept it cleanly shaven like a go-go dancer, whereas nowadays, he had matured, body as well as appearance. He was even stronger and taller. Never before was he so appealing or manly. And never before had I wanted to pounce on him as much as in this moment, but at the same time, my mind shouted, *DANGER! RUN! You stupid cow!*

However, reason usually played a relatively minor role in my life! Perhaps it was time to use more of it, just not right now...

Maybe if I was careful...I might be allowed to touch him once. I really wanted to! He was like a terrifying shark — lethal and stunningly intriguing. I longed to place my hand on his chest, feel his heartbeat, be assured I could, was allowed.

Briefly, I reminded myself of me when I was 17 at Chiemsee and I had been sitting thinking about kissing him.

Back then, I had been bold and fortunate...

So, I pulled myself together and gazed into his expressionless eyes with their infinitely long jet-black lashes and held the look that had stalked my nightmares in recent years. But he did not behave the way he had the last time we saw each other.

Tristan Sexy looked down at me, completely relaxed and unreadable. He had always been a god — just now, he was actually, absolutely unapproachable. "It must have been a long time since you've seen pure sex appeal considering your stupid gaze... But, one should not judge a book by its cover... You know that only too well, don't you?" he commented dryly. Now his mouth captivated my attention.

"And I would advise you not..." Suddenly he leaned in close, supporting himself by placing a forearm next to me on the car... His lips almost brushed along my ear. I heard his deep breathing and immediately mimicked him. The tip of his finger slid oh-so-tenderly over my bare, icy upper arm. "... to touch me." He emphasized every single word sensually and I envisioned his full pink lips as they formed each syllable, heard each note of his mesmerizing voice and became aware that he had always, even back when, been a master at verbally making me lust for him, turning me to putty in his hands. Albeit nowadays, his skills were simply divine. Basically, you could exchange the word god with Tristan — it was an equal statement. I intended to do that from now on.

"Do you really believe I would bang you after eight damn years and 34 days like nothing ever happened? I have better things to do! You might as well give it a rest with that damn lovey-dovey fuck me look, Mia Marena!" *Oh, my, Tristan!* He had counted the days! Why were my thoughts so obvious? Why did it still feel like we'd never been separated? And...

"Don't call me Mia Marena! You know I hate it!" I snapped as if a half an eternity hadn't passed.

I shouldn't have done it. Because *back then* no longer existed!

My impertinent mouth was to blame for him grabbing me by my left elbow and swinging me roughly around. I gasped as my face practically hit the crook of his supporting arm. A cry was fighting to escape, but his biceps pressed hard against my mouth, keeping it shut. My heart raced and I feared for my life. His hot troubled breath almost scorched the sensitive skin of my neck, when I heard ripping and felt a sharp yank.

Abruptly, my strapless dress fell to the ground and I heard an encouraging hiss, apparently, the sight of my body distracted him from whatever was on his mind.

I neither tried to free myself nor moved under him, instead, I simply remained still. Sort of like a deer caught in a vehicle's headlights. There I stood with my back to him, in my black hot pants, strapless stockings, high heels, and nothing else. The formerly balmy breeze felt icy on my bare skin.

"Oh, fucking hell!" Tristan whispered hoarsely in my ear and buried his face in my hair, panting.

"Fuck for me; luck for you... You will get fucked yet again," he announced frankly but tonelessly and I felt an oh-so-tender finger brush the waist of my hot pants — or was it only my imagination? Relieved, I exhaled, albeit, I was still shaky, but the touch was so brief as if it never happened.

"You'll get yourself killed if he finds out about this!" Firmly, he rubbed his cock over the fabric between my legs. Desperately, I gasped at *its* enormity.

Last night, I lay awake in bed – insanely longing for *him* – and now here he was pulling my hot pants down.

Thanks to Tristan, I had opted for them today, and thankfully, Tristan still loved my butt in them!

Annoyed, he pulled my hips back and me from the car. "It won't work like this!" In the next moment, he ruthlessly kicked my feet from under me so I hit the ground brutally, scraping my bare knees. My hands tried to break the fall and squeaked as they slid over the polished lacquer. Horrified, I yelped since it burned like hell.

Abruptly, Tristan was kneeling behind me, slightly bent over my back. He hovered above my half-naked from-cold-lust trembling body, fully clothed. Only his rock hard cock was pushing between my ass cheeks. He pinned one of my hands in the gravel. The sharp edges cut my skin, blood from the countless tiny wounds mingled with the dirt. The other hand roughly grasped my hair and pulled my head back before he whispered in my ear again.

"You won't so much as make a peep or you'll regret it, you understand?" As his hold tightened ominously on me, I felt tiny pebbles pressing even deeper into my flesh. I wanted to scream in panic, but with superhuman strength, forced myself not to, and instead, closed my eyes in an attempt to stop the flow of tears. There was no stopping them and they fell to the ground in front of me, staining the gravel dark as he released my hand to grab my hip.

It was like déjà vu. However, this time was more vigorous than eight years ago at the beach party when he deflowered me in the same position.

In the next moment, he slapped my butt with his bulging cock! This time, I suppressed a pleasurable moan, although, right then, electricity ignited throughout my entire body.

With one move, he pressed my on-button and inadvertently, my inner emotion engine revved instead of purring idly. Of course, he still knew which buttons to push even after eight years and 34 days!

"Still as horny as back in the old days..." He held *it* and rubbed it between my labia — let me feel it intimately. His cock against my pussy – marked me and at the same time, rubbed under my... snail – I was completely lost.

I could no longer suppress my whimpers and twitching and immediately the hand that held my jaw lightly forced my head around so I would look at him and see the warning... His gaze said it all. I instantly quieted down.

The following moment, Tristan pressed firmly against my entrance, groaned roughly when he felt a slight resistance, and then with a monstrous thrust, entered me all the way without letting go or breaking eye contact.

My knees slid across the gravel, but I did not feel any pain. It was as if I was drugged — by my own personal drug... thanks to his huge cock. It was deep inside me, hitting a wall and brutally stretching me while motionless.

During the recent eight years, I had not felt such intensity as I did now with Tristan Wrangler's outstanding cock.

"Shiiit!" he roared into the night and in the next second, came. I felt every single twitch, every pulse of its veins and nearly fainted because it was so indescribably exhilarating.

"Yeah..." Like a good horse that had done its deed, he gave my ass a satisfied slap, pushed off me, and stood up.

I was filled with irrepressible emptiness as hot goo ran down my thighs.

Dejà vu times four.

Humiliation: Check!

Doubt: Check!

Pain: Check!

And love? Four times, check!!!!

Breathless, I leaned back on my heels and stared up at him. Tristan raised an eyebrow and zipped up his pants as I bit my lip.

"Make sure you remember that this was a one-time thing. By the way, you really look like crap." He casually destroyed whatever hope there was as he glared disparagingly at my by-him ruined appearance.

Although I still bleed from my hands and knees, I was too aroused and near orgasm and only aware of the pain down there where his juices oozed out at intervals. As I rose, I slipped about with a grim expression and for the first time in eight years, I was almost able to enjoy his smile. Almost.

"You are still as finicky as ever, huh? I'm sure I'm not going to clean you up. You have to take care of my leftovers. Oh, don't give me that reproachful look. There was a time when I would have loved to take you in my arms and ride off into the damn sunset with you, which is what you probably are imagining right now, but, unfortunately, I no longer have that inclination. Your *snuggle-buddy* should be done with Mary by now. Well, then..." He squatted so near me with his forearms propped up on his knees that the tip of his nose almost touched mine.

He simply stared at me — I stared right back.

Yes, Mista Wrangler, even if you glower at me so condescendingly, I would still follow you to hell! I mentally told him, but would have never dared voice it!

He raised an eyebrow and chuckled derisively. Oh, I loved it when he did that!

"Your pussy is also no longer what it was. Nevertheless, today it was still able to save your little worthless life," he gently whispered in my face.

He couldn't be serious!

He was briefly inside me and immediately came! He might not love me anymore, but he still idolized my snail like he did eight years ago.

It meant only one thing to me: new game — old luck.

I would have to use Mia-power to win him back and for that, I already had a concrete plan. Grow old! With Tristan Wrangler! That was my goal in life!

Captivated by my sweet dreams, I smiled. "I'm not afraid of you and I'm ready. Now!"

He rolled his eyes. "You should be damn scared. Besides, you are totally stupid. Still," he announced unemotional and rose. Nonchalantly, he pulled out a 10-euro note from his pocket and tossed it carelessly on the ground in front of me. It said more than a thousand words.

He didn't believe I was worthy of another look, simply disappeared into the shadows a few parking spaces over, leaving me breathless, naked, with ripped clothes, smudged makeup, abrasions on my body, and exceedingly aroused.

Yes, this was a new, truly dangerous Tristan Wrangler...and I was still the old stupid Mia Angel because, despite everything, I still loved him the way I always had.

5. Fuck or Death

Tristan 'Musing' Wrangler

This evening, I really was a little fucking pussy who needed two joints to function somewhat reasonably because today, *she* would enter my kingdom.

On one side, my insides were eating me up, on the other... I couldn't wait to see her face once she recognized the life-size photo of the two of us. Even though I entertained anything but friendly feelings for her, I loved and hated that picture — more than anything else. Normally, I would never sell it, let alone display it in public. There was a reason it hung for years covered in a separate room to which only I had access. Even for me, it was difficult to look at because it had been a long time since I last laid eyes on it. For a moment, I was tormented by emotions and almost threw it against the wall, but I wanted her to see it and shit herself while surrounded by other guests.

At least I hadn't spoiled *the* showdown.

In any case, this evening had been a success because she had been scared of me. In principle, that wasn't anything new for I had made her life a living hell starting with the first school year. HA! However, it was merely a prelude of what was to come.

Still, it was scary to realize that not much had changed for me too. In fact, it deeply troubled me because I would have thought that the spell she could spin around me would be restricted by hatred and a thirst for vengeance. But that was not the case. I had not totally messed up, even held back — although her immediate demise was the original plan when I noticed that her dear friend left her alone in the dark parking lot while she was close to a full-blown nervous breakdown.

Naturally, I used it to my advantage.

It had been easy to sneak outside and observe her from the shadows for a few seconds as she plunged deeper into a Tristan-is-going-to-kill-me panic. The defenseless prey was not even aware the hunter was already on her.

A dimly lit lantern illuminated her as she leaned against a car in nothing more than a short dress that emphasized her smooth legs. Her hair was clearly longer and those high heels...

Fuck! That dress! Those heels! In the old days, she certainly took better care of herself.

She might have lost a good 20 pounds, but her flawless feminine curves, which her body already possessed back then, were still there — somewhat! Somehow, still there...

At that moment, I realized I still longed for her body or, better said, my cock still idolized her pussy.

And *that* was a problem! A huge, hard-rock one, as a matter of fact! Then again, that fucker up in the sky never made it easy when it concerned Mia fucking Angel.

Whatever, the past was history — now I would no longer let myself be deceived by her. Impulsively, I took a few steps into the light and leaned with my forearms on the roof of my car in clear sight.

"Afraid?" I deliberately broke the silence, making my entrance perfect.

She looked around panic-stricken and I happily inhaled every shred of her fear.

She played her role well...I had to admit.

Her declarations of love didn't interest me one bit and for her to use them to calm me down had definitely not worked.

Love was a damn overrated word. In actuality, you were always alone, no matter how many women told you they felt that way. I had to find it out the hard way for when I started out as a drug dealer I became involved in a turf war and almost croaked because some stupid chick betrayed me... Meanwhile, everyone knew better than to mess with Tristan Wrangler.

Yet what she was doing?

Exactly that!

Once again! I don't fucking believe it?

I created all sorts of torture fantasies — each one I believed would be painful for her — planting ideas in my head, while she still looked at me like *that*... She was as sick as before — as sick as I was.

It made me see red, so I combined the beautiful with the even more beautiful and ripped the dress off her with one powerful jerk. A long time ago, there was something to hold on to, now, I might end up with splitters while fucking. *But* her skin was still pale and delicate; her figure small and fragile, her soft rounded ass...packed in damn hot pants!

For a second, I wondered if she knew she would meet me and thus, intentionally went with black panties. However, that couldn't have been the case, could it? I wasn't known by Tristan Wrangler at the boxing gym or by the general public.

But there they were; her ass and pussy. I was inundated by images; sweat on her body, my cock inside; meanwhile my fingers cut into the soft skin on her hips. Ohhh...fuck!

While I was plagued by memories, my fingers wandered and touched the hem of her freaking hot pants. As if I burned myself, my hand abruptly recoiled.

In my pants, it grew moist and throbbed and I knew I would immediately come if I fucked her. Part of me had been longing for this moment for too long, the other still wanted to destroy her. Only my little brain did not want to play along and followed its own urges.

I wanted to take her as deep as possible, which was why

she needed to be on all fours. So, I pushed her to the ground like she was a cheap slut because that was all she was to me now. Every gesture and touch should show her how I felt about her, make her understand that it was all about me and not like in the past when I screwed her to seventh heaven on a regular basis!

Mia's pussy was so hot. Even hotter. The hottest.

The initial resistance was delicious and the tightness encompassing my cock was amazing. It felt as if she was still a virgin! She immediately milked me and I squirted into *my* pussy. At least that had not changed over the years: It was still my territory...

I came hard and long and I didn't care whether someone heard me.

Her muscles contracted around me so urgently, I knew she would come as soon as I so much as touch her clit. In this respect, nothing had changed either, like the old days; she was still susceptible to my charms. But I would not allow her!

No such luck! Not even a little ecstasy for Mia Marena — the miserable traitor!

Therefore, feigning disgust, I pushed her away and stood up.

She knelt there like a pile of misery, her makeup running in black streaks down her face and her hair disheveled. Except for high heels and strapless stockings, she was naked, utterly resembling — a little slut. To add to it, her knees and hands were scraped...

Yet her gaze was still open — almost pleading and absolutely devoted. I just threatened her, followed by screwing her like an asshole – like a sex offender – and she still gazed at me in that peculiar way of hers, like I was the fucking hero and not some fucked-up monster.

However, this time I would not fall for her little act. This time the roles would be reversed, that much was certain!

And so again, I pointed out that she didn't mean squat to me.

Granted, she reacted overly calm, presumably because the little bitch still thought she knew me. All she knew was the young naïve weak me, not the bastard I had been forced to become.

Oh...she would be on guard because I had a plan. It was genius...and fatal.

I would get my way and my vengeance and in the end, Mia Angel would either be dead, ruined, or at best, both... Perfect...

6. His Knife

Mia 'Musing' Angel

Francesco must have suffered a combination of myocardial infarction and stroke when he showed up approximately one minute after Tristan departed. Obviously, not because of me. He noticed the scratches first. He hopped around like Rumpelstiltskin, roared, dashed back inside the gallery and out again, only to run back in and out again — all the while on his cell phone, chatting rapidly in Italian. Then he noticed it wasn't only his car that was damaged...

I had just composed myself and was holding the remaining shreds of my dress in front of me. I had no idea what to say or do, so I simply looked at him when he turned the corner. How sick was that? I was more or less fucked-raped and had enjoyed every second. That was truly strange, but the worst was yet to come because I was standing in front of my boyfriend with my snail dripping like a faucet, but not because of him, oh, no... Insane — the only thing I could say!

"My God, Mia!" As soon as he had arranged for a paint job, he was at my side.

"I can't...not now..." I whispered.

Suspicious, he looked at me, but actually remained silent. He pushed a button and then me onto the passenger seat of his car. I tried my best to cover myself and stared outside into the dark...

It felt...empty.

Why wasn't Francesco inquiring about what happened? Why did he not demand an explanation? Didn't he care? And what had he been doing with Mary? How did he know Tristan? Dammit! Why didn't I run away from the latter instead of enduring everything without a struggle? Why was my body screaming, *you're safe,* yet my mind, *run*! Why did I want a repeat — right now?

Why was he still magnetic and I his counterpart? The incredible attraction between us was unchanged... Why would I go to him when, most likely, he'd strangle or destroy me somehow as he had already announced?

Was I really that crazy? Did I really want to risk everything I had created in my second life?

Robbie! shouted a voice in me! *You cannot simply abandon him!* I was all he had — and the other way around!

I had no idea if I should risk it. Perhaps there was no turning back. On the other hand, what was my life without Tristan?

Well, nothing, to be precise!

***

Once home, I had no desire to take a shower because Tristan's unique scent still clung to me. But Francesco carried me to the bathroom because, according to him, I looked like a rape victim. That was the only thing he said — otherwise nothing.

Later on, he did not inquire about what happened. It didn't seem to bother him, but perhaps his mind was still on the ominous Mary. Apparently, Tristan made sure she came on to him so he could fuck me in peace and quiet.

I had to admit, I didn't care if he had fun with someone else. Clearly, that alone should have told me I didn't have feelings for Francesco.

I was only interested in if I had imagined the encounter and, if not, did I have the guts to go to the photo shoot and confront him...

He was no longer his old self, but he was also not a completely new person.

So, would I go see him and risk total ruination or stay away and continue my life as it was? Without the love of my life? Yes, it was insane, yes, he had done terrible things to me...but maybe there was still a spark of the old Tristan left... perhaps I could somehow reignite it and keep it going. I had no idea.

In the morning, I sat next to Robbie's small bed, stroking his pale soft hand while staring at his delicate face, tormenting myself about what was right and wrong.

Should I listen to my mind or feelings? My heart had led me to him once before and even though it had been a rocky path, it had made us both so incredibly happy. Would it be like that now too — just much harder?

***

A week later, I still didn't know the answer; all I knew was that I wouldn't sleep a wink until I found out — pretty stupid. So, I took a sleeping pill — something I never did... and set my alarm clock. Francesco was already snoring, deep asleep next to me. He slept like a lumberjack, nothing woke him, not even if I rode another guy right next to him wearing a cowboy hat and yelling yee-haw.

Eventually, the pill did the trick. My eyelids fluttered erratically as I hugged my blanket, my wall of protection that separated me from Francesco. My dreams were likewise shaped — restless and unbalanced.

Tonight, they were as confused as my thoughts during the past week. Actually, like recent years. Well, okay... confused and...incredibly...erotic...and so, Tristan...

***

I woke up in the clearing, lying in the warm sunshine — completely naked and defenseless... Abruptly, frightening cold touched my body followed by goose bumps.

As I blinked my eyes open, a shadow hovered over me blocking the soothing rays of the sun. It was Tristan — in your fantasies, you simply know, in real life it doesn't work that way. Although, it wasn't entirely true. Tristan and I always had a subliminal connection between us, which was still unbroken, even last Friday. I knew he felt it too.

Confused, I looked up to admire my literal dream man in all his glory. Since the sun was at his back, I could not see him properly, which promptly annoyed me. "Tristan?" I breathed.

"Who else?" he whispered amused, instantly my old Tristan again, who idolized me. His devoted tone betrayed him and it felt simply glorious. Abruptly, I was overcome with a sense of security, closely followed by immense relief.

"Tristan!" I rejoiced and jumped nimbly up. Finally, I could give in to what I had longed for these past few years, was allowed to put my arms around his neck and snuggle my body against his. He was distractingly naked...and *hard...* He wrapped his arms around my waist and pulled me even closer.

Once again, there was only one thing to say: "I love you..." Tears robbed me of my sight and I pulled his gorgeous face down, covering it with delicate kisses while at the same time declaring, "I did not betray you. I was conned... You simply have to believe me!"

"I love you too, Mia baby, goddammit! It's not like I can help it, you know that, so stop crying," he murmured soothingly as if it was natural to love me — as it used to be in the early days.

All the while, he regarded me tenderly and lovingly. I stood on my tiptoes and grinning, his impertinent hands grabbed my buttocks firmly like they used to do. Panting, I cried out as he lifted me up and wrapped my legs around his hips.

His arousal pushed against the spot where it was best. "Ohhhh... God!" I sighed and threw my head back because his mouth gently brushed over my neck... He moved further down and soon reached the mounds of my breasts, where his tongue joined in. I arched my back...and moaned. Loudly...

"Fuck! You little hot thing." Tristan smiled admonishingly, his absolutely smooth pearly whites sparkling as he lifted me higher, but I trusted him. Tenderly, he bit my nipple and I gasped.

"Not so loud. Wake up, dammit!"

"What?" Tristan moved away and looked at me seriously, as I stared back utterly confused.

"You're supposed to wake the fuck up, woman!"

"Oh!" Abruptly, I was back in the darkness, snuggled up in my bed. What kind of dream did I just have? Sleepy, I rubbed my eyes and sat up.

"A..." My scream was not forthcoming because long strong fingers instantly covered my mouth.

"Be still!" he ordered harshly and I clutched my heart to process the shock. It was racing as if it was trying to burst out my chest. I quickly blinked tears away while trying to adjust to the darkness.

Tristan Wrangler, in the flesh, sat next to me on the mattress as if he belonged there. I smelled his cool manly scent in my contaminated bedroom.

Panic escalated. I was scared and my adrenaline level skyrocketed. Hastily, I glanced at Francesco, ominously asleep with his back to us, quietly snorting. I looked back at Tristan. I could see his outline, the messy hair, the muscular shoulders, and his arrogant aura he always exuded where ever. Carefully, I reached over his lap and turned on the small salt lamp on my bedside table.

The entire time, his finger lay on my lips. Each of my movements, he meticulously watched with his attentive penetrating gaze. I did not dare break contact. Maybe it was better not to say anything at first. For some reason, I always said the wrong thing. The main thing was he was there and touching me. At that moment, I realized I need him as much as I had eight years ago. No matter how.

I raised an eyebrow questioningly and he smiled, not in an outgoing way, but rather demonically. Nevertheless, it was better than nothing.

"Why do you think I came?"

Clueless, I shrugged. His grin widened and his gaze quickly darted to Francesco before looking at me again. Out of nowhere, he placed his denim-encased leg over my naked one.

"Spread'em!" His hand reinforced the brief command, like I wouldn't immediately obey when he spoke to me that way. His harsh tone made my heart and snail ache.

My breathing quickened and my fingers grew clammier when he released my lips and knelt between my legs and slowly leaned down low until he was extremely close to me.

"I simply want to make sure you'll actually show up this evening..." he whispered close to my ear and sat up a bit to look at me. There was confused chaos in his eyes behind a wall I could no longer see over and when my gaze melted in his, I felt something cold against my thong. *Rats!* The fabric quickly surrendered and fell aside. I wanted to squeal, cry, fight! I had no idea what to make of it, but, at the same time, his proximity alone was an aphrodisiac. Breathlessly, I stared at him. He wore a tight black shirt that accentuated his sculpted chest and his ripped abdominal muscles. The sight made me wish I could rip the fabric off him and explore his new build. However, doing so would mean putting my life at risk, meaning, *more* so...

He also watched me — mainly my face while I visually studied his entire body.

What do you have in mind? I inquired with my eyes.

"I honestly don't know what I'll end up doing to you...if we continue this here, but..." he said somewhat hesitantly for the first time since our reunion. It sounded slightly forced before he switched back to amused mode. "...I think I'm going risk it."

"What?" I whispered, unable to believe I was lying alongside him, my sleeping boyfriend next to us in bed, while I quietly talked with my in-the-flesh dream man about whether he would destroy me now or not... To make the thriller perfect, he followed the script and toyed with the knife in his hand...

"Will my hatred for you win the upper hand or my desire for your pussy?" Resting one arm beside me, the pointy tip of the knife followed his gaze down my body. The sharp blade almost scratched my skin...down between my breasts, on to my stomach, over my pubic mound, and then...a tortured groan escaped him while the blade idled at the beginning of my labia.

"Fuck! I've missed *this* sight!" he stated and his breathing quickened. Oh, my God! Did I still have that effect on him? How did he mean it? Was he up to something? Could he please remove the knife from my snail! One wrong move...just his hand trembling! *Oh, God...*

"Be quiet and don't move, Mia Marena! I'm warning you!" Teasingly, the fingers of his free hand slid between my labia. They almost forced me to squirm and twitch — and injure myself on the sharp blade. I whimpered. Tears flooded my eyes... *Oh, no, please...*

With force, he thrust the murderous weapon directly into the mattress next to my hip. I was barely able to suppress a sigh of relief, but on the inside, I was devastated. Sweat poured down my forehead in rivulets.

Sneering, he moved down and leaned his face against my inner thigh. The tips of his hair tickled me and I had to hold onto the bed frame in order not to arch my pelvis toward him. His smooth cheek wandered down my leg. I felt him inhale deeply and looked at the sight of his wild hair between my wide spread knees. Once again, he inhaled my scent.

"M'm," he hummed happily and my breathing became erratic as his nose nuzzled my labia. The touch alone sent hot flashes through me. My hands had a mind of their own as they tried to mangle his silky strands, but I managed to restrain them at the last second like so many times in the past. I wouldn't have been successful anyway because his hand surged upward and grabbed my wrists. At the same time, he threw me a warning look and I clenched my jaw to stay quiet, yet still whimpered.

He held me and bit my pubic mound — not hard, but in a way I definitely felt. Painstakingly, I managed to prevent a faint cry from escaping.

"I said be quiet!" he commanded again and I clamped my jaw tighter together, pinched my eyes shut, and let my head fall back.

When he blew on me, he chuckled, presumably because my body broke out in goose bumps. He was as playful as in the old days, which only made me hornier. I realized that despite his unpredictability, I was growing wetter and thoroughly messing up the bed.

"Long time no see..." he suddenly whispered and ran his index finger up and down my clit. Exceedingly lightly — *too lightly*. Almost snarling, I thrust my pelvis toward him. He should stop horsing around and do it already! It had been eight frustrating years since I had an orgasm and I was still aroused from last Friday. Now, I was more than in urgent need of one!

"You're simply incorrigible!" Exasperated, he frowned and I almost cried because at that moment, he looked like my former Tristan. Nevertheless, he wasn't because the coolness abruptly returned. "Has that son of a bitch also done this?" With that, he lowered his face and with an outstretched tongue, licked between my lips from bottom to top and then firmly flicked my clit. Again, I threw my head back and used all my strength to suppress the cry of lust that wanted to burst from my lips.

Oh my, *Tristan*!

It was too intense!

I quickly fell silent. No one had licked me as deliciously as he did! Well, okay, actually there was no one else but him who did it properly...

"Better not have," I felt him mumble against my snail, followed by taking my clit between his lips, causing my whole body shudder. Sweat now gushed forth, but not only that...I thought I might faint as he tenderly and sensitively sucked on and licked it.

"Ahhh, Tristan..." I panted in a whisper for somehow, I had to let it out or I risked exploding from pleasure.

That was when Francesco responded to my voice and we both froze. Tristan still had his mouth on me, but didn't move it — I did the same. I stared at my boyfriend's back and almost panicked when he rolled over...onto his other side and flung an arm over me. His huge hand landed perfectly on my breast, the one where my heart pounded much too fast and traitorously.

Shocked, I stared at it, thinking it couldn't get any crazier, could it?

Tristan watched the development through narrowed eyes and I could honestly say he did not like it at all. The flashes in his irises made that perfectly clear. Helpless, I shrugged my shoulders. What could I do? If I removed it, Francesco might wake up!

Again, Tristan seemed quite annoyed, so he sat up a bit, grabbed the monster paw, and carefully placed it next to Francesco's face.

Then, he pushed up my body and over my snail. I was certain it was leaving a trail behind. He pushed his crotch between my legs so his tip was right on my clit and began to rotate his hips.

"I don't want to see anything like that again!" His face was so close to mine, I only had to raise my head slightly to kiss him. But I didn't dare.

"It...it...wasn't my fault!" I stated defensively, but Tristan locked my lips with his fingers. *Really* hard.

"I don't give a shit! If he grabs you again while I have my head between your legs, I'll slit his throat!" Shocked, I sucked in my breath and Tristan chuckled quietly. With one hand, he pulled my tank top down, exposing my breasts and teasingly kissed my bare nipple, which immediately hardened.

My eyes rolled back into my head as powerful feelings

coursed through me because Tristan was now gyrating his pelvis with his tip still on my clit. I started moving in unison. As in the past, he knew too well what my body needed and how to give it to me. He was still so damn good...

However, it was more than I could bear. Any second now, I might come. And how! After eight years, it'd probably be the orgasm of the century and I wasn't known for being quiet.

"I... I..." I stammered.

"I know," he grumbled, pressing his fucker even more mercilessly against me.

"Ohhh, I...!" The first wave washed over me. Abruptly, he bit one of my nipples so hard that the pain displaced and overtook my climax. At the last moment, I failed to come... Shocked and beside myself – between pulling in my breast, the throbbing between my legs, and my missed salvation – I glared at him. Then I grew angry.

"Tristan!" I quietly cursed and for a few seconds, forgot the knife that protruded from the mattress beside me. He laughed hoarsely and gave the sore nipple a chaste kiss before unexpectedly disengaging from me and jumping up.

Panting like a steam locomotive, I lay there, face sweaty, hair sticky, eyeing him with a furious heart. Reproachful. He could not possibly be serious. In this condition, I definitely would not function properly!

Tristan was more than amused when he squatted next to my bed and brushed a wet strand from my forehead.

Between my legs throbbed and I experienced an unpleasant twinge.

"It hurts!" I hissed and he grinned wider, looking like the devil himself.

"I know," he replied quietly.

"You're so..." I growled, twisting around, rubbing my thighs desperately together. Warningly, Tristan raised a distinctive eyebrow and I immediately fell silent, ceasing all movements.

"If you want more, show up this evening," he murmured softly and stood up. "And you better not touch yourself!" I wanted to laugh at him because I most certainly would relieve myself. It was unbearable!

"Do you think you can fool me, huh?"

Oh, oh! Elated, he strolled to the door, but before he left my bedroom, he suddenly picked up my slipper. What did he need it for?

"If you get fingered by him, you're dead," he stated.

I still had no idea why he said that because Francesco was asleep and I could just as easily have taken care of it myself. But then, he unexpectedly hurled the shoe at Francesco's face and slipped out of the room grinning demonically.

"What the hell?" The actual complete stranger next to me sat up with a jolt as I heard the thump of the front door while he stared angrily at me.

"What was that?"

Inconspicuously, I pulled the blanket over my body so

he wouldn't discover the knife and slit panties. "Um..." I was far too bewildered. "Nothing, honey, go back to sleep." Thank goodness the footwear bounced off him and landed on the ground!

I wondered if he would go back to sleep when the alarm buzzed.

Preferably, I would have liked to freak out loudly because now I had lost the opportunity to put an end to the unbearable throbbing between my legs.

***

I was still quite upset when I was about to say goodbye to my pseudo-boyfriend to go work. He stood there in the bathroom with a towel wrapped around his waist, frowning while inspecting his split lip without the slightest clue how it occurred. I almost felt sorry for him because Tristan must have hurled the shoe forcefully.

Francesco regarded me skeptically, like he suspected I beat him during the night. I let him believe it for what else could I say: *uh, my...psycho lover did that... He became a little upset when you place your hand on my breast as he was going down on me while you unwittingly slept next to us.*

Not a chance...

***

Today we were going to bake. Daniel and Steffen, twin brothers, age ten, were cutting apples; Heike and Susi prepped the dough because at 12, they were the oldest, and Robbie was sitting on my lap. Armed with a huge chef's hat and a big wooden spoon, he was the one giving instructions for a change. He was so happy being in charge that most of the cake he was eating crumbled out of his mouth because he was laughing so hard.

After cleaning up the mess we made, we went into the garden where I chased the children with the water hose.

Then they took a bath and afterward, I read a bedtime story to each child followed by a peck on the forehead before I headed home. Francesco was already waiting for me — equipped with lip balm.

"Hey, Tristan Wrangler called again," my friend told me excitedly. Hastily, I slammed the door shut behind me and ran into my small but cozy living room.

"What did he say?" I inquired casually. Did he call to cancel? Shit, I didn't think I would survive it. Although, more likely, I would not handle it well if he didn't cancel, then again, it would significantly increase my chances of survival. Confused, I quickly blinked and disregarded my inner thoughts. No matter which, my heart would not survive, so it didn't matter.

"He had asked if he could borrow you until tomorrow because he has some compelling ideas for the photo session!"

Oh, God! My cheeks felt red. Hurriedly, I turned away from Francesco and leaned down to my most loyal companion in the world, my sweet black Chihuahua Stanley and buried my face in his fur. Actually, he was the only one left from my old life.

"And you should wear the shoes you had on last time."

Could it get any crazier? Images from the last time popped into my mind, setting my insides on fire.

"Anything else?" I asked rather uninterested and gave Stanley, who was now a little gray around the muzzle, a little milk bone before gently scratching his nose and ears.

"Yup, I am supposed to tell you that, uh...wait, how did he put it...?" Francesco was his usual carefree innocent self. "He has enough ass cream, so don't worry, or something like that..." Perplexed, he shrugged.

Ohhhh, that would mean I might be sore after tonight! The idea was enough to make me change my panties. "All this time I've been wondering what he meant by that?" Francesco mused thoughtfully. My eyes widened and I wrinkled my forehead. Dammit, I had to work on controlling my expression. I urgently needed a distraction!

"I don't know. Anyhow, I have to go to the bathroom!" I murmured as I quickly disappeared into the bathroom to shower and remove all unwanted hair. Surely, Tristan still loved it shaven and if not, he'd certainly tell me in no uncertain terms. I was as excited as a 14-year-old before her first date with the school hunk — basically, like in the old days. My tension increased the closer the imaginary pointer on my cell phone clock approached eight.

Incidentally, I seriously wondered if Francesco had become suspicious. After all, such a photo shoot rarely lasted all night. But, knowing Tristan, he had come up with an excuse that sounded logical. Back in the day, he was already quite skilled at manipulating people and I had an inkling he had become much better at it by now... It turned me on as well as frightened me.

***

I was dependent on a bicycle and the subway because I still didn't own a car despite a valid driver's license. Francesco was notorious for not letting me drive his luxury car for something could happen to his expensive Ferrari. So, I had no choice but to pedal vigorously away — uphill, my goal always in sight.

The closer I came to the ostentatious settlement, the more nervous I grew. Meanwhile, I was convinced I might throw up or pee my pants once I stood before him again. But no matter the cost, I planned to stay in control of myself because, personally, I found the risk of him turning away from me in obvious disgust too high. I was sick — without a doubt, but it was not like I ever claimed differently.

Today, I would not wear exquisite clothes like I had at our first meeting. I was hoping, actually suspecting, he might cut me out of them again. Naturally, hot pants panties were mandatory— this time in white, like the bra. The color of innocence. Yeah, right, who was I kidding? As if that would stop someone like Tristan Wrangler!

In addition, I selected low riding skinny jeans and a skin-tight black turtleneck sweater. Since I had bought the clothing from a thrift store, I had no problem sacrificing them. For the sake of simplicity, I pulled my hair into a

– 94 –

ponytail. Honestly, I had no time to blow dry and style it properly — or perhaps my frail nerves were to blame or both. Either way, it was the only option other than running around with a bird's nest on my head. My handbag – a practical dark shoulder bag – held everything a woman in today's age might need: cell phone, wallet, high heels, and an extra pair of panties... My light jacket and Chucks complemented my outfit. Obviously, it looked quite funny, but I couldn't peddle in high heels.

At one point, I eventually managed to get to the top of the damn hill even though I dismounted halfway up and pushed the bicycle the rest of the way. It was hell, but finally I was standing in front of Tristan's gallery. Again, the surrounding area was illuminated by gently flickering torches, whose light reflected off the extravagant vehicles in the parking lot. Puzzled, I noticed I couldn't see anyone in the entire, fully glazed ground floor except for a few wonderfully illuminated treasures. Unsteadily, I changed into my high heels and slowly approached the front of the building, which was easily accessible from the road. From afar, there was no sign of a doorbell, making me wonder if there even was one or how I would get in. As soon as I stepped up to the sturdy door, a buzzer sounded.

I quickly opened it and was greeted by a bunch of security cameras in the foyer — unquestionably, just like the control freak he had been in the old days.

Music welcomed me as I entered — loud and breathtaking. It was one of my favorite pieces. Nothing else greeted me except for the instrumental background music. The hall felt deserted except for the unique photos I had admired last time. The picture of me and Tristan in the clearing was also on display, illuminated by two spotlights to emphasize the scene. Mesmerized, I walked toward it. I wished I could take it down and hide it somewhere. Unfortunately, it wasn't possible. Where could I even put such big painting?

Nevertheless, it was beautiful, so passionate, without coming across as offensive. Representing erotica in such a way was an art in itself. One he had mastered quite well.

Wistfully, I thought about my old figure. Nowadays, I know I had never truly been fat, I merely thought so.

At the time, I never believed Tristan, even though he always made an effort to explain it to me. It was strange how differently humans perceived themselves. Insecure people oftentimes regarded themselves as ugly even though they were not. What was the saying: one desires what one no longer has. As one ages, one yearns for one's youth completely ignoring the fact that one did not like oneself at the time. A vicious cycle of dissatisfaction.

"It's not for sale, Miss Angel."

Ohhhh! There it was again! *Miss Angel*, emphasized in that soft, flattering, and yet provocative velvety voice. Instantly, my underwear dissolved into nothingness. I whirled around and saw him on the upstairs landing of the open-air staircase that led from art gallery to the second floor.

His appearance was simply...*breathtaking.*

The dark hair — the usual relatively short mess. The body – its usual sexiness – and Tristan Wrangler – his usual arrogant self.

His elegant dark slacks hung much too loosely on his hips. A totally black shirt — top three buttons undone... sleeves rolled up... He most likely knew there was nothing more attractive and compelling than the tendons on his muscular forearms...as well as his relaxed pose, although he was still as graceful as a predator on the hunt.

Wow! Tristan in a suit...

In the old days, he would have blown me away, albeit now I was at a loss for words. No wonder with an idling brain. It was difficult not to drool. Jeez, I needed to ensure I maintained my composure and did not behave like some pubescent school brat. I certainly was no longer one! I was now a grown woman!

But...God, he was *so* handsome! And I still loved him *so much*!

When he raised a brow, I noticed a brief little smirk scurrying across his cool smooth features.

"I wasn't thinking of fucking your mouth just now, Mia Marena, so you may as well close it!"

Dammit! Quickly, I sealed my lips and promptly froze. "You've never called me *Mia Marena*." I had no idea why that popped into my mind now because back at the exhibition, he had used my full name. Presumably, I was too shocked by his presence to register it.

He tilted his head slightly to one side and analyzed me. "What did I call you?" Unexpected and in slow motion, he strolled down the staircase as if on a catwalk without breaking eye contact. He walked right up to me, almost touching me and I began to tremble with anticipation. Finally, he whispered, "What should I call you?" I craned my neck in order to look at his perfect face.

"Like you don't remember," I whispered.

"Indeed!" His index finger brushed up and down my carotid artery, causing me to shiver violently. It was a silent threat. Breathless, I felt the warmth of his skin, counted the seconds, waiting for the attack, all the while not daring to swallow, too afraid he might take it as an affront — and, at the same time, silently cried out for him to finally do it.

No such luck.

"These past years have changed me... It made me look at things from a different perspective...reconsider my ways... abandon inappropriate behaviors...accept certain realities..." He said everything in a mysterious, barely audible murmur. "I know you would love for me to call you *baby*...but that name is reserved only for the woman I love. And she died a long time ago for me, along with my old self. They no longer exist..." *Ouch!* That hurt! I was standing right here — *before him!* My heart beat only for him! Still...

"It's not...what you think. It was supposed to be different than..."

"So?" He only glanced at me fleetingly before focusing on my neck again, almost rendering me incapable of thinking logically. "Was I or was I not sentenced to a two-year prison term because of your statement?"

"But..."

I was threatening to hyperventilate as he finally looked directly at me. However, now his smile was gone as if never existed. "Did you or did you not make a statement?"

Feverishly, I wondered how I could explain everything, how it was a big stupid mistake, that I had been set up by my father without it sounding totally implausible.

I had years to think about ways to tell him in case we met again. And now, I couldn't utter one syllable. From sheer nervousness, I began to gnaw my lip and gazed at the floor. Crap!

"Answer me!" The rest of his hand joined the index finger and cupped my chin, forcing it up with a jerk so I had to look at him.

His presence, powerful build, and inner strength intimidated me. I could not find any resemblance to the old Tristan. There was nothing soft and inviting about him. Instead, I was confronted with rejection and hardness.

"I had to..." I sobbed and squeezed my eyes closed. Before I could break out in tears, he distanced himself. As before, he was still speaking softly, almost seductively, but his words couldn't have been crueler.

"That innocent maiden from the country does not work anymore, understand? You might want to think about your actions and what you say; otherwise, I cannot guarantee I'll remain as nice as I am now..." If this was him being *nice*, I didn't want to see him angry. Only I was afraid I would have to deal more with the ice-cold Tristan than the supposedly *nice* one.

"Come!" he ordered and towed me upstairs, not watching out for me until we stepped onto the plush carpeted hallway. We turned right, climbed a spiral staircase, and finally stopped in front of a white door. Tristan punched in a code on the keypad, whereupon a green button lit up and we could enter. Again, we walked along a hallway — this time with black carpeting. Here too, he didn't give me an opportunity to look around for he was relentlessly tugging on my wrist. He stopped at the last door with a sign in gold lettering:

Godfather of Fuck

Was he serious? I felt like rolling my eyes and snorting sarcastically, but I refrained because I could not assess the new Tristan. That excessive megalomania he was displaying so obviously topped any grandiose behavior he had years ago. He might have been full of himself in the old days, but now he was definitely at a new level, especially so openly.

My first impression upon entering the room — decadent. Soft golden flooring and many artistic elements dominated the expansive area. Tristan headed directly to the minibar, which was not out in the open. Questioningly, he looked at me. As I shook my head, he imitated my gesture – quicker – and casually uncorked a bottle of ice wine.

Yummy... He still had distinctive tastes. As he dropped ice cubes into *two* glasses and poured the sparkling liquid, I continued inspecting the strangely alluring office. A huge kinky coffee table grabbed my attention. I was staring at a detailed vagina under a polished glass plate. Behind it, I noticed a dark leather couch and a large executive desk chair.

The walls, completely free of cabinets, were adorned with various frames. The captured breast and hand seemed eerily familiar. Maybe I needed to ask Tristan how many more pictures of us were in the impressive building. In one picture, I recognized his brothers and father with a giant black gorilla. Irritated, I stared at the animal.

Although overwhelmed by all the impressions, I said nothing, yet I wanted to know everything. I was simply too curious, but I took great comfort in knowing that at least his family was still part of his life. Maybe I could manage to get Vivi's number, after all, I hadn't heard from her since that dreadful day eight years ago. Not that it surprised me. My gaze wandered...another picture...

I almost laughed at it had it not been for my intuition warning me not to make a peep. It was god himself, enthroned on a cloud with outstretched legs, looking down on earth, grinning devilishly, where everyone was naked and participating in an orgy. The boss of heaven was, obviously, none other than Tristan, who held an oversized joint between his fingers while his other hand seemingly caressed the shiny dark gun resting on his thigh like it was his new baby number one.

The recessed golden ceiling lights provided the appropriate divine ambiance. Again, I had to stifle a giggle that immediately vanished as soon as something out of the corner of my eye demanded my attention.

Behind his desk, dead center in a beautiful frame, hung the picture of our clearing. It warmed my heart and drew me closer as I stared, mesmerized by the grass, trees, stream... At the last second, I managed to stop myself from touching the two shadows I had sketched in shortly before that terrible day.

"Why didn't you ever tell me you were the artist?"

Slowly, I turned to him. Embarrassed, I wiped the tears that had trickled down my cheeks unnoticed. "I don't know."

"Well, that wasn't the only thing you lied about to me." Now, he sat in his chair in the middle of the room. One foot rested on his thigh with the leg angled sideways as he, probably lost in thought, watched me while gently swirling his crystal glass. Unreadable and utterly unloving, yet still beautiful.

Naturally, I was aware of the heat rising inside me, which always gripped me when Tristan Wrangler looked at me. I peeled myself out of my coat and carefully draped it over the back of a chair along with my bag.

The entire time, he didn't take his eyes off me, not even for one second, skillfully rattling my nerves.

Yes, this truly was a new Tristan. Dangerous...

Undecided, I stood in front of him as he handed me the unwanted full glass. I was never a person to fight losing battles, so I grabbed it with sweaty hands.

"So..." My trembling voice reflected my mood. "What do you want from me?"

Another round of in-depth scrutinizing followed before he spoke — calmly and at ease, yet furtive. Like a predator about to pounce.

"Actually, the question is what do you want from me?" The whole thing almost resembled a hypnosis trick considering his velvety deep voice, intense look, and minimal movements — almost slow motion. I felt more than queasy and as I answered, it felt like I was hearing myself from afar.

"I want you."

"You want me, you say?" he repeated sarcastically. "So you can betray me again and destroy me a second time around?"

"No! It wasn't like that! I never wanted anything bad to happen to you, you have to believe me! I want you back, whatever it takes..."

Humorlessly – with a hint of disbelief – he laughed. "So, you actually came here because you want me back even though you knew I'd like to see you dead?" His jibe wasn't lost on me and seemingly brave, I nodded.

His grin was diabolical as his eyes sparkled challengingly. "You really are not normal... Okay!"

"Okay, what?" I pressed before I realized his pun.

"Okay... your wish is my command..." Before I had a chance to enjoy my inner sigh of relief and smile, he added tersely, "But I have one tiny condition."

"Yes?" My heart pounded so loudly in my chest, I was sure he could hear it. "Which is...?" Again, he bowed his head, but there wasn't the slightest smile on his lips. "For the next three months, both your mind and body belong to me to do with as I please. You will oblige my wishes — *no matter* what they may be. I am allowed to do as I please, whereas you have no rights. Now..." The corners of his mouth twitched mockingly. "...if the mood strikes me, I may be inclined to change my mind and believe your fucking lies..." Judging his face, it was beyond all eventualities.

"If you destroy me, it won't do me any good!" I had no idea where I found the nerve to be sarcastic.

"I'll honestly try my best not to let it go that far." Tristan winked at me.

It was absolutely and completely insane. I, him — the whole conversation!

"So...let me see if I understand correctly: If I bend to your will and do whatever you ask or have planned for me, I will be given the opportunity to explain myself?" I wasn't interested in anything else but his forgiveness, for which I'd actually do anything. Even if only so that everyone involved could shake off the demons of the past to live their lives unencumbered and, eventually, go without regret and a clear conscience into the light. His now rather brown eyes looked provocatively at me from under his long lashes. For a brief moment, they flashed, but it was gone before I could capture it.

"Yes," he replied plainly. Even if I didn't believe him, it was my only chance and I would use it!

"Okay," I agreed, regardless that I suspected I had agreed to a Faustian pact and therefore welcomed hell on earth. Tristan looked at me with an almost honest, open bright smile.

"I knew you would agree. It's your naiveté and simplemindedness."

"That's not me!" I exclaimed. "I agreed to it because I never stopped loving you."

"Yeah, yeah, yeah, whatever...let's get down to business."

"Get down to business?"

Lithely, he got up and headed to his desk.

"Well, obviously, we have to put it in writing."

"WHAT?" When he realized I hadn't taken a sip of my drink yet, he smugly held the glass to my lips.

"Drink!" he commanded, grinning mockingly. I downed it in one gulp.

He removed a black manila folder from the top drawer. Apparently, he was completely prepared — making me wonder how long he had been planning his revenge. Upon opening it, he directed me to his executive chair. He pushed me roughly into it and stood behind me. Wordlessly, he shoved the documents into my sweaty hands as he leaned over my shoulder threateningly –delectably scented – and grabbed his anti-stress ball off the table and kneaded it. For a few seconds, I was mesmerized by his slender fingers before focusing on the text in front of me.

"First clause…" I read softly to myself, "…no kissing... What?" I turned my face to him and was shocked at how close he was for my lips almost touched the corner of his mouth.

Oh, God! My cheap pants couldn't hold back the waterfall much longer. Tristan rolled his eyes as he stared unabashedly at my breasts. "No mouthing off! You see it written in black and white; I won't kiss you!"

"Why?"

"Simply because just like using pet names, I only kiss when I'm in love. Obviously, it doesn't apply to sluts."

OUCH! Once again...his indirect insult made me cringe, yet I still intended to do everything to make him change his mind about me. I may be many things! Naive! Gullible! Dreamer! Absolutely smitten with him! But definitely not a slut!

"I cannot even touch you?" I yelled after reading the next clause.

"That's right, unless I command you."

"Is there anything I'm allowed to do?" God, this man was so frustrating!

"Continue reading and you'll find out," he countered dryly.

Oh, yeah, he certainly was having his fun with me. However, he tried his best not to let me see his satisfaction.

"Third clause," I read next, which was written in big bold capital letters, followed by ten exclamation marks. "No fucking other guys...? Are you serious?" I mockingly probed. Slowly but surely, I grew mad.

"Do I look like I'm joking?" he suddenly asked sharply. Again, I turned to face him. As I bit my lip, he frowned, so I stopped instantly. However, it was good to know it still had the same effect on him as in the old days. "Uh, since then...somehow...I have...had...no sex..."

"What?" For a change, it was his turn to be shocked. He abruptly stood up straight and stared at me with his mouth agape. "Your pussy has seen no cock for eight years? For eight *fucking years*!?"

"When I said you're the only one for me and it would always be like that, I meant it!" The expression that scurried across his face was too brief to classify. He leaned back over me and rested his smooth cheek against mine, which almost made me purr...

"Keep reading!"

Confused, I looked at him and tried to come to terms with the closeness and my newly arising hope, when my gaze traveled back down to the slightly rough paper.

"Fourth clause; you are the only one who may bring me to orgasm?"

"Yep!" Tristan seemed quite pleased with himself.

"Who else would do it? I just explained to you that since..."

"I intend to make you so fucking horny that you're willing to kill for an orgasm. You're not allowed to take matters into your hands or, should I say, fingers, no matter how much you want it!" he interrupted, breathing in my ear. *M'mmmm...* Frantically, I suppressed a whimper when I felt his moist tongue, followed by his warm full lips underneath.

"You are mean!" I pouted.

"I know." He sounded as if he was congratulating himself, which really made me angry. However, I refrained from replying sarcastically and instead returned my attention back to the weird document.

"Fifth clause; I will only moan, talk, move, or squirm when you've given me permission. Tell me, am I allowed to breathe?"

"Nope!" I wanted to respond, but I was too distracted by his lips brushing against my neck and I had to close my eyes. It was sweet and malicious torture because everything felt so intense since I had desired his caresses for so long. I wanted to wrap my arms around his neck and...

"Forget it," I heard him mumbling against my heated skin when he sensed my intention. I tried to hide the effect he had on me, but unfortunately, my trembling betrayed my intense emotions.

"Continue, Miss Angel." Now he actually sounded amused and carefree, like the way I loved him...*more than anything*!

For a second, it felt like we had never separated, yet still as exciting as with a stranger. An intoxicating mix. His cheek continued snuggling against mine as his chin rested on my shoulder. He was so damn close and yet, I was not allowed to touch him, only receive. It reminded me of cuddling with a wild predator. Any wrong move might lead to the destruction of this magical moment.

"If I sign this...am I also allowed to make rules?" I directed my attention back to the document in front of me.

"Absolutely not!"

"Why?"

"As I said; continue reading." One finger pointed at the document.

"In other words, I should always be submissive and never ask questions. Which makes you what, a damn dom?"

"How do you know that term?" he asked somewhat baffled.

"Perhaps you remember that we covered that topic. By the way, I read FanFiction..." With that revelation, I turned beet red.

"Huh, I can already see...I will have my fun." He grinned broodingly. "And no, I'm not a damn dom. I simply do what I enjoy. I don't abide by any of the usual rules or whatever crap. However, I cannot deny that I found it quite stimulating back when I dominated you in my own way. And, I plan to expand it quite a bit."

"Reassuring to know," I muttered ironically.

"Nevertheless, that's not my goal because I find it fucking exhilarating when you're scared. This is not a goddamn fucking joke," he curtly informed me, signaling that our casual moment had come to an end. I swallowed hard – not at all thrilled – because honestly, I didn't find it exciting! Well, okay, perhaps a bit... Anyway, I didn't want him intimidating me even more. So, on to the next clause:

"I have to shave my entire body. I expected as much. And eat my meals at your discretion? What does that mean?"

As I finished the last syllable, Tristan swung my chair around. He placed an elbow on the armrest, grabbed my jaw with one hand, and applied so much pressure to my cheeks that it almost hurt.

"You're too skinny!"

"In the old days I was fat, now I'm too skinny. Who cares?" I mumbled indistinctly.

"You've never been fat. Goddammit!" he growled softly, accomplishing as much as if he had yelled. Unfortunately, I couldn't move backward because he had a hold of me. For a few seconds, we merely stared at each other until the rage in his eyes abated and he roughly released me.

"You will be at my disposal every evening, Friday through Sunday, and always reachable. There will be no safe words or whatever lifelines for you... It says so further down below. So, let's cut to the chase; are you in or out?" With that, he distanced himself and hurled the ball forcefully (which apparently failed its purpose) against the tabletop. He crossed his arms in front of his chest and eyed me with an unreadable expression. Oh, upper arm muscles alarm! Not to mention the imperious way he looked down on me...

Crap! A considerable part of me wanted to spontaneously tear my clothes off and let him fuck me right here on his desk. Knowing how he looked naked didn't help one bit. Just to mention it.

Then, there still was the little voice that was truly afraid of the man, who might resemble my Tristan in many ways but didn't at the same time. I have never known him to be this ruthless and cold — at least, not toward me.

"If not, then go. The door is over there..." As our laden with meaning looks traveled to it, the door opened as if on command and a little blonde nude elf with long curly hair and bouncing breast implants sauntered into the room. Dammit! What was she doing here so perfect, naked, and with... What were they? Did she have piercings in her nipples?

"Mary?" He looked at her with a raised brow as she froze upon seeing me in the chair. Was he fucking her? A stupid question — obviously, he was. Why else would she come charging into his office naked without knocking? The thought of him with another was so painful that it had the potential to kill me. My blood boiled while I tried to hide it. "Um, I'm supposed to tell you that...in the basement... Who's this?" she blurted out.

"What's it to you?" he replied.

Oh, okay. Now I was truly puzzled, garnished with a small dash of satisfaction.

"Sorry, boss..." she mumbled sheepishly. Boss? The situation grew increasingly perplexing. What was going on here? Now my inner turmoil was joined by curiosity.

So, Tristan was the...*boss*...of the nude nymph with the angelic face...?

Driven by the sparks his narrowed eyes spewed, she hastily fled the room.

He was still standing before me with his arms crossed – resembling a disturbingly beautiful statue – looking almost dreamily after her ass. Naturally, with his head tilted.

God, I wanted to kill him until he was dead!

As the door closed, he looked provocatively at me with a condescending smirk.

That ass knew perfectly well I had a jealous streak, how it would eat at me, yet he shamelessly toyed with my feelings! Something inside of me exploded! If he wanted to play it that way, so could I! He would discover the consequences for setting such rules and believing he could intimidate me. Since I was impetuous, I tossed all caution to the wind. I wanted to know now! Everything!

Therefore, I rose and ripped the manila folder out of his hand. Flabbergasted, he watched as I slapped the paper on the desk and grabbed the heavy expensive-looking pen lying there. Before I could resist the temptation to reconsider my decision, I zestfully signed my name on the contract line.

And that was that!

Speechless, Tristan stood behind me. I felt his breath on my neck as I finished and simply waited for a few seconds with my arms braced on the tabletop.

I'd just dedicated my life and soul to the devil. That was the only way to put it.

"And now?" For some reason, I simply felt exhausted.

"Now..." He wrapped an arm around my waist and pulled me a bit to the left so we were facing a golden velvet curtain, which, honestly, I had not noticed until now. "The party can begin," he whispered in my ear and the curtain slowly opened.

What I saw made my knees go weak because clearly I no longer knew Tristan. I no longer knew his world either and yes, it might be too much for me. Yes, I just completely shit my pants...

Because he, the man to who I had just signed over my body and soul, was the owner of a sex club!

7. Second Submission

Tristan 'The Dominant' Wrangler

I was still somewhat perplexed because she signed the crap and I believed I would have to bait her some more, woo her — perhaps even be *friendly*. What normal person would unconditionally agree to something like that without batting an eye?

I guess it was thanks to Mary's inappropriate naked timing... If she hadn't stormed in and I had not used the moment to make Mia jealous, she probably would not have succumbed to her emotions.

It was...such a hot feeling. I had no problem seeing her eyes erupt with jealousy when she noticed Mary's virtues and how natural she stood unclothed before me. It was commonplace for me and not worth another look. Nevertheless, for an outsider, for someone who might be as presumably innocent as Mia Marena – holy shit, what a crappy name, but not surprising with such parents – the scene must have been shocking.

It was hilarious; she hadn't changed a bit and still acted outwardly the same as before, shy and naive. But I wasn't fooled for a second — if she wanted, she could extend her claws and do damage. I had experienced it on my own body/heart.

There was still lots of spirit under that seemingly tranquil surface and I knew exactly how to bring it to a boil so it would finally spill over.

That had always been my specialty, but now I would be a bit more brutal simply because I had waited eight fucking years to live out my twisted fantasies and desires with my personal perfect *avenging angel*.

Though...she wasn't all that perfect anymore — it was clear I had to stuff her like a damn Thanksgiving turkey! She was only breasts and thighs. The question of whether she, like I, still suffered from the events of eight years ago, wasn't to be discussed.

However, something was on her mind because she looked downright exhausted; the dark circles spoke of many nights without sleep. Who the fuck knows what kept her up at night! Or was it because she was afraid of me? The idea had some...

Otherwise, there was no reason to worry about me. Whatever we had was half an eternity ago and she had a great new life with her great new boyfriend, apartment, dream job, pool, yacht, fucking personal trainer, and whatever bells and whistles — compared to me, she was moving in the light! Everything else was merely show.

Apart from the club, gym, photos, and my annoying yet somehow – yes, I had to admit – damn cool brothers, there was *nothing*. Otherwise, I was frustrated and bored — in Tristan mode.

The old pattern repeated itself...but it would stop — right fucking *now!*

With satisfaction, I recalled her horror when I showed her my empire — my personal heaven and her future hell.

She had not expected me to be a *true* sex god now. Presumably, she had suspected that I was merely a hobby photographer, which actually represented the fact, only slightly twisted because I was indeed an artist — it was simply that the subject was uncommon and anything but harmless. The word did not exist in my vocabulary!

That she had signed, despite everything, took time to digest. So, I left her seemingly fossilized figure alone in front of the glass and I threw myself across my three-seater couch to relax and enjoy a smoke — some things never changed. I had the best grass in the city and if she knew how much I kept in the safe, the little slut might call her daddy and rat me out again. Nevertheless, I was always careful so he couldn't touch me.

What a crappy thought to have now!

Whenever I recalled what she did to me, I felt the anger in me rising and wanted to strangle her with my bare hands. Especially now that she was finally within reach, the notion was even stronger than before.

For that, the time had yet to come. On a side note, my pecker still vehemently protested when such ideas popped into my mind. It did not care whether she was skinny or fat, if she had betrayed us, or if she was a slut, or my... It simply wanted to get in there because her pussy still was – no matter if the rest of her was thin or thick – the tightest it had ever felt.

Silently cursing, I shifted the impatient bum in my pants to a more comfortable position as I eye-fucked her back and blew different sized smoke rings with one of my lower arms braced over the angled leg with my leg stretched out over the entire length of the couch.

She still had not moved, was lost, with one hand against the cool window glass, staring. I considered throwing something at her so she would turn around. It reminded me of how I had tossed her slipper at Francesco's face this morning – the idiot – and I grinned with satisfaction. But what was that prick thinking, putting his hand on her tit while I was going down on her...?!

Oh, how she had tasted... To have such ideas right now was absolutely wrong because it made me rock hard. Not to mention, I was afraid it might burst the zipper of my pants at any moment now, kind of Rambo-style in camouflage and persuade me to fall over her uncontrollably. Tsk, tsk... I would *definitely not* give the impression I was still an 18-year-old, hormone-driven absolute imbecile, which I had portrayed back then.

Although, when it came to her, it seemed I was still quite hormone or fuck-driven, although now I could control it. In the sex industry, it was inevitable that you learned it over time.

Besides, this evening I was definitely not going to do her the favor and fuck her. *Because* she was yearning for it! She should know from the start that she couldn't control me — not even with her powerful pussy muscles. She should know that now, without exception, I was in charge. Of course, for that I had to put a mental chastity belt on my pecker, otherwise, it would ruin everything.

Yeah...that was the plan... So far, so good... I even had already played the James Bond intro in my head.

I took another long drag and watched her from under lazy lids. However, I wasn't quite as relaxed on the inside; appearances were deceiving.

"And I'm supposed to swallow your hilarious statement that I'm the only one you have had sex with?" I really couldn't wrap my head around it! Especially since she was together with teeny-weenie for what must be eons and I was sure in all that time she couldn't have kept him at bay. No normal man would put up with that for so long... Not that that bastard was normal... But at least now I knew why he visited my club once a week. Naturally, I was perfectly aware of his preferences and I could not help but feel relieved because it was obvious he wasn't getting it from her. Even if I wanted to torture and break her, no one else was allowed! That was my job!

My words ripped her from her paralysis. She turned around and gave me a look I had never seen before.

She seemed cautious, scared...just fucking hot...

"So...you're the owner of a sex club?" she enquired hollowly.

"Yes... Why haven't you fucked someone else?" I took another drag from the joint and sat up as she cautiously sat down next to me. In a way as if she really didn't trust me anymore because I earned my money through sex... She obviously didn't care that she was at my mercy, that I had just psychologically humiliated her, and announced several times to end her existence. Maybe she didn't care about me making good on my threats...but the fact I was a sex club owner awakened her distrust and intimidated her the most. That woman would forever remain a mystery to me.

"Because just the thought felt wrong." She gnawed on her lip again while staring at mine as they wrapped around the joint. I ignored her and casually gazed at the ceiling. "How long have you had this club?"

"About six years now. Why? Something wrong with it?" I watched her out of the corner of an eye as she closed her eyes and dropped back against the backrest.

"Because it wouldn't have been you," she whispered softly, but I still heard it and rolled my eyes. Holy shit...did she think I was buying all that crap? "What goes on in here?"

I made myself more comfortable and stared at the black ceiling in my office with its many spotlights, as well as her.

"H'm. What do you think happens in a sex club? People certainly don't come to buy asparagus or whatever seasonal crap," I replied. Seeing she wouldn't leave it alone, I told her. "People come here to fulfill their most secret fantasies, to feel what they cannot perceive in everyday life. Or, to get what they think they are missing out on in real life — yet, in actuality, they are simply blind and chase fantasies that do not exist outside in the real world... Anyway, I offer them the illusion of erotic, like it's written in the book."

"Have you ever...visited your club to live out your fantasies? With Mary? Have you broken her or someone else in?" I automatically smirked whether I liked it or not because there she was again: little jealous Mia... Marena — bitch.

Now, I sat up sideways and placed one leg under my body. She opened her eyes and turned to me. I grinned at her as I as casually played with a strand of her hair that tickled my fingers while my arm rested on the couch back. Everything about me screamed openness, but that was the subtle difference: even if I had people convinced I was charming — deep down I had a dark nature... No one was aware of my inner blackness unless I wanted them too and now I could keep it hidden, even from her. "I simply cannot live out my fantasies."

"Why not?" she inquired, downright curious, brought on by our *frank talk.*

"Because it feels wrong." I almost used her exact same words in a silkily perfectly trained breath.

"Why?" she inquired yet again, confused and agitated by my pseudo-seductive tone.

"Because you weren't here." I raised a brow provocatively to take the game to another level...and yes, as expected — her cheeks blushed, thinking I was wooing her. Stupid little cunt!

Rather than roll my eyes, I stood up, leaned down to her again, and brushed a strand behind her ear.

"I have only one single fantasy that I've been longing for all these years." She could not have looked happier...until... "Let yourself be surprised."

Suddenly, her cheeks paled... "Are you serious?"

"Oh, yes!" Grinning broadly, I pulled her to her feet. "When the time comes, you'll know." With these words, I dragged her out of my office.

She let out a breathless, insecure, actually slightly hysterical laugh.

Let her... I loved playing with her uncertainty.

Whistling, I led her across the entire floor to the staircase and down into the club.

My statement seemed to affect her control over her body for she stumbled behind me. However, she had always been that way.

Her eyes dilated, probably never to return to their normal size again, as she surveyed the scene before us. In addition, her mouth hung open when she noticed the entertainers preparing backstage for their performances. Female dancers stretched to warm up and applied glittery oil to each other. The male dancers, wearing only thongs, did push-ups or pull-ups to emphasize their muscles. Lara, the fire-eater, ran out of her dressing room, looking around frantically for someone with her breasts covered with some flimsy material. Naturally, I stopped and without a word, skillfully laced up her corset. My fingers were watched the entire time and her eyes narrowed when Lara received a light slap on the ass once I finished.

"Thanks, boss!" she called cheerfully after me... I smirked inside.

As Mel ran by us with her giant boa wrapped around her shoulders, Mia Marena clung tightly to my arm as if we were in a jungle, afraid she'd end up a snack. Ha! Just wait until she stepped foot into the official part of my palace because that was where the *real* beasts lurked. She seemed to forget she was hiding behind the cruelest hunter for protection.

Crazy...

Everyone greeted me respectfully, I responded casually, causing many to look a little puzzled, standing there dressed only underwear, if at all.

By the time we reached the red curtain separating the back area from the actual club, Mia Marena seemed almost turned on. Still grinning, I kept pulling her along the side of the elevated platform, stopping briefly at the rear of the stage so she could absorb the full extent of the crap she had unerringly dived headlong into.

The strong smell of sex, sex, and more sex. Half-naked

and fully exposed people. Booming music.

The obvious ecstasy between flashing lights.

"Oh, God..." was the only thing she mumbled as we made our way to the main bar.

Out of the corner of an eye, I noticed Garrett approaching, as usual, completely naked, except for a leather collar with an eyelet... aha. Tonight, he already belonged to a happy lady. Not at all pleased, I noticed Mia Marena staring at him, blushing. The way she took in his oiled muscular form, his black short hair, his sparkling blue eyes, the perfect smooth hard-trained appearance...and how she stumbled as he grinned at her and joined us.

"Hey, boss..." She could not stop staring at his abdomen.

"You like what you see?" I whispered into her hair and she instantly stiffened.

"How's it going?" I immediately inquired.

"I have already serviced two ladies. One fell in love with my ass." He turned around and showed me his red, recently spanked ass cheeks. Mia Marena panted and, I believe, mumbled a little prayer as she stared at the ground, turning beet red. I rolled my eyes.

"Ouch," I announced, amused. Garrett simply dismissed it. *It* was merely foreplay to him.

"Who is the young lady by your side?" He eyed said night owl from head to toe and up again, probably thinking she was a new whore. I intentionally did not introduce her because I wanted her to feel like one.

"This is just Mirta." Immediately, she stiffened and shot me a dirty look because she had always hated that name.

"Hi, Mirta!" Garrett mumbled politely and offered her his hand. I roughly pinched her side so she understood that from now on, her name was *Mirta* and, although she glanced up in frustration, she sighed and agreed.

"Hi, Garrett, nice to meet you," she grumbled sullenly, but still tried to be friendly. Typical...

"And?" he asked casually as he leaned against the bar we had arrived at. "What is your talent? Mistress? Slave? Blowjobs? Handjobs, tittie jobs, urolagnia, scat, squirting? Blood? Tantra? ..."

As Garrett was rattling the list off, I was taking her oh-so-slight nuanced expressions in with irrepressible satisfaction. The woman was still incapable of hiding a single emotion...

"I'm not sure yet, but a small test in your presence should provide clarity," I interrupted. Next to me, Mia Marena gasped and looked at me pleadingly. With raised eyebrows, I merely nodded emotionlessly and finally gave her the shock of her life.

Recently beet red, now cabbage purple.

"Let's meet after your shift in Bloody Hell..."

Garrett's eyes lit up and obviously eyed her small body while licking his lips... At that moment, I debated whether he could work for me without his cock.

"Can I do it?" he asked, hopeful because besides him, Georgi was also my new slut tester. Luckily, she didn't notice my murderous mood that briefly distorted my expression.

"No," I replied.

"So, Georgi gets to do it?"

"I'll do it myself."

"*You?*"

A warning look from me was enough to make him bow in front of us and quickly disappear into the crowd of sweaty bodies, which, clearly, was healthier for him.

I towed *petrified* directly to the bar and ordered her a Coke. After all, I didn't want her fainting on me.

"Test?" she whispered, her expression slightly distant.

"Yep!" Suddenly, I pressed her against me as one of the waiters squeezed by. She was being pushed around quite a bit because right now all sorts of idiots were flocking to the bar.

Fuck, she was so fucking tiny... Automatically, I grabbed her by the hips and placed her on a stool behind me so she was protected by the UV light lit bar and my body. Such small gestures stifled her desire to escape...or slap me... *I* wanted to play with her; I didn't want someone else ruining her.

I casually placed myself next to her, leaned on the counter with an arm, and signaled the bartender with a finger.

"The usual, boss?" he asked immediately.

"And a Coke."

In the next second, the refreshments were in front of me. Suppressing a smile, I leaned in close to her to take the drinks. She gasped close to my neck, her warm breath tickling me.

That crap still felt fucking good — I reluctantly admitted.

However, before I was tempted to pounce on her, I quickly reclined back on my elbows – away from her – and held the cola out for her.

"Drink!"

It went unnoticed for she was busy staring at the couple next to us. The woman worked for me and could have performed in an R&B music video. A black-haired Spaniard with the longest legs I had ever seen thrust her nipple at some guy in a suit so he could play extensively with it.

Without further ado, I grabbed Mia Marena's chin to turn her attention back to me.

The music played here!

It was a lot for her to take in for one evening — that I could understand. Naturally, a small part of me knew what was going on inside her, but I had promised myself to disregard whatever signals she might send my way.

"Did you like Garrett?" Again, her eyes widened and her gaze shot up to me as if I'd caught her.

"Um..." she stammered, squirming uncomfortably. She would do well not to remove my fingers from her chin because if I wanted to hold her, I would hold her. I raised a brow when she didn't reply.

"Yes, well, he has quite a...*body*... That's unmistakable..." As she mumbled, she blushed again.

"You mean cock," I coolly corrected her and she winced. "Are you betraying me already, little slut?" I murmured warningly and released her chin to run my index finger down along her neck and over her sweater between her breasts.

"God!" She threw her head back and moaned as I touched her erect nipple. Yep! Clearly, I had missed the little slut. But she shouldn't think she could deny me the answer merely because I drove her crazy.

"Speak!" Before she realized it, I had firmly flicked her hard nipple. Shocked, she expelled her breath. "Ouch!" She touched the battered place and stared at me reproachfully. "What are you doing?" she growled furiously, as if I was stupid and didn't know what I did. I laughed heartily. The way she glowered was too funny. It was only the beginning and she was already whining about pain! What would she do once I was finished with her?

"That's not funny!" she snapped and my laughter died.

She definitely still possessed too much self-esteem, was too cheeky, and had too much defiance in her voice. Those would soon be things of the past.

"Oh, yeah?" I growled as I grabbed the hem of her sweater, pushed it up a bit, and ordered, "Take it off!"

"No way!" I looked mercilessly down on her and did not

relent when tears came to her eyes. She had signed...so, no choice.

Besides, Mia Marena was stupid enough to stick to our agreement just to keep her pride intact.

"Please, Tristan," she whispered.

Okay...I guess she didn't understand the contract – everything it entailed – not to mention the fine print... That she resisted me pissed me off

"You don't want anyone to see you taking off your sweater? Okay!"

This time the usual question *okay, what?* was not asked.

Her visible relief vanished the moment I placed her on the counter and kicked the stool out of the way. The customers around me cheered euphorically. Actually, for hygienic reasons, fucking on the bar was forbidden, which the meaningful sign above us clearly stated, but since it was my place, my rules applied. Always!

Now she could be certain *all* eyes would remain on her.

Her shocked expression was unlike any prior. It seemed downright worrisome.

I casually crossed my arms in front of my chest and ordered again, "Take it off!"

She would learn she shouldn't fuck with me under any circumstances! All decisions were mine to make because I was the game master. Each time she resisted, she only made things worse.

But Mia Marena realized her resistance or pleading simply made her situation worse and relented. Once again, she forcefully exhaled but caught herself just in time. Defiantly, she pulled her sweater over her body and sat there in front of me in her flimsy see-through undershirt and white bra.

Hastily, she tried to cover her breasts, but I quickly restraint her by the wrists — because I was definitely not tolerating anything of the sort. As soon as I touched her, her face radiated familiar information — even if she was humiliated at the moment...it turned her on.

For a change, I smiled at her. Seeing her panting excitedly in front of me while simultaneously afraid truly amused me. At the same time, I was sure any guy would love to switch places with me. I had to restrain myself so I wouldn't fuck her right now just to mark her as *mine*. But it wasn't time for it yet. To satisfy my revenge and to make her demise tormenting, her humiliation had to happen gradually. I couldn't come on too strong, sending her running because the danger certainly existed and – at least I knew – the contract had no merit.

I slowly rubbed my thumbs over each joint while I expertly held her gaze. Still not immune to my grin, she gave me a shy, absolutely in-love smile. Perhaps she thought this was it, just sitting here on the bar half-naked — like a pigeon on a perch.

Well, she would be mistaken.

I gestured for her to lean back and brace herself on her arms. She did not oblige, so I grabbed her hair and hauled her into the asked-for-position, which coerced a silent scream from her. Those who didn't listen had to feel. Then I grasped her little firm ass and pulled her forward to the edge so she could feel my cock again and her tits were at the ideal height. Her frantic gaze flew over the audience, yet repeatedly sought contact with mine. With a shake of the head, I made her understand she should *not worry about what the others thought. I was the one she should worry about...* and I encompassed her delicate neck with my fingers.

She closed her eyes when she understood the meaning of my mental message and forcefully stifled a whimper. She wouldn't persevere for showing restraint was not one of her strengths...

Her eyes popped open as I grinningly ripped the undershirt off her. They appeared even bigger. She gasped loudly and looked shaken... However, she held still!

The fabric fell apart on both sides. Except for the music, everything around us became quiet. You could hear everyone holding their breaths. I was convinced a few of those fuckers were rubbing one off. No...I couldn't think of that right now, so I focused on the woman in front of me and slid both hands up her sides. Really felt her form. When I arrived at her flat belly, I started moving downward.

Oh, fuck!

She still felt awesome even though I didn't like to admit it. Besides, even though she tried to suppress it, I continued to hear Mia's specific groan-whimper-combo, which had driven me crazy in the old days, especially as I brushed down her inner thighs and on toward her knees. She winced. After all, she was too aware of the attention she was receiving.

"I lied to you," I whispered as my hands traveled the route in reverse. But this time along the outside of her thighs and further along her tailbone, all the way up to her bra clasp.

Any desire she had displayed instantly disappeared to be replaced by panic. Because she suspected I was about to expose her in front of the assembled club members.

Her silent pleading didn't escape me, but didn't I want to nor could I consider it. I brushed along the bottom hem of her bra toward the front.

"Not everything about you is ugly." With those words, I yanked it down so her tits peeked out. Oh, yeah...so fucking helpless...

She almost sobbed as the cool air played with her fully erect nipples and the spectators' eyes burned her skin.

"Oh, God, Tristan, stop!" She was no longer able to stop herself and wriggled around, trying to cover herself with her trembling hands before attempting to jump off the bar, where she might have hurt herself. Before her feet could touch the ground, I caught her with one arm around the waist and lifted her back up onto the bar. Shocked, she stared at me wide-eyed, looking absolutely frightened.

"If I were you, I'd stop... Otherwise, I'll chain you up and have every guy fuck you!" I warned. Although I wouldn't dream of it, having delivered the threat with a poker face had the same effect as its implementation.

"No..." I watched a tear run down her cheek, but her protest abated. Instead of continuing to fidget, she leaned against me and buried her hot face against my shoulder. I gave her a few seconds to brace herself for it would get worse.

I had to perform a balancing act since I knew I could not expect too much of her.

Playfully, I let my fingers dance over her back and chuckled when I saw goose bumps forming as she silently cried on my shoulder. When she calmed and dealt with her initial shock, I positioned her so everyone could get a good look. I even took a tiny step back and regarded her with my head tilted.

She pinched her eyes shut.

I took everything in, every whimper, every tear, and each lip quiver... It was too beautiful...

Unexpectedly, I grabbed her breasts so my hands covered them and placed a kiss between them. She must have read more into my tenderness than intended for she relaxed somewhat. I spoke directly against her delicate fragrant skin. "Forget the others. Forget everything around you. Only *I* stand before you now. You will only look at me!" She nodded breathlessly. I huffed ironically and began to massage her tits, gently and intimately — in absolute contrast to the stark scene. She was brave and relented to me and my efforts — but she had always been good at that.

Fucking-A!

Even I had to suppress a moan as I slid my lips slowly over her soft skin.

At first, I left my tongue out of it as I continued kneading. Then I took her right breast in my hand, offering me perfect access to the nipple. I licked it only lightly with the tip of my tongue, causing her to shiver, then harder...circling it, teasing the center, and then my lips encased her perfect dark skin and started sucking it rhythmically.

"Ah," she groaned as expected and I decided today she could scream as much as she wanted. Nevertheless, under no circumstances would I let her come.

I grinned devilishly as I continued my constant rhythmic sucking and licking, driving her so crazy so soon, she forgot about her surroundings...

Unable to control myself, one hand slid over her belly. I had to know if she was as horny as her noises indicated. She immediately pushed her crotch against my fingers as they slid probingly over the solid fabric of her jeans. My suspicion was confirmed because the area was saturated like the Great Flood had come again.

That did it. I had to reposition my cock for it was demanding room. It had a mind of its own and wanted to play, wanted to hide in her hole from the apocalyptic mass of water. *Behave yourself, you impatient asshole! You'll get yours, don't worry!* But it couldn't be restrained and with every passing second only throbbed even more.

H'm, come to think of it, since I had her sitting here before me...topless...with free access to her tits, which were still pretty full and soft despite her skinny figure...I might as well increase the level of humiliation, right?

Screw restraint! This was silly Turkey! She would *never* run away from me regardless of what I did to her!

I moaned throatily against her nipple as I imagined what my cock wanted and abruptly decided to let it have its way. It was not like she ever said no in the early days!

As I disengaged from her and took a step back, she whimpered and quickly gripped my hips with her legs. Almost angrily and with a hint of lust, she opened her eyes and acted shocked again when she noticed me opening my belt. Slowly, a look of horror spread across her face as I pulled out my rock hard boner. Again, she writhed around as her gaze scurried over the onlookers, which I had long since blanked out. I didn't give a shit about the others; this was my home, my kingdom.

"I think it's time to start round two...how about a tittie-fuck?" I grinned, roughly grabbed her hair, and yanked her head back so she had to lie down on the bar.

"No!"

All of a sudden, she used all the strength she could muster to push me off her — obviously filled with rage. I noticed it when she glared at me as she hopped off the bar, whereupon I had to catch her because her legs were apparently wobbly.

"You're taking it too far!" she yelled in a quivering voice as she tried to shield her upper body from the eyes of strangers with her hands, looking utterly humiliated.

It went down perfectly!

As she started headed for somewhere else, I followed her laughing. It seemed she seemed didn't find it funny at all and rushed straight toward the stage exit, the only route of escape she knew. *Stop the damn chase and fuck her already before she runs away forever*! my cock urged grimly... I repositioned it again with the implication it had to give it a rest for now.

Slowly, the situation was growing dicey because she put her bra properly back in place and grabbed some coat as she passed the employees' dressing room, threw it on, and ran, ran, and ran...

I was a *little* pissed off by the time we reached the picture of us in the gallery!

So, I leaped, grabbed her wrist, and used my body to press her against the nearest wall.

"What do you think you're doing?" I hissed.

"What does it look like? I'm leaving!" She eyed me angrily as she clenched her jaw.

"What?" Was she already challenging me? "Why?" But it wasn't only rage coursing through her. Again, her eyes were pools and her lower lip quivered, but she still sounded firm and resolute.

"This is not you, Tristan! And it's not me either! This here is not us, it's not right! In the old days...you were an ass, didn't give a shit...but at least I meant something to you! You know me quite well, whereas it seems I no longer know you! It *really* makes you dangerous... I can no longer trust you, not one bit! You're too unpredictable, too ruthless and cold... It's too much for me to see you like this...I just can't handle it..." she rattled, sobbing.

My fingers arrested her quivering lips. It was remarkable that she actually realized I was no longer the same — what a fucking great surprise! Hello, bitch! I had to spend eight years boxing my way through proverbial crap! What the hell did she expect from me?

"You can't just leave, you've entered into an agreement," I stressed firmly. My voice trembled slightly for I was furious on the inside.

"I don't give a shit about your damn contract!" she yelled past my finger, writhing and squirming, fighting me like a lioness. She even kicked my shin, which impressed me, goddamn fucking crap!

But it was easy to just push her harder against the wall so that she couldn't move at all. I needed her full attention for what I was about to say.

"If you leave now, there will be no coming back! You will not get another chance...Mia Ma..."

She bit me.

"Fuck!" Automatically, I yanked my hand away and stumbled back a step, stupefied, while I inspected my finger. Because, fuck, no slut had ever dared something like that! She used the opportunity to push me backward by the shoulder and slipped by me, sprinting...like coming off starting blocks.

"Dammit!" I cursed indignantly through the entire gallery. I was hopping mad and my finger throbbed wildly.

She ripped open the door and banged it shut exactly at the moment I was about to storm through it. The massive glass pane smashed into my nose — that woman would be my end! And yet, at the same time, she was never hotter! Fuck!

Again, I lost a few seconds because I had to pinch my nose and, wobbly, like I was fucking drunk, opened the door and almost fell backward.

Although she left her bag behind and was in high heels, she was already mounting her bicycle. She wouldn't actually take off, would she?

"For Christ's sake, WAIT!" I yelled, but she did not respond and simply pedaled out the exit and down the lamp-lit street with a pained expression... There was no way to follow her. The key to my car was in my fucking office...

"FUUUUUUUUUUUUUUUUUUUUUUUUUUUUUUUU UUUUUCK!" I shouted into the silent night with my fists clenched. Some of the windows or balcony doors from neighboring houses opened a crack, the peeping Toms hoping to witness something tragic.

"Come back! Goddammit! Mia!"

She did not...

While rubbing both hands over my face, I cursed like there was no tomorrow.

Disappointed, windows and doors closed, curtains slid shut. Naturally, all had *waited* for some disaster – whatever it might have been – only to *afterward,* righteously bitch about the decline of civilization. Well — as long as they had something to nag about... Fucking people...

My arms felt tired and hung limply down my side as I clenched my jaw. My nose and finger hurt. And my head was pounding... It was not the way I had planned for the night to end.

I realized I had gone too far, clearly. I was experiencing confusing, conflicting feelings in my chest: uncontrolled anger, desire for revenge, but also for something familiar...her smell, her body, her soft skin, which was astonishing.

It was all too much and drained my energy... My view of the world picture collapsed.

Mia Marena Angel had stood up to me. Turkey had actually pecked away at me with her beak...

Well, I guess both of us were no longer the same.

I really had not expected the complication.

The woman always surprised me — whether I liked it or not...

8. Conditions

Mia 'Scared' Angel

Everything went totally wrong. Absolutely wrong!

Who the fuck was Tristan Wrangler? Where was the man who could rob me of my mind by only giving me a little smile? Where was the man whose touch felt like a preview of what paradise on earth must feel like. Who was the man who exposed and humiliated me inside a sex club in front of a bunch of lust-filled eyes?

Were there any *boundaries*?

I had no idea for nowadays I could not read him, which was why my flight instinct prevailed.

Besides, everything about him was quite different, he simply went and took what he needed without the slightest consideration for me. Right then, I had needed him to have his hands from way back when. I needed their gentle touch, as if feathers were caressing my skin; if I wanted them rough, he used to grab me so that I seemingly felt every brush of his fingers inside me.

And now?

Now, I only found a blank expression in his eyes, which used to be vibrant and full of love. And that hurt — so much so!

It wasn't like he no longer knew how to get me aroused or how to get me to paradise again. He knew perfectly well that I got excited when he whispered dirty words hoarsely in my ear or that I lost my mind when a bit of his breath caressed my neck. The same went for when he batted an eyelash, smiled crookedly, or moved his hips even slightly against mine.

It used to be one of his natural instincts, knowing how to handle me or to be seduction personified...

Oh, yes...constant seduction — those words described Tristan Wrangler perfectly. That only made the conflict worse because, as before, my body still responded to him – playing the willing whore – while my mind screamed flee.

At that point, it seemed as if I would split in half.

Not to mention the whole sex club story. It was all too much. All the naked flesh, the self-indulgence and shamelessness, whereas I only let my guard down with him. I was definitely not one of those wannabe sex bombs he referred to as his staff. Only as far as he was concerned, I was a temptress...regardless I that didn't have the skills the other women in that milieu practiced. I also didn't have breast implants, a perfect figure, a tan, or know how to apply makeup perfectly to look wicked.

I worked in a children's home and he was a sex god!

Good... Tristan's preference had always been female naked flesh — because he lived for sex. But I would have never expected – considering how he used to protect and carry me around like I had been his personal goddess – for him to treat me in that manner. The way he looked at me while using me like I was nothing but some hole to stick his dick in.

In the old days, we might have been as different as Sweden and Africa, yet nowadays, it was more like the Gobi Desert and Antarctica. We simply didn't belong together, even less so than when I had been a loser and he the school hunk. Now, the gap between us was insurmountably deep. And, apparently, he had no more real feelings that might allow him to bridge the yawning gap.

So, I gave up...fled! For the first time in my life. Because betraying Tristan...letting him go – with the hope he might find a normal life without me – moving in with my uncle, all *that* had been a real battle! Not me running away from him!

My love for Tristan Wrangler had kept me away from him...

But now I was fleeing for my sake!

Then...my facade crumbled and I cried. I cried for everything I thought I had, what I believed I'd gain, for the hope that was destroyed, and, from my perspective, was catapulted back to reality. Thank God Francesco had been at work most of the week and did not notice my depressed brooding state the few times we saw each other.

As so often, two voices argued in my head. One disregarded the facts and was not yet disillusioned, not caring about what he had done to me. It was still strongly convinced Mia and Tristan formed a unit. Yet the other, filled with rage and shame about the evening, wished him to hell. Was there even a chance for us if he didn't even respect me a little?

All I wished for was a tiny glimmer of hope — no matter how minute. At least it would have told me he still had some feelings for me.

His threats triggered fear in me and his whole demeanor was downright cold, all in all, quite disappointing. I certainly did not imagine our big reunion turning out — that way.

Honestly, I thought he had grown into a serious and successful businessman because he had always been ambitious. Therefore, I always assumed he was living in similar proper conditions. Yet here, with this Tristan, nothing was normal or the way he used to be.

Now he was like stone – unfathomable – even more so than in the old days. And although back then he also intimidated me, somehow I knew he would never cross my invisible boundaries no matter how extreme his games had been.

Nowadays, I sensed I could not trust him anymore at all, like any wrong move could be my last.

***

Sighing, I dropped my head into my hands while sitting on one of the uncomfortable tiny children chairs, painting a stormy sea with a pod of colorful breaching whales with watercolors. The children were amazed and gave their creativity free rein, as it should be... I managed another week of worrying and brooding without hearing from him because one thing was clear; I would not make contact! Most likely, he was long ago over me thanks in part to the friendly assistance of his five other girlfriends who looked like Playboy bunnies and didn't freak out when he fucked them in public, but bravely indulged his appetites...no matter what they were...

"Mirti... don't pout!" Robbie's forefinger made an appearance in front of me and I smiled weakly.

"Don't wave your hand around if it has paint on it..." I caught his little sausage finger and held it down, "...use it to paint. It seems the fish needs a pair of eyes."

He looked quite charming standing there with his head slightly tilted and lips pursed as he regarded his painting. He was so cute. Every time I looked at him, my heart warmed and I unwittingly smiled. Today, Robbie wore a dark blue shirt and black jeans. This morning, I combed his hair into a moderate gangster style because he liked pretending to be a tough guy.

"I have to pee," came right out and he looked pleadingly at me with his big green eyes. "Can you come?" He didn't like going to the boys' toilet alone because the long empty corridor always frightened him... Of course, he immediately reminded me of Tristan... Oh, man! I was at work and needed to concentrate on the children instead of constantly thinking about my psycho ex-lover!

"Sure thing, boss!" I tousled his silky soft hair and he jumped up. "Yeah!" he yelled and I giggled.

With a running start, he stormed out of the common room and, like a small bundle of energy, roared down the corridor. I had to hurry to keep up and smiled at his exuberance. Compared to adults, children had it easy. It didn't take much to make them happy: a ray of sunshine, a colorful snail shell, a black stone, a flying plane — often sufficed. I wish I could also be happy about the little things life had to offer but, unfortunately, with age we lose that ability.

As always, I waited outside the boys' toilet, inspecting my un-manicured nails and fiddling with the cuticles. Luckily, the corridor was not dark because it was painted a bright yellow, but I still felt slightly nervous and repeatedly glanced down both directions.

No one was there. All was silent.

But the oppressive feeling would not go away. It crawled from my toes all the way up to the top of my skull and persisted — even after repeated controlled breathes. Comparable to what you feel when venturing alone into a dark basement or when visiting a cemetery at night. You are not truly sure why you are frightened, but it doesn't change the fact that you are. Perhaps the unknown you conjured up because of the inability to see in the dark.

I had to calm myself because I was not a 12-year-old that obsessed about her fear until she ran crying to her mama.

My gaze darted down the hallway when I suddenly heard the echo of slow approaching footsteps. I listened intently, pressed against the wall, when the sounds receded again...

Okay, I understood Robbie now! I found it also eerie and could no longer just stand here, so I opened the door a crack and looked whether the kid had done his business.

He was still hunkered on the throne, singing happily *a little man stands in the forest* to himself.

"How much longer do you need?" Considering my state of distress, I sounded unusually irritated.

"Close the door! It stinks terribly!" he cried almost hysterically. Under normal circumstances, I would have laughed, but I didn't feel like it now.

"Please, hurry up!" *Or I might have a heart attack out here...*

Sighing, I closed the door and leaned my forehead against the cool frame.

Everything is fine... No one here who shouldn't be here. There're cameras watching the entrance, I will be safe here... I repeatedly chanted, breathing deliberately slowly, hoping Robbie would come out soon. Rather than calming down, I felt increasingly panicked. My neck hairs were standing on end...

In the next second, two hands grabbed me from behind.

I instantly froze, my heart pounded in my chest, and my eyes widened in shock.

However, the fear faded *at once*.

A nose brushed through my hair, a smile pressed against my neck... He inhaled my scent deeply into his lungs and exhaled sharply. I shuddered and inadvertently leaned my head back against the strong shoulder behind me.

"You still smell like the old days..." he whispered against my temple and delightfully ran his nose along my hairline. Oh my, Tristan...

"What are you doing here?" How did he get in or know I worked here?

I merely received a moderately mysterious laugh as a reply.

The first touch instinctively told me the *aggressor* was Tristan. But now...to smell and hear him, to really feel him standing behind me after all the fear, was a relief. And yet just moments ago, I believed he posed the greatest threat... Nevertheless, I could not manage to suppress a faint sigh as his hands pulled me backward more firmly.

"Listen...I don't know what else to say, dammit. You would refuse if I ordered you to come back to the club as agreed. Unfortunately, even if I threatened you. So, I want to offer you something else; go to dinner with me." He pressed his hard masculine body against me and ran his thumbs down my sides. God!

"You mean like a normal date? After *that* fiasco?" I asked with one raised eyebrow, trying to remain calm or rather, get there.

"Yes." Then he must have believed he could reinforce his request...with the rod in his pants. With his soft lips caressing my neck... his intoxicating scent, surrounding me like fog...and his knowledgeable hands traveling over my body...

"I won't say I'm sorry since that crap was fucking awesome." He pressed my ass against his lower body, moving slowly and sensually against my pelvis, eliciting a breathless low moan as he kissed down my throat and nibbled gently on my neck. "And, if you want to come, I will let you come... Here. Now. I cannot give you more," he whispered hoarsely.

I could literally see a good Tristan on one shoulder and the evil one on the other arguing with each other...but for the moment, he was keeping the new Tristan at bay — for me.

Now, his hands moved upwards and kneaded my breasts in that firm way that made me horny and got the blood pumping between my legs.

"Dammit," I whimpered as I rubbed myself against him while pressing even harder against his lower body. He made me just as weak as I was addicted to him, and at that moment, I hated myself for it.

"I will not go out...with you..." I formulated between my embarrassing moaning and pressed my hands against the wall. "You don't deserve that privilege... Mista..."

"Mia, dammit!" he hissed at my neck. I stiffened, fearing he might bite me again.

But he didn't...because someone cried out.

"Let MIRTI go!"

Surprised, Tristan removed his lips from my neck and I froze when I recognized Robbie's voice.

"You can't hurt her!" As quick as a little monkey, the boy ran to Tristan and before I had a chance to comprehend, he kicked him in the shin and adopted the stance of a tiny karate fighter.

A hysterical laugh escaped me when I saw Tristan scrunch up his face in pain – for he was quite aroused – and slipped out from behind him.

"No, Robbie, it's all right, he didn't hurt me!" Grinning, I squatted in front of him and stroked his thin arm.

"No, it isn't! He bit you in the face! I saw it with my own eyes!" My little savior was still eyeing Tristan suspiciously, reminiscent of a jealous husband. I looked up over my shoulder at the big guy and giggled again because this little male coming to my defense completely overwhelmed him. It was not like he could knock him unconscious the way he would any adult who came at him like that.

As I replayed the attack in my mind, I couldn't control myself any longer and started to splutter. Tristan narrowed his eyes.

"MIRTI is always so sweet. You are not allowed to hurt her. Do you hear?" His little hand stroked my cheek and just for that, I wanted to take Robbie in my arms and shower his face with lots of tiny kisses.

"MIRTI?" Tristan chuckled abruptly and squatted down next to us. Puzzled, I stared at him. "MIRTI? You really call her *MIRTI*?"

I rolled my eyes when I saw Robbie immediately falling for the relaxed friendly tone. Children were so easily manipulated. Their openness was a blessing as well as a curse. "Yes, MIRTI, and I'm Robbie, her boss!" He was visibly proud, standing there with his small arms crossed in front of his chest like he was emphasizing his words.

Now Tristan laughed and again threw a meaningful glowing look.

Oh, wow...

What was that?

"Are you okay with me being your second in command?"

He had him hooked and knew it. Robbie's eyes...suddenly glowed and his cheeks turned red.

"I can be your boss?" he asked Tristan excitedly with that cute childish pronunciation and his bright little innocent voice.

"Do you allow chocolate to be eaten during working hours?" Tristan asked seriously as if his life depended on it. Where did he learn how to deal with children by using tag words? Had he perhaps already fathered a few? The thought made me miserable, but at the same time, I was overcome with a warm feeling as I watched how he...almost downright...lovingly and at the same time seriously...conversed with the little boy.

"Did you bring some?" was all Robbie was interested in at the moment. His joyful expression caused Tristan to laugh again. I grinned like an idiot when I heard the honest carefree sound for the first time after so long.

"Unfortunately, no...but next time I'll bring some with me, scouts honor!" My stupid grin vanished. *Next time?*

It was also a new side of Tristan! It was his first new trait that actually took my breath away because he was quite good with kids! He didn't use foul language! He knew what he should say and he obviously had *fun* talking to Robbie! I would have never, never, never, never, never expected it.

And that went for the little one as well for the kid usually wasn't that outgoing from the first moment. He suffered greatly from a fear of loss, which was why he didn't easily make friends. But just the tiny fact that Tristan had lowered himself to his height when he talked to him made a great difference on a psychological level. Especially combined with the way he used appropriate issues and treated Robbie like an equal.

Oh, he was good... *so good...*

Naturally, he was aware he had just earned himself a dinner with me.

The friendliness he had for the child, which meant so much to me, didn't seem fake or dishonest. He had a shine in his eyes, the one I'd been sorely missing. It bespoke of compassion, empathy, affection, warmth...he still possessed all of it... clearly!

Some of my old Tristan still existed!"

There was still hope!

I became quite dizzy as the love and devotion I felt for this special man filled me. Preferably, I would have thrown myself around his neck. I definitely had to restrain myself from doing so!

I took Robbie in my arms and turned to Tristan again, who also slowly stood up while looking down on us with a weird expression on his face.

"And?" he asked almost...hoarsely...

I could not help but grin as I brushed my nose through Robbie's scented hair.

"I will go out to dinner with you, you sneaky devil." Tristan twisted his lips to a tiny crooked smile and desperately tried not to look triumphant. He failed miserably and was never more beautiful... Had I not fallen in love with that smile half an eternity ago, I'd be *really* blown away right now!

"Can I take your assistant out for dinner?" he gallantly inquired with Robbie. His wide child eyes stared at me questioningly and I replied smiling, "You decide; it is entirely up to you."

"Okay, but take good care of her!" He again waggled his finger warningly under Tristan's nose and I laughingly pretended to bite it. Lately, he really waved it around a lot... Squealing, he quickly pulled the finger back to his chest.

"Friday, nine o'clock." Tristan's soft voice drew my attention away from Robbie.

As he brushed his knuckles against my cheek, his face couldn't have been more readable. Like the time he stormed my room at night via a ladder, just to make certain my father hadn't laid a hand on me... My heart pounded in my chest. I clung to the little compact body of the child.

"You're red in the face!" The little one stroked my other cheek making me blush even more.

Tristan laughed softly. "You should see how red she gets when I...oops...um...!" He snapped open his eyes and in a panic, quickly fell silent. I giggled. His filthy mouth almost got him in trouble, but thankfully, he caught himself in time. It was a major step forward for Tristan Wrangler.

Robbie looked at him curiously and at the same time, demanding, waiting for more wisdom to come out of the mouth of the big strong man.

"Go on, Tristan?" I teased gently.

"When I...um..." Distressed, Tristan frowned and then grinned. "When I tickle MIRTI!"

I rolled my eyes, expecting that Robbie would tickle me for the next few hours just to see how red I would *actually* get. Well, thanks a million!

"Call me if anything comes up." Tristan handed me a stylish business card while looking intently into my eyes. His thumb stroked the knuckles of my fingers as soon as I grabbed his hand and I could feel my legs taking on the infamous consistency of Jell-O. Presently, he really was determined to mess with my head. Obviously, he was successful...

"Okay, Mista Wrangler. See you soon." And with that, I turned around and walked away from Tristan. Robbie waved at him from over my shoulder and laughed loudly in my ear.

Ouch! I didn't even want to know what gesture Tristan made behind my back to lure him into making that rare sound again. Okay, perhaps I did want to know, I mean, it seemed to have been really funny... Robbie had a great sense of humor.

All of a sudden, I was on cloud nine. Tristan wanted to take me out to dinner...

It definitely presented a chance, maybe the first step in the right direction that I intended to use.

Robbie had ignited a spark and I had to turn into a fire.

9. Food of a Special Kind

Mia 'The Virgin' Angel

Francesco ruined my great plans.

Friday evening, he came home in a good mood, whistling and confronting me with the fact he wouldn't be playing squash today, but wanted to have an absolutely romantic – his words – dinner with me.

Great! Really great! My mood, which so far was floating on cloud nine, immediately dropped into the basement.

Now I wouldn't be able to see my psycho lover because my other pseudo lover wanted to take me out to dinner. Nevertheless, I couldn't just blow off Francesco; after all, I was officially together with him... So, I had to cancel with Tristan...or, at least, postpone.

Crap!

***

I was completely frazzled, especially my nerves. Francesco waited in the hallway while I visited the toilet again.

Fortunately, *he* had given me his business card...

Chewing my lip, I sat on the toilet lid, armed with my handbag, and fished my phone out. I kept the number in my wallet between old invoices. With trembling fingers, I dialed, quickly took another deep breath while watching myself in the mirror across from me, brushed through my hair, and pressed CALL.

My heart beat violently in my chest – only for him – yet I would cancel. With the one man who would certainly not just accept it...

My eyes narrowed when I noticed how my hands shook as I listened to the dial tone.

Full of sadness, I recalled how it had been back in the early days when I called him when I had arrived home too late or when he stayed longer at the boxing gym. I heard his gentle young voice breathing happily in my ear, *Miss me, Mia baby?*

It rang a few times and I was about to hang up when he answered, irritated. "Yes!" and all my wonderful memories vanished down the drain...

Wherever he was, it was loud. Music was blasting in the background and I could hardly understand him. He was probably in his funny establishment. Just then, I had a hard time swallowing...

"Hello?" he yelled, more than annoyed. I decided I should say something and not simply stare at myself stupidly.

"Hi, it's me...Mia," I whispered into the device.

"What? I can't understand one damn fucking word! *Speak properly*!" Crap! I could not talk any louder with Francesco so close. Tristan must have left the room because the music softened until it was barely audible.

"Mia! Hurry up! Or we'll be late!" Francesco called impatiently from the hallway.

"Yeah, yeah, Rome wasn't built in a day!" I shouted back. "Tristan, can you hear me now?" I whispered quickly, using my other hand as a shield.

"Did something happen?" he immediately asked, not sounding annoyed at all anymore. I shook my head and rolled my eyes until it occurred to me he couldn't see me.

"No!" I whispered again into the shielded phone... "It's just that Francesco insists on taking me out today. Did you get that?"

"What?" Tristan snapped, clearly annoyed again. "Where?"

"Doesn't matter."

'Doesn't matter?" he growled menacingly.

"Yes, it does...not matter...not really. Well, it is kind of... *shitty*... but we cannot see each other today..."

"Tell me right now where you are going!" he demanded firmly, which was just like him.

Nervous, I slid around on the seat, rubbing my face and sighing. "Tristan, please...just accept it."

"The fuck I will! Mia Marena, last chance or I'll have your cell located!"

"Then I'll leave it at home!" I almost stuck my tongue out at myself in the mirror. I could sense his menacing expression. Then he breathed deeply.

"It won't be like last weekend..." he conceded slightly hoarse.

"What...?" My voice broke because I had to think about the feeling I experienced when his fingers touched me while *the* murmur put me over the edge. I cleared my throat and pushed the distracting memories into the back of my mind.

"What do you mean by that?"

"Fuck, woman! I will let you come, okay!" Now my slow-wittedness had annoyed him again.

"We're going to P&T," burst out of me.

"Okay." He grinned. Definitely.

"Okay, what?"

"Okay, you're in for a surprise." After repeating something he had said at an earlier time, he hung up.

I still *hated* surprises!

I stared stupidly at the phone until the pounding on the door startled me, causing me to almost slide off the toilet seat. Oh, man...now what did I get myself into?

***

Half an hour later, we were in the exclusive quarter of the old city in front of P&T, an expensive, trendy restaurant in the area. Now I knew why Francesco had insisted I put on evening clothes. I did as he had asked and wore a dark blue, knee-length, V-neck dress adorned with many different chains, and matching earrings, which stood out nicely thanks to my pinned up hair.

When I started dressing, I still assumed I was doing it for Tristan because honestly, I would have never gone through so much trouble for Francesco. Since it was raining, I wore high boots, which was for naught because my boyfriend almost parked his flashy car inside the restaurant vestibule.

Graciously, I accepted his offered arm and he grinned broadly at me. I grew suspicious when he leaned over and his lips brush my temple. Oh-oh...

The interior was upper class with live piano music. Expensive pictures adorned the walls. Gold and black decorations. Chandelier. High stucco ceiling. Beautiful staff in gold-colored suits and dresses. All and all, a pleasant atmosphere. Fairly unheard of for trendy restaurants.

As always when I was on the road with Francesco, I was blown away by all the luxury. In Africa, people were starving and here they had nothing better to do than paste banknotes to their foreheads. How could people be so decadent?

Despite the artificiality, it seemed quite comfortable, although I was irritated by the reserved table in a secluded corner — quite unlike Francesco, who always liked being center stage. To make it even stranger, he slid over the bench to me and laid his arm across the backrest behind me.

Oh, no!

That was pushy and all I could think about were bright green-brown eyes that I would not see today... Tristan must be upset being stood up for another man...

Gloomy, I imagined what he was doing now and how he looked as I pretended to choose an appetizer.

However, I couldn't come up with anything concrete — for there simply were too many factors.

Was he fucking three porno sluts at once while nude and beautiful? The thought made me want to throw up and triggered an ominous tingling sensation. Unbridled rage rose up inside me when I thought of his beautiful hands on some other woman's body. Eventually, my jealousy might kill me even though I actually had no right for such sentiment.

Or was he wearing a suit, enthroned at the bar in his club, where he almost humiliated me to death, smoking one? I saw him in my mind, how he sat casually on a stool, his full lips holding a cigarette as he inhaled the smoke deeply. The way his gaze traveled over the club, longingly resting on the spot where I laid last weekend.

Was he standing in his office, looking at the picture of our clearing from happier times as he recalled that I was a damn traitor?

I really had no idea what he could be doing right now, which made me sad. Unexpectedly, I raised the menu a bit higher and shielded by it, wiped the evidence of my weakness from my face.

Crap! Why did he have to make me cry when he wasn't

even present? Why did he have such unbridled power over me in any given situation?

"So, Mia, tell me, what did you do at work today?" Francesco asked attentively. Confused, I looked at him. It was a workday like any other. Since when did he become interested in it? Honestly, it scared the heck out of me!

"Same old same old," I announced, glad the waiter appeared at that moment to inquire about our choice of drinks.

I ordered a Spezi, which was unusual to see in such a classy joint and I immediately earned an angry look from Francesco. If it were up to him, I would do without sugar, but I won the fight quickly. He went with flat water.

Bored, I sat back and played with my napkin.

Why was I even still together with Francesco? He was never more than an excuse to keep other men at bay and a means to an end to get over Tristan. I wanted to prove to myself that I could enter into a relationship with another... that was no life...

"Cavalli? Miss Angel?"

My eyes shot up because for a moment, I thought I was hallucinating again. A stupid mistake for in my daydreams he still called me Mia baby... Green-brown eyes settled on me.

Now I *knew* what he was doing.

He was standing here before me — stunningly beautiful. Stunningly confident...and drop-dead gorgeous in his black pants that hung low on his hips and the same color shirt with rolled up sleeves, his wild glossy hair, his athletic male body, his slightly arrogant smirk, and that roguish twinkle.

"Tristan!" I could not stop myself from exclaiming aloud, in a way that made Francesco wince and guests from neighboring tables stare at me, which prompted me to turn beet red and embarrassed, slid back and forth on the bench... "...Wrangler... what are you doing here?" I added softly and felt Francesco's haunting look on my hot cheeks, convinced I had just given myself away.

"Making sure all is well." Nonchalantly, he dropped onto the chair opposite me and turned to Francesco. "What are you doing in my place?"

My jaw dropped. *His* place? Oh, man! What else did I not know about him? *What* else did he own? Maybe I should actually Google him!

"I wanted to treat my sweet little mouse." What was I? A little girl? To underline his message, Francesco laid his heavy arm over my shoulders. I flinched and with difficulty supported his weight so I would not hit the table.

"By the way, how did the session go? I haven't found the time yet to ask my mouse about it." Couldn't he give it a rest with the mouse thing? It was no longer funny, actually quite embarrassing! *Hello!* Tristan Wrangler was sitting here! The man who had deflowered me! The man I was currently fighting for and whom I wanted to see me in the best light. The man of men and here I was embarrassed at being compared to a rodent!

Tristan must have seen it my way for his jaw visibly clenched as he eyed Francesco's arm around me. His fingers crept close to my cleavage and with a look, I made my psycho lover understand that, for a change, he should keep his temper in check. I should not have done that because suddenly his foot traveled up the inside of my leg and I gasped for air.

Holy shit!

Calculatingly, he eyed me because he knew he broke my concentration and drew my attention to him. In a panic, I barely shook my head and opened my eyes. His eyes narrowed warningly. *Shut the fuck up, I'm in control,* his look said!

He seemed to be busy thinking about something. Maybe he was imagining grabbing Francesco's head and forcefully slamming it down on the tabletop so that the bridge of his nose did the rest... Unobtrusively, I took his hand, linked fingers, and pulled it from my shoulder. Then I discreetly released it and took a sip of my drink.

Tristan smiled smugly at me before he consented to reply.

"The photo shoot..." He talked pretty damn smoothly and I tried to push away his foot with mine — however, he simply braced against it, "... went fine...but we're not done yet."

Skillfully, he managed to catch my foot between his.

Before I knew it, he moved one hand inconspicuously under the table and pulled me closer by my calf. Francesco was busy checking out a waitress' ass, which was why he didn't notice my continuous descent until Tristan had my heel on his lap.

"Aha...but I hope you bring her back as unharmed as when I drop her off. We wouldn't want to harm her virtue!"

If Tristan had something to drink, he surely would have spilled the contents considering his eyes almost popped out of his head. Then he had to fight down uncontrollable laughter.

"Virtue, you say?"

"What kind of subject is this anyway?" I growled gruffly while trying to free my foot, but he kept a grip on it...and slowly opened the zipper on the boot.

"Yes, she's still totally untouched. My Mia...a steadfast woman... In today's times, it's rather rare!" Francesco leaned conspiratorially toward Tristan, who merely grinned at him overbearingly, pretending to be happy for him. At the same time, he pulled off my boot and it landed on the floor, the noise concealed by Tristan's cough.

"Miss Angel, the iron maiden, huh?" he asked and caressed my smoothly shaven calf and strapless stockings.

Oh my, Tristan! So, it's Miss Angel! He grabbed my thighs tightly and with each touch, let me know I was his, regardless that I was sitting next to another.

And I totally agreed with him. I was melting from his tenderness and had to bite my lip so as not to moan as his hands gradually and slowly moved upwards — as I continued to gradually slide further under the table.

Moisture was now pooling between my legs – hot and steamy – as those two discussed my virginity as if I wasn't present.

"Do you also value the perks of being the first?" Apparently, Francesco was fascinated by the fact that he should be my first and really felt the need to discuss it right here and now...

Tristan glared at me and grinned briefly.

"Oh. Fuck. Yes!" And I felt exactly how it twitched in his pants. *Oh, yes!*

"Well, considering how quickly you go through women, I guess you had the pleasure numerous times!" Francesco was so focused on the waitress who brought us our appetizers that he remained oblivious. I was glad because now Tristan left my foot resting on his semi-hard boner and was no longer touching me.

I felt like pouting when he leaned back comfortably in his chair and took out a toothpick. He hung it loosely in the corner of his mouth, chewed oh-so-sexily on it, and gestured to the waitress to bring him a drink.

Abruptly, out of nowhere, his foot...was shoeless! In a sock! It oh-so-slowly moved up my thigh... Oh, God!

Startled, I winced and barely suppressed a squeal.

Meanwhile, I tried to push my legs together because I knew perfectly well what would happen if he touched me *there*. I would moan! Most certainly.

Warningly, Tristan raised an eyebrow, but remembered he was still speaking to Francesco. "Eight years ago, I had one and the perks were endless. You can mold them how you please; she was so fucking tight... They act like saints, but watch out, the shy facade usually hides a sinful core. The body might be untouched, but in the mind, a nasty slut..."

Oh, Tristan! *His autocratic and yet soft voice. His foot! His gaze! Me humbly before him on all fours. He behind me on his knees, his hands on my hips.*

At that moment, his head injury had not mattered for the power of our lust had always been something special and once unleashed there was no turning back no matter what was happening around us. Nevertheless, there were more important things in life than dealing with stupid questions such as how he had managed to have sex even with a head injury and stinking drunk — he was Tristan Wrangler, with him, anything seemed possible.

I almost climaxed at the memory, but I restrained myself. My breath, however, I was unable to control, which was why I was glad Francesco was focused on his curry/leek cream soup and fried prawns.

"Oh, Mr. Wrangler, you are here too?" A deep female voice ripped me out of my reverie. Immediately, I noticed a hand with blood-red fingernails coming over his shoulder from behind. The same color wavy hair covered his upper body as she leaned down and put her nasty lips on his right and left cheek before he had a chance to respond.

Slowly, I set my cutlery aside...then stared at her through narrowed slits while every cell in my body started to shake...

Warningly, he squeezed my foot so hard it must have left a bruise. Message received. I remained sitting on my butt and refrained from immediately taking the handsy woman apart. I was so tense, my toes curled.

"As you can see..."

She used her nasty thumb to wipe the dirty lipstick off his cheeks as she whispered, "Well, have fun..."

He grinned broadly and murmured, "Same to you! And please say hi to good Ute for me!"

Huh! Who was good Ute? And who was the woman sauntering away in her tight black dress, swaying her hips?

"Well, hello..." Francesco obviously couldn't resist.

Tristan waved him off. "You don't stand a chance. She's the biggest bull dyke on the planet!" He smiled at me mischievously, which again made me feel completely out of place...

His lustful game instantly went to the second round.

Forcefully, Tristan spread my legs and slid along the seam of my strapless stockings. He grinned as he touched them and I had to bite my lip as he slid them down a bit.

"Where were we?"

"Discussing the perks of a virgin!" Suddenly, Francesco was focused again and gave me a kiss on my flushed cheek. At the same moment, I felt the ball of Tristan's foot between my legs. Oh, God! His grin grew even wider when he noticed how hot I was.

My panting was drowned out by Francesco's declaration of affection and I averted my face.

"Okay, let's steer this conversation toward a normal topic!" I ordered curtly.

As a warning, I wanted to nudge Tristan's pecker, but it would have unnecessarily turned him on, so I figured I might as well torture him also a bit. With my toes, I traced the contour of his hardness and quite deliberately went slowly up and down...up and down... He certainly had trouble keeping his reaction in check, which only encouraged me. Tristan gritted his teeth and adjusted his foot so that it was at the highest point between my legs...

Right on my already swollen clit. He lasciviously bit his lip... Oh, God, if Francesco noticed what Tristan was doing all hell would break lose.

I choked on my soup as a wave of excitement surged through me. Francesco patted me on the back while almost smacking me down on the table.

Tristan threw me a warning but passionate look, so I pulled it together and quickly resumed eating, unable to avoid moving my hips.

"Mia, you're so flushed...are you hot?" Francesco asked concerned. I froze.

"Yes, you do seem red, Miss Angel... Why is that? Is the soup too spicy?" Tristan whistled amused from across the table, having a good time, and I pushed firmly and aggressively against his boner.

"I'm *very well*!" The last word I squeaked out at least two octaves higher than normal because Tristan also intensified his efforts. He chuckled devilishly and I gave him the evil eye. Francesco seemed completely oblivious. Only when he suddenly stood up, did I focus on him.

"Please, excuse me... I'll be right back!" he announced and I stared at him, shocked. He could not leave me alone with the aroused, unpredictable Tristan Wrangler!

But he did...

"Oh, Miss Angel... Now we are completely alone," Tristan muttered softly and increased his touch.

"P-please stop..." I stammered incoherently, but gyrated my hips more intensely now that Francesco was not here. I closed my eyes, leaned my head back, and completely relished the moment because lust coursed uninhibitedly through every cell, merging in that one spot.

"You complained that I never let you come."

"Yes, but I didn't mean for you to get me off with your toes while my boyfriend is sitting right next to me!" I hissed, barely able to control my shaky voice. He did have talented toes! And here I was not even into feet.

Desperate, I sighed. "Tristan, I merely called to cancel!" and grew a shade darker.

"I'm not being cancelled on!" Suddenly, his foot was gone. He sat up, leaned forward on his elbows, and captivated my gaze skillfully. Brutally, I gnawed my lip.

"Am I making you nervous, Mia Marena?" His voice was quite rough and promising...

"Please stop!" As I slid around on the bench, he was visibly enjoying torturing me. In whatever situation.

A diabolic smile spread across his adorable features. He leaned forward so we were almost face-to-face, raised his hand, and circled the rim of his glass with his long index finger and with half-lowered eyelids whispered, "Fuck... You have no idea how damn sexy you are sitting here...at my mercy, your eyes begging me to put you on the table and fuck you right here." I almost hyperventilated as I stared at him, speechless. He smiled complacently, leaned back, and with it, broke the spell.

If he stopped now, leaving me hanging again, I swear I'd run amok, whether Tristan helped me — or not.

He chuckled softly. "You want it, you'll get it. Here and now, in front of all these people and your...*lover*... who's sitting next to you and who would never do such a thing! You will not let on! Eat your food and make small talk while I show you who you truly belong to," he finally proclaimed coolly and stood up.

Then he disappeared because he dropped his fork and went down on his knees to retrieve it. Next, he actually appeared under the tablecloth that almost hung to the ground. He wouldn't actually dare, would he?

"Yummy, what have we here?" *Oh, yes, he would!*

I wanted to kick him, but he grabbed my knees and spread them apart. "Don't you dare!"

"No, Tristan! I cannot do it! He'll notice!" I tried to

slide back up the bench out of his reach, but he kept a steely grip on me making certain I stayed in place.

"Relax, Miss Angel! Or I'll go down on you while you are *on top of the* table, I swear to that fucker in the sky!

"Please..." My hands slid down to keep him away from me by pushing against his cheeks because I knew better than come close to his hair. I had lost that privilege.

"Put your hands on the table and keep them there. He better not become aware of anything!" he proclaimed firmly. He audibly slapped my inner thigh, which made me squeak again and startled the other guests, who already seemed somewhat annoyed by my strange impulses. By now, they must think I was mentally challenged or something. Then again, it wasn't too far-fetched.

Since it was useless refusing him, I prepared myself for what was to come. Okay, at least I tried. If he brought me to climax here, there would be no more denying anything. Everyone would hear my noise and put two and two together! How was I supposed to control myself after eight years of abstinence? Help! He was such a manipulative bastard! Yet he had such power over me.

But he always had and always would.

I wanted him. No matter where. No matter how. No matter when. Which he knew perfectly well!

Actually, I hated the way he behaved around me. I hated that he didn't show any emotion and became a complete asshole so that I softened and acquiesced, unable to help myself and gave into completely to him.

And then I felt his fingers traveling up my inner thigh.

"Fuck, your stockings make me so damn hard!" Sure, his porno sluts probably wore nothing else. "Uh-oh, you're already soaked through again, you little virgin. You don't even know what's in store for you and yet you're as horny as can be..." he chided gently. I felt his cool breath on my heated snail.

"Yummy..." He placed his lips on my panties and everything down there started vibrating.

"Argh!" I used both hands to claw at the bench just as Francesco returned.

"You look much worse than earlier!" he gasped, wide-eyed and tried to take my hand, from which I pulled away.

Tristan graciously paused and gave me a minute to explain his absence to my boyfriend. Breathing deeply, I tried to calm my pounding heart and ignored the hands on my knees that were keeping my legs spread apart.

"No, everything is okay. I have a little...circulatory problem. I simply have to drink something." I made up some crap and downed my Spezi. Francesco stared at me with raised eyebrows as he slowly sat down again.

"Where is Wrangler?" he asked as he ordered salmon fillet on a bed of spinach with parsnips and couscous for the both of us. "Um...he...had to..." Tristan sighed quietly. "...go to his office...had to...call his...accountant!"

"Aha. Thank God he's gone... I cannot stand him and the way he looks at you! Like you belong to him..." A silent grumble came from where Tristan's lips were and I quickly coughed as a distraction. Francesco looked at me skeptically, but did not inquire any further. If only he knew! Tristan wasn't gone but now was really getting down to business.

His right hand traveled leisurely upward to the hem of my panties, right above my labia and I stiffened in my seat. Fortunately, Francesco wasn't too close to me at the moment.

"So, I invited you to dinner because I wanted to talk to you about something important, regarding our future..." Francesco said while focusing on his plate.

"Oh, yeah?" I gasped, unable to control my voice.

Tristan had just pulled my panties aside, exposing me... With the index finger of the other hand, he stroked my wetness, quickly making it disappear deeply inside me before continuing upwards.

I flinched violently and Francesco looked at me confused, yet chose to ignore it, and frowned as he continued.

"Yes, we've been together now for several years...and I think we should strengthen our relationship. After all, I'm a man...if you know what I mean."

GOD! *His* hair was tickling my inner thighs and I felt his tongue... Oh, yes...Tristan Wrangler's famous and by many women equally revered, as well as dreaded tongue. Finally, he gently circled the tip of his tongue around my clit, sending flashes coursing through my body, neutralizing all pathways in my brain.

"Okay!" I cried and avoided looking at Francesco or moving around too much. Under the table, I curled my toes — in plain sight, I balled my hands into fists so that my knuckles turned white.

Tristan was humming against my snail, which probably meant he liked what he tasted as he licked me in the opposite direction. Extremely slow with pressure. Then determined fingers spread my labia before he began to fuck me with a stiffened tongue.

"Oh, my, God!" I gasped as my entire body twitched.

"What is it?" Francesco asked, startled and glanced around the restaurant confused, trying to locate the reason from my outcry. He even dropped the cutlery in his hands.

"Here comes the food!" I said as an excuse, which was actually true.

"Yeah...?" Apparently, according to his questioning tone, Francesco didn't share my enthusiasm. Then, he briskly turned toward me. "Are you sure you don't... I've no idea... but, Mia, why are you breathing so fast?" He felt my forehead. "Do you have a fever? Chills? Your entire body is shaking!"

"I...I'm just so excited... the food is finally here! Can we eat now? I'm really hungry!" Tristan's tongue most probably would be sore tomorrow.

"Okay, so..." Annoyed, Francesco rolled his eyes and took a tiny bite of fish like he was a woman. Then, he startled me by taking my hand and again turning to me. I couldn't take it anymore, so I reached under the table and pushed Tristan's face away with all the strength I could muster in my non-functioning state. At the same time, I was hoping he wasn't going to bite me again.

"I wanted to tell you that I'm finally ready to do it today. I want to make love to you... I've been waiting for so long..." Oh no, right now I felt like I was in a low-class romance movie because Francesco was so sickening sweet. "I respect your virginity, but I cannot wait any longer! My loins yearn for you..." Where did he get that from?

Before I could laugh at his last statement, he stunned me by pushing my hand on his penis.

"Can you feel it?" Saying what first came to mind might not be appropriate: *What?* I really had not expected that right now!

My body froze in its confused state as he rubbed my hand against his crotch.

I could think of only one thing: Tristan must be freaking out under the table. So, I reassuringly stroked his cheek as I removed my hand from Francesco while trying *not* to look disgusted. He was already breathing heavier.

Tristan didn't react. I inspected his smooth face with my fingertips and felt his jaw firmly clenched.

Oh, holy crap!

"This is not a good idea!" I replied breathlessly. I had no idea what I to say. "You know what we agreed to... You were fine with it." Until now, he had respected it, but I saw in his eyes he no longer would put up with excuses. Tristan took my fingers and flung them away from him.

Okay...not just angry — *super irate*.

Francesco was about to say something when suddenly his cell phone rang and he moved away from me. I breathed a sigh of relief.

"One sec!" Francesco read intently and cursed. Something he usually never does.

Abruptly, he jumped up.

"There are problems...at the bank. I have to go! Here is some money!" After eyeing me nervously, he tossed a one hundred euro note on the table and gave me a fleeting peck on the cheek (like he always did...) before slipping on his coat... Okay... Off to the bank? ...He'd probably amuse himself with another. How fortunate!

"It's nine-thirty on a Friday night," I pointed out, trying to make him a little more nervous. Not that I minded, given my raging psycho lover was waiting for me under the table.

"Yes it is!" Francesco was already heading toward the exit, running his hand through his hair and licking his lips. "I'm sorry, okay? I'll give you a rain check! I promise!" Then he turned and hurried out the door. My expression must have looked a bit confused.

As the door shut behind him, it changed to relief. But I was also...afraid. I braced both elbows on the table and rubbed my hands roughly over my face, until...

"Tristan?" I picked up the tablecloth and peeked underneath. I almost laughed when I saw how he was squatting down there. Only almost because his eyes sparkled with anger, robbing me of my saliva.

"Aha!" he exclaimed and came out from under the table. He was seen by the other guests, some dropping their forks and knives from sheer shock once they put two and two together. An elderly gentleman sitting with his 20-year younger woman at an adjacent table whispered to her that he wouldn't mind if she were to do that too.

"So, he wants to fuck you, right?" Tristan bellowed angrily, yet softly. With clenched fists, he took a step around the table, then braced them on the table in front of me and hissed in my face. "You will not fuck him! Do you understand me?"

"Whoa!" I shouted as he grabbed me by the upper arms and practically pulled me around the corner onto my legs. The other guests could no longer keep their mouths shut and gasped, horrified. Tristan didn't care and pulled me closer so I could feel every single muscle, stiff or not.

"You're mine! And only mine. Goddammit!"

"I know!" I quickly muttered, sounding fairly desperate — completely overwhelmed by his anger. Besides, I knew from experience not to stand in Tristan's way when he had such an outburst...

"You won't do it?" He raised an eyebrow and his whole body trembled.

"Not if I can help it," I pleadingly breathed for merci without lowering my gaze.

"I swear to you, Mia Marena! Don't mess with me!"

"Never! Francesco is actually more like my roommate..."

Tristan snorted sarcastically. "Will you stick to our agreement?" he asked again, sounding anything but calm.

I bit my lip. "I...honestly don't know... Can we talk about it? When we have peace and quiet?" At the moment, I realized we had anything but that, and now, other guests had stopped eating and were staring at us, outraged.

"Do you prefer him to..." I quickly covered his mouth because I didn't want anyone here to fall off their chair, hearing more of Tristan's obscenities. Naturally, he didn't care that a managing director wouldn't behave in that manner.

"Goddamn fucking cunt shit," he swore. Now, I had gone too far, but in the next moment, he tried to get himself under control — for me. I knew that. Everyone in the restaurant gasped in disgust and, resignedly, he rolled his head back. I smiled because his cursing constantly reminded me of my old Tristan and I liked that.

"Get your ass outside, Mia Marena!" Now he was ice cold. I shuddered: *goodbye old Tristan, nice to have seen you...*

He released me and stormed outside. If there hadn't been a doorstop, it would have slammed forcefully against the wall.

Unsteadily, I followed because I knew he would drag me out by my hair if I hesitated.

Okay, right now he was only pretty angry and common sense told me that, perhaps, my next lesson was awaiting me in the parking lot...but my heart...my damn heart...didn't care about common sense.

Which said lots about it. Tristan had hit rock bottom, caught in an intricate game of sex, and possibly, violence. He was aggressive with even less respect for his environment than during his best asshole times.

I had to find emotions in him or else I couldn't fight for him, could I?

Did I even have a choice? Now that I was an adult, could I stay away from him?

Yet...I needed a little proof that my fight would not be for nothing.

He had to give me as much!

10. The Giant with the Small Dick and my Slut

Tristan 'Pissed off' Wrangler

I was pissed off.

Actually more than that! Everything had gone wrong. That big dumbass with a small dick was getting serious and wanted to fuck my Goddamn slut!

Okay, so she was the slut who had betrayed me, who ignored me for one whole week, and who didn't come back after I humiliated her in the club... But still!

I wanted to show her who was in charge and that ass-hat fucked it up for me when he informed her that he would like to stick his tiny noodle in her while I had my tongue in the opening to hell, fucking her like there was no tomorrow.

Without further ado, I sent him a message that the Greens (the damn cops, even though they now wore blue) were on the way to his warehouse because I knew he would panic and leave. And that was exactly what happened.

However, even though he left, I was already utterly furious with a tendency to surge!

After all, he contaminated my damn slut's palm!

I stormed out, but not even fresh air could soothe me.

Since he stated he would no longer wait and had placed her fucking fingers on his micro pecker, I saw only one image in my mind.

His massive body over hers...his dick inside her. And the worst part of it all was that she had her legs wrapped around his hips, pulling him deeper, the way she had done it in the old days with me, her hands scratching his back instead of mine...her voice moaning his name loudly.

"Freakin' bitch in heat!" I growled right in front of the upper-class restaurant, which belonged to Phil and me, and kicked one of the huge candles in front of the entrance. Mia Marena flinched, startled. The candle tipped over, went out, and the gleaming white wax spread over the expensive carpet. Phil would have a hissy fit.

Where was that damn slut anyway? My gaze wandered back and forth searching for her. Finding her next to the candle – with the clear intention of escaping – I stared at her intimidatingly...

"It's too late to run away."

She even took a step back when I approached her, which didn't bother me.

I grabbed her arm firmly to let her know how upset I still was. It was her fault he wanted to fuck her now! It was her damn fault that he even considered it! After all, she was living with him!

Francesco saw her in her underwear regularly, perhaps even naked. They shared a bed. Maybe they even showered together! Oh, what was I saying, she probably had already blew him and let him touch her everywhere! Once a slut always a slut! That drove me insane!

"Tristan... I..." she stammered but I wasn't in mood for it when I dragged her around the building in the direction of the rear courtyard.

"Shut up!" Two sharp words and a warning look was enough to silence her. I kept towing her. She valued her life and offered no resistance.

I had no idea what I would do once we were in the shadows because I was still undecided between *sticking my pecker in her mouth* or *giving her ass a good spanking.* However, she'd most likely enjoy either one...which was why I really tried to control myself. My damn fucker down there screamed at me that she wouldn't dare fuck small dick Francesco, only me. It clearly leaned toward option one... Then again, something could be said about number two...

As we stood in the small alley between houses where no ray of light fell, she tried to free herself from my grip... "Now let go of me already!"

That was the moment where I lost a little more of my composure and growling, pushed her against the brick wall. She gasped as her back made contact and I cornered her by bracing an arm on either side of her.

The woman, who obviously played with her life tonight, looked deliberately to the right, which I put a stop to by grabbing her chin, forcing her to look at me.

My gaze fixated on her delicate quivering lip and I involuntarily recalled how the deep red full sweetness tasted and how sensual it felt when I took the tender flesh between my teeth and nibbled on it as she groaned. Back then, there was no nicer reward for me when Mia Marena whimpered, sighed, groaned, pleaded...directly into my mouth. Suddenly, it was the Italian bastard who had raped her palates and my anger blazed anew.

I almost felt ashamed that she still had the power to distract me with her damn female attributes...it only made me even more aggressive.

And even though she was visibly scared because she stared at me with wide chick-eyes, as if I was going to eat her, there was also trust in her eyes. That phenomenon puzzled me for quite some time. She behaved as if she expected me to have the upper hand in any situation, yet I presented the greatest danger...

Crazily enough, she growled and she even grabbed my chest and tried to push away from me... "Tristan...I cannot...breathe..." Somehow...her absolutely useless opposition made her a crazy cute slut.

"Stop it, dammit!" I cried and grabbed both of her cheeks, pulled her back, and stared at her.

"What?" she asked confused.

"Stop behaving like you did back then!" That did it! I

was in no mood to recall the past because it was not the same and would never be again. It had taken me eight fucking years to come to terms with the fact that my first and absolutely only love had betrayed me. Now, here she was, pretending like nothing ever happened!

"Stop pretending you are someone else!" she whispered and her eyes welled-up. I wanted to scream, pull out my hair, go absolutely berserk; instead, I punched the wall as I said, "I'm no longer your fucking hero!" Forcing myself to remain calm, I continued hissing, "I want to enter into a crazy sex contract with you. I want to humiliate and destroy you. That is suitable for the role of a villain, isn't it?"

She didn't answer. The first transparent pearls broke free and trickled down her face before she closed her eyes and with it, cut the connection to her soul. Yes, that pissed me off too. She was still so open and predictable. And why did it seem I could see actual goddamn feelings in her eyes. In every single look she gave me? How could she be that good of an actress?

My vengeance should finally begin! I should own her every night! To break her, so I knew her better than she knew herself. That was the plan and my patience was at its end.

Now!

"Will you agree to the deal or not, dammit!" With a jolt, I jerked her chin upward once again and she opened her eyes, gasping. Her hands balled into fists and she started to tremble like a leaf.

"No!" she answered, more sobbingly than anything else.

"No!" She sobbed louder... In a semi-satisfactory perverse manner, I knew I intimidated her...but she looked so appealing, so fragile and, so...h'm...the possibilities... I had no idea why it turned me on so much when she was crying and all desperate like now. When her lower lip quivered and her expression was pure fright. Why I was rock hard again and desiring to fuck her right here in the courtyard was also beyond me.

"Tristan, listen to me!"

"Don't you dare make demands on me! Not you!" Dammit! ... I had to turn away and really force myself to keep calm and not yell at her, so she finally ran for her worthless, fucked-up life. But all that was immediately suppressed. That was the way the old soft Tristan thought. A small reminder of what I had endured due to her was enough to drive away any compassion for the conniving slut.

"But, I will demand something from you and you'll damn sure listen to me!" she suddenly screamed, almost deafeningly loud, and her hand shot upward and grabbed mine. Huh, Turkey was fighting back! "Don't you dare threaten me again as if I were one of your..." Her eyes smoldered ominously at me as she quietly continued, "and yes, you're right, it's not like it once was! I too changed! I can no longer be possessed unconditionally. If you want me for WHATEVER, then you must first prove something to me. She was shaking all over, but still managed to keep a firm grip on my hand.

"I would advise you to take your hands off me," I whispered smoothly, yet nevertheless threateningly, and signaled with my eyes my exact meaning. Apparently, unlike the early days, now she did care about her existence for she let me go, albeit oh-so-hesitantly.

"What do you want from me?" I asked curtly and decided it was time to give her some space, so I stepped back and crossed my arms in front of my chest.

"Um, Tristan..."

"What?"

"Your hand is bleeding."

"Nice for the hand. Talk!"

Mia Marena looked up at me. Her gaze wandered a couple of times back and forth between my hard eyes and the cold asphalt, before opening her mouth and barely whispering, "I just want you to love me again."

Sure! What else would she want than Tristan-cuddly-flower-sex-I-fuck-you-to-seventh-heaven-and-do-anything-for-you-Wrangler. Spontaneously, I chuckled. She was so dense!

"I'm not kidding! You mean something to me. Correction, not just SOMETHING — I still love you! Because time has not erased that. Do you think the last eight years have been as easy for me as you imagine? Do you think it was easy to get used to having lost you while I was constantly thinking about you all the while knowing full well you *hate* me?"

The mood to laugh left me. I looked down at her tear streaked form with her clenched little fists on either side, regarded her glossy hair and glowing eyes — rosy cheeks. Dammit...to hell all that I found fucking unholy: I wanted her... So much... If only for three months — at which end... should I have gotten my revenge, I would let her go and the spell would be broken.

But if there was one thing I had learned, especially when it concerned Mia Marena Angel, was to put on my poker face, no matter what happened... "You are not in a position to make me feel guilty, Mia Marena. You did all that yourself.

"I know!" Her obviously guilty conscience instantly made an appearance and she carefully took a step toward me while eyeing me closely to gauge my reaction. As I raised my brows warningly, she stopped, frustrated and huffed. Her shoulders dropped and as she continued speaking, her voice sounded somewhat spent.

"I just want...one night... One night with the old Tristan. I need to know if there's still something left of him. One night...and then I'll be a new Mia for you... I will endure everything... do anything for you... just one more time... *please*..." The last word was hardly audible, but I heard it anyway, damn fucking crap...

"So, frankly speaking, I fuck yo..."

She interrupted again. "No, you *love* me once and then I'm yours." Eagerly, she blinked at me, her eyes already aglow, and her tears ebbing away.

Could I do it? Could I actually be intimate with her? I had no idea. But I wanted those three months with her as my personal slut more than anything. Thus, I would give it a try...

Frustrated, I sighed and ran both hands through my hair as I stared down at her. She was actually quite modest and still so naive. Willing to trade one night of bliss for three months in hell. Nothing more. The devil himself should love her, which was utterly illogical...but worth a try.

"I'll *try* to be nice to you."

She shook her head.

"Don't make me say it!" I hissed threateningly.

"Will you sleep with me? No fucking? Make love...like a man and a woman, not a monster and its slave!" Oh, fuck! That sounded pretty damn scary — at least the first part! How would it be to *do* that?

"Yes, dammit, if you'll give it a rest!" I hissed from between clenched teeth and stared over her shoulder at anything, just as long it was not her face.

"And I'm allowed to touch you like I feel without hearing *don't touch me here or there*?" she asked expectantly.

"If you wash your hands first."

Now she smiled, a broad smile showing all her bright teeth, looking damn dreamy.

"And kissing?" My gaze was icy and pierced her brown eyes...

"Whores aren't kissed on the mouth!" I immediately stopped her because I wasn't quite sure my lips could even come close to her seductive cherry traps. I already made that mistake once; after all, everything had started with a damn kiss!

"Too bad!" Now pouting, she longingly gazed at my lips. I resisted smirking when I saw how happy she was suddenly.

Did she even know what she was getting herself into? I guess not — I didn't even know myself yet!

"Will you be at my disposal tomorrow evening so we can get this over?" I asked and Mia Marena warningly raised a brow.

I sighed heavily...got over myself and wrapped an arm around her waist.

"Do we go to your place or mine?" I inquired softly and wistfully. She sighed dreamily and leaned against me.

"Naturally, yours," she whispered and I chuckled softly...

"Naturally," I muttered and led her out of the courtyard and darkness to my car...

This should get interesting!

11. Sex with the Ex

Mia 'Happy' Angel

Even at night, the main street was well traveled, but Tristan safely steered his battleship through the heavy traffic.

I was probably even more excited than when I visited Tristan's club for the first time. I was unsure what awaited me, if he would be able to abandon his negative feelings toward me for good and open up to me.

At least he wanted to try and that alone showed me that I had to mean something – at least a little – to him...

He must be telling himself that everything was part of his plan. However, if that were actually the case and I didn't mean anything to him, he would have forced his will on me. He was strong — I was weak...

But, finally, he did ask for my permission to own me for the next three months, which ultimately showed he cared for me. Subconsciously, he made himself believe he was quite the bad boy, but there still was something of *my* Tristan in him...perhaps just a bit more psychotic.

A little surprise, I noticed we were heading for his club, steadily uphill where there was less traffic. I took my forehead off the window and looked questioningly at the dark man on my left.

"Don't you agree a sex club is more about fucking? About screwing? About banging? Even if it is your place, it has little to do with feelings!"

Tristan snorted and glared arrogantly at me.

"That's where I live."

"What? There?" The gallery came into view and I pointed at it, outraged.

"Yep!" Oh, Tristan...you don't even have a decent home...

He briefly appraised me as he steered the car into the parking lot, which again was half-full of luxury cars.

"Oh, please!" he snorted derisively. "It's purely voluntary."

"Okay." He must have seen the tears in my eyes and as usual wanted no pity — thus he didn't get any.

As soon as the car stopped, I got out and almost broke my legs because I forgot I was wearing heels. How embarrassing, I actually fell on the ground... Tristan was neither kind enough to help me or suppress his laughter. Actually, it didn't really bother me. If it would cheer him up, I would inconspicuously lose my footing every other step. For my taste, he was much too serious and grouchy lately. However, if everything went according to my renewal plan, I would soon put to an end to it.

My grin widened, the closer we came to his office. Maybe the place wasn't the right one, but it didn't matter anymore because, as before, the reason was crucial. Here, we would get close to each other again.

For years, I had longed for it and now I would get it.

Tristan actually led me into his office, earning him a strange look from me. He didn't actually sleep here, did he? Rolling his eyes, he pressed a button under the desk and pulled me aside. Instantly, electronic folding stairs descended from an opening ceiling hatch.

Impressive!

Grinning, he let me go first and hissed. Apparently, he still couldn't take his eyes of me, fat or skinny. Deliberately wantonly, I climbed the stairs step by step as memories of the past overwhelmed me.

Visions of Tristan and me in the locker room, gentle echoes of the way he assured me I had a beautiful body as he held me and gazed lovingly at me. I smiled dreamily as I automatically compared his present physique to his earlier one. Back then he was tall, slim, and slightly muscular, never too much, but also not too little — definitely a sportsman through and through. Today, the contours of muscles were clearly defined. He acted more manly, but not in a forced way, and still had the grace of someone in complete harmony with his body.

I angled my head a little and watched him climb nimbly up. He looked at me questioningly and in a slightly mocking way, raised an eyebrow.

"What?"

"Nothing...it's nothing..." I tore my longing gaze away from him and looked around.

Wow! Now I could no longer hide my amazement. We found ourselves in a winter garden bedroom under a clear starry sky. There was a huge bed and a wardrobe... The floor was carpeted in soft white and only one wall was not transparent, probably the one abutting his bathroom. It was made entirely of red Plexiglas. When Tristan snapped his finger, it began to shine in various shades of red and cast warm light on the seemingly open space. Here and there, the light reflected off various elements, kind of reminding me of the northern lights. It was absolutely fascinating.

I had never seen anything of the kind.

"Wow," I whispered and looked at the now reddish shimmering clear starry sky. Tristan walked around me to the freestanding fireplace.

However, the main part of the room was occupied by a simple canopy bed. It too was dominated by gold ornaments, which I also noticed in his office. Curious, my gaze traveled to the large sliding door wardrobe, whose entire mirrored front reflected the play of colors on the opposite wall. These tones, together with the pure sky, the huge bed, and Tristan, catapulted me into a world of erotic dreams.

"If you want, you can use the bathroom." Tristan was suddenly standing behind me. The crackling fire was evidence the man was successful.

Breathless, I shook my head.

Tremendous tension in the air accompanied the crackling flames. This here was something special — a turning point. For me, he was trying to be my old Tristan and I intended to appreciate every minute because I knew in the future there would not be any more.

His large hands snake around my belly. It was amazing to be touched by him without the anger and hatred and my breath faltered. His thumbs gently caressed my skin. I felt his nose in my hair, heard him breathe in deeply and sigh softly. Slowly, much too slowly, he let his fingers travel over my waist and upward. Laboriously, I remained still so I wouldn't miss a thing and closed my eyelids, thoroughly enjoying each tiny caress. He took my breasts in his large hands and kneaded them gently.

"H'm," he muttered and lowered his face to brush his lips along my neck. "You are aware that you've entered the lion's den?"

I smiled because I had heard these words before, seemingly a millions years ago. I was happy he seemed to remember our good times as I did.

"Yes," I whispered and angled my head to the side to give him better access. His grin tickled my skin as he obliged my subtle command. "But it's a nice and warm den... I'm sure other woman like it too." I simply could not help myself, although part of me didn't want to know how many women's breasts he had already fondled here while spoiling their necks...

Tristan laughed hoarsely, which made me pretty angry. "You can rest assured...you're the first woman who has been allowed up here."

"You are not serious!" Surprised, I turned to face him. A mixture of satisfaction and surprise.

"Absolutely!" He looked down at me patiently and eventually his expression of amusement changed.

"I don't know if I can do this crap..." he finally whispered. Fear rose inside me since I didn't want it to stop. But what could I say to make him feel better so our plan would succeed? I wanted to kiss him because back then it dispelled all his concerns. However, today wasn't then.

"I love you, Tristan. You have no idea how much this means to me!" Carefully, I cradled his smooth cheeks and ran my fingers close to his hairline, and simply held his precious face. I wanted to read his thoughts, wanted to know what he felt for me.

But he closed his eyelids, pressed his lips into a thin line, caught his breath, and spoke with a controlled voice,

"Go to the bathroom!"

What had I expected?

Sighing, I turned and obeyed the command... Here, thankfully the walls were not glass, albeit the ceiling was. Above me, stars sparkled and on all sides of the hill on which the building was built at its highest point, the luminous city spread out. A huge whirlpool tub on a pedestal in front of a window and an oversized washbasin perfected the room. What was I even doing in here?

Drained, I braced my hands on the marble and regarded my mirror image.

I was freshly shaven and showered...okay... I became a little sweaty in the restaurant, but freshening up in here would feel strange.

Since I was now in this private location, I might as well snoop and smell his cologne. I loved it... It was so strong...so masculine...so naughty — like him. With my fingertips, I brushed over the gleaming white towels he used to dry his body. Of course, they were embroidered with his initials. Discovering the ass cream in a wall cupboard, I chuckled softly and took a deep breath to keep my excitement at bay.

He was probably still using it as lip balm.

I stood there for a few minutes, no idea what I should do next. Finally, I washed my hands and decided to go back.

The fire was still blazing pleasingly in the fireplace and the roof was...open.

OPEN?

Retracted. In any case…it was no longer there. Just like that! It was still cozy; I could feel the pure late summer air and watched the stars without any reflection. I even heard crickets chirping like I was in a clearing.

Confused, I looked around. The room was large and meticulously tidied — old habits die hard. On one hand, it felt funny to be in his private rooms, yet on the other, it was so familiar.

My eyes searched for the man I loved and found him despite the lack of lighting. There was no light source except the soft red and the flickering fire.

For a moment, my heart contracted because now I saw nothing of the old Tristan. This one here was broken, had dark shadows under the eyes. His eyes were empty and dark. Only the flames of the fireplace reflected life in them. The corners of his mouth failed when he attempted to smile because he probably noticed me looking straight at his burned out humiliated soul. His strong jaw muscles bulged, the jugular vein throbbed fiercely, and I couldn't stand it any longer.

In four-liberating steps, I reached him and gently ran a fingertip over the evidence of his discomfort. Tormented, he exhaled.

"Don't be afraid..." My fingers wandered up as if on their own, trying to brush away the exhaustion under his lashes. "You look so tired...Tristan..." He merely snorted sarcastically and one corner his mouth lifted almost derisively. Otherwise, he didn't stir.

My heart beat loudly and quickly. He would shower me with kisses, not bites while looking at *me* not just my body, and caress me rather than grab.

I smiled weakly at him and mustered all my courage. All I had to sway things were my courage and curves, thus I would use them. Slowly, I ran both hands down my waist and his eyes narrowed a bit. I grabbed the hem of my dress and happily noted Tristan held his breath. Without haste, I pulled the fabric upward bit by bit and finally over my head.

He clenched his jaw and turned his face away as I stood before him dressed only in lilac panties and matching stockings. Tons of necklaces covered my breasts, nothing else.

"Look at me," I quietly demanded and he reluctantly obliged, eyeing me from head to toe. I saw desire flicker in his eyes, but at the same time, I also saw something like panic. My legs softened and the inside of my belly contracted with anticipation.

Oh, man!

It was harder for him than he would ever admit. That was why he had added an even tougher shell. I would love to crack it, set him free, regain his trust, but knew it was going to be a long path and that I would also have to sacrifice much of myself to save him... But I would do it without hesitation because this destroyed, beautiful man was worth it.

Questioningly, I gazed up at him as my fingertips connected with every inch of exposed skin visible under the three open shirt buttons. Outwardly, it seemed he was looking me calmly in the eyes, but I knew deep down he was overwhelmed with emotions. Uncertainty, lust, and conflict were recognizable. I wanted to eliminate anything negative, would love to turn him back into the old Tristan who had completely trusted me, who had been at peace with our relationship. Obviously, it was not possible. After all, he was no longer eighteen and had a long, difficult journey since our separation...

"I'm scared too," I whispered as I shakily began unfastening more buttons without heeding his reaction. He merely snorted again and continued staring at me, still superficially unmoved.

"I'm afraid it won't work, that I'll lose you. I don't want to lose you. Not again," I whispered and my breathing increased. Each new button revealed a bit more of the tanned skin stretched over his abdominal muscles. They were really clearly defined... Very clearly!

And then there were those hairs as I opened the last buttons and pulled the shirt slowly out of his pants that disappeared in a fine stripe under the waistband in a beautiful V... My swallow was heard throughout the room as the last barrier was conquered and I bit my lip because then I could push back the shirt and expose his bare torso completely.

"Stop it," he suddenly mumbled hoarsely and I looked at him confused. His eyes almost burned. Abruptly, he raised his hand and when he made intimate contact and pulled my lower lip from between my teeth, I realized what he meant.

Blushing again, I gazed at the ground and felt the hot tingling sensation as his thumb brushed over my lower lip. When I looked up, he released me and I joyfully licked my lips, unable to resist tasting his flavor. Then my hands slid over his chest and stripped off his shirt.

Abruptly, his finger shot out and grabbed my wrists. Surprised, I visually freed myself from the few hairs on his well-defined chest and focused on his face.

His expression appeared pained; I lifted a brow questioningly.

He lowered his eyelids, took a deep breath, and let go of me again. His arms fell lifelessly to his sides and, frowning, I carried out my plan by standing a bit on the tips of my toes because he was so tall.

The material fluttered to the ground and I gasped...

Covering the spot where his heart was beating were the delicate fingers of a woman reaching around his side. Her index finger flicked a genuine-looking heart...filled with deep cracks and that crumbled up one side of his chest down to his ribs. It was a beautiful but devastating tattoo. Its importance was immediately clear.

It was *my* hand! A flick of it had destroyed his heart!

"Oh, God..." Completely speechless, tears filled my eyes.

His grimace intensified and it seemed as if he wanted to cover up, but I was faster. Without being aware, I leaned forward, hugged his hips, and buried my face against his rock hard chest. Erratically, he exhaled his lips in my hair...

No, no, no! I would have never imagined it was so bad, that he had suffered so much because of me!

"Tristan..." Tears ran down my cheeks, his pain was simply too excruciating for me. His hands still hung limp, perhaps even floated over my back. He didn't pull me into an embrace or push me away as I flooded that cruel tattoo with salt water. Then I gently pressed my fingers against it and freed the skin from the wetness. I wish I could wipe away the agony as easily.

"I'm sorry. I'm sorry. I'm so sorry!" was all I managed to sob.

"Baby, stop it!" Tristan seemed stunned and didn't know how to deal with me because I was crying hysterically. Finally, he pushed me unusually gently away by the upper arms and at that moment it struck me... He *actually* called me *baby*! My tears dried up immediately.

He rolled his eyes. "That's not how I'll make damn love with you!" Then he did something absolutely incredible! Effortlessly, he picked me up into his arms and carried me to his bed.

Whoa!

"Love, whatever that is..." he muttered as I clung to his neck.

I was sure he simply wanted to distract me from the fact that I had ripped out his heart and it worked. Completely. I was overwhelmed! Being carried by Tristan Wrangler really was an uplifting feeling and it let me forget everything around me.

Quite unlike him, he set me down on the golden blanket with great care while smiling devilishly down at me, which I returned a bit uncertain.

At that moment, I felt exposed and seventeen again... As

a distraction, I let my eyes take in every inch of perfectly brown muscly dream skin. He was simply...incredibly sexy.

And he knew it.

"You like what you see, huh?" he teased and his hands covered my knees. He pushed them apart and slowly bent over me, supporting his weight on his arms that he positioned on each side of me. The situation was too much for me. His impeccable muscles, the six, respectively, eight-pack demanded attention, but so did his biceps. Perfection almost lulled me into a dream state were it not for the tattoo that, despite ignoring it, was ever-present out of the corner of my eye.

I quickly forgot about it when he pressed his pelvis against mine and slowly started grinding his hips. That was our only physical contact.

"I like what I feel," he muttered in his deep, haunting, velvety voice.

I smiled broadly up at him and let my hands travel up his arms, felt the firm warm texture under my fingers, and brushed down the back. His scent was forbiddingly seductive, not to mention his gaze... *God...*

"Now if I die, I would be happy," I whispered as I risked moving toward his belly, touching the few hairs leading downward while taking great delight seeing his muscles contracting under my fingers.

"It is possible that I come uncontrollably as soon as you touch it," he warned, smirking and lowered his face to start sweetly torturing my neck again. Part of me wished my lips were what he was spoiling, but the other part loved Tristan's mouth anywhere on or inside me. He licked, nibbled, and kissed like a world champ, which he clearly was in these things. However, he did not bite, for which I was grateful. My heart started beating faster as he pressed his groin more firmly against mine to show how much he was excited.

The familiar heat coursed through me.

I gasp and pushed him a bit away because if he dry-humped me now, I would never be able to free him from those stupid pants.

He growled indignantly in my ear, but didn't resist when I let the highly stressed button pop free. My breathing quickened when I pulled the zipper down. Without any warning, I reached in his pants and directly into his shorts and…there it was.

My cock!

Only now did I realize how much I had actually missed it.

I wanted to cheer and shout as I touched the straight shape I could barely get my hand around. Slowly, I pulled the foreskin back and enjoyed feeling the unyielding hardness and subtle throbbing between my fingers.

"Fuck!" Tristan growled loudly and uninhibitedly thrust his lower body. "Oh fucking fuck!" He threw his head back and I stared mesmerized at his lust-distorted face, bulging tendons, and veins in his neck as I reciprocated his hip movements and felt my snail literally dripping, completely soiling my panties.

"Tristan," I whispered hoarsely.

"What?" he managed to say from between clenched teeth and partially opened his heavy lids to look down at me as I jerked him off. His expression looked slightly mad with lust, his breathing intermittent.

Help!

"I want to blow you."

His body froze and it took a few seconds before he moved again to grab my hand and stop my movements.

"Please!" Since seeing him again, I had wanted it. So, I lowered my head a bit and from under my eyelashes looked at him pleadingly. Thinking about his cock in my mouth made me bite my lower lip and lick it.

"Wow, Mia!" Suddenly, he completely disengaged from me and sat back on his heels. He gasped sharply – quite forcefully – his eyes dark and filled with lust. His heavy boner hung out his pants, leering at me. *Blow me. Blow me. Come on already, blow me.* I frowned. *I'd love to, but the decision is not only yours!*

"If you take it in your mouth, I'll come instantly. I'm almost there already!" Tristan announced straight out, just like him. Then, he grabbed it and calmly rubbed it up and down a few times. I swallowed hard because it was completely...unnerving to see him like that in front of me.

I loved the dark carnal glow in his eyes when he looked at me like he did now. Because then I felt...desired and so...*alive*. Unlike recent years. I executed a pout worthy of an actress and he grinned mockingly.

"Stop pouting, Miss Angel!" *Oh, he even called me Miss Angel. Today must be my lucky day!* He slapped me between the legs with his flat hand, which alone brought about a moan. Overbearingly, Tristan smiled and jumped up to take off his pants. I merely stared, hypnotized by his perfect butt, which was small and firm, just asking to be bitten!

He chortled.

"You really are incorrigible. You better come over here before your eyes pop out of your head. You only have this one chance to do with me as you please. So, just do it, Mia Marena!" I didn't have to be told twice and jumped up, but instead of assuming a position in front of him, I placed myself behind his proud back and looked at his raised eyebrow in the opposite mirror.

"May I touch you?" I whispered carefully.

Tristan rolled his eyes and gestured welcomingly. "Help yourself..."

I smiled.

"Your body is so beautiful," I muttered, full of awe and looked at my own small pale hands as they slid around front to his stomach. My breasts pressed gently against his back and my nipples hardened as I lightly traced each of his abdominal muscles with my fingertips. His eyes followed each move.

"I've missed feeling your skin under my fingers so much," I whispered and continued running them upward.

"I've always wondered if my time with you was a dream. Whether it was real, something unique that I experienced with you, found outside books and movies, outside the fantasy world."

Meanwhile, I arrived at his chest muscles, which I also touched tenderly and felt his heartbeat under my palm. It was racing. Luckily, I didn't leave him as unaffected as he would like me to believe. Tristan glanced at me in the mirror with burning eyes.

"Do you still remember? Back when? Our dream of sharing an apartment? All the plans we forged?" Tristan's entire impressive body tensed, but I continued to talk softly and quietly.

"I haven't forgotten. Not for one minute. I still dream about it every night. So, please, let me see some of the old Tristan come to the surface because he needs air to breathe, otherwise, he'll suffocate...and I too...need you...Tristan Wrangler." My words caused goose bumps across his back, which in turn caused a tear to run down my face. Tristan's breathing accelerated.

"I still adore you – like back then – still completely smitten with you, still willing to do anything for you. Deep inside, you know it." I touched his chest again.

In one lightning-fast move, he whipped around — his eyes burning, but...*in such a way*...it made me take a step back and raise my arms defensively.

"This was a SHITTY IDEA!" he initially whispered and was screaming when he finished, while kicking the ancient and massive armchair next to him, which tipped over with a loud bang.

I cringed before him.

Why didn't I know when enough was enough! The last sentence almost caused the barrel to overflow. And that was exactly his main concern! He was afraid of the feelings he had for me, afraid of being hurt again if he allowed himself to get back together with me. And here I rubbed it in his beautiful face that he still felt something for me. Feelings that could break more than just his heart and for which he wasn't yet ready. Feelings that he'd rather transform into hatred than to accept them for what they actually were. Oh! Dammit!

"You know what? FORGET IT!" He ran passed me like he was hit by lightning, picked up my dress and threw it against my body. "Just forget it! Okay? You go your way and I'll go mine!"

"But..."

His eyes were so cold I froze under his gaze and quickly slipped into my dress. He dressed as well. In a hurry, he zipped up his pants with his back to me at the window and looked down at the city. His shoulders sagged and his usually strong appearance seemed weak and broken.

"Never again will it be as it once was, Mia Marena," he remarked quietly and bitterly. "I cannot and will not offer it to you. The Tristan you dream of, the one you once knew, no longer exists. You destroyed him when you ended us... You trampled him with your feet and shamelessly exploited his goodness and love for you... You were the one who ruined him, just like that!" and he snapped his fingers, "... and you tell me you love me!" He laughed mockingly. "You don't even know me anymore! You merely hold onto to what you once knew about me, of which there is nothing left anymore. I'm a changed man! I'm a fucking stranger! So, never in your life can you love me! And I...I...can no longer love at all. You've seen it yourself! I have no fucking heart and apparently, it's required for crap like that!

He spun me around and *now* hatred exuded from his beautiful eyes.

"Do you know how it feels when the one person you trust most in this world betrays you?"

"That was never my intention!" I cried desperately.

"What wasn't your intention?"

"I never wanted to testify against you!"

"So, it must have been your alter ego, the one you share your body with, who commanded you..." The tone was saturated with sarcasm! His hand shook slightly as he ran it through his hair and tugged on a few strands like I'd seen him do a thousand times. "But honestly, I don't give a damn! I'll give you only one chance to leave this building unharmed before I lose fucking control of myself..." His soft voice shook as he clenched one fist then the other.

Oh, no! He couldn't throw me out. This was my chance to establish something like closeness with him. If I went now, it would be over. There would be no new chance. Just the thought of never seeing him again made me nauseous and sweaty. And my heart spontaneously felt like resigning its commission.

I had to make him change his mind...somehow!

"I've always stood by your side and I won't stop now. No matter how much you humiliate me. So, come on, start! I know you still want me. I'll do it, okay? I'll agree to whatever. I'm all yours."

Then, I simply dropped to my knees in front of him, stretched out my arms, and symbolically offered him my wrists.

For a few seconds, he stared down at me dumbfounded — I firmly held his gaze.

"I will endure whatever."

He raised a brow — a good sign.

"Whatever? Are you sure?" His voice was no longer cold but a velvety grater and immediately sent me goose bumps scurrying down my spine.

"Yes, whatever," I replied softly and suddenly felt intimidated by my own courage. It was not a good idea, but what other choice was there?

Suddenly he grinned devilish yet beautifully.

His sinister expression made my heart skip a beat.

"You shouldn't have said that!" *Yeah, like I didn't already think of that.* He grabbed my hands and pulled me up in one smooth move onto my wobbly legs.

12. Lesson Number One: Forget Your Inhibition!

Mia 'Open' Angel

"Are you afraid?" Tristan *Insanely Sexy* Wrangler was standing behind me. His hands were lightly holding my hips, his lips against my ear, his warm breath caressing my neck.

I shuddered violently.

Was I afraid?

YES! Because I had no idea why we were here — in one... *classroom* with six two-seater benches in two rows that were facing an old fashion green chalkboard. Up front was a teacher's desk, on one side a sin and pictures of the human body hung everywhere. Mainly about the union: penis and vagina described in detail, various techniques, and practices were depicted in detail. I immediately felt like I was back in school — incredibly kinky...

The room was obviously only one of many located in the basement of the building because there was one colorful door after another, all in a row. Some had peepholes and a few labels, but I did not dare peek inside.

The door behind us was labeled *Learning*.

***

I was quite relieved when we left the club full of frolicking members behind and made into the basement via a red-carpeted staircase. Through an oversized sparkling curtain with two darkly clad sentries stationed in front — we stood in a seemingly endless corridor. One side was made entirely of colorful Plexiglas, kind of like in Tristan's bedroom. The light mysteriously swept over the walls, bundled itself, and separated again, like bodies of lovers.

This was topped with aesthetic black and white photographs by Tristan, over which the light show also played. All in all, everything seemed classy and at the same time, mysterious...

Right now, I was glad it was only us in the hallway and not full of half- naked people who were uninhibitedly living out their fantasies.

Tristan opened a door almost at the end on our right. After glancing through the peephole as a precaution, he pulled me inside.

"Georgi, I need you!"

Oh, God! Only when Tristan turned on the light did I realized we weren't alone in the room. A man stood in the middle of the room like God had created him and on his hard cock hung a woman...with her lips.

"Oh, hi, boss!" The dark blond man grasped the hair of a young red-haired woman who was kneeling in front of him in one big hand and continued to move inside her mouth like he wasn't talking to his boss. Tristan was unperturbed. I, on the other hand, felt like digging a hole to crawl into and disappear, so I leaned my flushed face against his broad back.

"Finish up here and in five minutes come with Mary to the classroom," Tristan ordered curtly. The woman blinked her heavily mascara eyelashes lustfully at him and grinned suggestively as his gaze absently wandered over her. She was completely naked, skinny, with tattooed rose vines climbing up her left side, which weren't ugly...once I saw the gleaming red.

Grinning, Tristan shook his head and pulled me out of the room.

I clenched my jaw. How often did he get such offers? And how often did he accept? I almost questioned him, but he was too busy directing me into the classroom where he assumed a standing position behind me and shrewdly asked if I was afraid.

"That depends on what you have in mind for me." I had barely finished when I felt Tristan's lips move into a diabolical grin.

"Oh...Mia Marena...there are quite a few things I have planned and I'm certainly leaving you in the dark." His fingers gently brushed my hair from my shoulder.

"Why do we need the other two?" I was sure he could hear the tremor in my voice.

"To humiliate you," he replied, bored, then suddenly jerked me around to him and took my flushed face in his big strong hands.

"To humiliate me?" My fear increased somewhat. He smiled lopsidedly, which was equally breathtaking.

"Oh, yes!... I will make you my personal whore because that's all you mean to me. However, considering your current disposition, I know it won't work. I know you're still shy in front of others. You have to get over that. And that is to be lesson one. Get rid of your inhibition and regard sex for what it is; a normal physical desire that corresponds to human nature."

"Lesson one?" What had I gotten myself into? Why was there so much longing bubbling in my stomach?

"Ahem." Thoughtfully, his lips slowly brushed over my temple and he inhaled my scent deeply.

Then the door opened and Georgi...still completely nude...and Mary...the blonde porn chick who had stormed into his office the last time and who was responsible for me signing the contract...entered, horsing around. She had just pinched his side and he jumped out of reach. When they realized Tristan stood behind me with his hands wrapped around my middle, they stopped horsing around and looked quite shocked.

It gave me the opportunity to check them out more closely.

Mary truly was a classic beauty. She looked like a Botticelli angel, but even more stunning. Her face was delicate, her body petite. She had elegant curves, big breasts, a small waist, and completely shaven. Her smooth blonde hair hung over upper body down to the tailbone.

She wore red high heels, making her legs look incredibly long. Her makeup was dark, which only seemed to make her more seductive. She made me feel insecure... She pursed her full red vampire lips as she inspected me — especially the area where Tristan's fingers were interlinked over my stomach. Her envy was unmistakable. She definitely would have loved to switch places with me. Automatically, I laid my hands on his forearms and held on to him... M.I.N.E! With a huff, she turned around, apparently message received.

That was good!

Georgi had shiny short hair and intense, light green eyes, and an intelligent expression. He might have Slavic origins, but despite his soft flowing contours, he seemed unyielding... His gaze was focused on Tristan, which was why I could unabashedly look at his smooth oiled muscular chest all the way down to his... GOD! Why did everyone here have such giant penises? Okay... he wasn't as big as Tristan, but still impressive... And he was completely shaved, resembling a Greek God. The kind of man every girl on the street would look after. Considering his high cheekbones, full lips, and those intense eyes, he even took my breath away a little regardless that I was already standing next to the most beautiful man on earth!

As I looked at Georgi's face, he winked at me, which made me blush even more because he caught me staring. Tristan growled in my ear as he wrapped his arms tighter around me and squeezed me against his hard erection. I bit my lower lip.

"Um?" Mary was the first to raise an eyebrow.

"This here is Mirta... From tonight on, she works for me. Only for me!" Tristan stressed while focusing on Georgi. He pretended to be thoroughly pissed, even slammed a fist ape-like on the ground, but no backtalk.

"This is Mary and Georgi. They've been with me the longest, basically, since the beginning. They are responsible for normal sex, which is why those two will participate in the first lesson...anything else would be too much."

"Okay," I stammered, not knowing where to direct my gaze. Anyway, the linoleum was actually...quite interesting. Its grain...yes, quite symmetrical...

"First and foremost, you need to understand that a sexual union is quite natural and therefore, the most common thing we practice in our lives. The inhibition and embarrassment you feel right now are but a product of your counterproductive education. It assures you feel inhibited when you show yourself as the fucker up there created you. You are desirable and born solely for the purpose of pleasuring a man, forget that, pleasuring me. Abandon all those hypocritical rules. That will be the goal for the next three months." Tristan grabbed my chin and gently tilted it upwards so I had to look again at Mary and Georgi.

"They have beautiful bodies, so why should they feel ashamed of them and cover up with clothes?"

Mary had her lips pressed together, Georgi waved at me. I liked him. He was a typical pretty boy, I already knew that much. My erupting giggle almost became stuck in my throat as Mister Teacher took me aside.

"Sit down here!" Tristan grabbed a chair from the last row and pulled it out for me.

"You guys use the desk to teach our student how to fuck properly!" He pushed me down by my shoulder until I was sitting. Okay, so I inspected the wood grain.

"Eyes front and center," Tristan muttered firmly and grabbed me by the hair. My breathing accelerated as he ripped my head upward so that I *had* to look forward and watch...as Georgi smiled softly at Mary, stroked her hair back, and kissed her. He spread her long legs and placed himself between them. They were at an angle to us, which allowed us to see everything.

His butt... God... so hot!

"That's how it should be... Watch everything closely. Those two get turned on when someone watches."

Tristan pulled a chair over and turned it with its back forward so he could straddle it and whisper in my ear from behind.

Mary moaned softly in Georgi's mouth and arched her back as one of his tanned hands stroked her upper thigh. I swallowed dry because their act was actually highly erotic. It was obvious they were familiar with each other and that both enjoyed it to the fullest.

As well as I was...for, embarrassingly, I felt myself growing wet again between my legs.

Of course it did not escape Tristan and he brushed aside a few lose strands of my pinned-up hairdo.

"It turns you on, right? See how he kisses her? How their tongues play?" I glanced up and actually saw them tongue wrestling. Their narrowed eyes, the completely lustful muted noises they made...

"You see how he touches her? He adores her curves and completely gives into the feeling her soft skin under his hands... Do you want me to touch you like that too, Mia Marena?"

Oh, God! Yes!

Georgi's long fingers traced circles on her thighs. She spread her legs wider as she slid forward to the edge of the table and thrust her shaven snail at him. He smiled teasingly at her mouth and brushed over her lower shiny lips, which she eagerly offered him. She groaned; Georgi groaned, even I groaned as a sensual feeling coursed through me.

Without my help, images flooded me as Tristan seduced me in that manner.

"Your pulse is already racing...that's hot..." His nose brushed the skin under my ear.

Suddenly, Tristan's fingers wandered to the front of my legs and slid upward. My heartbeat increased again as he pushed my dress up, simultaneously exposing me. Determined, he spread my thighs... I didn't know whether to cling to him or run away...

My belly contracted fiercely as his talented fingertips dance along the waistband of my panties.

"M'm," he growled lustfully in my ear. "You're even wetter than she is... Using only your imagination, you have such vivid fantasies...so passionate... In your mind, it's us you're looking at, right?"

Instinctively, I opened my eyes again, which I had kept closed until that moment, just in time to see Georgi's finger in action... Slowly, he pushed it in as he nibbled on the tender skin of her neck. A shiver coursed through me as she arched her back and contracted around him. I did the same and a short embarrassing whimper escaped me.

"Yeah, baby. That's it... She simply gives into the passion... Fuck, I love it when you do the same and you whimper and moan full of lust..." His hot breath robbed me of my mind, but it was nothing compared to the words he spoke...

Georgi withdrew after he had fingered her a few times and spread the wetness between her folds. He grabbed his cock and positioned it in front of her entrance. They eyed each other and I stiffened.

Tristan was still lightly caressing my soaked panties, but not hard enough to bring me over the edge. As I pressed against his too slight movements, he laughed softly and throatily. The sexy tone he used made me shudder.

"Watch how she takes him, how she wraps herself around him... Imagine it was my cock in your...pussy... You remember how it feels when I stretched you the first inch? When I slowly started moving inside you and suddenly thrust so deep you seemed to feel it in your belly?" My focus shot back to the two up front as I clutched the seat and shamelessly rubbed against him...

Oh, God! It was as if he was already in me — absolute insanity...

At that moment, Georgi thrust into her, but not forcefully, rather slowly and gently. He rolled his head back... Mary dropped back onto the table, moaning ecstatically as he penetrated her deeper and deeper until he completely filled her.

"God..." I moaned breathlessly in unison with the other two. My head fell back on Tristan's broad shoulder and I closed my eyes, almost coming — from Tristan's hoarse sexy voice and the thoughts he planted in my head and the fuck performance by Mary and Georgi.

"Fuck..." Tristan growled hoarsely as I rubbed myself more firmly against his fingers and shuddered.

"Tristan, please!" I kept my eyes tightly closed and concentrated on his, for a change, unsatisfactory finger play, all the while, listening closely to Mary's loud lustful noises, Georgi's hesitant panting, the slapping noises their bodies made and mixed rough breaths. It was enough to drive you over the edge.

"Please what?" Tristan used his other hand to grab and lightly knead my breast. No, I could not possibly say it in front of the others. No fucking way.

"Get rid of your damn inhibition and articulate what your body has been conveying the entire time. It literally begs me... Say it... loud and clear!" he whispered roughly and suddenly his finger pressed more firmly against my entrance. "Then, you'll get it."

My moans were as loud as Mary's and when I opened my lust-veiled eyes, everything was blurry. I was hot and my entire body shook because I needed him so much! Meanwhile, I no longer cared that we weren't alone! The other two were much too absorbed in their passion.

"Fuck me," I whispered hoarsely.

Again, Tristan rubbed my entrance. "What? I couldn't hear you. You have to speak up."

"God! Fuck me already!" I screamed at him.

"There you go!"

And he grabbed and lifted me up. Whoa!

I melted away under his lecherous dark gaze. His fingernails dug into my ass cheeks as he carried me forward.

He plopped me down on the table right next to Mary. I gasped as she sat up and held onto to Georgi's neck and kissed his throat. Georgi grinned at me briefly, but kept pumping into her body while massaging her breasts with one hand and holding her upright with the other.

Way too many impressions...

Closing my eyes, I felt Tristan tugging my panties down. At least he didn't ruin them.

"Eyes open!" he demanded softly and pushed against my crotch.

"Ah," I gasped and arched my back as lightning bolts shot through my starved body. I fell backward and obeyed his command. When I noticed Georgi staring lustfully between my legs, I moaned, wrapped my legs around Tristan's hard hips, and pulled him closer.

I was so excited it was almost painful.

Quickly, I looked up at Tristan, who was biting his lip as he pushed two fingers into me. Luckily, he was too focused on me to register what was happening around him because Georgi's attention was still directed on me, well, at least parts of me.

"You're so damn seductive...the way you lay so eagerly beneath me..." he groaned and pulled out his fingers with a smacking sound. "...I love to watch how I finger you, but I much prefer seeing something else in you."

Mary next to me ripped open her eyes and eyed him eagerly. She was about to reach for his hard cock he had just freed from his pants and which pressed wonderfully against my thigh.

"No!" I immediately protested and Tristan grabbed her wrist before she could touch it.

"This here is our game!" With a relieved smile, I reached down and grabbed it myself, and as a thank you, rubbed it back and forth a few times.

Annoyed, Mary snorted and kissed Georgi more aggressively.

Tristan gleefully rolled his head back and gasped...as I massaged it.

In that moment, he was even more desirable.

I needed it/him. In me. Now!

Knowingly, he grinned at me. Apparently, my expression spoke volumes. His beautiful eyes gleamed at me as he positioned his tip at my entrance and remained like that for a few seconds.

"This time I'll make sure to enjoy it more," he mumbled and held my knees far apart...

And then he thrust into me...

Without paying attention to our audience, I screamed my pleasure.

Tristan was finally inside me again. The wonderful stretching... oh...it was the greatest of all sensations. He filled me all the way to the stop and we were so close that not even an inch separated us. Which, despite my arousal, at first, was still unfamiliar and then quickly evolved into a kind of *homecoming*. Just like in the past, my pussy and his cock matched perfectly. The feeling was downright overpowering, reminding me more of our past than the degrading incident in the parking lot — of better times, hope, and happiness.

I arched my back and wrapped my legs tighter around him. He hissed as I gyrated my hips against his and then he used both his hands to keep me from moving.

"Oh...Tristan..." I moaned as he painfully and slowly pulled out of me while keeping a hooded gaze on everything.

"Fuck, baby!" he moaned roughly and again slammed his hips against mine as soon as I only felt the tip inside me. In that way, he never really severed our connection. Incidentally, I heard Georgi and Mary still going at it. That Tristan called me baby again in his rough, I'm-in-the-middle-of-sex-voice, in combination with his moaning, made the whole act so exciting that I could not even begin to come up with something comparable.

"I love fucking you!"

These words alone almost made me come. Tristan grabbed my knees, pushed them apart, and adopted a more vigorous pace. In that manner, it would not take long until I exploded. Already, my insides were contracting.

"Look. At. Me. When. I. Fuck. You. Mi. a. Ma. re. na!" Tristan hissed between thrusts.

The vision of him almost did the rest. I choked out a groan, helplessly stretched my arms over my head, and squirmed around...almost bursting with lust... offering myself completely to him, body and soul. He could have it all...

"Wow... Now I know why only you fuck her," I suddenly heard Georgi's rough voice. As much as I was captivated by the lustful pleasure, for a moment, I actually forgot about those two being present, even though now and then, Mary and I knocked knees...

Breathlessly, I met Georgi's eager bright green look. Tristan growled as I bit my lower lip, but it was just too hot to look at two beautiful muscular bodies during sex while being adored by two pairs of eyes at the same time.

Anyway, I was glad Tristan was focused solely on me while he fucked me to heaven.

"How about switching?" Unexpectedly, I suddenly felt strange fingers on my leg and I gasped. The veil of lust around me instantly dissolved...

In the blink of an eye, the hand was gone...along with Georgi...

Completely taken aback and confused, I watched as Tristan slammed Georgi against the closest wall and pressed his forearm against his neck.

"Try to touch her again and I'll break all your fingers! I don't give a damn what the customers think!" he hissed, enraged. He had never even talked to me like that, so deadly and scary quiet.

"No one but me will ever touch her! Nowhere! Unless I explicitly permit it! Understood?' Georgi gurgled a reply while clutching Tristan's taut arm with both hands.

I sat up. Mary jumped off the table, but didn't dare say or do anything else. She couldn't have helped Georgi anyway unless he allowed it.

"Tristan," I gasped in shock, "let him…go!"

He stared warningly at his opponent for a few seconds and then slowly eased him down the wall. Hunched over,

Georgi grabbed his neck and gasped for air.

"Out! Now!" A harsh whisper was enough to send the two fleeing from the room.

I looked at Tristan, but no longer moved because he still so damned angry. His gaze burned my eyes, he shook all over, and inspected me like a wild lion.

Oh...oh... Run away?

No! Don't run away! That's exactly the wrong thing! Don't move!

I'M RUNNING NOW!

NO! the voices in my head screamed as I cautiously watched him.

Tristan started to move slowly and came at me like a predator that had finally cornered its chosen prey after all kinds of initial back and forth. I was paralyzed and could barely breathe, yet I was still pulsating violently between my legs. My heart raced as he stopped in front of me and grabbed my chin so that I could no longer lower my gaze, which I had no intention of doing. His shockingly beautiful face directly in front of me, his flashing eyes, the full mouth, everything was so close. I could feel his breath on my cheek as he leaned down over me.

"And you even liked it..." he whispered, ripping me from my lethargy. He placed his finger between my legs...directly on my clit. Whimpering, I tried to shake my head, but he was still holding my chin.

"You are not to like it if someone besides me touches your pussy! All that belongs to me!" Slowly, he began to rub me without breaking eye contact.

Oh, my, Tristan!

"This is my hunting ground."

Was he joking? That was obvious!

"Or do you think someone else can get you going like I can? Do you think someone other than me knows exactly what buttons to push?" He shifted his fingers slightly so it massaged the special spot on my clit, where it felt the best. I clamped down on my teeth to keep from screaming. Panting, I clawed his upper arms, felt his muscles move under the shirt while he was satisfying me.

"Ahhh..."

"Only I know how to make you explode within seconds. That's one of the few facts that will never change between us." His touch grew more intense – more demanding – absolutely knowing. My insides twitched and I prayed he would let me come this time. His velvety voice continued to do its magic. "Only me! Is that clear? Answer me!"

"Yes, Tristan... Yes..." I confirmed and pushed even closer against him. I was so close... "Only you...as...always..."

"Now, look me in the eyes when you come."

I exploded — moaned...really loud...and twitched all over. Waves surged through me, rendering my brain completely useless and pulled me along. I lost the ground under my feet, completely immersed... It was such a relief to finally reach the peak of pleasure. It felt as if I had been reborn by the time I made it to the surface again and panting, gasped for air.

"Fuck!" was all he said. And then he surprised me by doing something to me in the middle of my fading orgasm that completely robbed of my almost non-existent breath...

"I love your orgasming pussy!"

With one thrust, he filled my pulsating heat completely and I cried out again. "Oh...God!"

At once, he adopted a fast tempo while greedily kissing my neck, on to my chin, and then the corners of my mouth. I whimpered and clutched his neck helplessly, hoping he might kiss me properly in the heat of pleasure, but he merely grinned mockingly.

His strong arms held me upright. Had I not been on the verge again, I would have cried... It was too exquisite, to once again feel him so hard and assertive inside me.

"Tristan... Oh, God...!"

He adjusted the angle a bit so he hit that special spot inside me, the one that even in the past made me scream uncontrollably.

"Ahh!" I felt myself contracting again and closed my eyes, a bit leery...because I could not possibly survive coming a second time!

"Please, don't..." I moaned weakly. I shouldn't have done it because Tristan grabbed my hair with one hand and jerked my head so he could kiss my neck again. The other grabbed my butt to push me and my hole tighter against him... Every fiber of my being felt his hard muscular body.

Then he thrust properly...

"Oh, yes, Mia Marena!" he grunted through clenched teeth. Exactly at the moment, I shuddered again.

"God!" My whole body tensed – I could not stir – as I foundered this time. Tristan was kind enough to remain still and filled me deeply with his hardness as I contracted around him. His lips rested against my temple; his breathing was shaky as he forced himself to remain motionless and in control. Every muscle of his was rigid. I fully enjoyed the second orgasm. Felt it with every fiber...

But I was barely finished when he suddenly pulled me by my upper arms onto my knees.

Open your mouth!" He grabbed my hair again and tilted my head back. His other hand grabbed his cock. Still half-woozy, I opened my mouth and instantly felt like exploding again as soon as shoved his hard warm cock between my lips.

His look, oh...*that look*... No one could fuck me with his eyes like Tristan Wrangler did.

"You better swallow every drop!" he threatened and rammed it once down my...throat...I choked...as he immediately climaxed. He held me in place as he twitched violently in my mouth and I struggled to get the rest down.

"Oh, fuck, fuck, fuck, Mia, fuck!" Tristan completely stiffened as he emptied himself in my throat and looked deeply into my eyes while roughly holding me in place.

Once he was done, he released me and backed away from me.

I tipped forward and caught myself in time before landing on my nose. I would have loved to lie there in the fetal position, I was that spent.

My wheezing sounded as if I had just finished 20-hours of labor while sweat ran down my face in torrents and moisture down my legs. I longed for a bed because this had been hardcore training and I was so out of shape. No wonder, I hadn't been worked like that in eight years.

Tomorrow, my entire body would ache and I would have sore muscles in places I had long forgotten.

No orgasm in eight years and then immediately two in a row and with Tristan Wrangler! Hallelujah!

I heard running water. Then I saw Tristan's designer shoes coming into my field of vision. He crouched before me and amused, smacked a cool wet washcloth against my head. Before it had a chance to slide down, I grabbed it and wiped it over my forehead, heated cheeks, and cleavage. *Ooh*...that felt so good...

Cautiously, I smiled to myself as I watched his face and cleaned down below. He looked down on me mockingly, but absolutely distant, so I had no way to get through to him...

"Come back tomorrow night at eleven!"

I frowned. "Wha..."

Tristan merely raised an eyebrow.

"Okay," I whispered and shakily handed the washcloth back to him.

"Okay, what?" he snapped and ripped the fabric out of

my fingers.

"Okay, I'll be here." Now I had to resist a smile.

"I had not expected anything else. Not after what just happened." Tristan straightened up. I followed and soon after stood in front of him on rubbery legs.

"So, tomorrow at eleven. I'm having dinner with a few business partners and you will be my personal slut. Until then, I want you to read again and memorize the rules... I won't tolerate any mistakes."

"Yes."

"Yes, Mister Wrangler," he curtly corrected.

"Yes, Mista Wrangler." I saluted. Tristan rolled his eyes — probably because of my special ending.

"Just as it's not Tristan — at least not in front of others," he said unusually resignedly.

"Also, from now on you won't wear any underwear when you see me. That crap is just annoying."

"Got it!" It'll at least save me some money.

"You can go now." I remained standing. "What else do you want? You had your fucking orgasm and not just one..." Tristan stared at me like I was an idiot.

"Um...can you call me a taxi?" He frowned and annoyed, ran a hand through his hair.

"I guess I'll have you driven home. It's not like I want anything to happen to my slut, right?"

That slut calling business really irritated me, but on the other hand, he did not want anything to happen to me! I was torn, but since I had agreed, I had to oblige.

In addition, he had let me come twice today!

I could not wait for tomorrow to come around — I was already longing for it even though I was still with him.

Because my curiosity regarding lust and his fantasies were definitely roused... The way he probably planned it. One thing was certainly clear...no one but he could put my body into such a fierce state of ecstasy. No matter what he did! It was always kind of...shocking, breathtaking, and fascinating at the same time.

Part of me knew it was a mistake because part of him still hated me and because he was a psycho lover...but still trusted him. Completely…

13. My Slut

Tristan 'Fucking' Wrangler

What was I thinking yesterday? I shouldn't have let her come so soon but made her wait — torture by controlled orgasm. But when Georgi touched her – the body that responded so hypersensitive to stimuli... damn – *my* hot body – I saw red.

Once again.

Maybe my goal was actually only to humiliate her, but that didn't change the fact that I was to be the only one who drove her to unbridled ecstasy and gave her more than simply pushing the right buttons. The bastard who just by using his voice, words, and last but not least, touch, could make her explode. And, at that, as often and as intensely as I deemed fit.

It was up to me if she came or not — only me! Which was why I did it.

And fuck...she seemed quite grateful and awestruck — which her veiled eyes and entire manner betrayed.

She was so infinitely erotic, so feminine and cuddly when I filled her and she gave herself completely to me. The way she squirmed under me, clawed me, moaned devastatingly, screamed helplessly, and always equated me with none other than God. Her warm wet pussy that tightly grabbed my pecker. The sight of it sliding in and out of her wetness that bathed us both.

When she was under me, it was actually the most fantastic picture on earth...

It should always be like that. But, only with me!

However...could I be sure considering the giant with the pencil dick wanted in her panties? No! Which meant that man had to be removed at once. However, if I had I gotten rid of him – I was still searching for a final solution – she would have grown suspicious, although no one would probably miss such a small sausage. However, why spill tears over lost opportunity when new ones would present themselves. Maybe a more — subtle one.

The point was to show her her true face without him looking behind her curtain. Otherwise, the whole matter would end up a serious catastrophe. No one was in the mood for a furious friend when you are the secret lover!

I was greatly annoyed at being the fucking *lover*. *Owner,* in my opinion was much more appropriate...

Today, I would show all to who Mia Angel actually belonged, who controlled her, as well as her body, but above all, her soul.

Killing a few birds with one stone. That way would be easiest.

Usually, I had my crazy little trophy girlfriend accompany me to such dinners to negate the rumor I was gay. I had known her for years and honestly, I had no idea why I bestowed my favor on her. Maybe on a subconscious level it was part of my revenge on Mia Marena, proving to myself I did not need her... Besides, quite simply, it had been the best solution because she didn't ask for anything in return. That chick was in seventh heaven just hearing me introduce her as my girlfriend. Currently, she was on some shoot in China. As a model, she traveled a great deal and damn she looked great, but that was it. Whenever she opened her mouth, I always questioned my sanity and pondered why I didn't boot her to the curb, despite all rumors. Fortunately, *Mirta* stumbled back into my life. I could not deny myself the satisfaction of presenting her as my current slut.

Thinking back on yesterday – the tightness, her moans, the wriggling around – made my pecker twitch in my pants.

Quite inappropriate because, presently, I was sitting with my family in our restaurant having lunch.

Quickly, I repositioned it and suppressed the image of it in her wet pussy.

"Hello! Earth to asshole! Earth to asshole!" My eldest brother Phil threw a piece of his homemade olive ciabatta against my forehead, unkindly ripping me out of my reverie. "I' m talking to you!" Annoyed, he dodged aside when I immediately tossed his ammo back while cursing, "You bum, food is not to play with!"

Yeah, yeah...a penny for your thoughts right now! You seem so heated, little brother..." the dark red-haired, blue-eyed ass teased as he placed his arm around the shoulders of his blonde snake. She was four months pregnant and shoveling tons of potatoes into her mouth. Someone must have told her carbohydrates were good for the unborn child. Unfortunately, she didn't seem to like veggies for she was rather listlessly poking them. I was sure she would have preferred biscuits for she usually stuffed herself with them when she thought no one was looking.

"I'm not heated, you lummox!" I hissed and rolled my eyes at Tom who was sitting on the bench with his redheaded witch, grinning from ear to ear.

"Actually you kind of are...and why are you constantly fumbling around with your pants. Are they too tight? Why are you so nervous, Tristan? Look...your hands are shaking, you're your eyes are all shiny... I haven't seen you like this in recent years," he listed in detail as he immediately jumped onto the let-us-stress-our-little-brother-out-simply-because-we-have-nothing-better-to-do bandwagon.

I felt like banging my head against the table! All these years and *nothing* had changed! "I have no idea why I do this to myself each week!" Finishing my statement, I emptied my glass of wine in one gulp.

"Don't always drink so much!" Vivian, the witch, nagged.

"Lick my..., babe!" I rolled my eyes and grinned inwardly.

"And since you're 27, it's time you stop all that cursing. If you were still with...um..." Vivi fell abruptly silent and I raised an eyebrow.

"...with Mia, I'd still be cursing as I do now because she loves my dirty mouth, you hear?"

Naturally, my faux pas was noticed.

Now, everyone was staring at me, not saying a word. For the first time in eight years, I had mentioned her name! Just like that! In addition...

"She *loves* it, Tris?" Tommy, the stupid psycho, asked immediately. Sure, a lawyer promptly looked for any damn subtext.

"Heavens! She *loved* it," I emphasized theatrically. "Now, shut up!" One by one, I pointed my fork at those present. "You, you, you, and especially you!" Which was meant for Vivian because she had her head tilted to the side and was eyeing me much too intensely.

"You only fill my head with stupid shit. Eat your organic crap and take care of your idiot!" Yes, Tom and Vivi had become...organic fanatics par excellence. Terrible!

"You should lower your aggression a notch or you might end up choking on it. And maybe you should give organic a try! I think all those preservatives go straight to your head," Tom murmured and chomped down on another piece of fucking broccoli. But Vivi wouldn't take her eyes off me and sat there with her arms crossed in front her mini breasts. I gave her the fuck off finger and focused on my beef tenderloin... Nobody cooked steaks more tenderly than Phil.

Given we are a much employed family, we made it habit to at least once a week, usually Saturday afternoons, to have a meal together. Okay. Because of the restaurant, Phil and I also saw each other during the week and on Mondays Tommy always visited the club to check up on things because he was part owner.

So, always on fucking Saturdays, I had to endure the concentrated idiocy all at once.

Although they often went on my nerves, it was also reassuring to know they were there because Tommy, Phil, Vivi, and even Katha the pregnant snake would do anything for me. I could count on them and in the world in which I momentarily lived, that counted for more than I would ever willingly admit.

So, for the rest of the meal, I refrained from being an ass even though it demanded great self-control on my part.

By the time we said goodbye to each other, they were looking at me funny. Obviously, I was in for a thorough interrogation or two. The next time I encounter them, they'd make Swiss cheese of me because even I noticed this morning how treacherously shiny my eyes were and that my face had assumed a healthy reflection.

Naturally, it didn't escape their notice, except for Katha perhaps because she felt sick once again...you almost felt sorry for her. *Almost!* Still, she was an arrogant bitch who was unaware of how lucky she was being with a man like Phil.

Well...she looked perfect. That was the most important thing for him and I was sure some sexual crap played a part, but I didn't want to know anything about that...

Was there anything still connecting me to *her*? I wondered as I sat in my A7 and raced homeward — pedal to the floorboard. If you had plenty of horsepower under the hood, you should also enjoy it; anything else was pure blasphemy...

What a stupid question! Had I gone completely nuts?

It was an eerie erotic tension, a flickering. It was as intense now when our bodies were pressed together as it was years ago...if not even more so.

Now, it was much more exciting for me than before because where scruples had been now lived the joy of discovery. I had to see her and my brain was in sexual overdrive. Lately, it was creating fantasies with possibilities – and that meant something – I had never even imagined.

I was eager to explore her limits and eliminate them, dominate her completely, and could not wait to carry out every single theory with her.

The one I had planned for this evening had something special about it. It was still unclear whether she would break the leash again and run away sobbing. She had managed yesterday's experience quite well, which was probably because I was exceptionally kind enough to allow her to come for a change. If a few orgasms kept her from leaving me and I could still implement everything that popped into my mind, then that was a small price to pay.

I still loved it like I did before when her muscles contracted around my fucker as I looked at her lust-distorted face and felt her entire body tremble. The little slut was already turning me into an addict again and all that had been required were a few fucks...

It was obvious.

And yet, here I was unable at all to stop the process somehow...

Well...some patterns simply continuously repeat...

***

I was so looking forward to her arrival on Saturday evening at eleven that I could almost burst. A small part of me actually doubted she would come, but a larger portion was certain. Naturally, it was right.

Two minutes before eleven, I observed her rushing toward my office on my monitor. In a hurry, I jumped for the door and yanked it open. She did not expect me to be so fast because she was busy looking at her compact, reapplying lipstick. Caught, she grew beet red.

"Do you think it makes a difference?" Without another word, I pulled her into the room and slammed the door shut.

She seemed unsure as she put away her lipstick and nibbled on the freshly painted, quite appetizing thing. I shoved my hands into my pockets, leaned against the door behind me, and watched her peel off her long coat — deliberately using my look to make her nervous.

She uncovered an attractive brown – fairly tight – dress. Her feet were in black high heels, which made me hot again. She had tamed the hair into a simple ponytail, probably didn't have time again for blow-drying. That was so typical of my slut.

After she draped her coat over the back of my executive chair, she glanced shyly up at me. Embarrassed by my intense gaze, she played with her fingers.

"Here I am," she whispered.

"Here you are," I confirmed with a smirk and pushed off to join her. "Let's have a look and see if you followed my instructions. Dress up!" She blushed a shade darker because she was embarrassed that she had to immediately show me her pussy and in such a baring gesture. But she did well, didn't hesitate, and lifted the material with both hands.

"Good." She dropped it again while still gnawing on her lower lip. She had done that even in the past when she had been nervous.

"Upstairs?" and I stroked the spot where I suspected her nipple was. It immediately hardened under my touch, making Mia Marena grin in satisfaction.

"You actually are as dumb as I thought...now take off your clothes!"

That *really* caught her off guard. Her mouth was gaping, but she didn't obey.

"Okay, let me rephrase that... Am I talking like a little dick? Take off that crap before I cut that outfit off your body!" I firmly demanded again.

"Okay! Okay!" The threat worked because instantly she peeled off her dress and stood before me naked and vulnerable. I skillfully suppressed the urge to touch her for if I did, we definitely would not make it to dinner on time.

Instead, I strolled to my couch where I had laid out an outfit of my choosing for her. When I approached her with it, her eyes widened. No idea why...it was only a latex dress; black, tight, with binds on the side, a zipper up front, and hot as hell. I knew she had never worn such clothing. The item didn't leave anything to the imagination.

"Put this on!" She glared at it suspiciously as if I was forcing her to wear a strap-on dildo.

"Damn...it's nothing but latex!" I held it up for her. Gently, she stroked the sleek shape. Then she leaned forward and sniffed it. I really had to hold back my laughter when she wrinkled up her tiny nose and with attitude, yanked it out of my hand.

HA! But that was not all. As she squeezed into it, she made no real attempt to hide the angry glances she threw in my direction. Actually, she failed miserably in her attempt to visual stab me as I sat comfortable down in my chair and silently watched. Eventually, she won the battle, although it was much too loose on the sides.

"Come here!"

As I tightened the lacing, one or two gasps escaped her. However, I made sure not to squeeze her together too much because I didn't want her fainting this evening.

She would not look at me. She must have felt embarrassed and under normal conditions, I would have had to listen to a lecture about women, sex symbols, my club, my job, and whatever else she didn't deem appropriate. But then, we had these rules she was obviously trying to obey. Therefore, she merely clenched her hands into small fists while acting as innocent as a lamb...

Oh, fucking yeah... Sex would be amazing if she continued being this angry.

Obviously, I'd do my best — but when didn't I?

"So!" I slapped her ass as soon as the dress was tight enough and stood up to grab the piece de resistance.

I grabbed a large shoebox next to my desk and produce Roman sandals with 12 cm heels and buckles that ran up to just below the knee. Naturally, in jet-black lacquer.

Her eyes narrowed, flashing hatred at me. She took a step back when I approached her with the shoes.

"I'll look like a whore!"

"You *are* a whore," I replied frankly and grabbed her around the waist as she continued trying to escape me.

Next, I pushed her into my chair, knelt before her, and without hesitating, removed her heels. This time she was wise enough not to kick me when I put on the other shoes. She sat there like a little princess on a pea with her arms crossed in front of her, and tried to look down on me with a look that could kill. When I had closed all buckles, I glanced up at her and grinned.

"Oh, come on! Don't act like that..." I stroked her upper thighs with both hands. Her expression flickered from anger to uncertainty due to my gentle words and she bit her lower lip as my fingers wandered further northward.

I liked how angry she was, which was why I loitered at the uppermost part of her upper thighs and earned a renewed glare.

If she continued that behavior, it wouldn't be long before I went up in flames...only to rise again from the ashes like a phoenix so she could bring about my end once more.

"You will feel like a whore once I fuck you on the dining table in front of our guests, believe me." The words transformed the sparks into a forest fire. As she stood there seething, I rose to put the last accessory on her — a long black hair wig. I ignored her quizzical look as I tugged a few strands while taking great delight in seeing her increased confusion and annoyance.

Kindly, I held out my hand, but she refused it. I didn't care. I simply grabbed a wrist and marched off.

She stumbled after me and I knew she was busy silently cussing me out.

My grin was evil... This would be an evening completely to my liking!

14. Power Demonstrations

Tristan 'Provoking' Wrangler

I had decided to have dinner in the winter garden, which I had added to the park. Here, the atmosphere was relaxed and open. It was needed for the kind of feasts I held here regularly.

As we walked along the path of red pebbles, I fished in my pocket for the icing on the cake and pulled out a black and gold Venetian mask, one that hid everything but her beautiful eyes. I wasn't in the mood for *someone* to recognize her.

"Here is the last item of your outfit." We stopped and she looked at me skeptically before I put the item on her and said next to her temple, "I don't want anyone to recognize your face," I admitted and smoothed out her hair once everything was perfect.

"Like I said, you are my slut only and it shall remain that way. Tonight, you will keep your little mouth shut unless I order otherwise...understood?" She snorted wryly — but nodded.

"Perfect!"

I grinned when I felt her shiver as we entered the upper class dining room with my arm wrapped around her shoulders. I didn't know whether it was because she was angry or excited, in any case, it was going to be interesting.

The others had already arrived.

Leo and Vincent, the two top Mafia bosses in the city, who had secured a monopoly on drugs and prostitution here, and, in my opinion, should start thinking about retiring, sat at the end of the long table, and expertly inspected the curves on my companion. Always on the lookout for fresh meat. Of course, their eyes began to shine immediately, full of lust, as they took in the quite skinny, yet beautiful body of Mia Marena. Long legs and not too small natural breasts...small waist, wide hips... Yes, her appearance equaled that of a whore perfectly without her knowing it.

But the two almost-retirees were out of luck...

I pulled her against me and shot them warning glances, which would have been absolutely useless if they had any real interest in the woman. Make that...with anyone else except me. Her gaze traveled over the assembled guests and she stumbled and gasped when she realized *who* exactly was present.

Down the length of the table sat two more men, Francesco... and his partner, who she already knew from the bank and opposite them, Garrett and Georgi, the two who usually did dirty work for me, were – armed – responsible for my safety.

Then again, everyone was carrying and not one had any fear of using their gun. It was customary in the business. *Welcome to my life...*

Mary and Lena would serve us. Naked, naturally — how else? Mia Marena could be glad she was allowed to wear clothes at all. I disliked the thought of blatantly presenting her to the public.

"Ahhh, our young whore king..." Leo faked happiness as I stepped up to him and firmly shook his hand. His dark eyes continued to gaze at my companion's curves and he licked his chapped lips. "This your new one? Truly exquisite!" He was about to reach for her upper thigh, which presented itself at an ideal height, but I unobtrusively towed her along behind me.

"This is Mirta," I announced impassively while staring at his long spidery fingers that now floated in space, uncertain.

"Mirta!" He clapped his hands. "That name is unusual in this industry!" Once again, his bloodshot eyes traveled to her and back to me.

"How'd you come by this diamond?"

"I met her at a beach party, deflowered her, and then she immediately agreed to do *anything* for me." I shrugged as if it was nothing special.

"H'm, like a fairy tale," the older man with long black hair that was pulled tight and bound at the neck mused.

"Yes, of course, fairy tales...are our job." I replied wryly and tried to pull her along. The tiny resistance made me realize how uncomfortable she felt being ogled like an animal in the zoo and how much it threw her to find Francesco here. I ignored it and continued to welcome Vincent who had more white hair with every meeting and, as usual, acted annoyed. His hair was as long and bound like his cousin Leo.

He offered me his limp hand and did not even acknowledge us with a look when he mumbled, "Hello". Although each man was no longer youngish, the way they carried themselves in those expensive designer suits and whatever other exquisite accessories made them look powerful. They embodied the Mediterranean princes of the underworld. If you posed a problem for them, you might as well go ahead and put a bullet in your head.

Fortunately, Leo liked me a great deal and I enjoyed certain privileges. Somehow, in a twisted way, the top boss felt responsible for me, saw potential in me, perhaps even his successor...otherwise, he would have never tolerated my club because now, I was his main competitor in the city. We often exchanged girls — mine being the better ones, as I'd just demonstrated with Mia Marena. And if I didn't want it, he wouldn't get her. No one else would dare such a thing. When it regarded drugs, he had the right connections.

I needed him; otherwise, I would have eliminated him long ago.

Next, I welcomed Francesco and his errand boy, who sat relaxed next to each other chatting. Mia Marena stiffened in my arms as her man rose to shake hands with me. Inconspicuously, she slipped behind me and I rolled my eyes. Even if he recognized her right now and demanded I hand her over, he would not get her.

She was MINE!

My nerves were nicely on edge knowing how crazy dangerous the game was. She no longer meant anything to me and to torture her in this way — no, I simply wouldn't miss it for anything in the world. At this dinner, she would die a thousand deaths while under constant fear of being discovered.

Once I had exchanged a few quiet jokes with Georgi and Garrett, who were not naked nor in sportswear, but waiting for me wearing Italian suits, I sat in my chair opposite Leo and Vincent, and pulled her onto the chair beside me. Her chin literally rested on her breasts, her face completely pale. I let her stew and ignored her discomfort.

The appetizer was served.

"You've already gotten rid of the shit?" Leo asked and I nodded as I ate a piece of ciabatta that Phil served at these events. Just like the other slop...

"Yes, four days ago. I urgently need more. People are starting to bug me!" Well, not me directly. Customers never saw my face. Only Garrett's or Georgi's, but Leo already knew that. *Never reveal your true identity — except to those most loyal to you.* Rule number one in the drug business. "Also, I need 10 kilos of that lemon marijuana and 15 kilos of hash. The really good black shit. Plus three kilos of coke, the expensive crap. Not the cut crap ..." That should replenish my stock.

Mia Marena dropped her spoon in the soup and coughed, embarrassed when she heard me rattle off my order, thus drawing attention to herself, which made her thoroughly blush.

ARGH, that was hot... The same hue she had when having an orgasm.

It twitched in my pants and I placed my hand on her bare upper thigh. Frightened, she looked at Francesco who was digging in like it was his last meal.

"Of course. I'll send someone first thing tomorrow."

"Good." Taking another spoonful, I eyed Francesco. I had to show her what role he played.

"Will you come, Cavalli?" I asked coolly.

She immediately winced and I sensed her shocked expression.

"No, tomorrow is Alec's turn. I don't have time. My old lady wants to cook for me. Her slop is terrible, but that's what one puts up with for a good blow job..." He grinned salaciously. I merely thought, *Yeah right!*

My eyes narrowed and I flared my nostrils. Okay, mission accomplished. *You see! He's an ass!*

Out of the corner of an eye, I noticed her staring

gloomily at her plate. Okay...perhaps it was a little hard on her. Dammit! Why did it bother me? *She's a cunt! Forgot already?* I cooled my seething temper and forced myself to look away from her.

"Why else have a woman if not for fucking or cooking?" I inquired and winked at Francesco. That was precisely the opinion these fucktwats possessed. While stroking her upper thigh, I could hear her furiously grinding her teeth. Ohhhh, fucking would be phenomenal.

"It's best if they're good at both!" Francesco smirked and Alec the moron, who in his spare time tried to be a hip hopper, laughed along. Everyone else roared enthusiastically...

"Oh, really? Have I already told you about the shoot..." I wanted to annoy her some more when she committed a grave mistake, namely by determinedly shoving my hand from her thigh! For the grand finale, she crossed her arms and legs.

What the fuck!

The last of the sentence remained unspoken, and instead, I let go of my spoon, wiped my mouth with the napkin, ignoring the others who continued their cheerful joking, and turned to her while at the same time placing one arm on the back of her chair. Unmoving, she continued staring straight ahead even though she should now be able to sense my fury.

How dare she remove my hand and close her legs! Had the contract been unclear or was she *totally* suicidal? She probably never closed her legs on Francesco...did not shove his fingers away.

Now, I was shaking with anger and she was gnawing her lower lip again.

Okay, that was it!

She gasped when I suddenly came very close.

"You know, Mia Marena, you just crossed the finish line at high speed?" I whispered softly. Her look overflowed with anger and humiliation — which I ignored.

"You will not close your damn legs to me! That there is *mine*!" And with that, I grabbed her knees and pushed them apart before I put my palm on the velvety flesh. Finally, she turned her head to me wide-eyed.

"Tristan..." she whispered and I smiled charmingly.

"And I'm going to fuck that now." Slowly, I let a middle finger disappear into her. She panted and hastily looked over the table.

No one was paying us any attention because, at that moment, Mary and Lena served the main dish and were groped extensively.

"In front of your friend and those other horny fuckers! You will not move and will not let on! *And you will not come*! Now sit on my lap," I growled and opened my pants.

Her pleading stare only pissed me off more, so I grabbed her hair and turned her face a little so my nose brushed over her temple while I smoothly whispered, "If you refuse, I'll rip that damn mask off and fuck you on the table!"

She gasped in shock and immediately jumped up. She

tried to preserve her dignity by sitting sideways on me, but I grabbed her hips and directed her to sit on my cock with her back to me.

While I held it with one hand, I used the other to push her down. Despite her anger and desperation, she was soaking wet, which was why it slipped easily into her. I gritted my teeth so as not to gasp as she surrounded me. She clutched the edge of the table and I raised her legs so that all her flyweight was on me, giving my pecker deeper access.

"M'm," I mumbled, leaned forward, kissed the smooth skin of her back, and moved my hips a couple of millimeters. I knew she could feel every bit and had control her expression...

"Now...eat!" I ordered between kisses and licked her sweet skin as she obeyed. Her hand was shaking when I gyrated my pelvis.

The conversation continued as if I wasn't in paradise.

There were discussions on market prices and the latest techniques of the newest girls while I was deep in my slut, who grew increasingly wetter and started to contract around me. Suppressing my guttural moans, I leaned my forehead against her back.

"Do that again," I whispered roughly and held her thighs wide apart under the table. She contracted again. I gnashed my teeth and pushed deeper into her.

Almost choking on her food, I chuckled demonically and swiveled again. It almost robbed me of my damn mind because she was so hot, so open, and, at the same time, so tight.

"Again, baby," I whispered and stared at the goose bumps my breath raised. This time too, she was obedient. Nervously, she reached down and frantically clutched my hand that held her thigh.

Fuck! I was going to come here and now and no one could stop it. Not even me...

I was lost...and at the same time, I wanted to do it right in front of her boyfriend and those other foreign bastards.

"I'm going to squirt now," I whispered breathlessly and again felt her shiver. The fingers on her thigh dug into her flesh. As her muscles contracted again, I suppressed a groan and came right inside the middle of her divine tightness. All the while, my forehead was on her back and I kept her firmly pressed against me. My breathing was fairly rapid and it was truly difficult trying to silently catch my breathe. But I managed.

However, if she thought now she was out of the woods, she was mistaken!

I stroked up her thighs and along her lower lips. Panicking, she tried to jump off me and I placed a hand on her stomach. The other was stroking her clit.

She winced — my fingers were not moist enough, so I dash to her entrance where I was still buried, to get the wetness I needed. Then back up, where I noticed her increased breathing when I touched her clit again.

As she lightly arched her back, she firmly set aside her cutlery. But she was a good sport. Dessert was served and still no one noticed what we were doing.

Currently, I had no idea what was going on outside our bubble of lust and frankly, I wasn't a damn bit interested as I circled her clit while continuing to increase pressure. Her despair was proverbial; I swear I could even smell her as I was working her divine clit, which progressively swelled under my fingers.

Slowly but surely, she tightened around me and if I had not grown hard again from her contracting muscles, she would have pushed me out.

I was so lost in her and the feel of her pussy that I almost jumped when Leo slapped the table and stood up.

"We're out of here," he proclaimed, satisfied.

Hurriedly, with my expression under control, I squeezed her legs together and rearranged her on my lap so he could neither see nor get an idea of what was going on when he offered me his hand. Grinning, I gave him my completely soiled fingers.

He didn't notice anything because he was staring down Mia Marena's cleavage.

"And, do you think we can change things up? You can have Lilly?" She was the best he had at his club and honestly, the second hottest broad I had ever laid eyes on. These last two years, we had often bargained for her...but he had not relented.

"No," I merely replied.

He did not expect that response, yet he wouldn't officially show his pissed off state. However, the skin around his eyes crinkled.

"My friend...what do you want." He patted my shoulder and I sensed this was only the beginning... My scalp tingled and I increased my hold on Mia Marena. "Tell your brother the food was molto bene..." He emphasized the words with the typical Italian forefinger-thumb movement. "He can cook for me!"

"I'll tell him..." Phil would never agree to his offer for he did not fuck hookers because he already had one. Vincent nodded briefly at me and followed Leo outside.

Francesco also got up and his curious gaze shifted to Mia Marena's face. Alec – already shit-faced – also rushed to stand.

Fuck...what else did I miss?

"Do I know her from somewhere?" Francesco mused and I narrowed my eyes.

"I wouldn't think so!" The words came out harder than intended, but it was the truth. He had no idea about the woman on my lap!

"Well..." He shrugged and offered his sweaty hand, which I shook again with the one with his girlfriend's cum on it. That brain fuck, without him the wiser, I was getting hard again. Francesco and Alec left us quickly because the latter had to puke and the former had to accompany him.

"Happy, boss?" Georgi asked, dropping his napkin and loosening his tie...

"Yes, now get out. ALL OF YOU!" Because I actually felt my fucker growing hard again since it grew limp during the farewell ceremony.

"Okay!" Garrett and Georgi rushed out of the room, slamming the door behind them.

"And now..." Abruptly, I raised my hips and Mia Marena released the moans she had been holding in for the last hour. Hurriedly, I opened the front zipper as her body came alive and she wriggled beneath me and tugged at the dress with enormous effort – clearly a disadvantage of latex – yanking it down so that her tits popped out. "...let the pleasurable part of the evening begin, Miss Angel..." Determined, I grabbed both mounds and kneaded them as she rotated her pelvis against me as I thrust upward.

"Yessss!" she gasped when I hit her sweet spot. But that wasn't enough for me, no way. I wanted to see her face. So I picked her up from my lap and turned her around to face me. She swayed as I pulled her hips to me. Bending forward, I swept the plates and cutlery off the table behind her, sending them clattering to the ground.

"I told you I wanted to fuck you on the table." I grinned as she looked at me with incredulously big yet charming eyes. I lifted her onto the tabletop and spread her legs wide, finally able to look long and hard at her pussy.

"Oh, fuck, Mia! Oh, fucking fuck..." The sight of her wet thighs almost made me come.

"You're so hot," I announced and couldn't resist tasting her. So I held her knees apart and stuck my tongue into her problem free. I actually tasted both of us, which turned me on even more.

"AHHH!" She arched her back all the way. I almost buried my face in her throbbing flesh as I licked devotedly upward to her now almost big cherry clit. And her cherries were back...

"OHHHHHHHH TRIIIIIIIIIIIIIIIIIIIISTAAAAAAAAAAAAAAAAAAAAN!" she shouted while clawing at her hair. Her hips beneath me twitched uncontrollably and I grinned, sucked harder, and pushed two fingers into her. She jerked and almost came. At the last moment, I let go of her and sat up. My fingers still had our wetness on them...I smeared it over her wonderful tits. She held her breath and my gaze. Grinning mockingly, I leaned forward and used my tongue to again remove all traces before I stuck my finger in her mouth.

"Suck on it..." She obeyed...while staring into my eyes from huge lakes of warm caramel. I almost came just from the sight of her lips, which closely embraced my flesh... I recalled our first time in her room on her rickety bed and flared my nostrils... Oh, fuck...

Timidly, she raised her pelvis toward me. I could not say no to the invitation — not now. Doggedly, I grabbed my fucker and pushed into her with one thrust. Once again, we were in complete harmony.

"FUCK," we both groaned and I abruptly leaned over to torture her nipples as I pushed into her heat. She started to contract again when I sucked on her left nipple.

"Don't you dare come," I breathlessly warned and thrust deeper and harder into her.

"Please, Tristan," she whimpered and bit her lip so hard it bled, then dug her nails into my back.

"No, Mia!" Because I was a mean man, I changed the angle of my hips so I once again hit that special spot. Her moans grew louder, more urgent. She grabbed at the artificial hair again and pinched her eyes closed. Her teeth nibbled deeper and deeper into the soft flesh as she fought the orgasm. All the while, she contracted tighter and tighter around my fucker so that I also had to restrain myself.

I wanted to torture her for a while longer.

The sight of her wrestling with herself so as not to succumb was divine. The sweat on her heated skin, the wild strands caked to her intense face, her trembling beneath me.

I was in heaven…and she was my angel and devil all in one…

Our sweaty bodies kept slamming into each other.

"Please. I'll. Do. Anything," she squeezed out in complete despair and I laughed breathlessly. Okay…I would provide relief, but not without benefitting myself.

"If you come, I will punish you the next time!

"T…Tristan…p…please!" she gasped because I let my fingers travel up her thigh and stroked her lower lips. She ripped open her eyes and glared at me in shock for she was aware that one skillful touch and she would erupt like a volcano of lust.

"No!" she screamed.

"Oh, YES!" I grinned nastily and gently massaged her...

"AAAAAAAAAAAAAAAAAAAAAAHHHHHH
OOOOOOOOOOOOHHHHHHHHHHHHH
MYYYYYYYYYYYYYYYYYYYYYYYYYY
TRIIIIIIIIIIIIIIIIIIISTAAAAAAAAAAAAAAAAAAAA
AN. She shrieked so loudly, I was certain people in the club heard.

Everything was pulsating! *Everything!* Her entire body!

I knew exactly how intense that crap had to feel considering how long she had been abstinent. I even felt the echoes on my cock for she had never come this violently. The effects drove me over the edge and I also let go. My sperm shot into her unhindered thanks to the pill, which I had seen during my nightly visit.

Presently, she clung so tightly to me like she was drowning and for quite some time...I briefly debated whether to make her come again, but then she would definitely lose consciousness.

Thus, I showed mercy and simply buried my face against her delicate neck once it was over.

She held me tightly and wrapped her legs around my hips.

Slowly, I brushed my nose over her wet fragrant skin and felt my stupid grin, which I already knew was there. Back then, eight years ago, I had worn it every day because, at that time, the world had still been whole. Now, everything was different.

I imagined she was mine, but she wasn't. Officially, she was *his* property. A thought that almost made me run amok each time.

"You came, Mia Marena," I stated and she winced because she sure as hell didn't expect me to adopt a murderous tone right after such awesome sex. "I did warn you."

She did not object and we both knew there was no way out for her anyway.

Her mind might be strong, but her body was still weak.

Slowly, I sat up so I could look at her. She returned my gaze with glassy eyes. I could feel the heat in them and realized what feelings they betrayed. Yes...I knew perfectly well and for a tiny moment, she actually touched my heart as her hand reached out and tentatively rested on my chest exactly over my tattoo. It seemed as if she was stabbing a thousand small needles directly into this so vital organ.

But I closed off whatever remained of it. I locked it up by thinking about how I had seen those deep emotions in her gaze way back when and in the end, they hadn't meant anything. *Absolutely nothing!*

Abruptly, I disengaged from her, causing her to gasp.

I zipped my pants as she sat up and I tried to save her wig. I pulled her off the table, reserved as before, and repacked it skillfully. Cautiously, she peeked up at me, but I avoided those treacherous eyes.

She didn't say anything. I didn't say anything. And that was just as well.

Without a word or another look, she turned and went to the door.

"HEY!" I called after her and she cringed before turning to face me. Now, her expression was blank, all feelings suppressed.

"Don't you want to know what your punishment will be?"

Wordlessly, she shook her head.

I understood why she was so distant all of a sudden. *I* had every reason to ignore her.

"What's your damn problem?" I couldn't help asking just so I would know if she would come tomorrow.

"Not a thing, Tristan. I'm simply tired," she stated and her shoulders sagged.

This made me pinch my eyes shut.

"You will come tomorrow," I stated and the ambiguity did not escape me. As a response, I merely received a forced nod.

I let her go and continued watching her swaying hips, long legs, and overall appearance, which fascinated me so much.

Even if I did not intend to bring feelings into play, I was simply powerless against some.

She pulled me under her spell. I adored her. However, I would never ever fucking *love* her again!

15. His Dominance

Mia 'Thinking' Angel

Oh my, Tristan! was the first thing that came to mind when I woke up Sunday morning. Leisurely, I wriggled around and stretched out, accidentally pushing Stanley off the bed. He yelped theatrically and I peeked over the edge to apologize, which was when I noticed that all my muscles were sore, even the intimate ones. H'm, Tristan Wrangler had made me sore... I literally still felt his hands on my body. His fingers branded my upper arm and I touched the marks of passion he left on me.

Yesterday...had been absolute madness. How he had shown me in front of everyone else that he could do with my body as he pleased. The way he had set me down on his hard cock and thus, showed his dominance over me while my current life partner sat directly across and curiously watched us. The entire time I was paranoid my true identity might be uncovered. That he would jump up and pounce on

Tristan. Nevertheless, *if* he did notice something, he was great at hiding it.

No... Francesco certainly did not notice anything.

Not a thing!

At any rate, it was what I told myself the entire time so as to come across as normal, which was almost impossible. At least by the time I felt Tristan come inside me – each squirt – I could not respond! That was plain torture!

Naturally, I was already aware Tristan was getting a kick out of tormenting, shocking, and pushing me to my limits until I eventually broke. However, I would not let him destroy me. Although skillful, he did not torture me obviously, inflicting bodily harm... Tristan chose much more subtle methods.

He used certain looks, small words, and his reserve to *really* hurt me, which I knew well.

Tristan wanted to see me suffer, but I was stronger than he suspected. In my youth, I had endured much worse. After all, I had grown up with a sadistic piece of shit for a father and I was a pro at clenching my teeth and putting up with things so I would endure. Right now, I was doing the same; I was enduring.

Well...until he was inside me again as I lay on the table with him standing between my legs. However, when his magic fingers joined in, I surrendered.

I came...like *never before!*

Having to hold back an orgasm simply turned it into the most intense climax I had ever experienced, which he made happen as if it were nothing. But then it never took much for Tristan to drive me insane with his touches. It meant so much to me to feel him inside me, to be so near and united with him. His eyes, however, betrayed that it was merely a means to an end, to show me how he was the dominant one. What great control he had over me and that I was nothing more but a sweet little sex toy.

In that way, he spoiled my body and ignored my mind. My soul and thoughts didn't matter to him. *That* was also a way of punishing me.

I, Mia Marena Angel, the woman he once loved and idolized, no longer existed for him, which was clearly visible on his chest. The moment I placed my hand over his shattered heart tattoo, he confirmed my theory because he pulled away when the situation grew too intimate. Hello? Actually, it was hard to believe. There was so much of him still in me, yet that simple gesture was too intimate for him. It was grotesque...however, a suitable symbol for what took place between us.

And it made me so sad.

After that memorable evening, I went home and spent half the night awake — almost resigning myself to the thought that he actually *could* no longer permit any feelings.

Could I ever make him whole again? Could it ever go back to the way it used to be? Even if only slowly?

Or was his pain too deep? Had too much time elapsed, during which he became used to his new insensitive self?

Was I even still able to get through to him and would three months be enough?

I was clueless — it happened often lately. Before I drifted off, I decided to continue trying because, every now and then, the old Tristan appeared. Like when he possessively pulled me behind him, always ready to protect me, or when he was overcome with lust and accidentally called me *baby*, or when he looked at me affectionately. Or when he devotedly kissed my body and obviously enjoyed it, or when he smelled, felt, or tasted me... There were those moments, albeit brief, but they were definitely there.

Now all I had to do was capture those moments and hold onto...

Unfortunately, I could not immediately implement my plan because Sunday morning I woke up with terrible abdominal cramps. As punctual as if a timer had been set, my period arrived. Immediately, I grabbed my phone from the bedside table and pondered feverishly about how I could explain this fiasco without losing credibility.

"Hi, Tristan..." *No, that sounds stupid.*

"Good morning, Tristan..." It was nine, he might have already been up for a while, so also not good...

"Tristan, I have to tell you something..." *Also crap.*

"Please don't freak out..."

"Hello."

"Ahoy..."

I pondered a while longer and started a text message.

We cannot see each other until next weekend. I'm truly

sorry — Mia. Before I changed my mind, I sent the message and went into the bathroom to put in a plug and take a shower. When I finished, I checked my phone. My heartbeat quickened, I had received a message.

It seems you have a problem understanding, Mia Marena! was the only thing he wrote. I rolled my eyes. Oh, man! Even his writing sounded dominant.

Okay. If you have to know: I GOT MY PERIOD! I typed and hit send again, blushing. My phone remained silent for the next five minutes. He might first have to digest the shock after hearing about the cruel condition called menstruation.

So, I sauntered into the kitchen and put on a nice strong coffee. Stanley was petted extensively, like every morning, and once he was reassured that I loved him greatly, he also received his breakfast. Once he was finished, I took him for a little walk to do his business and then sat on my tiny balcony to enjoy my second cup of liquid food. Naturally, I had my phone with me...and it beeped soon after.

I really don't give a damn! I should have known... But I *did*! First, during the initial two days, the cramps were so bad I thought I'd die and second, because it was uncomfortable for me to have sex during that time. Not to mention, doing it with I-look-so-perfect-Tristan while Mia completely soiled him — over my dead body!

Sorry, Tristan...not going to happen. I have cramps. Could it get worse?

Fuck you! Obviously, considering his ravishing reply. A few seconds later, my phone beeped again. *"Do you need medicine? Should I have a doctor visit you at home?* Oh my, Tristan! I could not prevent a nauseous smile as I stared lovingly at the phone... I still mattered to him; there he was again — my old Tristan. Although, his mood swings were cause for concern.

No, thank you. I'll be fine. I have Stanley to keep me warm and a bottle of wine to relieve the pain. Thank you, Tristan, that was really sweet of you.

I'm no damn plush bunny! I could literally see him narrowing his eyes.

Yes, you're the uber-bad-boy. Happy now? I texted back and chortled. I felt somewhat cocky, for which I immediately received in kind, because no reply came.

So, I went back inside and snuggled with Stanley on the couch. After listlessly surfing the TV channels, I settled for *The Nutty Bombshell.* Okay...a nice funny Sunday program...the right show to complement lazing about while impatiently waiting for a message from my psycho lover.

But there still was no reply.

Overcome with disappointment, my eyelids drooped heavily and threatened to close when it beeped again.

Was that just now sarcasm, Miss Angel? Ohhhh, Miss Angel! I immediately grew hot as I frantically contemplated how to reply. I definitely didn't want to risk him coming here like a berserker, wielding his knife again... That mattress had been really expensive! On the other hand, it really would be nice to have him here next to me on the couch, in my arms, him eyeing me worriedly, maybe gently rubbing my stomach – although I still didn't care for it, but I digress – while inquiring whether I was in pain, kissing my temple, and his minty breath tickling me...

The doorbell rang.

My heart started to race as my gaze slid to the clock. It was eleven Sunday morning.

Who could it be...*him*?

My pulse raced, palms sweated. Anticipation and nervousness were battling inside for first place. On shaky legs, I crept to the door. I could do nothing about the automatic glow plastered on my face as I opened it. However, it automatically dimmed because it was Francesco standing there grinning broadly.

"Oh, hi!" My disappointment was so obvious even he should have noticed. He entered without removing his shoes, ignoring them, and brushed his lips across my cheek. He smelled of some expensive perfume that I'd never noticed.

"Hi, little one. I forgot my key." Spontaneously, I thought about everything he said about me last night. He had been hurtful, something I never believed he was capable of. Unfortunately, I could not confront him about it or alleviate my aggression in some other way because it would give me away. Although, seeing his face surely would have been worth its weight in gold.

"I brought you some breakfast." He presented rolls from behind his back as I fell listlessly back onto my cozy couch and slipped the phone between the cushions after switching it to silent mode.

"Well, that's great," I replied, not exactly thrilled.

Although I always assumed Francesco would never snoop around in my phone, considering what I heard yesterday, I couldn't be sure. Thank goodness Tristan was not saved under his real name and who would look under *TtF*, alias; The true Fucker.

I braced myself for the eventuality that my friend would not leave all that quickly. So, I spent Sunday with him. We ate breakfast and watched comedy shows, basically, behaved like an old married couple. We didn't talk much, only trivial stuff. It gave me to time to think. I was quite astounded by the fact that I actually didn't care he had a second face.

Meanwhile, I dragged myself outside the house twice for Stanley's sake, took a couple of naps, and when I woke up in the middle of the night, I was glad to find Francesco gone.

***

Monday morning I returned to work.

Robbie had missed me terribly; it was unusual for me not to be there on a weekend. But, I had asked to be off for the next three months each Saturday and Sunday. In exchange, I had to work extra shifts during the week. I had also missed the little man with the beautiful green wide eyes.

I was close to tears as I sat with a guilty conscience next to his bed, stroking his hair and he sighed in his sleep "MIRTI..."

He was as beautiful as an angel with his rosy cheeks and smooth facial features.

The resemblance to Tristan was uncanny; he could easily pass for his son. Also in character because in Robbie's small chest beat the pure heart of a fighter. It was simply that his tough life had not yet taught him to harden it.

The week dragged on, every day stretched to infinity because I never heard back from Tristan. I tried to distract myself, stayed at the home, even fell asleep on two evenings next to Robbie's bed because he was often plagued by nightmares. Unfortunately, he refused to talk about it, so the only thing I could do was keep him company.

With each passing day, autumn grew stormier. The fewer leaves adorning the trees, the more colorful the ground in gardens and streets. It grew noticeably colder and I had to don more layers each time before heading to work early in the morning.

Secretly, in the farthest corner of my mind, I longed for Friday to arrive. The day I would look into *his* eyes again and he would transport me again into the world of pleasure. I missed him. Very much.

Over the weekend, I missed Robbie when I was alone. During the week, I hunkered down next to Robbie's bed and thought about Tristan while I stared out the window at the night. Why couldn't I have them both? Why did neither completely belong to me?

The boy and man both had difficulty opening up. They merely showed bits and pieces of themselves, small fragments. However, I wanted everything from them, needed them all for myself. It was just with the one it wouldn't work and the other was too stubborn.

On Friday evening, I was excited and at odds if I should just wear the terribly wicked dress from last time and shock Tristan by putting my makeup on porn starlet style. But then I chickened out and left it hanging in the closet. His world had not yet rubbed off on me that much. Even though I had to admit, that piece had not looked bad on me. It had an outrageously sexy flair about it and to feel latex against the skin was something else. However, I didn't think I would develop a fetish for it. I had only one and that was Tristan Wrangler!

It was eight o'clock and I got ready in peace. I brushed my teeth, put on light makeup, and shaved my whole body, when the doorbell rang. Frowning, I went down the hall to answer the door with my toothbrush in my mouth.

It was Francesco! Again...

I thought he was playing squash for an hour. And why did he ring? Did the dodo forget his key again? And *why* was he toting a suitcase?

My eyes almost popped out of my head when he waved a city map around and grinned happily at me. I regarded him skeptically, unsure if he had finally lost it completely.

Then...I had a very bad premonition.

It was promptly confirmed by Francesco.

"Pack your hottest things. We're flying to Prague for the weekend!"

And my wonderful plans were shot to hell...

***

Two hours later...

At the time I should have been entering Tristan's office, I was sitting on a plane, bitchy and irritated.

What was Francesco thinking inviting me to that beautiful historic city? The exact weekend I planned to meet my psycho lover for uninhibited sex? I definitely had better things to do. Why did he have to be in such a good mood and hold my hand? I was so annoyed I didn't exchange a word with him the entire flight.

Even while packing, I had nothing more but brooding silence for him. What could I have said, *Um, no, it's a nice idea, but I'm tired of Prague. Could you leave again so I can get ready for Tristan in peace? Remember him, the guy who went down on me during dinner. Oh, that's right, you were too oblivious. Or, how about when he fucked me in front of you and a couple of drug dealing bosses. But there too, you were too dense. Instead, you preferred to talk bad about me.* Naturally, I uttered nothing, so he had to put up with an ungrateful bitch, which didn't bother me in the least.

At the last moment, I even remembered my cell phone that I had forgotten all week long because I usually never used it. No wonder I hadn't heard from Tristan. When I fished it out from the depths of the couch, my eyes widened in amazement at the 101 missed calls and, without exception, all were from him.

Oh, no! And now I had to cancel on him this weekend because Francesco had discovered his romantic side! Everything had already been paid for; flight, hotel, all sorts of bells and whistles, and I just couldn't bring my heart to say no because he really seemed to be looking forward to spending a couple of private hours with me.

How was I supposed to confess to my psycho lover that I was standing him up — again? I was glad to receive a little reprieve because my phone died when I pushed the button. Charging was only possible once Czech soil was under my feet and then I would be far away from Tristan, his anger, and his knife.

I really had no idea how he would react when I canceled the whole weekend, but I had a hunch. Anyway, I had no choice or else Francesco could become suspicious.

In between, I asked myself why I didn't just break it off with Francesco, I mean, I knew he wasn't the right person for me. On the other hand, he had been there for me all these years and really helped. I wouldn't want to lose that.

Ultimately, I had to admit I didn't want to end up alone because I couldn't be sure of anything with Tristan. Obviously, I hoped I could get his old self to make a comeback, but it wasn't guaranteed. Selfish, but the truth.

Upon arriving in Prague, it was already late at night. We checked into the Hilton and Francesco carried our suitcases upstairs. Beaming, he showed me the luxury suite, about which I could not really be happy about. For me, it was kind of a forced vacation and logically, my optimism fell to the wayside.

And when Francesco, in good humor mode, picked me up and swung me around like in those embarrassing, predictable American films, I would have loved to have thrown up because all I could think about was that Tristan was so far away. After successfully avoided whiplash, he set me down and disappeared into the bathroom, finally giving me time to charge my phone.

Eventually, I had to do it...

Oh, no! Ten missed calls and eight messages. All from Tristan.

PN 1 23:03 *Mia Marena, it is three minutes past eleven!*

PN 2. 23:10 *Are you fucking with me?* That was what I had intended to do!

PN 3. 23:20 *I hope you broke your leg and are lying in the hospital or some other acute emergency exists that keeps you from coming to me!* Emergency, yes, but not one he might be imagining.

PN 4. 23:30 *I called all the clinics. You haven't been admitted to any of them. Damn, what's going on?* Uh-oh.

PN 5 23:35 *Go fuck yourself!*

PN 6 23:44 *No... Don't fuck yourself... I want to fuck you! COME OVER!* I'd love to, but I was taken to Prague.

PN 7 23:50 *Okay, you are fucking with me!* Dammit!

And lastly PN 8. Point 12 *I'm driving over to you now!* Oh, God. I winced. He had sent the message half an hour ago. Now I was really in trouble. He must be at my place by now. So I hurriedly typed. *No, Tristan, I'm not fucking with you. I'm also not sick or don't want to be fucked by you. I would love to lie under you right now! Or ride you! Whatever you like!*

But Francesco had the glorious idea to kidnap me. I'll get in touch tomorrow. I'm sorry, baby! I hit sent and quickly turned the phone off as Francesco came sauntering into the room.

I swallowed hard because the only thing he had on was a towel wrapped around his large muscular body. Relaxed, he sat down next to me on the couch and placed his arm around my shoulders.

"And? Do you like it here?" He placed his other paw on my knee. Automatically, I placed mine on his to keep it from wandering.

"The hotel room is really great," I replied somewhat sarcastically, barely able to restrain an eye roll.

"You silly little girl. I don't mean the room, the city! It is an architectural masterpiece mixed with contemporary accents... I thought you liked art..." His nose brushed through my hair and I stiffened because his loud hot breathing sent goose bumps scurrying across my neck, but not from desire...more like disgust.

"H'm-H'm," I replied and resisted the urge to bite a finger, preferably, the one that slipped up my thigh. He grabbed my hand that was resting on his and lifted it up to his thin lips.

"You know what this town is perfectly suited for..."

"Touring castles and drinking beer?"

Francesco laughed. "No."

"Eating Bohemian dumplings?" I wanted to sink into the soft couch cushions as Francesco's rough mouth rubbed over the back of my hand. My forehead broke out in cold sweat and I lowered my lids. I had to distract him from his purpose, so I resorted to unfair means.

"Francesco?"

"H'm?" he hummed softly, grazing my forearm with his nose, inhaling my scent, and then kissed the crook of my arm.

"I feel sick!" He recoiled as if receiving an electric shock.

"Sorry!" I jumped up and ran into the bathroom because I couldn't take the closeness for one second longer. My throat felt closed off and the sweat-dampened clothes clung uncomfortably to my body.

In my new refuge, I sat down on the toilet lid and suppressed my tears. At the same time, I was hoping he would be asleep by the time I came back out.

But he wasn't, he was no longer there at all. Also fine with me. Let him go to a brothel to get what he needed. For example, a woman he can use for cooking and sex! Having seen that side of Francesco had shocked me and completely changed my opinion of him. Okay, actually, it didn't matter to me; I was merely upset with myself for not having seen him for what he was sooner. My father and uncle had been excellent tutors in that regard. Sick pigs could be found everywhere and Francesco...was no different... Now the veil was lifted and there was no turning back.

When he returned, I was already sound asleep... Luckily!

16. Escape or Attack?

Tristan 'Stalking' Wrangler

FUCK! Yes, actually FUCK! It was eleven o'clock Friday evening and she never bothered to show!

And here I had just started carrying out parts of my Mia fantasies. I still needed her! The feeling of hatred was still there, which meant; I had yet to overcome the issue. She should suffer like I had suffered — only then would I be able to abandon my resentment and maybe even forgive her.

Yes, part of me *wanted* to forgive her...a part that, admittedly, was growing stronger and stronger. A part that had never really been able to resist her and that would love her, dammit, always.

But, if she capitulated now, my deserved revenge and everything that might follow would look bad.

Next, I thoroughly freaked out under the guise of retaliation.

Of course, there was also this tiny but absolutely nerve-racking part in my mind that worried. Was she sick? Did Francesco find out about us and beat the crap out of her? Did something happen to her? Did Leo simply abduct her?

Dammit! So, I texted her.

I was angry, which was why at times I wrote only shit...and then I even apologized, in my way, for the crap. To say the least, I was a little confused. Then, after what seemed like days, I received a response!

No, Tristan, I'm not fucking with you. I'm also not sick or don't want to be fucked by you. I would love to lie under you right now! Or ride you! Whatever you like!

But Francesco had the glorious idea to kidnap me. I'll get in touch tomorrow. I'm sorry, baby!

WELL! First off! How *dare* she play with my fucking mind movie if she wasn't even here? *Lie under me? Ride me?* Was she trying to kill me?

AND THEN: *Francesco had the glorious idea to kidnap me?* What? Where? To the mountains? A cave? His apartment? Dammit! Why wouldn't she say *where* she was?

And then the absolute stumper! She texted... *I'm sorry, baby!*

BABY!

Roaring, I kicked my beloved coffee table, then cursed some more because I almost broke my toe in the process, ruffled my hair, punched the window, whose pane, thankfully, didn't shatter (bulletproof glass), and tossed a few papers in the air.

I really had expected to see her. Last Sunday was ruined because of those shitty women's problems and now that damn pecker-head had abducted her!

Was he fucking her already? Was she lying *under him*? *Riding him*? Oh, FUCK! I was so mad! If she were within reach, I would...no idea.

Presumably, I would have put her in the cage at my club and left her there to rot, but not before screwing the brains out of her skull until it left her an empty shell that would be available whenever I wanted her.

All damn night long, I tried to reach her so I could yell and express my anger. But I wasn't merely angry, I was also worried about her, which literally ate at me. During those miserable hours, the only I thing I heard was the same shitty announcement.

The party you're trying to reach is out of the area. Please try again later.

At some point, I fell asleep on the couch in my goddamn office and woke up the next morning with a stiff neck because all night long I had kept the phone pressed against my ear so as not to miss a call.

"Damn dirty whore!" I cursed as I blinked sleepily, rubbed my aching neck, and stretched.

I stared intensely at my phone as if telepathically telling her to call or perhaps send another text. But, neither happened. The screen remained dark and empty.

So, I pulled myself together and went upstairs to change

for an hour of jogging in the gym to work off my frustration.

Actually, purely out of principle, I wanted to leave my phone at home because the silence was almost deafening. It bugged me enormously and was extremely distracting. However, I was weak and turned around to get it after all. Maybe that fucker with the pencil dick was up to no good or another emergency had arisen. Thus, I should be available, so, perhaps, I could run properly amok. I didn't like the first thought at all, but the second one provided satisfaction when I imagined wiping the floor with him.

But neither happened, not when I was jogging nor when I was pummeling the punching bag. Once I was up in my studio in my second office and finished a bottle of water in one gulp, I finally had had enough. I would call her one more time and if she didn't pick up, then I was finished with her!

In my head, I made a complete idiot of myself. Ah, humbug, *she* made me do it. Once again. Like I was still a pubescent 14-year-old who could be seduced!

I fell heavily onto the couch, towel dried my sweat-soaked hair, and searched for *my slut* in the phone book. I was convinced I would hear that shitty announcement again, which now I could recite in my sleep, but instead, my heart almost stopped when I *actually* heard a dial tone!

"Pick up! Come on, pick up." As soon as realized I was *pleading*, I banged my head against the wall. I was such an idiot!

"Hello?" her voice rang out after the fourth beep and, initially, I was so relieved and so damn angry, I was at a loss for words.

"Hi, little one?" she asked when I said nothing. *Little one*? Had she lost her mind?

"Just. Tell. Me. One. Thing." I could barely get my teeth apart and pinch the bridge of the nose hard. "Have. You. Lost. Your. Mind. Completely. Now?"

"Oh, no... I was merely kidnapped, know you, and I could not contact you earlier..." Why was she talking to me like I was a fucking toddler? I heard her take a sip and then rustling noise in the background.

Then his shitty corrosive voice. "Who is it?"

"A boy from the home. Eat your food," I heard her say away from the handset and then it dawned on me. In a feeble attempt to calm myself, I blew the held air from my cheeks.

"I'm only asking you this once... Where. Are. You?" I still sounded quite curt and I really had to make an effort to stay reasonably friendly and not scream into the handset for her to get her ass back here so I could send her off to the desert.

"Yes, we can watch *Cinderella* next week..." she stressed. *Cinderella*? What? The Czech play she had loved so much when she was younger and had actually tormented me with? So, what? She was in the Czech Republic?

"Be more precise!" I barked.

"No... Paris *HILTON* is much too grown up for you, sweetheart..." she replied lovingly. With my free hand, I rubbed my face. Oh, God. I was so annoyed and here she was making me play a guessing game.

"Give me your room number, Mia Marena!" I growled.

"Yes, Christmas is on the 24th of December, we can watch it then..." Oh, man! I huffed deeply. One time. Two times. Three times. Then I dared speak again.

"You do know that I will rip your little ass apart, right?"

"Yes, of course, my darling..." she murmured sweetly, although her voice trembled slightly.

"What were you thinking? Just leaving like that?" I couldn't help myself.

"Sometimes, things just happen...you have no control over... I will be back soon." She tried to remain calm. However, she sounded very insecure after my not so subtle announcement.

"We'll see each other sooner than you think. And don't you dare switch off your cell phone again, understood?"

"It is all right." It wasn't lost on me that she tried to sound carefree.

"I'll find you!" I barked and abruptly hung up before I kept her on the phone for hours just so I could hear her shitty voice.

Next, I dialed Markus' number who, as usual, picked up after the first ring. When the boss called, everything else could wait.

"We're taking a plane to Prague!"

After giving my orders, I went ahead and packed...

***

Two hours later, I set foot on Czech soil (then the second one). Garrett and Georgi would take care of the club. Phil would see to the restaurant and John the boxing gym. Markus would accompany me. He was sort of a bodyguard even though I could handle myself just fine and also a good friend.

The air in the foreign city was corrosive. As always, when I was here on business, thick smog covered everything and I coughed extensively as we walked to the rental car that was waiting for us at the small private airport on the outskirts of the capital. Beautiful old town...my ass. Here, one died from the stale air faster than one could say beautiful old town! That in turn made me recall Naples... That city really stunk! It was no wonder considering the garbage problem, which the Italians did not want to or could not solve.

But all that made no difference. I was only here to make it clear to my bitch who was in charge — that was it!

The nearer we got to the hotel, the more excited I became. Initially, I tapped the ball of my foot nervously on the floorboard, constantly ran my fingers through my hair while I searched the streets for her in case I needed to jump out of the car and drag her into it. It was no way to live. I forced myself to relax and forbade any thought of her from entering my mind. With questionable success.

By the way, I had to calm down in general. On the inside, I was still seething. Something minor would probably be sufficient enough to make me explode. A red traffic light or the like. Therefore, I continued breathing deeply. It wasn't Mia's fault Francesco had dragged her away. No, of course not. It wasn't like she had free will. Damn slut. Besides, she should now no longer be with that puke-face! But that was too much to ask. The teeny-tiny little word *No* was simply too incredibly difficult to pronounce. *The ability to think prudently. That little slut. Let the pisser up in the sky show mercy on her when I get my hands on her.*

In fact, I really had no idea what I would do when I encountered her. But above all, I had no idea how to approach her. Should I wait in the lobby? Knock on the door? I leaned toward the latter option, followed by immediately taking down the fucking door like a raging bull. Unfortunately, I refrained from doing just that because of Francesco, the little weenie. And how would I react when she answered the door — half-naked, with mussed hair and swollen lips, like a freshly fucked Turkey? Okay, calming down wasn't quite working. It was equally a blessing and a curse that I had not taken my gun along, otherwise, there might have been a bloodbath. On the other hand, I presently had no idea how to get rid of my frustration.

As I continued to breathe deeply, I decided not to leave it to chance and pulled my phone out of my tight jeans.

"Where are you now?" I merely texted and hoped she

wouldn't dare once again not respond.

We stopped in front of the hotel and I reluctantly got out while Markus took care of the luggage and left the car with the valet... My phone beeped, it was her. Nevertheless, I first took my time and lit a smoke before I opened the message.

"We're going to the market and then I'm getting a massage..." BINGO, BABY! Slowly, a grin crept across my face and I jumped into action ...

17. His Kiss

Mia 'On Top of the World' Angel

Why in God's name did I feel so hunted since I texted Tristan my whereabouts? Did I actually believe he would come for me – an unimportant little bitch – in Prague? Was I deluded enough to think he would run after and secretly watch me?

Yes... I was.

Yes...it seemed so for I had that tingling on the back of my head — as well as along my back. I was constantly looking furtively over my shoulder. Francesco must think I had gone completely crazy. For some reason, I couldn't help myself. It was just there, that tingling sensation, the tension. I only felt like that when *he* was nearby.

I decided to get a massage later at the hotel because I was clearly overworked, over fucked, or obsessing about Tristan too much. In any case, I urgently needed rest! Even from Francesco.

He was unbearable, always wanting to hold my hand,

kiss me, and feed me cheese and grapes. Basically, he was completely... corny. I wasn't into that. Besides, I could not forget how he talked derogatorily about me while eating not knowing I was there. Naturally, I understood why Tristan invited Francesco and steered him into a conversation about me. I wasn't as stupid as my psycho lover repeatedly tried to make me believe. He wanted me to see Francesco's true face and how rotten he was.

On the other hand, Tristan should have known I wouldn't just throw two years away.

Francesco was security. He had protected me during a time when no one else had been there for me and he would do the same now. I was too scared, yet, with him, I felt safe...

In addition, he had money, was financially secure. No, I didn't want him to buy me expensive knick-knacks, but if necessary, to intervene in case of an emergency. But he already demonstrated that, for example, when Stanley had been ill! Yes, in some way I was using him, which constantly bothered me. Otherwise, I had no one — no family, no friends. Francesco, however, was always there for me, even those times when he did not share my view and had become difficult.

Therefore, I could not possibly leave him simply because Tristan wanted it. And though I was at first extremely angry with Francesco, over time it slowly diminished. He might have said a few rude things, but it didn't mean he was an overall nasty guy. No one could be pushed into a single category or drawer. Everyone has certain attributes, but also shortcomings. After all, I let someone else fuck me.

That had always been Tristan's problem. For him, everything was black or white, nuances or other opinions didn't exist. If you didn't share his views than that person was simply wrong...

***

The market visit wasn't really calm, just like the drive back...

"So, I'll go get us something to eat and be back in half an hour, after you've thoroughly been kneaded, little one." Francesco tugged a strand behind my ear and I smiled shyly.

"Okay," I whispered, glad for the little break and waited until he had left the room before I completely undressed and lied down on the soft massage table in the huge bathroom. I turned on the relaxing meditation music and closed my eyes as the soothing tones worked on me and consciously breathed in and out deeply.

H'm, it already smelled lovely.

Sighing, I placed my face in the opening and relaxed, stretching slowly. Actually, I merely wanted to forget for a tiny moment...e*verything*.

However, I failed miserably.

Tristan, Tristan, Tristan... What was he doing right now?

At the same time, I enjoyed the comforting and unique

fragrance around me. It smelled so fresh. Of honey. And a bit of...lilac...and um...sex?

SEX?

I frowned and opened my eyes. I knew that smell too well! But it *couldn't* be? Now I was hallucinating again. Oh, man...

Unnerved, I shook my head...closed my eyelids and tried once more to unwind.

I was beyond help. Absolutely hopeless.

The door opened quietly, steps approached...

It must be the masseuse. I stretched a little to assume just the right pose and waited for words or first contact... Nothing happened... For a very long time! Don't tell she was standing there ogling me? Nude? And defenseless? Alone... Irritated, I was about to look up when a hand suddenly grabbed my neck.

"Not a word!" I shivered as the familiar voice whispered in my ear. Unable to move, every fiber of my being sensed his presence. His tight grip eased up and began to knead me. "Do you even have the slightest idea how angry I am?"

He spoke softly against my ear as his long, knowledgeable fingers almost...*caressed* the skin on my back and his gentle voice made me passive. "You're lucky I didn't get my hands on you yesterday. I'm certain I wouldn't have been able to control myself and it would have been the end of you."

Horrified, I gasped, but he kept massaging me, working his way down each side of my spine.

Comforting goose bumps spread across my body. I whimpered softly when he grabbed my tied-up hair, suddenly pulling my head back so my throat was stretched and said more intensely, "Do you really want it to be over already, Mia Marena? Then keep it up! Continue playing with my temper... Play with me...if you like...but with me as an opponent, you will only lose."

"Do you think I simply flew here to provoke you?" It obviously worked, but I finally had had enough! He always assumed the worst! I didn't care that he was a thousand times stronger, angrier, and more unpredictable. I didn't care about being naked, so I turned around, straightened up, and glared at him.

Tristan sat sideways on the lounge next to me wearing a white shirt with the top two buttons undone and pair of bright colored, low riding jeans. With his glorious hair tousled and a well-proportioned face, he looked at me somewhat astounded as I me knelt before him and cupped his stubbly cheeks in both hands.

"Do you really think I would willingly miss the time I was supposed to spend you?" I was serious. My heart opened when I realized that he apparently felt the same way, although he tried not to show it, but he was only here for me!

"Why haven't you told him to get lost and to stick his tiny dick into someone else? Has he fucked you, Mia Marena?" Purposefully, he removed my hands and held my wrists.

"No, Tristan!" I quickly shook my head before adding sheepishly, "He has tried..." Instantly, I realized the consequences of my revelation. Pain stricken, his face contorted as if I was torturing him. "He wants to...but..."

Tristan snarled suddenly and held me captive with his gaze. His face expressed various emotions — anger, jealousy, possessiveness, pain, and desire. His beautiful, long fingers were still coldly clutching my wrists.

Abruptly, he let go of one, grabbed my neck, and suddenly pressed me against him. My mind could not fathom as quickly as my heart what he was doing, when he pressed his lips – possessively – against mine.

Everything was too grotesque! Tristan Wrangler, the man who would like nothing more than to gaze down at my lifeless body, was kissing me with such ferociousness and with *so much* longing that I grew dizzy.

Then, he did something he had promised never to do again.

My tense muscles relaxed and with a sigh, I leaned into the kiss, attempting to suck in more and more of the incredible taste, which was about a million times better than I remembered. It was my elixir and necessary to endure the next humiliation. Tears burst from my eyes. I had longed for this for eight years. His divine lips on mine...

As hard and demanding as the kiss was, it quickly transformed into lovely despair when his tongue brushed playfully over mine. I moaned with pleasure as I felt his slight smile and clawed at his shirt while suppressing the urgent need to crawl on his lap and sink my fingers into his glorious hair.

To my amazement, his hand slid from my neck to my cheek, and he gently pulled me closer. His thumb traced little circles on my skin and he groaned hoarsely into my mouth as our tongues touched again.

The power my body possessed over him was incredible... amazing how fast a kiss that was born out of hatred and anger could evolve into loving and glowing passion.

Interestingly enough, he didn't even notice that I touched him, pulled him towards me, and held him.

But before I could finish moving my hand across his chest toward his collarbone and around his neck, he abruptly pushed me away.

After he squeezed his eyes tightly closed for a moment, blazing fire in his irises flashed. Although the passion scorched me, at the same time, the iciness of his gaze made me shiver.

I wrapped my arms around my body and whimpered helplessly because I had lost his beautiful lips and when I heard him cursing, I knew my old Tristan was gone.

But he *had* made an appearance, with such power and intensity. It was at that moment, I was convinced I had a real chance.

Now, he was infected! He had broken his number one rule — for me!

HE KISSED ME!

"Goddammit," he cursed again. He was still so near my face and so beautiful. I stared at his shiny full wet lips and wanted to... just one last time...very briefly...taste them...

"Forget it! FUCK!" Unexpectedly, he jumped up as he ruffled his hair. "I hope you now know who you belong to!" he yelled and rummaged around in his pants pocket without looking at me. Because of me, Tristan Wrangler was absolutely beside himself. I could barely resist a satisfied smile. A small bottle landed next to me on the lounge.

"Pour this into Francesco's drink and meet me in the lobby at eleven," he ordered curtly.

"What is it?" Carefully, I picked it up and looked closely at the clear liquid.

"It will give us a few hours to ourselves. Ass-fresco will sleep through the night like a damn baby." Shocked, I looked up at him, immediately tormented by remorse. Could I take it that far?

He rolled his eyes. "That crap is absolutely safe!"

"Okay!" I whispered, although I was anything but convinced about the undertaking. What if something happened to Francesco, perhaps the potion affects some people differently? Was I willing to feed him drugs just so I could have uninterrupted time with Tristan alone?

Tristan snorted again, not dignifying me with a look, which was probably due to the tent in his pants and my nudity, and then he disappeared, leaving me breathless.

I couldn't help but smile and run my tongue over my tingling lips.

Tristan had indeed just kissed me! And he might do it again! But would I be willing to do whatever for it?

18. His Story

Mia 'Touched' Angel

Francesco came back soon. He had grabbed some Chinese take-out, which could be found on every corner here, for which I was grateful. Because he actually didn't care for Asian food, yet I loved it.

Naturally, he had an ulterior motive. The entire vacation served only one purpose. He finally wanted me to come around...which obviously wasn't lost on me. Happily, I remembered the sleeping potion in the pocket of my black skinny jeans.

"And...did you have a nice massage?" he asked as he dropped next to me on the comfy couch and poked around his fried noodles.

Oh, yes! That tongue gave a really awesome massage...

"Yes...it was very...stimulating..." I almost giggled. *After all, Tristan had kissed me*, I thought to myself and with a grin, dug into my noodles. When did I become such a slut?

"Just wait until I thoroughly knead you, little one..." Determinedly, he pushed his food aside, slid closer to me, put his arm around my shoulders, and caressed my cleavage. Oh, no!

I slipped away. "Did you bring something to drink too?" I asked, trying to distract him while I debated if I would give him the sleeping potion.

"Uh, yes..." Francesco frowned somewhat indignantly and I smiled apologetically at him because I had evaded his touch.

"Dry throat and whatnot..."

"H'm..." he merely muttered and for a man his size, stood up quite gracefully and walked over to the dresser where he had left a bottle of water. It was the only thing Francesco drank. I was pleased when he also grabbed two glasses and placed them on the table in front of us. He poured, handed me my glass, and raised his to toast me.

"Here's to us..."

"To us..." I did not sound as euphoric as he did. He emptied the glass in one gulp and I silently cursed him for immediately attacking his food again.

Oh, no, I had missed my opportunity, although I still believed it was not right. Besides, I had no idea what Tristan was thinking. How was I supposed to implement his oh-so-great plan? I felt I was going insane and decided I needed to make up my mind quickly if I wanted to take that step. If an opportunity presented itself, then I would attempt it. If not, then not. Yeah, who was I kidding? Basically, I had no choice. The need to be with Tristan grew increasingly stronger and outshined any principles or possible risk. Therefore, I feverishly pondered about a pretext to get rid of Francesco.

Finally, I had an epiphany. I took my glass and acting extremely clumsy...spilled the contents over me and the couch.

"OH!"

"Oh, wait!" Francesco immediately jumped up and ran to the bathroom. Now was my opportunity!

Quickly, I grabbed the bottle of water and unsteadily filled his glass. I dug for the vial in my pants pocket. *Crap!* Why did the jeans have to be so tight? Once I had it out, the damn cap wouldn't come off, and I started to sweat all over.

Finally, I succeeded and poured the transparent contents into the sparkling liquid — exactly at the moment I heard Francesco returning. Quickly, I shoved the evidence between the couch cushions and tried to look innocent as he sat back down next to me and started dabbing me with toilet paper. My heart was racing.

It was sweet... I had to give him that much... At the same time, I prayed everything would work out. However, he was getting a bit too involved with cleaning my breasts so I gently fought him off.

"Thank you, Francesco...it'll be fine! It's just water..." I smiled shyly and took a large bite of my food.

DRINK! DRINK! DRINK! Grimly, I stared at his drink and his gaze, dashing back and forth between his glass and the almost empty bottle.

"Oh, now we're almost empty. Here, you can have mine!"

Crap! Why did he have to be so damn courteous all of a sudden? Oh, yeah...he wanted to get me into bed!

"No, thank you. I'm not thirsty!" I quickly stuffed my mouth with food.

Frowning, he eyed me. "But you just asked for a drink?"

"Yes... But I'm good now!"

MAN, JUST DRINK!

He shrugged...and emptied his glass...in one gulp. Seldom before had I felt such relief and panic at the same time. He grimaced in disgust and examined the empty crystal more closely. Nevertheless, it was too late.

I noticed I was staring at him expectantly and quickly focused on my food. Now the stuff only had to work. Hopefully, it was actually harmless. Just in case, I continued watching him out of the corner of my eye while I stuffed myself with noodles.

"So...what would you like to do tomorrow?" he asked, setting his plate on the table and pushing the food around while looking at me with his big brown eyes.

"Uh..." *Fuck my psycho lover.* "No idea." I shrugged, disinterested. Francesco rubbed his eyes and blinked vigorously a couple of times. The suspense almost made me hold my breath, but I harshly reminded myself to behave normally and continued eating.

"Well..." His speech was slightly slurred. "How about..." He gulped loudly and rubbed his eyes again. He dropped the fork in slow motion and braced himself with one hand on the table. Now I held my breath and set aside my cutlery. Francesco blinked unnaturally, trying to focus his gaze...unsuccessfully. He looked at me bleary eyed.

"Uhhh... I. Think. I..." And with that he fell forward so that his face came to rest on the table next to his plate.

"Oh!" Unsettled, I wrestled his massive body up and placed his head on a pillow, where he leisurely smacked his lips. It calmed me because he merely seemed to be asleep. For a while, I watched him. His breathing was even and he appeared to be fine.

Would he really sleep until morning and maybe realize I had tampered with his water?

What was done was done, so I hurried to make the best out of our deviously obtained time.

***

Hastily, I went to the door, slipped on my sneakers, and put on my coat because it was cold outside. Before scurrying out and softly shutting the door, I double-checked the room keycard in my pocket.

I took off down the classy hotel hall to the elevator like I was fleeing. Only when the door closed with a subtle *Ding!* and the typical elevator music enveloped me, did I relax somewhat and breathe deeply.

Escape successful!

I suppressed my thoughts about the sleeping Francesco and concentrated on my meeting with Tristan, which promptly made my face beam and excitement enveloped me in its beckoning arms.

By the time I arrived on the ground floor, I was humming because my mood increased the further away I was from the hotel room. My heart beat to the rhythm of my nervousness.

In the lobby, I scanned the crowd of bustling guests. When I did not find him, I felt the onset of disappointment.

Did he stand me up? Simply forgot?

"M'm... I love it when you wear a ponytail..." Someone tugged on my hair, stepped close behind me, and the warmth of a well-known body caressed me. The incipient flicker revived me and I couldn't help but smile even wider. Full of anticipation, I turned around.

Oh, Tristan! Each time his appearance hit me like a hammer.

"And again that stupid grin!" Tristan rolled his eyes and looked down at me amused. "Is that giant baby sleeping?" Instantly, my conscience reappeared. I convinced myself Francesco was doing fine and stopped myself from bombarding Tristan with questions about the potion's harmlessness.

"Deeply and soundly..." I merely replied and blushed under his intense green-brown gaze.

"Stop that," he demanded drily, albeit, deep down he was pleased.

"What?" I whispered, pretending not to know what he meant.

"You're no longer 17 or some groupie facing Channing Tatum!

"But," I whispered and chuckled.

"But what?" He raised an eyebrow.

"Yes, I am a groupie...yours," I grinned, slightly breathless. *Now* Tristan was unable to hold back his laughter.

"Well then, come on, let your idol abduct you," he announced and chivalrously offered me his arm. There he was again — the old Tristan. I smiled wider as we strolled outside with my arm hooked in his. I hoped this evening I would be able to hold him for a little longer than usual...

***

The sweet Tristan departed after a few steps when I stumbled and almost dragged him down. Was it my fault there were cobblestones everywhere here, on which I regularly almost broke my ankles? I didn't think so!

"Too clumsy to walk," Tristan mumbled, annoyed as he led me into Prague's night... I blushed and clung tightly to his arm as I twisted my ankle, for a change, in sneakers. Tristan huffed, got into a taxi, and pulled me in after him.

The ride through the never sleeping traffic progressed silently. I could tell he didn't want to talk and was quarreling with himself. Something he did often lately. It weighed on me when he seemed so detached at one moment and the next, created the impression he would have to carry all the worries of the world on his shoulders. I would have loved to share some of the burden.

Two sharing a load was always easier...

I sighed...Tristan was once again cool, reserved, and nasty. So I had to watch what I did and, above all, what I said. That was why I remained quiet and let myself be surprise.

But even if he was no longer the former man I knew, I was sure one thing hadn't changed: Tristan was anything but normal or even predictable, therefore he would not abduct me to take me to an expensive restaurant to feed me tidbits, soup, and a 10-course meal. I was certain he would come up with something special...and, as expected, that was what happened.

Because, Tristan Sexy would not be Tristan Sexy if did not do something for me that a man usually did not do for a woman.

***

"Oh my God!"

"I'm presently not working, so you can call me Tristan." He leaned with his back to the city, his elbows resting on the railing, leisurely smoking a joint. His hair blew slightly in the wind, the well-defined moon with a visible crater made his face appear downright inhumanly pale. It was only with difficulty that I could tear myself away from his fascinating sight to admire the lights below us. It was unique, but could not compete with the man next to me.

In his tight, thick gray turtleneck, hip-hugging jeans

with deliberate tears, and his unique sexy leisure look...but especially that overwhelming expression and that mouth, he was the dream of every sleepless night...

Fiercely, I bit my lip as I eyed him intensely and blushed as soon as I reached the goal where a raised eyebrow awaited me.

"If we get caught up here, we'll go to jail..." I announced as a distraction from my pining.

"*I* will not get arrested. Just relax!"

"But we are on the Petřín Lookout Tower! And it's midnight, no one else is here!"

"And..." Carelessly, Tristan flicked the roach behind him out the window... "Paul is here. He is the head guard who coincidentally learned how to be a chef from Phil, which he was before he switched to the security sector back when he took boxing lessons. Guess who taught him everything?" Tristan grinned at me arrogantly and I sighed.

"So, you didn't break in! And here I was so scared!" I scolded him indignantly.

I almost peed myself during the 299 step climb, I was so afraid of being caught and my love-hate relationship for heights...and Tristan had enjoyed it.

Now he grinned dirtily. "I told you before that I find it hot when you're scared." Nonchalantly, he shrugged his broad shoulders.

I wanted to inform him that he was an ass. Old Mia would have done so immediately with the old Tristan, but this one here was the new dangerous one. So, I narrowed my eyes, took a few steps, and placed my hands against the windowpane where the wind strongly whistled given the height. It smelled good above the roofs of Prague...and it had *nothing* to do with Tristan's expensive cologne, whose brand he had not changed in all those years.

I smiled to myself as the tower beneath my feet swayed slightly in the fierce wind... Despite my fear, I enjoyed it because I sensed Tristan's presence in every cell. It breathed life into me and released endorphins and adrenaline.

He leaned next to me on his elbows and let his head sag forward. I stared at his long neck and Adam's apple, but quickly finished my eye fucking because the sight triggered throbbing in my nether regions. He looked exactly like he did when he was deep in me...

OH, GOD, I WAS LOST! NO, MIA! DON'T THINK ABOUT IT NOW!

Instead, I asked myself for the gazillionth time how he ended up the way he was nowadays. At some point, I would have to talk to him if I want to make progress and get to know the new him, to win his confidence again.

"Tristan Wrangler," I whispered, mustering my courage... "Owner of a classy sex club...a fancy restaurant chain...world-renowned photographer...with contacts all over the world... beautiful and dangerous..." Tristan opened his eyes and eyed me vacuously. "...what made you become who you are today?" I added and watched the city. I knew direct eye contact would make it harder for him to open up. My gaze betrayed too many of my feelings for him. And that unsettled him.

"Is this some shitty interview?" *Yes, yes, Tristan...your sarcasm cannot always protect you.*

"No, I'd just like to know." I remained serious as he ran a hand through his hair and sighed. For some time, he simply stared straight-ahead looking lost...then he breathed deeply in and out...

BINGO! He started to talk softly without taking his eyes off the city.

"Where shall I begin? Oh, yeah...the betrayal..." I did not flinch, although my insides twisted into a tight knot, but he didn't pay attention to me and just talked to himself.

"There was your statement, dickhead's testimony, add to that a colleague who allegedly testified seeing my car at the edge of the forest when my brothers and I, who were left completely untouched, gave Chief Dickhead a beating. The evidence was crushing, especially when you said all that crap in court. But, my lawyer was good and Tommy learned the trade from him. Otherwise, I probably would have been longer inside... Your father...arranged it all very cleverly...with your help... And no, I don't want to hear your side of the story now... It's hard enough telling you this crap without having to listen to your stupid excuses... So, just listen or don't, okay?" He threw me an icy look and ran his fingers through his hair again. I pretended to lock my lips and toss the key away. Again, he glanced up at the sky, then stepped away from the railing, and started pacing back and forth in front of me...

"I was allowed two visits a month. Mostly, my entire family came for a half hour and that was it... Sure, initially we also exchanged letters, but over time, I wrote them less and less because I met new people in jail and I even got used to the confinement, loneliness, and bleakness. It was hard in the beginning; the other guys didn't know me. Once I confided in my roommate, he told the others that I was doing prison time because of a woman. Promptly, I was the loser and not taken seriously, considered a low-life wimp. I hated you! You, the whole affair — everything! They teased me about being so devastated because of a stinking pussy.

After a month, I had enough and beat Carlos, the top guy, hospital ripe. He stayed three months in the infirmary and it had been TOUCH and GO when they patched him together so he wouldn't end up a cripple..."

He shrugged, but his flexing hands told me it still haunted him. "But that wasn't enough. The others came at me numerous times to finish me off, but I took down one after the other. In a rage, I was invincible and the guards gave me free reign. They hardly ever intervened, so I did everything to earn respect. Do you really think I would let myself be fucked in the ass? That guy ended up eating his fucking soap!" The memory made him smirk a little, but then he sighed... "The first half year in that cell was one of the toughest times in my life."

With burning eyes, I stared at him. Was it so far-fetched that he hated me so much? After all he had been through? All that time of loneliness, alone against an army of bad men who wanted to break him?

Oh, no, clearly not.

"Eventually, they didn't just accept me, they looked up to me. It made it a little more tolerable. I no longer constantly expected to be ambushed... At some point, I even got used to not being able to go where I wanted. That was probably also for your benefit... just saying...otherwise, I would have looked you up immediately... When you have no alternatives in life and nothing to lose, eventually nothing is important..." He stepped in front of me and looked sternly down at me. I shivered.

"Someone who has not experienced it cannot imagine how crappy it is when you cannot even walk through a normal door and go outside, to experience *life* ...

Anyway, after I showed those fuckers the worst but understandable means who was running the show, I was bored and started training like a madman... But what other useful way was there to kill time? In addition to my mini job, I could have taken all kinds of drugs or whatever crap, but I had a goal. I became acquainted with a few useful people who helped me when I was finally released...and, unfortunately, not early parole for good behavior..."

Tristan turned away from me, once again leaning on the railing, letting his empty gaze travel over the rooftops of Prague.

He inhaled deeply and I knew he was enjoying his freedom because he knew it was precious.

Tears welled up in my eyes. A locked up Tristan resembled a dead Tristan...and I was the one who did it to him. It was impossible that I or he would forgive me, yet he still managed to keep resentment out of his soft voice and I gave him credit for it.

"When I was released, everything was lost. It was as if I had walked into a completely new world, like some fucking helpless baby... My coach said I could forget about a professional career. He dropped me as soon as the verdict was in. Generally, a two-year prison stay is not good to have on your resume. My family was scattered all over the country, but even from afar, they provided assistance and money. Nevertheless, I've never been someone to ride other's coattails. I wanted to do it alone." Yes, I knew that. His gaze became calculating as he continued cooling.

"And I *have* made it alone. I knew this guy, Pete, who had been released two months after me. At that time, I was living in some low-life dump, surviving by washing dishes... Can you imagine, me cleaning dishes?" Humorlessly he laughed. "He was hardly out when he connected with Leo... Pete got me the drugs, I distributed them. Then, he died — unexplained reasons. But before that, Pete he had taken me along a couple of times to see Leo... Afterward, Leo approached me personally. At the time, I had already made him a few hundred grand. I was always adept at manipulating people, dealing with numbers, and not being fucked with, which is necessary in that business.

Leo apparently recognized my talent and sponsored me. I was only out of prison for a year when I already had enough money saved to become self-employed. Naturally, I focused on what I did best: SEX." He eyed me provocatively and I did not evade his gaze, although it was growing increasingly uncomfortable. He challenged me to take him on, counter. For example: Why didn't you become a decent businessman? But he no longer knew me all that well because I would never hold anything against him — never. Had he forgotten I was the one who always took his side, no matter what it was about?

Obviously...

"Yes...you certainly know about sex," I confirmed, seemingly unmoved. His lips changed into a mocking grin and he turned away from me again.

"In the beginning, I only had Mary and Georgi... they cost me a bunch of dough, but I simply had to have them! The club had been small and in shambles, but the customers always came back... Over the years, I expanded bit by bit, each month making more money and on the side, made a name for myself as a photographer. Phillip moved back to the city from abroad, where he acquired the best culinary education money could buy. Next, I invested in his upper-class restaurant chain.

You cannot invest your money diverse enough and you damn well better go with the times and constantly reinvent yourself... Two years ago, I remodeled the basement and hired Lena and Garrett. I expanded everything. I became the best — even better than Leo. At least, regarding hookers. Fortunately, he grew fond of me. He is fascinated by how I can make money out of crap and wants me to be his successor... Unfortunately, Francesco is..." I cringed... "... his nephew and I expect...will claim the position."

"Francesco is Leo's nephew?" I exclaimed, shocked. Tristan raised one eyebrow to remind me I should keep my mouth shut. I was still staring at him stunned when he continued, unmoved.

"Now, I've amassed a fortune in the seven-figure range. I could never lift a finger again, but I enjoy what I do. It gives me something to do. And, I like my staff. I like it...simply...being in charge!"

He shrugged, ran his fingers through his hair, and turned to me wearing a crooked grin.

"And now I'm standing here on shitty Petřín, 380 meters up in the air...with you, Mia Marena Angel. I cried my eyes out on your shoulder... Something...I never believed..." he mused as his gaze searched my face, stopping at my eyes and piercing the curious brown.

"I told you my story, now you tell me how you got here!" he demanded with a gentle undertone that sent goose bumps over the body.

I closed my eyes...and armed myself to relive the past eight years.

But he had revealed everything to me. Now it was my turn.
Fair was fair…

19. Mia Marena Angel

Tristan 'Confused' Wrangler

Mia Marena Angel was no longer her old self. Under normal circumstances, she would not have put up with any of my crap but directly kicked my ass. The reason she didn't do so now was she was afraid I might completely freak out. But above all else, she endured it because...for some reason...she loved me.

Because, yes, I could not close my ignorant eyes to the specific looks and touches. No person was that good of an actor! Not even her!

She was a strong little person who put up with the insanity simply because she knew what she wanted.

That was why she was here and stuck around — no matter what I did to her, which was reassuring. Still, curiosity nearly ate me up and my fascination with her transformation from pudgy Turkey to the strong independent woman in recent years preoccupied me.

Intelligence, she always possessed. I simply called her out on imaginary stupidity to hurt her. And she was funny. We had always shared the same crazy humor. Just as, all along, we had fit well together. And even if I did not want to admit it, nothing certainly had changed regarding the latter. Together, we were perfect. Even after eight damn years... But nothing could douse the pain and seemingly constant simmering anger within me. I still wanted to see her suffer and was suspicious when she begged, which downright verbally and mentally implored me to forgive her. Yes, why? So she could destroy me completely? It seemed as if I was split in two. One, tender Tristan, who wanted nothing more than to hold his girl in his arms and never let her go and the other, who could not forget and was determined to exact his revenge – an eye for an eye.

Nevertheless, I controlled myself because inside me damn hope grew like a nasty cancer, even though it did not erase her guilt. I wanted to know everything because so much time had passed where I had not heard from her.

What had she been up to during those eight years? Had she even thought about me, maybe even lay awake all night long like I had, pining for me? Was she aware what I had to go through because of her?

NO! She had no idea because after my girlie confession she looked shocked. Obviously, she had not let on. Earlier, she would have cried openly. Now she furtively wiped the tears from the corner of her eyes as she gazed out at the city without focusing on anything in particular...

"Where should I begin?" she asked herself and her expression seemed so infinitely pained that my damaged heart violently contracted.

"Tell me everything that happened beginning on the day I was put away..." I whispered because everything else I already knew. I was not yet ready for her flimsy excuses why and how she had acted at the time. Besides, I could not possibly continue maintaining a calm expression while listening to her words.

For long time, she stared at me before sighing and lowering her head into her hands.

"After the... *event*, my uncle took me to this city. Okay!" Immediately, she caught me off guard. She didn't notice I was staring at her because she buried her face in her hands.

"He was better than my father, he didn't hit me. That was it — in regards to anything positive. Nevertheless, he honestly threatened me and Stanley all the time, even your siblings, your dad, and you too, so I would testify in court against you...and I did...it was incredibly difficult for me! But I still thought it would be better for you, and I wouldn't, in this way, destroy you...that you would somehow make it... My uncle...can be quite manipulative, more so than my father. It is a requirement in his job. During the day he is a mailman and in the evening, a drug courier. The small two-room apartment where we lived was always packed with junkies and other people that I was supposed to serve..."

Oh, FUCK! My hands were already clenched into solid fists so that the veins stood out.

"I got my high school diploma here and after several internships in various institutions, I realized it was my calling to work with children. So, I wanted to become a social worker. Painting...I had only done for myself. I didn't want to make my leisure activity my career because it would have been more difficult to live on that and I had to get away from my uncle. I drew on the pavement to earn a little extra. During the day, I drew funny cartoons...in the evening...only you. Your face. Your hands. Your body. Every detail of you. I had to capture you somehow so as not to forget you... I had written you so many letters and wanted to send you so many drawings, but I had never been able to do it... Oftentimes, I stood for hours in front of the mailbox..." She faltered and I noticed she was crying softly. Crap!

I turned away because I couldn't nor wanted to see her so broken. Breathing deeply, I again focused on her remarks; after all, I wanted to know. Damn, ignorance could be damn blissful because she touched something deep down in me that actually should no longer exist.

"My uncle...helped me a bit financially so I was able to do my studies, but, naturally, not without a trade-off. In my family, no one does anything out of pure selflessness as you may recall...so, initially, I stayed with him and took care of his apartment and everything else in his life. He was the man of the house and his word was law. As I said, it was better with him than my parents. Better than with my father..." I only had to think about him and I saw red, so I was glad when she changed the subject.

"During my college years, I met Francesco... He was an administrator at my uncle's bank, which was why he came over at times. He never took drugs, was always calm. I always wondered why he hung out with drug addicts...

Now I find out he had been supplying my uncle all along. At the time, I was naive and simply thought he was nothing more than some boring banker... He...once came to my rescue, so to speak... and I was so grateful I went out with him on a date even though I couldn't care less about men.

He fell in love with me, made my life a whole lot easier, and yes, I took advantage of him because I felt safer knowing I had a protector at my side. That hasn't changed. He gives me security, which is something I need..." How true. In this respect, I had spoiled her, had always protected her, and would have even given my damn life for her...

"Well...I aced my studies, which was why it was rather easy to get a position at the home. I wanted to work with children because they are so carefree. They regard everything as uncomplicated, unlike me. It's good for me to be around them... especially Robbie."

"Your little boss?" I had to smirk when I thought about the little rascal with the insanely intelligent eyes, the one who had so gallantly protected her and kicked me in the shin. Now she laughed...a little.

"I would like to be much more to him than a care worker at the home who only engages him every so often. It is almost impossible to say no to him when he looks at me pleadingly with his green eyes and little pouty mouth... When I first saw him, I was totally shocked...because initially I thought... I repeatedly asked myself if...he…" She stopped short, grimaced at me as she straightened up, and supported herself with outstretched arms on the railing.

"You thought?" I pressed.

"First, I thought he was your son because the resemblance is uncanny..." she exclaimed and shocked, my eyes widened. Luckily, my dismay escaped her.

"He has many of your traits, kind and loving, he wouldn't hurt a fly, which is why others tease him...just like..." She swallowed hard. "…what you had to put up with." I froze and fervently hoped she wouldn't dwell on that chapter of my life, which, fortunately, she did not. Maybe she sensed my reluctance.

"I try to protect him, be there for him to take that huge load off his small shoulders. If I had my way, I'd adopt him. I even talked to the home's administration, but as a single person, I have no chance, nor could I afford it. Together with Francesco, it would be more feasible, but he has no heart for children, doesn't even want his own. So, that won't work either. I would love to give him a normal life with a normal family. With a strong father who protects and loves us both... You remember the names we had picked for our three children? The boy's name? Sometimes I think meeting Robbie was fate."

Her eyes swam in tears and she gnawed her lip. Unprepared, her wistful gaze hit me hard.

"N...no... Mia. Don't even think along those lines!" I shrunk away from her and, yes, I stuttered.

"I know, Tristan..." Her gaze returned to the city. "...but a person can still dream, can't they?"

OH, FUCK! What should I say? Stunned, I stared at her as I slowly came to terms that she actually wanted a relationship, children, and a damn house. WITH ME!

She would cut herself and bleed to death if she came just one millimeter closer. All that was left of me was a wreck with rusty corners and edges. Thanks to her. So, what was this now?

"I would not make a good father," I replied harshly, "or a good husband. I make money selling drugs and sex — morally speaking, I'm the lowest scum. First and foremost, in this world, it's hard enough to protect myself and rose-tinted fantasies certainly have no place there!"

Ironically, she snorted. "Even you don't believe you'd let the...people you love come to harm. No matter what world! I'd say you're deceiving yourself, Tristan Wrangler!

"In there..." and she tapped a finger against my chest, "you're still a *good* man. I know it." She placed her hand flat on my chest and looked up at me. I stared down at her, distressed.

"You don't know anything! Not anymore." It sounded both disparaging and desperate.

"Tristan, I know perfectly well you're not ready for that and I understand I lost my chance with you, but *please*, please let us not continue wasting whatever precious time we have together... We've already wasted so much of it," she begged hoarsely and moved her small fascinating body closer to me. "I need you to believe me..." she croaked and a single tear trickled down her smooth cheek."

Oh, God... Yes, the name of that fucker popped into my mind because she was staring at my lips. She wanted…that which I had forbidden. *No kisses!* No matter how much I long for her cherry lips, which felt so soft, warm, inviting, and so damn hot...

Screw it. Dammit! Just once more... Really, one last time! And then *never again*!

Unwittingly, I put my hands on her upper arms, brushed upward, held her by the shoulders, and instinctively, leaned toward her because her lips pulled me like a magnet. *She* magically drew me in...

She really wanted me, *had* been thinking and never forgotten me, and she did not lie to me, instead, was still honest, open, and lovely, and so *damn sexy*! What about all that? I'd never been more confused. A state I strongly hated. But right now I had no time to deal with it and instead focused on those sweet parts in front of me.

Fuck it! Just one more time snacking on the cherries... I was crazy about them!

She must have risen up on her toes because suddenly her hands cradled my cheeks and her heavy breath was on my lips. It was fast and urgent as she stared into my eyes. Her heat was mere millimeters away. I closed my eyelids in torment and enjoyed brushing my mouth over hers.

She groaned oh-so-softly.

Fuck! Now I was lost!

My fucker took complete control as soon as it heard that unique sound!

I was about to press my mouth to hers and take total control when it vibrated in my pocket. Dammit! I held her in place and blindly reached for the phone while watching her face, which was a mere millimeter away from mine. Her closed eyes, those incredibly long black eyelashes, and that annoyed frown because we were interrupted.

"Just be patient for a moment, Miss Angel, and then I'll kiss you senseless," I whispered gently. She made me so soft, but the smile I received was worth it...

"What?" I growled into the device and froze as soon as I recognized the voice on the other end. Not the overly skinny tramp!

"Trisi? Honey, can you hear me?" Mia's eyes flew open. Static on the line, but she definitely heard TRISI because first her gaze was disbelieving, then hurt...and then...*fucking angry!* She tried to escape our embrace.

"Hello, Tristan?" Shaking her head, Mia retreated.

"YES, DAMMIT," I snapped into the phone. I wanted to grab and hold Mia's arm, but she was quicker. The way she glared at me now! Her lips quivered...and she clenched her small hands.

NOT GOOD! NOT GOOD AT ALL!

"Can pick me up at the airport?" the swamp cow murmured. *"I'll be there in 10 hours!"* Mia continued shaking her head as she stared at me hurt and angry. Then she simply turned around and marched off.

"NO, DAMMIT!" I screamed into the phone and hung up.

"WAIT," I yelled and rushed after her, trying to grab her by the upper arm, but she forcefully pulled away from me and ran in the direction of the spiral staircase.

"MIA! BABY! PLEASE!" Fuck! I gritted my teeth and resumed pursuit.

I finally caught her just before the landing, whirled her around, and pinned her with my entire body against the chilly railing post, where I felt her trembling, and her eyes blazed hatefully.

"Let me go! *Immediately!*" she screamed. I had never heard her sound so murderous.

"Let me explain, *dammit!*"

"No, you don't have to explain anything! I understand perfectly well! I will not ruin a relationship! That you haven't fucked another..." She giggled ironically, "...I honestly did not believe! BUT IT HAD TO BE HER! It proves one thing will never change! You were and still are a fucking ASSHOLE!" I sucked in air as she stumbled backwards and freed herself from my grasp.

"You're completely off base!"

She laughed again...even louder, shriller, and with less humor. Oh-oh. It seemed as if she was about to lose her mind.

"How many more girlfriends do you have? How many do you tell your heart-wrenching stories of LONELINESS to? Who do you have during the week? Sabrina? Maria? Lena? MARY? HUH? How many PUSSIES are truly yours?"

"I don't have to explain myself to you," I growled.

"NO!" Now she came at me, and oh man, she was furious... I almost took a step back. And again her index finger tapped against my chest. "You have taken it too far! How could I ever hope to be the only one?" she whispered, gnawing her lip. She stumbled backwards and nearly collapsed. Exhausted, she leaned against the wall behind her and closed her eyes. "This must be great for you, isn't it, Tristan? Hurting me this way? You like that, don't you? Do you finally feel better? Is this here your true revenge? God... I'm so stupid..."

"Stop it!" As I approached her, she opened her eyes and the usually warm liquid caramel was frozen, warning me against taking even one more step. "*Stop it, baby...*" I sounded soft and velvety. I could not nor wanted to see her like that. So profoundly ruined! At that moment, all I had to do was admit that, even though I subliminally already knew all along, I could never win the battle to ruin Mia. Not when the end result looked like that and stood there with tears in her downcast eyes. Fuck...

"I cannot stand *this*..." Abruptly, her rage abated and tears glittered in her eyes.

It was like before: her pain was mine and it went deep — like everything between us.

"Mia baby," I whispered roughly as I closed the distance between us and cradled her cheeks... She continued sobbing as I called her that name again... "I would never do *that* to you. There has been no other woman in eight years... You're the only one... Always have been..." And then I just did it. I again pressed my lips against hers as if it was the ultimate proof of my sincerity! I no longer wanted her to believe there were others besides her. Only for one reason: I was a sadist and an asshole, but not a liar!

In addition, something else would emerge: I was still obsessed with her. In all those years, I could not possibly forget her because she was a drug that I immediately became addicted to. An addiction that was, despite being dormant the entire time, nevertheless always present and incurable. Now it burned even hotter within me. No matter what I tried, I simply couldn't escape her. She was my Achilles heel. It had been and, the way it looked, would always be like that. To ruin her was to ruin me.

My great plan shattered into a thousand pieces... But my heart...piece by piece healed when she suddenly sobbed and clung to me desperately.

She wanted to believe me, but unfortunately, she didn't. I couldn't blame her because our issue was far from resolved. I too wanted to believe and trust she had not intentionally put a stop to my life with the snap of a finger. And to get my point across I had to convince her that her jealousy was unfounded.

So, I intensified our kiss, touched my tongue to hers, and groaned throatily as her taste unfolded in my mouth and made me forget the present.

Marginally, I registered a slight movement and then raging pain! The little slut kicked me in the holy fucker.

"FUCK!" I roared over Prague as I retreated. Both hands traveled to my crotch and I cringed as the torment settled in my belly. In that way I was able to stand on my feet! In horror, but calculating, she backed away from me.

"Don't ever kiss me again! Who knows where your lips have been!" she warned.

That little slut could count herself lucky I was still paralyzed with pain and hurried out of my sight!

Callously, she left me writhing there because she had hit the center perfectly.

Once the pain had somewhat ebbed, I took off — always following my nose...because she hadn't made it far. After a few yards running on solid ground, I discovered her and screamed across the entire deserted park.

"Mia."

She only increased her stride, which I would have done too if I was in her shoes because now I was furious. Did I not call her Mia BABY? And, to top it off, did I not kiss her and in doing so, actually violate my immutable principles? Did I not get fucking involved with her? And as thanks I get a kick to my sanctuary?

NO! Why did a damn cab have to come by now, God-damn-fucking-crap!

She dove in front of the car so the driver had to come to a screeching halt so as not to hurt her. With a haunted expression, she circled the vehicle, ripped open the door, and slammed it shut right when I was within reach and out of steam. Before I could react, she pressed the lock button, and shouted something to the driver.

I narrowed my eyes and bared my teeth as the man shifted the car into gear.

And what did she do?

She gave me the middle finger... Next, she kissed said part with gusto...her gaze still ice cold... meantime, mine was rather stunned... and off they went...

And I was left behind, alone...

It started to pour. The wind blew fiercer. Yes...well...that was not the way I had imagined the whole thing! Cursing, I started walking since I saw no other taxi nearby. Of course not! We were here on a fucking mountain! I still could not believe that one happened to drive by!

On the way back to the hotel, I could not stop myself from cursing her. Vociferously!

Now she *truly* did not want anything to do with me! Then, she could have it. And she was absolutely wrong. I had not let another get close to me.

The cunt of cunts was a mere alibi girlfriend. I never fucked her, never even met up with her except on public occasions. She didn't mean shit to me.

But HER! Mia! MY DAMN FUCKING GIRL... Yes, she had been and probably always would be...did mean fucking shit to me!

So I cursed everything and everyone because I was sure about one thing, I was not crawling back. She did not want to hear my explanation, so she could kiss my ass and stay where she was. Goddamn cunt crap! What else could I do but curse the whole world and above all, her?

Nothing!

20. His Absence

Mia 'Strong' Angel

The next morning, I refused to wake up. At least I tried. I simple wanted to continue reveling in pleasant dreams, but the memory left me no choice. Relentlessly, it replayed in my mind.

As I grumbled, rolled on my belly, and buried my face in the pillow, I relived the entire disaster again. I was at the highest point in Prague...in the middle of the night. With Tristan Wrangler.

Finally, he told me everything he had done over the last few years. Granted, it was hard to listen to it with all that guilt on my shoulders. Important, however, was that he confided in me. Now it was up to me to open up, partially because I did not want to revive the ghosts of the past, not completely. Nevertheless, I told him most of it so he had an overview. However, the worst things I kept under lock and key so as not to unnecessarily burden him. After all, I had already done enough to him.

Since we had met again after the endless separation, I saw in his eyes that he wavered for the first time.

I sensed him softening, slowly but surely his hard shell crumbled and I was able to get through to him. It was so wonderful, as if I was again at the goal of my dreams...and then he even wanted to kiss me!

As his hands touched me, full of emotion and passion, like in the old days, I melted. With his lips on mine, I thought it alone would give me an orgasm at any moment...when his cell phone rang and ruined *everything*!

Everything! Because the woman on the phone actually called him *Trisi*. She sounded so shrill, it was impossible not to hear. I abruptly felt nauseous hearing her nasally voice, which clearly belonged to his girlfriend. The guilt in his eyes only confirmed it.

He had actually fucked with me! Quite so!

Probably, he was his club whores' best customer, fucked 10 different women every night, and probably received discounts from all the condom manufacturers, which would soon come out with special editions honoring his name.

And I, the stupid little cow, had actually thought I might still be his only one!

Yes, I *was* stupid! And naive and completely foolish, but, in particular, *angry!*

He constantly made me feel guilty while he had no scruples fucking his brains out! Oh, man... I was so fucked up! But then he always had his double standards.

My hope to permanently get through to him, to obtain his forgiveness, and perhaps have him again at my side, was once again razed, without me being able to do anything about it, let alone want to. Our future dissolved the moment the truth had been revealed. I was just one of many. There were only bits and pieces of the old Tristan that did not stand a chance against the new one. Besides being overwhelmed with desolation, I only felt rage and that needed to be released. It crushed me. The kick to his privates could not have been timed better, my farewell to his fucker.

At least I now knew what was what. I no longer knew the man I had once loved, nor did I want to. He lied, deceived, and manipulated when it was to his advantage instead of honestly stating his view. One of his greatest strengths – his honesty – no longer existed. Therefore, I decided to call it quits with him, excluding him from my life, my dreams, and no longer focusing on him.

I would build my future with Francesco. He was also not ideal, but he always took my side, supported me, giving my sad existence at least a little sense.

The man, who was presently lying next to me snoring like he had been for the past two years. Not Tristan Wrangler. I was finished with him.

Eventually, my heart would get used to the idea and the painful tearing would cease to exist. Now it was important to pull myself together and continue without him. I had no inkling how to be one of many, sharing Tristan with others would kill me in the long run. It was better to let go of him completely.

So, I woke my roofied boyfriend with a gentle kiss on his prominent stubbly chin and smiled at him when his dark brown eyes blinked sleepily at me. Francesco was a handsome man in the classic sense, with an angular face and an awesome body. Any other woman would long to wake up next to him. Maybe it was high time for me to think that way.

"Good morning, sweetie," I whispered softly and his full lips twisted into a smile.

"Morning, little one... Thank you for getting me into bed last night. I guess I must have fallen asleep. I'm sorry..."

Yeah, he had fallen asleep thanks to the drops I added to his water so I could have a romantic evening with my psycho lover, which had mutated into a nightmare.

He grabbed my hips and caressed my tailbone under the shirt.

"No problem." NO! I would not think about yesterday now! No, instead I would look toward the future and finally leave the past behind me.

"Sweetie?" I whispered and pulled his blanket back a little so I could trace circles around his brown nipples. Still groggy from sleep, he viewed my finger, his eyes grew large, and full of hope, he glanced at my face.

"How about we freshen up and meet back here in bed?"

He grinned and sat up abruptly. "YES!" And he cleared me like a hurdler and disappeared into the bathroom.

Giggling, I shook my head and stretched leisurely when I heard water running. I was considering putting something else on other than a sleep shirt and thong, but then I shrugged and also went into the bathroom to brush my teeth and at least comb my hair. Francesco was doing just that when I entered the room yawning. I giggled again and rolled my eyes. Seeing him so excited, he was almost cute. I was seriously hoping he would not be so excitable in bed.

He was done before me and left the bathroom whistling.

A minute later, I followed and found him striking a sexy pose in bed. I had to admit one thing: he was hot, his body nothing but muscle. And he knew it. Grinning overbearing at me, I promptly blushed.

At the same time, a little voice in my head was screaming that the body in front of me was nothing compared to *his*, but I ignored it so I could focus on my mission.

Let go of Tristan Wrangler, look toward the future, blah, blah, blah.

I knelt on the bed and smiling, leaned over Francesco. He met my lips and we kissed softly. He did not cause butterflies, but rather impending nausea, which always overcame me when I was intimate with him, but, surely, that was only a question of becoming accustomed. Rather, I focused on what I was doing so as to distract myself from the annoying discomfort. It worked quite well, especially since Francesco gave me time. Timidly, he touched me, kissing almost restrainedly and seemed to be in no hurry.

Without wanting to, I judged. Although I would have loved to remove the thought of Tristan surgically from my head, I could not help but admit Francesco was no match. He lacked tongue skill, but more importantly, the infamous tingling sensation was absent. Nevertheless, I didn't give up. At some point, it would work out. It simply had to.

So, I buried my hands in his hair and swung my leg over his hips so I could rub myself against him to get aroused. Francesco moaned throatily and I felt how excited he already was.

I was not feeling sick, perhaps even a bit hot, as it twitched between my legs, even though his size was clearly not in the same league as... Dammit, he will never measure up to *him*!

Francesco darted his tongue urgently in my mouth and coiled it around mine. I moved my hips somewhat and he grunted impatiently as he caressed my back, removing my shirt in the process.

Oh, God... he would soon have me undressed!

My heart was racing. But I allowed him to slide it over my head and even helped. As soon as I topless, we continued kissing. His huge hands grabbed my breasts much too roughly. He squeezed and kneaded them awkwardly, which was rather uncomfortable, almost painful. Francesco didn't seem to notice my discomfort because he cheerfully continued kneading as I repressed inconvenient thoughts about more talented fingers. I really had to stop. Right away.

My kisses grew more intimate, more frenetic, causing Francesco to think I was enjoying what he was doing. He gasped and swung me around, whereupon I eyed him expectantly. But I didn't get anything more than a slightly stupid grin, no dirty words to get me going. No hot fantasies to increase my anticipation. Dammit. Tristan was like a darn virus.

He kissed down my neck to my breasts, which felt nicer than his hands on me. But they didn't remain idle and without much ado went directly for my thong.

I stiffened slightly when Francesco sat up between my legs and stared at me lustfully. It did not make me feel coveted, rather cheap, although there was no reason for it. With *him,* it was always... *Stop!*

Francesco shoving a finger in me suppressed the unwelcome memories. I clenched my teeth because I was not the least bit prepared.

"OH MY GOD! You're so tight!" *Oh no? Really?* No wonder. Even the Gobi desert was wetter than I was at that moment. However, I refrained from commenting sarcastically since he now added a second finger.

OKAAAAAAAAAAAAAAAAAY! Automatically, I stiffened and still Francesco wasn't the wiser. He merely moved his fingers in and out while blatantly staring between my legs. He didn't seem interested in what I thought of his efforts and ignored the lack of moisture. He was only focused on his own arousal.

It started to burn slightly as he added a third finger, then a fourth, which was truly painful. I tried pulling away from him, but he held me in place and fumbled around with his thumb. Totally tense, I clenched my hands into fists and grew a little scared.

The extreme stretching was excruciating, especially since I was not properly prepared for it. Besides, as far he was concerned, I was still a virgin. This would not do!

Once again, I mustered up my courage to push him away and to let him know I didn't care for it. Just as I was about to speak, there was a loud knock on the door. I probably had been never been so relieved in my life. Whoever was intruding deserved a medal.

Mumbling, Francesco jumped up, quickly gave me a little kiss, and disappeared from the bedroom to answer the door.

"Wrangler?' He sounded quite surprised, but it didn't compare to the way I felt. Oh, God, what was he doing here? Immediately, those stupid butterflies fluttered in my stomach, causing blissful feeling. I cursed them and him because it was his fault.

Hurriedly, I stood and dressed. If he found me here naked, I could peel dead Francesco from the carpet fibers.

Tristan's reply was much too soft and quiet for me to understand, but it did not change the fact that I would have loved to fall crying into his arms so he could comfort my battered snail.

"Yes, this is a real coincidence!' Francesco laughed and Tristan hesitantly joined in. Then the Italian yelled into the bedroom, "Little one, look who's here!"

I swallowed hard and froze mid-movement for I was not quite dressed.

"Yeah, one second!" I screamed. Sweating, I hustled over to my suitcase to pull out a pair of pants, maybe even a thick sweater. I threw whatever pieces of clothing across the room as I searched for something appropriate. It made me feel horrible because I was no better than him, just a fraudulent slut.

It was hopeless. Worst of all, I could not deny it. After all, Francesco had greeted Tristan wearing only shorts and disheveled hair. He knew perfectly well what had happened, so I dispensed with my cover up attempts, slipped into a pair of pants and a T-Shirt, and went to the door with sagging shoulders.

There they were. The two...who could not be more different. One had divine, talented fingers; the other was kind, yet still made me feel nauseous. But then I was biased anyway. No one could match Tristan, no matter how much I hated it. In that way, I would never escape him. Even if everything was currently shoving me toward him. Dammit.

When Tristan looked at me, his eyes narrowed — his cheek muscles twitched. Right then, I wanted to run away.

"I see you've been having fun," he stated in a suspiciously soft but, at the same time, deadly voice... I winced as Francesco wrapped his arm around my shoulders and pulled me tightly against him.

"Yes, definitely. She literally fell over me this morning!"

Could you please, pretty please, keep your mouth shut? I glared at Francesco, which naturally completely escaped him because he too busy bragging.

"All right...then I will do something without you... I wish you... *lots of fun!*" The last bit he snarled at me and I shivered from head to toe.

Francesco was joy itself and kissed my hair.

"We sure will!" *OH no, we won't! A headache will promptly arrive!*

"See you, Francesco. Goodbye, Mia Marena!" His words brought tears to my eyes because his message was unmistakable: His final goodbye...

Without another word, he turned with his head held high and strolled gracefully away.

With all my strength, I pushed back the tears and pushed roughly away from Francesco as soon as he closed the door. All this here was so wrong! Francesco was not the right one!

"Francesco, I can't... I have a headache," I stated coolly and went into the living room. Consideration was at the moment not possible. So, he would not pursue me, I locked myself in the bathroom. I really needed time alone right now...

Then the cell phone I had left in my discarded pants

started to vibrate. I immediately knew who it was and I was afraid to read the message. Eventually, curiosity won and I opened it with trembling fingers. Three words glowed at me ominously. Three words that left me completely desperate...

You. Are. Dead!

How right he was...

***

Monday morning, I sat happily in the children's home next to Robbie's bed and I woke him gently. He blinked a few times and opened his big sleepy eyes.

As soon as I saw the deep green, my heart felt a stab.

"Mirti!" He beamed like the sun in miniature when he recognized me. My heart knotted up because he had a new bruise on his forehead, which I was certain was courtesy of the other kids.

"Hi, sweetheart..." I tenderly caressed his cheek and the spot — feeling the silky soft skin.

"Are you sad?" the observant boy immediately asked, yawning mid-sentence, which only made him more endearing. He scrambled up, ending on wobbly knees in his little bed, dressed in a shirt and red Superman shorts. I held him with both hands and caressed him.

"I missed you... That's all," I admitted and was glad I could be honest with him. Which was the truth. He smiled slightly and thoughtfully tilted his head.

"I'm here now, Mirti. So, you can be happy again!" With effort and with the help of his little finger, he tried to move the corners of my mouth up, making me giggle.

"That's right! Let's both be happy and make the most of this day, all right? So, let's get you dressed, okay?" Not waiting for his reply, I stood up and with much gusto lifted him out of bed, which made him laugh. For a while, I kept spinning with him in a circle, only to hear the beautiful carefree tone longer, after which I breathlessly sat down on the chair next to his bed, the one I always occupied when he searched for his clothes. He wriggled impatiently and like every morning, I asked him what he dreamt about.

Carefree, he yapped away because he was a little chatterbox, talking about some boxing gloves that had chased him, but which he had *completely defeated.* I laughed at his dramatic, wild reenactment.

Then I dressed him. I loved it when he wore red; it emphasized his rosy cheeks and made him look even cuter than he was already. Today he wore he red sweater. As I put his clothes on, he told me that his idol, Klitschko, had also been in his dream and came to his aid.

I almost cried again because I knew his subconscious was yearning for a stronger male to protect him. Which every child needs because having a male role model in their life made them feel secure. Children, especially boys, apparently from early on, feel responsible to protect the women in their lives, but they also need a person who cares for them.

I wish Robbie would get his Klitschko, someone who would speak up for him and keep him out of harm's way.

But for the time being I had to suffice and reinforce it with my love.

"You, Mirti..." He drew out Mirti and I had to grin because I sensed he was about to persuade me into doing something. His small hands flitted quickly and clumsily over my cheeks, but I loved it when he did that. There was nothing sweeter!

"Yes?" I asked and closed the last button on his pants.

"Can we go to the boxing gym again? Just you and me? PLEASE!" He leaned forward and hugged me tightly to emphasize his words.

Defenseless, I held him. "PLEA...SE Mirtiii. I'll be especially well behaved! You're the best Mirti in the world! PLEA...SE!" And I had already lost.

"All right. But you have to eat your broccoli today!" He immediately moved away from me and looked at me disapprovingly. I knew you should not place conditions on children, but I felt more like his mother than a textbook social worker and a mom can never completely adhere to proper rules because she had no objectivity when it came to the child.

"Only TWO PIECES!" He firmly showed two fingers. I chuckled for he was not just good at talking me into things, he was also a wheeler and dealer.

"Four." I knew we would meet in the middle, which was fine because I'd just give him the largest pieces.

"Three! My last offer." Oh, man, one day the kid would be a real tough businessman.

"Okay, boss." Grinning, I stood up and messed up his silky blond hair.

"YES!" he cried and charged full speed toward the bathroom. Shaking my head, I followed.

Yes, Robbie really had a talent for cheering me up.

At least for a few moments, then the corners of my mouth drooped again and my stomach knotted up. Because, basically, nothing had changed. Tristan Wrangler was still no longer part of my life...

***

In the afternoon, I spoke to Eric and told him I would like an hour alone with Robbie so I could take him to the boxing gym during break time. I wanted to arrange for the children to train there for free. As a social institution, we had small funds available to us and it would do the kids good. And if it required me to take down the owner, so be it.

Holding Robbie's hand, I entered the large gym. Both of us were drenched from the pouring rain, but it didn't bother us. At least Robbie. He exploited every single puddle, jumping in with gusto. I hoped his rubber boots were waterproof.

After I removed my coat, I peeled Robbie out of his rain jacket before we passed the reception desk at the entrance and entered the huge training hall.

Okay...clearly, in the afternoon it was much busier than in the morning. Guys faced each other in the two regulation size rings and each of the five punching bags were occupied.

However, I barely noticed because there was a bewitching scent that demanded my attention. The smell seemed to follow me so I started thinking I was paranoid. Presumably, I was suffering from some type of brain tumor that caused me to sense things that weren't there.

Crap!

Meanwhile, Robbie was dragging me through the gym, beaming and telling me everything he planned to do. Grinning, I let him tow me along as I searched for a trainer. Although I didn't see one, I found something else instead that immediately made me stumble as soon as I recognized the broad glistening back.

Only one had such flawless muscles. Only one had that sexy hairstyle, those biceps, and those bandaged fists that mercilessly pummeled the material... I saw it as if in slow motion. Tristan Wrangler boxing – *eventually,* the man might actually cause my demise – okay, probably sooner!

But a coat rack combined with a devious step, interrupted my ogling. I tried to catch myself but it was too late and once again, I stumbled awkwardly.

With a loud *AAAAAAAAAHHH* that *everyone* heard... I, together with the traitorous coat rack, rushed downward. One rod banged my forehead as I was buried beneath and a sharp pain followed.

Groaning, I stayed put for the time being and gently touched my head. I hissed when I felt blood, but since I was buried by clothes, I couldn't see.

"Mirti! Mirti!" Robbie called out in a panic and I felt his little hands pulling me onto my feet, trying to free me from the awkward and embarrassing situation.

"Ah, crap," I cursed uncharacteristically and hoped the apparition was simply a fabrication of my crazy mind. But the loud melodic laugh that rang out above me informed me otherwise.

"WOMAN, YOU ARE TRULY SOMETHING!" He couldn't pull himself together as he easily lifted the rack off me with one hand and exposed my bright red cheeks. Dripping with sweat and bare-chested, he looked at the disaster and squatted...

Oh, God, I wanted to dig a hole and disappear into it! Groaning, I wanted to get up and touched my head wound again.

"Keep your fingers off it!" Tristan slapped my hand and flashed a warning look before he gently took hold of my chin and turned my face so he could inspect my wound.

Oh, my holy Tristan! Obviously, his physical workout had pumped up his muscles, which were glistening invitingly...and so close! How was I supposed to resist or ever escape this WET-PANTY-DREAMMAN?

"Hey, you okay, sweetie? Your stunt looked quite professional..." one of the athletes who had gathered around me asked as Tristan casually waved him off.

"She's fine! Such falls are her specialty!" I grew mad because he had no right to humiliate me in front of everyone and he was flitting a finger over my face like an annoying fly and it tingled too much. I also didn't even want to know how many women there had been since Sunday morning in Prague.

"What are you doing here?" I snapped at him and tried to get up.

But for some unknown reason I grew weak, be it because of his half-naked presence or the fall, and in the next moment found myself in his strong arms.

OH, GOD! In his *sweat-soaked* arms, mind you! If he continued like this, he might as well put a bullet in me. His presence and scent were intoxicating my senses without me being able to control myself. The man would seal my demise.

"HEY!" I heard Robbie's squeaky voice. "Put Mirti down!" He tugged on Tristan's sweatpants just hard enough for them to slide down a bit and expose more of that adorable V, which had always made me weak.

Now even Robbie was stabbing me in the back! Clearly, it had to be a conspiracy!

"Robbie, stop it!" I hissed.

"Hey, boss, take it easy..." Tristan said to him casually and started to move away with me. "Will you help me bandage her up? Upstairs I have Band-Aid's with dinosaurs on them!"

Tristan grinned cheekily at me and I narrowed my eyes. Dammit! I completely forgot how good the guy was with kids because it simply didn't fit him! But then it seemed he never ceased to amaze me! Robbie rejoiced and hopped around and to top it off, clapped his pudgy hands. Traitorous pack! "YEAH! Can I put them on?" Effortlessly, Tristan carried me across the gym and up the spiral staircase behind the little one.

"Sure... I cannot perform such life-threatening surgery by myself," he joked with the boy, who laughed even louder.

"Dino Band-Aid's! Dino Band-Aid's! Dino Band-Aid's!" Yes, children really enjoy themselves on average 50 times a day and really, just about the little things. I wish I could do that too. At least once a week!

But I had an even more burning desire for this wonderful god to solely belong to me. Who was I kidding? Although I knew it was not possible, my feelings for him were still intact.

I had been pining for him ever since the first day of school and that feeling had not abated. He was always there and took care of me, even if he didn't feel for me what I felt for him. After all, there was who knows how many thousands of women wooing him. Abruptly, my mood darkened...and I glared at him angrily.

"I hate you!" I snapped as I thought about if I had ever told him *that* before. But jealousy gnawed at me like never before making me downright mad. He merely raised a brow as he pointed at a door that Robbie was to open for us.

"Mia Marena, *you* hate me?" he whispered drily, but lurking near my scalp so it tingled. "I *honestly* haven't fucked anyone else, unlike you!" At once, all warmth disappeared from his eyes and we glared angrily each other.

"I also haven't fucked anyone!" I replied sarcastically and quietly so Robbie certainly could not hear the words. In any case, he was busy looking through the huge window down at the gym, then threw himself on Tristan's chair and tested out how great it could spin...

The sweaty angry boxer god sat down on a couch in the office. Although it resembled the one in Tristan's club, this one was a bit simpler. Luckily, I was not confronted with a naked woman's pussy here, also not with nude photos of me or a dreary image of the Tristan-god and his gun. Also, there didn't seem to be evidence of his family.

Tristan didn't bother covering his model body as he grabbed a few things from the medicine cabinet while glaring lethally at me. He sat on the edge after placing me on the cushions, practically forcing me to lie on the sofa. I rolled my eyes because he was still so damn controlling.

Suddenly, Robbie leaned over me and blocked angry Tristan I-will-kill-you-with-looks Wrangler's view.

"Wow, Mirti, it is bleeding a lot!" Robbie was fascinated with the wound and itching to touch it.

"It's not as bad as it looks. Mirti has a thick skull." Tristan absentmindedly caught Robbie's finger and suggested he spin around some more on the office chair. He'd call him if he needed an assistant and that he should look in the top drawer of the desk; there might be a chocolate bar hidden inside. Was the man a magician?

Robbie did not have to be told twice and he immediately

forgot all about me all due to a chocolate bar. His anxious face disappeared from my sight lightning quick. Then I closed my eyes because I knew Tristan would soon bend over me again... and seeing him so close and focused was more than I could bear right now.

"And?" I asked impudently but softly so Robbie could not hear me when I felt him oh-so-tenderly dabbing the blood from the wound. "How many women have you DOCTORED?" I peeked through my lashes and noticed his eye roll.

"None," he answered bitterly. "And? How many times have you fucked Francesco by now?" he whispered. His fragrant minty breath blew across my face. Inconspicuously, I inhaled every bit deeply and just as dismissively replied, "None."

Triumphantly, I looked at him challengingly with a brow raised. Instantly, Tristan stepped closer and brushed his cheek over my...whoa...

"Mia Marena, don't overdo it with your rebelliousness. I know where you live..." he whispered softly in my ear and gently sucked on my earlobe the way he usually did with my clit... ARGH! His couch was officially threatened to fall victim to a flood.

"Nothing but empty words, Mista Wrangler. Just like everything else you've said so far!" I hissed, checking on how far I could push the issue and rubbed my cheek against his. My hand extended on its own and slid down his sweaty naked muscular chest. My insides were tingling again, but it was more intense because I was so mad at him.

"I haven't lied to you. Never. FUCK!" My fingers traveled down over the lucky patch that led to his fucker and he bit my neck. I gasped and slightly arched my back.

"I told you not to bite Mirti!" Robbie's stern voice suddenly sounded above our heads and Tristan got up. He was breathing heavily and I quickly lowered my hips back onto the couch. It was a mystery how they got there. Tristan shook his head slightly to clear it, the blazing fire disappearing from his eyes, resuming their usual iciness. Mine did the same.

"I'm sorry. She's just so tasty... So, how do you like it here?" He handed a colorful dinosaur Band-Aid to Robbie, one depicting a T-Rex. It passed Robbie's test. Tristan helped him put it on, the little one looking extremely focused, his tongue stuck between his white teeth. Just like Tristan... Their skulls were also tilted in the exact same way, even their frowns appeared similar. *It was scary* and...so fascinating! For a brief moment, I saw them sitting in front of a blazing fireplace building a model plane. But that would never happen. Tristan was no fluffy bunny, more like a wolf in sheep's clothing and a freaking crook. I didn't believe a syllable he was saying. Now I only had to get my body to listen to me.

"Thank you!" I snapped and sat up when they finished. Robbie looked at me in shock. Usually, I was friendly.

"You are welcome," Tristan answered just as toxic and Robbie narrowed his eyes. I couldn't help myself and stuck my tongue out at Tristan. My small guardian inhaled sharply. Tristan growled at me.

"Don't fight!" Robbie cried suddenly, ripping us from our silent confrontation.

"Mirti," he addressed me in all seriousness, "giving someone the tongue is *very* rude!" I actually blushed a little... Oh man...

"And Mirti taught me that guys should always be nice to girls! Growling is not nice!" Now he looked sternly at Tristan and frowned. My little one was awesome!

"So, make up," Robbie prompted with a wagging finger and chocolate smudged mouth.

"Okay," we grumbled. I giggled and Tristan rolled his eyes. Robbie looked skeptical.

"We are getting along, you see?" I took Tristan's big hand that gently wrapped itself around my fingers and shook it.

"No, not like that! Do it the right way! With spit! Or it doesn't count!" Tristan's and my mouth dropped. Robbie continued to look at me firmly and I groaned before I pulled my hand back, spat on it, and offered it to Tristan.

"With spit or it doesn't count, Mista Wrangler," he said as if I had just completely lost it.

"If you want to continue to play with Mirti...you guys have to make up!" Robbie nudged. Oh, God! I grew bright red and Tristan's lips suddenly moved into the dirtiest, most beautiful smile.

"Yeah..." he agreed. "...I actually still want to *play* with Mirti. So..." He spat a good wad in his palm and squeezed my hand. His warm saliva mixed with mine and I had to suppress a disgusted groan. Tristan stroked the back of my hand with his thumb as he held my gaze with his diamond look. My breathing intensified... My heart knocked louder...

"That's good!" Robbie professionally separated our hands and stood up, while we, repelled, wiped away the spit on our pants.

"Shall we go see the boss, Mirti?" It made me remember the actual reason we were here. Why were we in an office? Did Tristan know the owner?

"Um...do you happen to know who owns this joint? I need to discuss a few things with the owner," I asked and sat upright. Tristan grinned at me as if I made a private joke.

"What do you want from him?"

"I want to ask him if he's okay with kids training here. For free!"

"For free!" Tristan raised an eyebrow. Not for a minute did the haughty expression leave his face.

"YES! If I have to, I'll spread my legs! I'm a slut anyway, so I might as well make use of it!" I hissed silently. Luckily, Robbie was distracted again with the picture window, staring out over the entire gym.

"Oh, yes, you really are...*my* slut!" he stated in a hoarse, barely audible whisper.

"I cannot deny that..." I sighed hard, "...and I don't have

a problem with that! But, I won't be one of many... I want to be *the one*."

"You are," he mumbled, restrained, but looked at me seriously. No trace of uncertainty, murderous intention, or phoniness. "That was my alibi girlfriend," he continued in a whisper. "I don't feel anything for her. She accompanies me on official events. There are only two women I deal with privately — Vivi and Katha, and that's only because I cannot get rid of them!" I almost felt sorry for him...but...

"Alibi girlfriend? Why would she call you if you don't even need an alibi?"

"She wants more, I don't. You know I've *never* lied to you about that crap and I don't intend to start now. Calm down, dammit! I *only* want your pussy!" Ohhh... the way he said *pussy*, the way he caressed the word. He really idolized it... His gaze grew 50 degrees warmer. Then he cleared his throat and tried to change the topic.

"Well...I guess...the boss gives his consent, after all, you already spread your legs for him several times." Tristan looked arrogantly down at me, but his eyes were full of mischief.

"Huh?"

Purposefully, his gaze traveled around the office...

I followed it...and my mouth dropped.

"This is yours?" I waved my hands exaggeratedly around.

"Yeah. What do you think? It's where I first saw you."

"Here?"

"Yep, it was when you were standing right there in front of that window." I chewed my lip and glanced furtively around... Yes, clearly, this was Tristan's empire... Even the dynamic photographs of athletes on the wall spoke volumes. Why didn't I notice it earlier? Oh, yeah... the sweaty, distracting upper body of a model...

When I made eye contact with him again, his grin grew even wider.

"Did you fuck him?" he asked gently, but urgently. Oh, man... considering his tormented expression, it really had to be worrying him.

"No, Tristan, I didn't! I don't know, but he has some strange predilections..." Uncomfortable, I looked around, happy to see Robbie was still not paying attention to us, but busy spinning in the chair at the other end of the office. His laugh was the loudest sound in the room.

All of a sudden, Tristan nostrils flared and he began to tremble.

"HE FISTED YOU?" he whispered furiously and I winced.

"Fisted?" I mumbled questioningly.

"How many fingers did he shove in you? Three? Four? The whole fist? The head?"

Oh, oh, Tristan was about to explode.

"Relax!" Carefully, I placed a hand on his arm and stroked upward to his muscular shoulder. Having arrived, I lightly kneaded the hard muscles. He moaned softly and briefly closed his eyes. I was so glad he accepted my touch, which only made me wetter because he really was a dream man, especially when he made such devoted sounds. "Tell me, has that fruit-bag hurt you or stretched you out? If so, then that perverted bastard will get a bullet between his eyes faster than he can stick his fist into someone! How could he desecrate something so nice and tight with his shit?" he hissed softly, accompanied by moaning devotedly as I rubbed him. It would have been funny if he wasn't about to freak out.

"Tristan!" My gaze wandered to Robbie. He was still spinning...

"Don't distract me! He isn't going to hear anything and don't stop, dammit!" He grabbed my hand when I tried to withdraw it and immediately put it back on his warm bare skin...

So, I continued kneading his neck as he croaked, "Answer!"

Resignedly, I sighed. "Four fingers. You knocked as he was about to stick the fifth in...not a second too soon."

Tristan grimaced in disgust and appeared...tortured.

"Oh, fuck!" but then he contemplated the issue and relaxed a bit. "Well...I guess four fingers are not much more than my fucker..." he mused and puckered his full lips appraisingly. Yes, but when he put his fucker in me, I was already longing for him to do so... Francesco had not prepared me at all. I hadn't even been properly aroused. Obviously, I wouldn't rub Tristan's nose in it.

"This evening, I'm taking a plane to see Dad and won't be back till Friday. At that time, I'll examine you thoroughly!" That triggered a real flood and Tristan grinned nastily. "I hope everything down there in your paradise is still in good working condition. Otherwise, I cannot be held responsible for my actions!"

I rolled my eyes. "You know perfectly well that my PARADISE is a muscle, it cannot be stretched out just like that!"

"Yeah, more importantly, it's *my* muscle!" He peeked over at Robbie. Seeing the boy was busy scribbling with a pen on the desk pad, his talented hand went between my legs and gently pushed. Panting, I clawed at his neck. "I believe you now. But if he dares put his fat sausage fingers even close to you, I'll chop them off and shove them up his ass." I had difficulty swallowing.

"I love your dirty mouth, Tristan." He kissed a corner of my mouth and grinned mockingly.

"I love the way you react to it." I smiled. His lips brushed across my cheek to my ear, where he whispered hoarsely, "I cannot wait to have you naked, without any disturbances, underneath me, making you scream. Like that Saturday on the dining table. Will you come like that again for me, baby?" *Oh my, Tristan* ... Just then, my mind was in overdrive and he knew it... Also: *baby!*

"Tiny pupil approaching!" As his fingers disappeared, my favorite orphan came back into view.

"Mirti, you're so red again." Robbie touched my cheek,

seemingly concerned and Tristan chuckled. I closed my eyes and tried to calm myself as I was lovingly patted.

***

Did I believe him? Could I trust him?

I asked myself those questions repeatedly as I sat the next evening on my couch, listening to music and stroking Stanley.

Okay...I had no idea if I was Tristan's only woman, but I loved him and would never find out the truth if I stayed away from him. In addition, today's meeting reassured me that I couldn't escape my longing for him. I only had to think about his touches and everything inside me started to pulsate.

I closed my eyes, heard his voice in my head, felt his breath on my face, and I knew I might be able to run away from him, but I couldn't hide for long. However, I would observe him. I would watch him closely when he looked at other women to see if he showed interest in them. Until now, I hadn't noticed any longing glances other than toward me. Ironically, I could not expect him to have lived like a monk these past years — especially a man like him! Ha! But, apparently he had done just that...no sex in eight years... The idea was *crazier* than I wanted to admit.

Basically, I had to give him another chance. There was no other choice. After all, he was doing the same, considering he was willing to believe I hadn't slept with Francesco.

Francesco...the whole thing with him seemed to be too

much for me. His predilections deeply disturbed me and now, since we took a step toward sexual intercourse, he would be even more relentless. I had no idea how to keep him off me, especially since I had no way to judge him.

There was so much about him that irritated me and that I didn't know. Unlike Tristan. He seemed to be well informed about him whether it was the drug business or sexual preferences. Did Francesco actually go to a club for years to get what he did not get from me? It kind of made sense! And I wasn't particularly bothered by it. Now that I had a picture, I was glad I had been spared all this time. Also, I'd make sure there was no repeat performance.

My body longed for Tristan's hands and lips. There was no denying them, not one bit. In that respect, I guess I was pretty spoiled. But who would go with pork if they could have steak or normal tomatoes when cherries were available? Who would drink champagne instead of... Okay, I was hungry...

Stanley followed me into the kitchen. As I made a sandwich, I tossed him a slice of sausage, which he gulped down as if he had not eaten all day and promptly choked. Insatiable little lump.

When I walked back into the living room, my cell phone on the coffee table flashed.

Friday at 11. No underwear. And don't think anything between us has changed. No kissing. No Mia baby. My fucker is happy. I had to smile at the message. Typical Tristan. Not wasting an opportunity to be dominant and blaming his fucker for it.

I thought you had suppressed the fact that you had called me MIA baby and kissed me" I texted back, grinning. Now that he wasn't here to intimidate me, it was much easier for me to be honest.

It was my fucker talking. He was panicking. Yes, yes...

Before or after he got acquainted with my knee? Oh, I would have never dared utter such a thing in his presence.

Mia?

Yes.

Friday, you and I are going to church. Oh, church *and* Tristan! He wouldn't dare! Would he repeat *that*! Promptly, my heartbeat quickened!

WHAT?

You read correctly. You kicked me in my sanctuary; naturally, I will defile you in a sanctuary. Like eight years ago. But this time it won't be just my fingers. Initially, I was at a loss for words, read the message about ten times, swallowed loudly, and then texted back.

Can I somehow get out of it? I might not be a believer, but I wasn't sure whether I would survive the thrill.

No way. Punishment is a must! Should I list all your transgressions? Oh, I was sure he was grinning nastily. I could just imagine it. Even in my mind, his beauty was distracting.

I beg you.

You broke off the kiss. You called me asshole. You ran away from me. You kicked my privates and fucker...you even took off again. You gave me the finger and you let yourself get fingered by tiny dick! I'm sure you also kissed him... I don't even want to think about it... Enough reasons?

Oh, man! *Counterattack! Come on already, Mia, don't be a chicken!*

You deserved everything! You threaten me with all sorts of unimaginable things. You are toying with my biggest fears. You're a psycho lover. You never want to kiss me. You don't call me your girl, Mia baby, or Mia. You call me slut, tramp, whore, or whatever is worse than MIRTA. Then you think I'm stupid, too skinny, ugly... Shall I go on?

Two of your issues are wrong.

Which ones?

You're not ugly and you're not stupid, however, you are a bit too skinny. Whatever happened to my curves?

Great! I rolled my eyes because it was obvious he was amusing himself. Did I already mention that I loved it when he was so carefree? Apparently, it was easier for him to be happy when I wasn't around, when he wasn't constantly confronted with the face of betrayal.

Tell me. Why are you so skinny? he insisted.

Because you weren't around.

Aha, so it's my fault you were irresponsible toward your body?

YES.

I'm going to fatten you up like a turkey. I laughed.

Do it!

I will. I was sure he laughed too.

Okay.

Okay.

Okay, what? I texted back.

Okay, I'm going to fuck your brains out for your last sassy remark!

All I hear are empty threats, Mista Wrangler.

Continue like that and I will come immediately and I mean that ambiguously.

Like I said, nothing but empty threats.

Get undressed and lie down on the bed.

WHAT?

No other message.

OH, OH!

Would he really? He couldn't... It wasn't Friday and I was unwashed, disheveled, wearing baggy clothing, and my apartment looked as if a bomb had gone off in it! Panicking, I jumped up, almost flinging Stanley off me in the process.

"Oh God, oh God, oh God!" I ran around like a chicken with its head cut off thinking about what I should do first. Stanley was bouncing happily up and down next to me — apparently, he was having a blast. I hoped that none of my neighbors saw me or they might call the loony bin.

Whatever discarded newspapers lay about were shoved inside the wardrobe — the books that fell out had to be put back. Then I transported three plates and a glass from the small table in front of the sofa into the kitchen, adding to the mountain of other dirty dishes waiting to be cleaned... Crap! I simply closed the door and hurried back into the living room. I swept the cookie crumbs from the couch and used a hand to push them under the carpet, then tossed Stanley's chew bone into his dog bed as well as his little stick that he liked to gnaw on, then added the chips to the crumbs under the carpet... Panting, I looked up and surveyed the remaining chaos... Apparently, not much had changed.

Capitulating, I decided I couldn't change the state of the apartment fast, so I rushed at full speed to the next station: the bedroom and tore my clothes from my body. I jumped into bed, assumed a position on my side, brushed a hand through my disheveled hair and wheezing, caught my breath. The cell phone in the living room beeped. A new text message. Crap!

I jumped up and ran back.

It was freaking cold. My teeth were chattering as I opened the message.

You overlooked the pink chew bone... I read the text three times before the meaning sank in. It beeped again. *Don't open your eyes so much and close your mouth... Instead, spread your legs for me!* Oh my, Tristan! It couldn't be true!

In a panic, I searched the living room and disgusting paranoia creeped up my back. He couldn't have installed cameras in here, could he? Not finding any, I shakily texted back while inconspicuously pulling the couch blanket over me.

You did not do that!

In every room! Get rid of that fucking blanket! Frustrated, I threw it aside.

Since when?

Since Sunday!

Because of Francesco.

Him too...

Why else.

I just love watching you.

But I don't like being watched by you!

That's a boldfaced lie, Miss Angel. I can see how wet you are right now! I can zoom in.

Quickly, I closed my legs and peeked. I wasn't all that wet!

HA, HA! he immediately texted and I panted in frustration. *You are divine and now I'll rub one off. It's already in my hand...*

God... *Now* I was wet! Properly so!

Do it... He didn't have to tell me twice. Immediately, my fingers moved to the throbbing spot between my legs.

Legs apart, wide!

I spread them.

Yeah...and now imagine my fingers are... You know what they can do to you...how they feel...do you feel them, baby?

I groaned as I read the word *baby* and imagining what

he wanted to do to me. It was even worse when I visualized Tristan sitting in his office and using the aforementioned magic fingers to stroke the enormous length of his shaft, his head rolled back, eyebrows wrinkled, and his full lips parted slightly.

Should I describe what I'll do to you Friday?

Yes! I texted back. Then I completely surrendered to Tristan's dirty breathtaking fantasies while enjoying the tingling and knowing that Tristan was observing me from somewhere...

21. My Girl the Complete Whore

Tristan 'Every Woman's Dream' Wrangler

Today, the honeymoon would be over for I would take her to the brink of her limits without any regard for her. Her bold text messages broke the camel's back and showed her rebelliousness. Although, I could not deny being amused by our written banter, so much so, I did not intend on stopping it altogether. But it didn't change the fact that her conduct deserved a lesson. Because, in hindsight, I was annoyed, even though it required two. After all, I had gotten myself involved with her and always gave in when she tempted me with her charm. Ah, dammit. My lack of self-control made me not only angry, it would end up driving me crazy.

Probably, I should have focused on her misconduct for which there was plenty. For example, she kicked me in the fucker. I was still close to tears when I recalled the excruciating pain. I'd make sure she paid for that. Then there was needle dick. That prick compensated for his tiny fucker by fisting women. To each his own, but he would answer for planning to defile my girl's divine pussy with that crap. Ever since I found out, I could not get the horror out of my head. It was pure torture.

Speaking of stretching, I had planned for her to ride me while giving confession to the priest, but that would be too easy. Tonight would certainly not be easy because I was going to show her what it meant to be my personal slut...

I would treat her like all my other employees and draw the much-needed boundaries for me as well as for her.

If she did well, then I'd reward her at the end of the night. A special kind of experience.

However, if she resisted, bitched, or moaned, she would just make it worse for her. Like our first visit to the club, when I humiliated her in front of all those present.

I was kicked back on the couch in my office stoned and watching the raging crowd in the club in nothing but shorts so it would go faster later. Preparedness was everything.

It was two minutes before eleven, but all hell was already breaking loose. The room was filled to capacity, which was good... The bigger the audience the greater the thrill.

Grinning devilishly, I stubbed out what was left of the big joint.

Our outfits and other items that I planned to use today were already laid out on the office table.

Mia Marena's eyes would pop out. I was gloating and mentally rubbed my hands — and obviously, my fucker! All day, it had been thumping a wild rumba in my pants, more precisely, since I returned home.

The past week I had spent with my father and Phil and worked intensively on my tan. We wanted to expand our restaurant chain and my father would take care of everything on Gran Canaria. We made the necessary plans and visited various eligible spots. Unfortunately, we didn't find anything suitable, but could acquire land where the location was ideal for our project.

I rose and was about to run both hands through my hair when there was a knock. As usual, I rushed to the door and ripped it open.

This time she didn't touch up her lips, but she still was not prepared for my quick appearance for she looked shocked as she clutched her heart.

"Does your conscience bother you or what?" I inquired sneakily and she rolled her eyes, which made me want to slap her titty or ass.

Yes, okay...the week was stressful and I was not exactly in a good mood.

That was why she would have been better off if she had not fucked with me...but when was she *not* fucking with me?

"Do you always have to..."

Gruffly, I interrupted her and curtly demanded, "Get undressed. Completely!" She should not even get the idea she could complain and had to be reminded who was in charge.

Her eyes briefly bulged before she realized she should not hesitate and stripped in a hurry.

I did not turn my gaze from her because I loved watching her get nervous, nor did I give her the slightest smile or encourage her in any way. Let uncertainty ate at her because she was just too hot when I made her almost soil her panties.

Oh, fuck... Since when did I turn into a damn sadist? But the question was irrelevant because her shiny labia betrayed her arousal and pulled me under its spell. She loved me as dominant, deceptive, and brutal as I was...

Finally, she stood there completely naked, wringing her hands. I narrowed my eyes when she actually tried to cover herself, making me move her hands from her body.

"Never cover up for me, Mia Marena," I ordered quietly as I looked down at her as she bit her lip. "And stop chewing or I'll fuck you against the window."

Scared, she looked at the glass, but up here, we would not be seen anyway and if, it didn't matter because no one else but me would dare lay a finger on her.

Her mouth no longer moved, but she still seemed intimidated. H'm, actually, it wasn't good for her to be scared because she needed confidence for what I had planned for her.

So, I decided to be a little nicer... Obviously, self-serving.

"Are you a brave slut, Mia Marena?"

Hesitantly, she nodded and I smiled...partially.

"Then you may now undress me."

She countered by violently biting her lip again and I rolled my eyes.

"Come on, take that crap off! It's not like you haven't ripped my clothes from my body plenty of times..." Sternly, I pointed to my boxer shorts, which were taut. She hurried to hook her fingers under the hem and went down on her knees in front of me, pulling the fabric along.

FUCK! My fucker popped out into the fresh air and now was but a couple of inches away from her cheek. Seeing her squatting there so naked and absolutely...beautiful in front of me, I thought to myself: what the hell.

Unprepared, I grabbed her hair and directed *it* to where I wanted *it* to be. Her eyes were veiled with pleasure as she looked up at me, but she bravely took it in her mouth and immediately began to suck with relish. She moaned and closed her lids as soon as she tasted *it*.

"OH, FUCK!" I immediately pushed her away, otherwise, I would have come right then and there, and I didn't want to give her the satisfaction. It would only throw off the balance of power and today I had to prevail, even if it required everything I had within me not to continue giving in to her velvety lips and then fuck her until she did everything I wanted. Everything in its time. Frustrated, she huffed as I moved away.

"Bring me those biker pants!" She stood up, went to the

desk, and eyed the other items skeptically. I grinned secretly as I took them from her and slipped into the tight leather pants sans underwear.

Mia Marena swallowed and let her gaze travel longingly over me. Yes, I knew I looked absolutely hot. Earlier, I shaved my entire body just like in the old days.

"Pull the zipper up. With your teeth!" Again, she squatted in front of me, held my upper thighs, and actually moved the part in the desired way, all the while looking me in the eyes. Not so easy...because of that stiff prick.

"Leave the button undone," I announced dryly.

"Get the massage oil and rub it on me using your body." I couldn't help but grin because she regarded me in such a cute shocked way; however, she obeyed and poured a little in her palms. I rolled my eyes, grabbed the bottle, and upended it over her front.

"H'm..." I hummed as I spread it around. "Your tits are amazing. I love how your nipples still respond to my touch..." I briefly tweaked them between index and forefingers. When she groaned, I released them and lightly slapped her tits. I was aware it made her furious and clearly saw a twinkle of displeasure in her eyes.

"No moaning! We are not that far yet. You were to lubricate me with your body!"

"H'm!" was her only comment. She approached me and I clearly felt her quickening breath as she pressed her soft full tits against my chest and rubbed her entire upper body against me, distributing the oil between us.

Suppressing a hoarse groan, I wondered if someone had switched off the air conditioning... In regard to my arms, she could not help but thoroughly knead the muscles. I made a mental note to *definitely* reward her at the end of the evening given how hot she was massaging me right now. As I turned around, she did the same to my backside until I gleamed and looked like a professional go-go dancer... Then it was her turn. Slowly, I spread the oil over her silky skin and constantly stared at her and blew on her skin so she got goose bumps and shivered slightly. H'm...

Breathless and with reddened cheeks but infinite trust in her eyes, she gazed up at me.

I played extensively with her tits and took my time oiling between her legs even though there was no need for it because she already glistened so invitingly.

She squirmed and moaned, so I decided not to interrupt her.

After all, I was simply a horny shit who knew how to touch her, which left her no chance but to show me her desire. Besides, I didn't mind her moaning.

I loved those sounds. All of them! I would have loved to record them so I could listen to them every night as I fell asleep. Then again, I might end up masturbating all night long...

"If I had it my way, I'd fuck you right now. But you have to wait a little while..." Increasing the pressure on my finger, I made it disappear between her tender lips without penetrating her and rubbed it back and forth.

"Tristan..." she gasped devotedly and pressed her groin against my hand.

Abruptly, I withdrew and turned her around so I could oil her backside. Naturally, I worked and kneaded her small round ass cheeks thoroughly. Oh, yes... I could have gone on for hours!

At some point, and clearly much too soon, she was glistening just like me, looking like SEX on two legs.

"Get your outfit!" I emphasized the command with a smack on her butt.

She approached the table cautiously as if snakes where hidden in the clothes and grabbed without paying attention to them.

I accepted them. First, I put the black thong on her, then the mesh skirt, and closed the triangle bra.

"I..." Quickly, my index finger closed her lips and gently brushed over them.

"Sh... I won't let you out of my sight all evening and no one but me will touch you, okay, baby?" Smiling, I swept back her hair. By now, for some reason, I was in a...splendid mood.

"But..."

Gently, I stroked over her lower lip and tilted her head sideways. "Quiet now!"

Her mouth dropped and I laughed softly as I reached behind me to the dresser for the last essential prop, the one she hadn't noticed yet.

"Tr...!" My hand shot out and I slapped her delicious little chaste ass. She yelped and immediately used her fingers to cover her mouth. While I was laughing, she looked at me with utter outrage, groped her way to her ass cheek, and kneaded it reproachfully. Smirking, I showed her the black riding crop.

"You may choose. What do you be prefer? Being a dog or a horse?" I joked and she stared at me shocked.

"Is that a riding crop?" She eyed the thing in my hand as if it was something disgusting. She seemed petrified. With pleasure, I brushed the utensil over her stomach, breasts, delicate neck, up to her chin, and then used its tip to raise it so she had to look at me.

"Great observation, Miss Angel, it is a riding crop," I praised her and let the tip of the aforementioned item brush along her jaw. "I will use it when you don't obey. It won't hurt...but it won't be pleasant either, mainly because you will scare yourself. Preview?" Unexpectedly, the leather rushed to her hard nipple.

Mia inhaled sharply, cringed a bit, her eyes moistened, but mostly her irises darkened.

Oh, fucking yeah...she liked it...and I even more.

Her breathing quickened as she expectantly looked at my hand while I looked down at her amused. Oh...how her oiled up chest raised and fell...how she shivered...

Fuck!

It should be forbidden to be that hot! My fucker wanted her! *Now!* And I was now tired of controlling myself. It was simply not possible. Crap on my plan. I could still implement it later.

"Change of plans," I yelled and tossed the whip aside to grab her hips and pull her to me, to which her lower body smashed hard against mine.

"I want you!" and then I kissed her...on the neck. Even though I would have liked to put my tongue in her mouth and taste her, I was not yet drunk enough with lust to be carried away.

She gasped as our shiny oily bodies rubbed against each other and spontaneously grabbed my ass and pulled me closer. I mimicked her, cradled both of her plums, and increased the pressure of her pussy on my dick, which caused both of us to moan in unison.

Now, *I* clearly had increased the temperature!

She stretched her torso toward me, enjoying my lips and my tongue, which skillfully made their way down to her full breasts. At the same time, I thanked my foresight for having gone with edible oil because often times, anything else tasted purely chemical. Then I bit her nipple, which was simply tasty. But not hard... I didn't want to hurt her... at least not like that. All I wanted was to feel her around me.

"Tristan," she whispered into the silent office, which was usually only interrupted by our frantic breathing.

"Turn around!" I mumbled in reply, when her ass hit the glass pane. This time, I wanted her from behind. Deep...

Really deep and hard...really hard. In a hurry, I pulled the zipper down.

My little totally horny slut reacted immediately and turned around. I grabbed her hair and pulled her head back to be able to continue kissing her neck. I used my other hand to massage her breast while rubbing my fucker between her ass cheeks.

"Oh, fuck...baby... You know how hot you look when you're so close to coming simply because I slapped your tittie with my riding crop?"

She whimpered. Oh, fucking yes! At that moment, I could not decide which sound of delight I found the most arousing. Only one thing was clear, I was lost when she panted, moaned, screamed, or whimpered. Even her regular sighing undermined my self-control.

"Unfortunately, you won't be coming yet!" With those words, I grabbed her a little firmer and bent her forward so that her face was against the pane and slid my hand from her hair to her neck while I rubbed my knuckles over her dripping wetness. She squirmed impatiently. Her hands left oily fingerprints on the glass and her hot breath fogged it up.

"This is for me. You have yet to earn your orgasm!" I grabbed the damp fabric of her thong and pulled it aside to expose her smooth lips and died a few deaths as I positioned my fucker right there in absolute paradise.

"TRISI! I'M BACK!" I almost cried NO when I realized who was trilling at the door... Unfortunately, I was too shocked to do anything meaningful. Like, for example, immediately tell the broad to shut her yap.

But I froze as the door opened and my fuck-ending spoiler confronted me.

Mia Marena gasped and at the same time, shot up and turned around with momentum to see who was interrupting us so rudely...

My alibi girlfriend could not have chosen a better time to show up here. I mean, really! I planned to read her the riot act later on.

At the moment, she simply just stood there stupidly with her manicured hand on the doorknob and pink painted mouth wide open. Quite wide. Same as her eyes...

Actually, I was only looking at Mia, who clearly just now suffered a severe heart attack. I was sure of it. For a few seconds, the world stopped. Then it continued to turn...

Mia spun around to face me and *sized* me up... My heart stopped under her absolutely deadly expression.

And finally...she hissed.

"Tristan, I'll kill you!"

22. His Damn Alibi Girlfriend

Mia 'Jealous' Angel

I expected something, just not what happened. For example: Menderez becomes President, humanity realizes the meaning of existence, or a tsunami crashing over us. *But not that!*

I would have never considered that *this natural disaster* would descend upon my little world. I would have never thought it possible that he'd welcome her back into his life... Yes, hearing them on the phone, I already had inkling, but I pushed the thought aside! After all, there were plenty of potential candidates so to speak, the agony of choice! Surely, he didn't *actually* fall back on Eva Eber!

Well, that she just burst in was the ultimate proof of how wrong I was.

And *he* accused me of treason?

WOW!

Unable to deal with the absurdity of the whole situation, nor take my eyes off him, I did the only thing I was capable of at the moment; I slapped Tristan Wrangler, quite hard!

Somehow, the loud smacking sound jostled everyone out of their personal paralysis and all three of us gasped.

I...because my hand hurt.

Tristan because I actually dared hit him.

And *it,* because it must have been just as shocked by my presence as I was by hers.

Following the group horror, not much happened.

Tristan's hand rose in slow motion as he stared at me with an expression of pure horror in the eyes and just as slowly rubbed over his three-day beard, as if the touch would confirm what just happened. Furious, I stood before him.

It was still at the door and had not moved an inch.

So, I started and hissed forcefully...desperately.

"You know perfectly well...what we went through because of her! You know that she...would have rather turned earth to hell than see you and me happy together! That she...wanted to...ruin everything. And you let her into your life? Please tell me her presence is merely a coincidence. Tell me you have no idea what she wants here!"

"OH, PLEASE." *It* sounded nasally. Now, I honestly saw red. Oh, God! Her voice was so repulsive! My blazing gaze traveled to her or should I say, to the thing... It had not changed all that much: a gray, too tight dress – probably from the children's department – endless legs – unfortunately perfect – and monster jugs, which almost busted the neckline of her hooker rag. Contrary to how I remembered her, her nose was smaller and lips fuller. Probably recycled, for the sake of the environment. For makeup, a revival of flashy colors. I had missed that pink so much. Otherwise, the same disgusting swaying of the hips — trademark: how much was its nightly rate — combined with a nasty grin, which after eight years it seemed to have perfected, and the batting of the eyes, which demanded much from her false eyelashes. Simply, the ultimate catastrophe.

"What is Turkey doing here? Trisi?" She approached him and he took a step back while closing his pants, but I didn't mind... She would never again put herself between us! *Never!* Too much had happened because of her. I had put up with too much!

"Don't touch him!" Before she knew it, I had forcefully pushed her away by her bony shoulders. So hard, she crashed against the wall behind her and groaned. Her bright blue eyes flashed. Wild, almost mad...looking deranged, she was about to rush me.

But Tristan snapped out of his paralysis, pulled me close to him while at the same time shoving by me so that he stood partially in front of me when she tried to grab me. His other hand grabbed her fingers, which must have been going for my hair.

"Leave her alone!"

"But Trisi!"

"DON'T CALL ME THAT!"

"Tristan Wrangler. I'm your girlfriend, so I can..."

"You are my *alibi girlfriend*! Nothing more! No petting. No kissing. No fucking! Those were the damn rules!" he growled directly in her face and let go of her hand before he spun around to me. Apparently, he had himself under control again and finally realized that I had actually slapped him.

"And you..." he rumbled and I looked at him shocked as he looked down at me, all oily and beautiful, "...must have lost your mind!"

"Excuse me?" I yelled and shuddered.

"It's a nobody, Mia Marena." He pointed at the tart while he oh-so-quietly and ominously explained to me, "Just a cheap tramp. A means to an end. I don't even *fuck* her! *I don't look at her! I don't kiss her! I don't touch her!* Dammit. I'm here with *you* and after *eight years*, I *still* obey *your* fucking rules! Do you even understand what that crap means? I didn't tell you about her because, for a change, I wanted to spare you. It means *nothing* to me. Why complicate things? And you thank me by raising your hand against me? That will have consequences — now!"

He dragged me behind him out of the office.

I was so mad — my whole body was shaking and for a few steps, I staggered behind him on the velvet carpet. Totally stunned...until my anger finally found a way to channel itself just as he arrived at the top of the staircase.

What was I even still doing here? He was an asshole! She was Eva — the dream couple had reunited! I was bending over backwards for him and here *he* was stabbing me in the back? After everything she had done to *me,* to *us*?

"You are such an ass!" Without hesitating, I tore myself from him.

"WHAT?" Tristan stared at me when I came at him and just like with her, forcefully pushed against his broad shoulders. Unfortunately, he did not do me the favor of staggering, so I pushed his back against the wall and he rolled his eyes.

"You know what, Tristan Wrangler? Enough is enough! You finally did it! I'm here in a sex club, right? I'm here to have fun not to be constantly humiliated! I'm sure I can find men who wouldn't mind kissing me! And I'm sure there are guys who wouldn't mind loving me! Guys who won't lie and abuse me! Men who know what they have with me and who would believe me when I say I'm no traitor! Who wouldn't question my love! And who have the courage to admit their feelings even if that makes them vulnerable! So, I'll enjoy myself with them now. You can go fuck yourself! Our agreement is null and void! We are history! BABY!"

I felt my heart beating in my chest as I hurried down the stairs. Fortunately, he was...too shocked to immediately pursue me. I was almost all the way down and felt the deep rich booming bass of the club in my belly when he roared from above.

"HAVE YOU LOST IT?" I had already slipped through the curtain from backstage and placed myself among the pulsating lights, loud music, and half-naked people...in safety...

Well...I didn't feel safe at all, still like hunted prey. If he got his hands on me *now*, his punishment would be inhumanly cruel.

This was no longer a game; it had become serious! I told him I planned to have sex with some horny bastard in his exquisite fuck club. His hunting grounds! Dumb idea!

Hurriedly, I squeezed by the dancing bodies. Here and there, I received a *hey baby* and once or twice someone grabbed my ass. But I couldn't stop and continued to hurry, without a goal, without orientation. If he caught me now, no one could help me! Sweat ran down my forehead in beads as I pushed myself through heated bodies. I ignored the surrounding naked flesh and calls. The bass was booming through my limbs, my heart, and my chest.

When I reached the outer edge of the dance floor and eased past the last person, I bumped into something hard. Out of nowhere, the stage appeared before me. The *empty* stage...

Oh, crap! From the left and right side, club members were crowding me. I turned around and was confronted by blazing green-brown eyes. Deadly eyes! Only directed at me.

OH, NO! OH, GOD! OH, HELP!

Panicking, I let my gaze wander as I contemplated my escape … There was only one option. Before I knew it, one knee was on the edge of the stage and I was heaving myself onto it. Exactly at the moment his hands grabbed for me, I quickly I stood up and rushed to the center.

Hastily, I inspected my new haven. Below, a few noticed me and started to whistle and howl. The stage was not particularly big and only equipped with a pole. The floor was covered with black velvet and looked fluffy soft...

"Come down from there!" his quivering lips mouthed silently.

The hell I will! He looked like the devil himself, simply not all that trustworthy. So, I preferred to stay up on stage, towering above him!

A spotlight fell on me and the predominantly male cries grew louder and more enthusiastic. An unknown energy took hold of me. His gaze was on me... At once, I felt so...*powerful.*

"No, ASSHOLE!" I mouthed back and winked at him. What was it again he had taught me? To feel SEXY? Like a goddess! To abandon one's inhibition...blah, blah... It's just a body...blah, blah!

My lips formed a smile as my entire attitude changed. I squared my shoulders, loosened my steps...swayed my hips more...

I grinned wider when the DJ put on a new song and gave me a thumbs up. *It* must be fate.

Kings of Leon, *Sex is on Fire*

My pelvis rotated as if on its own, I was good at that! I was no rigid board... It was in my blood to use my feminine curves.

I prudently tested the pole and intrigued, felt the cold material under my fingers, stroked it up and down, and the sounds clearly grew louder before I turned, the narrow metal at my backside, deliberately seeking his eyes...

I found them. He stood there where I had escaped his grasp. His mouth was pressed together in a line, hands clutching the edge of the stage.

Here, Mista Wrangler! You asked for it!

The smoky voice of the singer started and the song became more intense. I felt the erotic vibes and slowly let my back slide down the pole, where I purposely spread my legs, knowing where everyone would stare. It aroused me so much that I had to close my eyes once I was squatting...

In one flowing movement, I went on my knees, aimed at the wonderful blazing dark look in front of me and crawled toward him... I did so stretching my limbs and raising my butt in the air. The shouts, as well whistles, became deafening. His eyes narrowed as I crawled toward him.

Oh, Tristan! He could no longer move. I had him completely captivated and it felt oh-so-good.

Then I discovered Georgi in the crowd, who was also watching me, looking quite shocked.

Grinning, I considered taking it a step further and, at the last moment, turned left, away from Tristan, toward Georgi. He grinned at me with raised eyebrows, clearly ready to jump up on stage... I winked at him. Tristan's head followed my eyes and he spun around to Georgi.

A blink of an eye later, he did something I did not think

possible and, thus, destroyed my feeling of superiority.

He swung himself...in biker pants...go-go dancer oiled...using his absolutely dream muscles, with one graceful flowing movement onto the elevated floor and with his fists braced on his hips, placed himself between me and Georgi. A side note, stole my breath way and grinned diabolically down at me. Now, women's voices clearly joined the calls of men — all who were pretty delighted.

At that very moment, I saw Eva trying to climb up on stage. Had she lost it? What was she even doing here? The god, who was standing before me so sexily, was *my man*!

I crawled two steps toward him when I saw his brown designer shoes, held onto his thighs and smiled shyly as I pulled myself up on him.

Oh-so-slowly...while I rubbed my breasts over his thighs, twitching fucker, his abdominal muscles and, finally, over his hard naked chest... My hands stroked over his hard slippery body.

Immediately, it shot through me like molten lava. He was a pure aphrodisiac.

Wow!

Tristan, the god, grinned superiorly... as I held his hips.

Right then in that moment, the lyrics a*head while I'm driving* played... His grin turned into the dirtiest, most beautiful thing I had ever seen. I had always loved asshole Tristan! Even back then in the car, when I blew him and his fucker had made violent contact with my throat for the first time... I was flooded by memories...

Then he grabbed me by the hair, just like in the photo, pulled my head back, pushed his lower body hard against mine, and rotated his hips. My hands traveled up his back and felt his smooth flesh.

Help! Were we in *Dirty Dancing?* Had he taken a stripper dance course? Where did he learn that? Was he the new Ricky Martin or what?

I gasped because he always knew exactly how to move and yet... I had not expected him to be so...yes, actually...quite professional. Then again, it wasn't surprising...just seeing him in those pants made you lose your mind...and the hip movements he had clearly perfected during sex.

The screams turned into hysterical screeches and I knew if he continued, everyone would storm the stage and the evening would end up in a big crowd orgy. Eroticism gripped us and we were turning the heads of those present. I clawed at Tristan's forearms and moaning, closed my eyes as I felt him between my legs. Slowly, his hand moved down my thigh to my knee, then he wrapped it around my waist, and pressed me against the pole while he, absolutely gracefully and superiorly, dry fucked me...

"You... Your sex is on fire..." he whispered in my ear in an angel's voice... Just like eons ago in the school locker-room.

WOW!

Of course, my lower body automatically moved in sync with his and eventually my arms raised themselves and with outstretched hands above my head I held on to the pole. Tristan securely grabbed my other knee and I swung both legs around his hips.

Oh, God!

Only my scant thong and his too-thin pants separated us.

"If it's not forever, if it's just tonight... Oh, it's still the greatest, the greatest, the greatest."

I loved it when Tristan used his beautiful voice to sing my favorite songs to me and arousing me on stage in a sex club... Resignedly, I moaned, let my head roll back and ground my pelvis in unison with his because now I desperately needed the friction.

Where was I? Why was I even mad at him? What was my name? None of it mattered! I needed him now! *In me! That* was enormously important!

The audience was completely freaking out, men and women alike. They made more noise than the music.

"Tristan...please...fuck me!" I whispered with my eyes half closed...

Well...he had been waiting for that because he immediately stopped moving. His hands dug into my ass cheeks — and held me. Oh, God. He was so muscular. He had no problem holding me like that... I could tell by how calmly he looked at me.

"Okay!" He took a step back. Panting, I let go of the pole and held on to his broad shoulders. He did not give me a single moment to clear my thoughts... Not a single one.

Because his lips moved over my neck as he led me off

stage. Calls and whistles of disappointment followed us...

"You are my slut," he muttered and pushed me harder against his lower body while easily carrying me to the back area of the club. A door opened, slammed shut, and suddenly, I was pressed against a cold wall. Tristan held me with one hand while the other slid between our bodies and fumbled with his pants...

"Yes, Tristan..."

"You don't want someone else?"

"*No, Tristan!*" I cried because he bit me in the neck.

"Who do you want, baby?" I felt that he had freed his fucker — how he slid it up and down. Unable to wait, I thrust my hips toward him. Now his knuckles brushed over my snail and I rolled my head back — whimpered... was completely lost when his hand came back up and the knuckles accidentally rubbed again over my middle.

"You, Tristan, *you!*" I cried desperately, "*please!*" more imploringly.

"Will you act up like that again once I'm done with you? Once you've had *me*?" He stopped rubbing himself and I felt the tip of his penis at my entrance. Purposefully, he pressed hard and firmly against my muscles. But not strong enough to completely overcome the initial resistance. It bordered on torture, again!

"No, Tristan. I WILL NOT ACT UP AGAIN!... PLEASE, DAMMIT, DO IT ALREADY! NOW!" I cried out indignantly and loudly. However, I stopped him before he entered me by holding him back by his hard throbbing fucker while I stared straight into confused lust-drunk eyes. "And if you want *me, you* will not act like that again either!" I yelled, trembling and slowly moved my hand up and down.

With a wildly beating heart, I waited. If not, I would leave, even now! Once and for all! Even if it tore me apart! He had to make up his mind once and for all! What did he want, who was he! I said all that without words...until that crooked grin appeared and my old Tristan looked down at me.

"You got it, baby!" That was all I needed to hear.

"Remember your wor..." I mumbled as he thrust into me and placed his lips on mine. My inner muscles gave way and welcomed him deep inside. They stretched...contracted a little... felt his hardness, his strength...his twitching when he was all the way in.

Oh my, Tristan!

We groaned in each other's mouth. My nails dug into his hard ass.

I felt him tensing his muscles as he pulled out completely only to plunge into me again with one forceful thrust, causing me to hit my head hard...

And then he did something unexpected because he protectively cradled the back of my head with his big hand as he thrust into me again, leaned his forehead against mine, and gazed deeply into my eyes... Wow!

Overwhelmed by emotions, I fought back tears.

I clung to his shoulders, wanting to thank him for being

the way he was. Cold and, at the same time, so hot, so indifferent, and yet, also so compassionate... Loving and, at the same time, so rough. I wanted to scream everything I felt for him into the world as he unerringly thrust into me, increased his speed, making our oily bodies slap increasingly harder against each other and our gasps and moans grew steadily louder.

Between each g-spot aimed thrust, a half-screamed half-whimpered word.

"I. Love. It. How. You. Fuck. Me. I. Love. It. How. YOU. Hold. Me. Tight. I. Love. It. That. You. Know. Exactly. Where... UHHHHH! AHHHH!" He quickened his energetic pace and changed the angle somewhat so he hit the spot better while his lips were on my rapidly throbbing carotid artery.

In the meantime, I moaned loudly, way past whimpering. It was impossible for me to control myself when receiving such continuous stimulation. It didn't matter to me. With Tristan, I could let myself go and I loved it. My body was an instrument that only responded to his knowledgeable fingers.

"You. Are. A. Sex. God!" Tristan laughed breathlessly against my neck and ran his tongue over my salty skin. Firmly, wet, warm. It was too much...it was honestly too much.

"You too," I thought I heard...because I had already left this world as I climaxed intensely and loudly.

"AHHH, I love YOUUUUUUUU!" Tristan was a lousy mimicker because he came a second after me and we pulsated, twitched, and soared together...

By the time we landed back on earth, we were not only oily, but sweaty and struggling for breath. I was gasping slightly more than he was despite his muscles having done all the work... Oh, man... I had to get in shape because tomorrow I was sure to have aching muscles in the most unlikely places. However, it was worth it.

I smiled when I put my lips on his forehead and couldn't deny myself a gentle kiss. He did not recoil...but closed his eyes.

I simply wasn't yet in the mood to think about something else other than his phenomenal muscles, which were still holding me tightly and unwaveringly. It seemed he had a different opinion because soon after his breathing slowed, I knew at any moment now, he would pull away without any tenderness and I would feel like a whore again.

"Never do that again," he said abruptly and I ripped open my eyes.

"What?" I pretended to be naive.

"Mia!" he merely growled and tried to break away from me. However, I was not ready for that yet, so I clung to him as if my life depended on it. And even though I should not say it, I did it anyway.

"EVA. EBER!" Was all I gasped and slowly...I started to boil again...because, slowly but surely it all came back to me: EVA EBER! First class slut and forever a dumb cow!

Next to Miss Robinson and Bianca, she was one of the ten most hated women in the world!

HER!

"Why, out of all girls, her, Tristan?" I asked and fought for self-control. At the same time, the dreamy part of me naturally noticed he was still holding me and that his face was now resting on my shoulder. He did not kiss or stroke me, but at least he was holding me...

"She was there when you were not," he replied tonelessly.

I pinched my eyes closed. "I would have been there. Always!"

"But I did not want you!"

"You wanted *her* rather than *me*?" I inquired bitterly.

"Yes," he said, absolutely honest.

"So, in the end, she managed to get between us after all!" "No!"

"An explanation would be helpful," I demanded, slightly indignantly.

Now, his eyes burned as he searched my eyes.

"She wanted my heart, but she could never have it because you had taken it along, you stupid little girl," Tristan replied unsmiling. He broke away from me and set me down on my feet.

I was digesting his words as he packed away his fucker, first zipped up, then closed the button and finally gave me an arrogant look.

"She was never for me, currently is not, and never will be. I want you to know that. Your jealousy is absolutely uncalled for. She will no longer be allowed here as long as you're here. It will be as if she never existed, okay? So, calm down, dammit and let us simply enjoy the time we have together. The clock is ticking."

Fucker! Now he used my biggest fear against me. To lose him after three months. Finally and forever. Calmly, he watched me, knowing full well I would break.

"It has long since expired." Was all I could say so as not to lose all of my dignity. Without a word, I turned around and opened the door that led outside. Tristan probably thought I would go home, but for today, I was not yet finished here. Not quite so. Now it was time to do something that was already years overdue.

Happily, I noticed her a few seconds later in the back stage area where she was conversing with Garrett, who wore a strange leather mask on his head that covered his whole face. When I approached them red-faced and freshly fucked, her eyes narrowed. I stopped in front of her with my chin held high and looked straight into her eyes.

"Eight years ago, I told Tristan Wrangler I would never hit another human being..."

Without another word, I raised my right hand, clenched it into a fist, and with all my pent up rage and strength smacked her cheek forcefully...

I almost came again.

H'm, the sound alone was almost satisfaction enough.

But then there was her stupefied expression as she actually staggered and Garrett had to catch her so she wouldn't hit the ground. Without batting an eye, I calmly finished my sentence.

"…but you are not a human being!" And with that, I turned and marched away swinging my hips.

Ouch! Frantically, I shook my fist because it truly hurt...

I heard Tristan's laughter behind me as I disappeared through the door and knew that although the countdown had expired, it did not mean I would lose Tristan.

END

Excerpt from the next book

I have included the next chapter! I hope it will give you peace of mind until the next book is finished!

1. The Merger

Tristan 'Helpful' Wrangler

H'm, today, my slut looked delicious enough to bite as she came to me. Her long legs were in tight black jeans, small feet in sneakers, which did not bother me. A dark blue pullover with V-neck flattered her upper body, which immediately captivated my attention. I liked it when she wore it because I loved her cleavage.

Her hair, as so often, was again in a ponytail, which nevertheless hung down below her shoulder blades. Her face was lightly made up, the mascara making her eyelashes appear even longer than they were. The delicate lipstick that matched her pink cheeks tempted me and did not free me from evil.

She was not styled, wore no designer clothing, high heels, or push-up bra.

Yet, she was divine.

Her curves always made me think nasty thoughts.

Then there was her pretty face with flawless complexion. Those expressive big eyes...the delicate neck...those beautiful small hands, which always instinctively touched me. I could have continued like that forever because there was not one single fragrant inch of her that I didn't enjoy.

Fuck, I already wanted her again and here she had just arrived in my office.

"Hi," she murmured softly and hung up the coat she had just peeled herself out of on the hook next to my door. I immediately noticed how unenthusiastic she had greeted me and I didn't like it.

"Hi?" I replied suspiciously, raised an eyebrow, turned completely around in my office chair, put my outstretched fingertips together, and looked over them.

She remained at the entrance, her gaze slid back and forth between my face and body. Her cheeks reddened. Oh, yes. Mia wanted me as badly as I did her. She also recalled our last time and she found me just as hot as I found her.

I also looked hot in my plain white shirt and low riding jeans.

"What have you planned for me for today?" she asked and I could tell by the tone of her voice that she was already quite excited. Naturally. She never knew what I had planned for her, whether I would send her to hell again by fucking her in front of strangers or if I would just fuck her in private and send her to seventh heaven.

Today...it would be seventh heaven.

Because honestly, I had somewhat of a damn guilty conscience about the Eva thing. I should not have tried to hide it from Mia, but I knew she would freak out and not forgive me if I told her I had allied myself with her worst enemy.

That she was still around was all the proof I needed: Mia Angel truly loved me. And that changed a lot...

Granted, Eva Eber also loved me in her own way, but her feelings oftentimes were quite pathological and nothing compared to Mia's unquestioning nature. Eva's tenacity alone was scary.

During my jail stint, she continuously bombarded me with letters even though I did not answer any of them. Once I was out and had opened my club, she found out and showed up one evening with tears running down her face. I sent her away night after night. Still, she did not give up. That was about the time the first rumors of me being gay started circulating because the fucker had not been in the mood for broads and vehemently refused to do its duty — oh, yes, I, Tristan Wrangler, was impotent with other women but not *her*! She had turned me literally into a limp dick! So, I decided, partly out of spite, but also to finally escape all those homophobic wisecracks, to take Eva Eber as an alibi girlfriend. Nothing more.

Eva was happy to be seen with me in public and could brag about it. Everyone who knew us also knew she was my girlfriend. She wallowed in my reputation like a pig did the mud, which was enough for her. Otherwise, she left me alone for the most part.

When she found out Mia had entered my life again, she suddenly became obtrusive, always calling unannounced, suggesting in her madness that she just *come over* and used every opportunity to touch me!

What was that overly skinny bimbo thinking?

I was so sick of her scheming. Even back then, but today she could almost drive a wedge between Mia and me. But I would not allow it. Never again. Slowly, we fell back into our old rhythm and our bond strengthened...

Because Eva's subconscious attempt to separate us was anything but successful. Mia Marena was finally here — with me.

The relief that she was not gone for good hung thick in the air yesterday. Just because of that, she was able to make me promise, not to be like *that* anymore.

Both of us knew what that meant...no humiliation or degradation... At least not where it would destroy her.

I stood up, walked over to my closet where I grabbed an already prepared basket and again felt like little Red Riding Hood and I offered Mia my arm without a word. She linked her arm without hesitation and grinned.

Amused, I rolled my eyes and led her through the gallery to the rear of the property, also called *Garden of Eden* and part of the outside grounds of my special club.

During the summer, you could enjoy the fresh air out

here, which was why large four-poster rattan beds and other fucking sites (for example *in* a tree or a cave, etc.) where plentiful. There were various scavenger stations, with love swings and bulls with dildos sticking out their backs, especially for women's rodeos. An amusement park for adults. You could even try it on a small roller coaster, which was for the more daring. Numerous paths snaked along the spacious grounds, benches hid behind huge tree trunks, and kinky statues lined the avenues. Everything was beautifully set in scene with floodlights and fog machines, reminiscent of a mystically wicked place.

Mia looked wide-eyed at me as I led her outside. Although it was not raining, it was rather cold and the air was full of moisture. At the end of the garden, we reached the planned destination.

She did not immediately realize where we were because dense fog surrounded us. Only when we were closer did she notice the hot thermal spring I led her to. Her gasp betrayed how impressed she was. I had forked out a couple grand for the installation, but then it was also a hit, especially with the play of color underwater.

The bubbling source lay somewhat hidden under the far-reaching branches of a large willow tree. Everything was made of smooth volcanic rock. There were no sharp corners or edges and it was gently illuminated. The colors alternated between red, yellow, orange, and purple. There was nothing cold, nothing hard (except my fucker), only warmth and heat.

"Wow!" was Mia's first comment, which made me grin. Of course, it certainly was *wow*. At least my world offered a few benefits.

"M'm-m'm." Unable to resist, I approached her from behind and wrapped my arms around her flat belly. Immediately, I undid the button of her pants and ran my nose over her neck. Smelled...felt... smiled... *Wow!*

She shuddered and squirmed somewhat, rubbing her soft ass cheeks against my fucker. Oh-oh, I had to get in there now... Obviously in the hot water because out in the open we might freeze vital body parts.

Fog wafted around us when she turned to face me and carefully undressed me. Button by button, she timidly opened my shirt, looked me in the eyes, and kissed every inch of exposed skin. I allowed it... She was particularly thoroughly with my left breast, caressed every inch below the tattoo, before wrapping her full lips around my nipple and gently sucked on it. With a harsh growl, I pulled the scrunchy out her hair, sending it spilling over her delicate shoulders and pert breasts. I rolled my head back as I gleefully buried my hands in her velvety soft brown-blonde curls and disheveled it. I loved grabbing it in my fist and pulling her head back to show her the desired direction. I did that now too because if she were to continue sucking and licking so thoroughly, all I would want was to hold her down. But we weren't that far yet. All in good time. After all, I wanted to undress her first, see her before me in all her glory. Urgently so!

I wasted no time and stopped the little minx. She gasped, but I released her hair, grinned at her, pulled the sweater plus undershirt over her head so that she stood topless and freezing before me.

"Are you cold?" I teased her because her nipples were as stiff as whipped cream. Before she could reply, I leaned down and paid her back.

"Yummy..." I hummed gleefully against her soft skin as I sucked on a nipple while kneading the other tit with my hand. Smoothly, not roughly.

"Oh God, Tristan! What is going on with you today?"

"I am merely sticking to our latest agreement..." I mumbled innocently, "...why, are you complaining?" and glared at her provocatively from down below with an eyebrow raised. I could also do it differently — if she wanted...

"*No!*" she immediately cried, arching her back. I laughed passionately against her increasingly cold skin and abruptly moved away from her upper body. Hastily, I squatted before her and released her from the rest of her clothes. As promised, she wore no underwear, which I happily noted.

As soon as I stood up, she relieved me of my pants, following my subtle command, to free my, as usual, impatient fucker from the confines of the fabric. I grinned as she forced the material down my legs and almost fell over. Eventually, she succeeded and both of us stood there naked, albeit unusually quiet. I had never spoken so little since I began fucking Mia. But today I just wanted... Yes, what exactly?

Silently enjoy...the past was the past...

I grinned down at her, unexpectedly throwing my arms around her, and grabbed her smooth bare buttocks. Trembling, she grinned at me as I lifted her up and she leaned against my shoulder. Absolutely instinctively, her legs wrapped around my hips and I carried her into the hot tub.

I leaned my back against the round stone behind me, sighed and rolled my head back, then watched her intently as she sat on my thighs. I sat comfortably as if in a chair because the hot tub was built so you could sit on the edge and swim in the center. Guaranteed to fit at least 15 people here, whereas the other end lay shrouded in fog and could not be seen. Colored lights danced softly across Mia's pale skin. Her hair darkened as it floated on the surface of the water. She was a sexy little mermaid...

Luckily, she was not an actual mermaid; otherwise, she would not have the appropriate orifices apart from maybe her mouth.

Slowly, I wrapped a wet strand around my fist. Puzzled, she snorted as I pulled her nearer, so close the tips of our noses almost touched.

Oh, fuck! Why was I torturing myself? Now *I* wanted to kiss her! It was prohibited. Even her eyes betrayed her longing for the same thing. But I didn't. I merely held her until I felt her excitement vibrating because I enjoyed toying with her even though I knew it was wrong to give her false hope. Nevertheless, I loved it when she looked at me like she did at that moment.

"Mia," I whispered against her little face.

"Yes." She sounded so fragile, so uncertain, so gentle and, above all, devoted as always... The sound went straight to my fucker.

"You may ride me now," I announced magnanimously and released the strand of hair to grab her hips with both hands.

Her wet upper body stuck out of the water briefly as I easily lifted her up. She gasped when the cold air hit her heated skin and closed her eyelids as I positioned her over me. I held it in place with one hand while I slowly lowered her. Divinely, she threw her head back, rolling her eyes. She arched her back as I entered her fully, thrusting her nipples toward me. I could not resist, sat up, wrapped her firmly in both arms, and sucked extensively on them while she, without prompting or guidance, started rotating her hips. She clung to my shoulders and made small gentle moans, mixed in with delicate whimpers each time I mimicked her movements.

Steam surrounded us, the water splashed softly. Otherwise, the night was silent and dark except for the hot tub's dancing lights and absolutely soothing noises. It seemed heavenly ... How had I ever gone without it for so long? How was I ever supposed to do without it?

I sucked harder on her nipple. She shocked me by

pulling me into a tighter embrace and moaning louder, only to push me back by my shoulders.

"Stop, Tristan! Otherwise I'll come at any moment now!" she explained choppily.

Oh, fuck!

I could no longer look at her or *I* would come!

So, I rolled my head back, put my hands on her thighs, happily closed my eyes, and just felt her...as well as listened. I loved the desperate noises she made, loved how she grew increasingly demanding in her movements, and idolized the way her fingertips dug hard in my chest while she forcefully bit her lip, her forehead wrinkled from frowning. Her legs were shaking and she was trembling on the inside, nearly triggering a premature orgasm.

Now *I* had to grit my teeth and claw at her pliable flesh because I wanted her to come first.

"Mia!" I growled because she intentionally held back and opened my eyes to glare at her indignantly.

What did she do? She smiled at me naughtily, knowing perfectly well what she was doing to me as I restrained myself just for her and how it tormented me.

"You little bitch!" I managed to snap half-laughing, half-moaning in torment because she once *fucking more* wrapped herself tighter around me.

Okay...she asked for it! I could easily bring her to climax despite her resistance. Proof? Gently, I took my fingers from her thigh and stroked her clit.

Shocked, she panted and grabbed my hand, but it was

already too late. The timer had been activated, the bomb would go off. Any moment now... Just a little gentle friction while she continued gripping my wrist...

"WHO... lives in a pineapple deep in the sea? Sponge Bob Square Pants! Sponge Bob Square Pants!" Suddenly, I heard an annoying voice pulling me out of my foggy state of lust.

It was a ringtone!

What was that crap?

And then she did something I would never forgive her for. *Never!*

She got off me!

"*What the fuck?*" I cursed and tried to stop her, but she evaded my grasp!

Meanwhile, she was rummaging in her pants pocket while the song continuously trilled on, riling me up even more. It wasn't until shortly before the grand finale did she finally answer.

"Hello?" Breathless, she listened while I continued staring at her. She was kneeing at the edge of the hot tub, naked and shivering and not making any move to return to me!

I had been *so* close, just as she had been!

"What?" she screamed and jumped up, her expression panicked. Searching, she looked around and gathered up her clothes. "Yes, I'll be there in 20 minutes. Tell him I'll be right there!" she cried desperately and actually started to pull up her pants with one hand. I was speechless! "Okay, see you soon!" And she hung up, totally ignored me, and forced her wet body into her clothes. I still hated it when Mia dressed. It was downright depressing.

With a jolt, I jumped out of the hot tub.

WOW! Was it cold! But it didn't matter. Freezing, I stood right in front of her as she tugged her undershirt and sweater both at the same time over her wet head.

"Hey, hey, hey... Stop!" I helped pull the items down because by herself she was unsuccessful. "What the hell is going on?" I asked as soon as her face poked through the neckline, unable to do anything for my shivering because it really was fucking cold.

Then, for the first time, I noticed her expression. She seemed truly concerned.

"Tristan, I have to go! I'm sorry, but it's an emergency!" She searched for her shoes and slipped them on without bothering with her socks for she found only one. "I have to... I have to go to the home..."

"What happened?" I handed her the missing sock. When she was finally good to go, she eyed me, her shoulders drooping and a fearful expression.

"It's Robbie..." Which explained her panic. He was her favorite child at the home where she worked — with whom she had a special relationship.

"I've got to call a cab!" She tapped her phone as if her life depended on it and I barely kept my eyes from rolling as I took it away from her. Not waiting for her protest, I threw on my clothes while at the same time I managed to ward off her small hands that were again grabbing for the cell phone.

"I'll give you a ride!" I announced and marched off. She seemed confused and hesitated for a few seconds before she followed me across the grounds, past the side of the house to my Audi.

***

During the drive, she seemed restless. I could tell she was literally cursing every red traffic light and wishing I'd use all the horsepower my baby number... I was not sure anymore... had.

Mia was excessively nervous and I was worried she might collapse, so I did something I had planned to never to do again! I calmed her, spoke to her, once again risked everything, and made a fool somewhat out of myself — okay, what else could I expect when it came to her...

"Mia..." Without planning to, I sounded soft and calm as I lightly squeezed her leg. "What's wrong with him?" Distressed, she looked at me and I noticed the smooth skin of her cheeks was covered in tears. Well, wasn't that wonderful!

"He's been throwing up for the past four hours. He won't stop crying and no one can calm him!"

"Oh." That didn't sound good.

"I'm sure I can calm him, I just have to get there and be there for him. He only trusts me!"

Well, let's see if that turns out to be a mistake...

"We are almost there," I merely replied because her last

sentence conjured up too many negative memories.

I rounded the last corner and as soon as I came to a stop across the street from the home, she jumped out and ran full speed to the entrance. I was tempted to leave and pretend I didn't care, but a small part of me that was already not so small anymore, whispered to me that my girl needed me and that I should not waste time and get my damn ass in there! So, I got out swearing and actually followed her.

When I entered the hallway of the huge converted farmhouse with its colorful shutters, she sprinted around a corner and I heard her rushing upward. The floor beneath my feet creaked just like the door did when I closed it behind me. The wooden staircase also protested under my feet and although I had misgivings, I followed her up to the second floor and down the corridor to the end, where she ripped open a door and disappeared from sight.

By the time I entered the room, she was already sitting on the edge of a small old bed, wiping the forehead of a pallid Robbie.

"Mirti?" he asked in a fragile voice and lifted his tiny hand to reach for hers.

"Yes, my darling. I am here," she whispered and bent down to put her full red lips on his sweaty temple. I swallowed hard. Tears were running down his cheeks as he closed his eyes and breathed deeply.

"I feel so sick... I must have eaten something bad..." the little one muttered and snuggled against her palm. Oh...fuck!

The way he looked at her, as if she was his queen. And the way she was looking at him...as if he was her personal little prince, for whom she would lay the world at his feet.

"What did you eat?" Mia asked softly, a slight trace of a smile on her beautiful face.

"Grass. Johann and Stefan said it would be good for me," Robbie replied and I huffed. Both looked at me, surprised. Apparently, they just noticed me and I felt awkward, shifting my weight from foot to foot.

"Um... I..." I had no idea what to say. I felt like I was sticking my nose where it didn't belong, but then the corners of Robbie's pale lips turned upward before he briefly closed his eyes.

"I'm glad your friend is here too...Mirti... Just don't start fighting again!" Mia stared at Robbie. Then me. Then Robbie. Then me. And I smiled devilishly. *Let's see how you talk yourself out of this one, baby...*

"I did not tell him you're my friend," she said defensively and right then, she was my girl again, the one who had won my heart with her uncertainty. I released the doorframe and sauntered over to her. Before I could reply, the boy continued.

"It's so obvious. It's yucky the way he looks at you with his lovesick gaze. I hope you are not going to kiss now!" He certainly was on to us. I was about to sit down in the old rocking chair next to the bed when I stumbled my last step. Mia was completely overwhelmed; probably scared I might get angry. But even I was a bit taken aback.

How did the little shit arrive at that? I may find her seductive, sometimes even charming, and occasionally even sweet, but I did not love her! Hadn't in a long time!

"That I can promise you, boss," I laughed and finally sat down. Robbie smiled a bit more contently as he looked back and forth between the still-shocked, beet-red Mia and me.

"So, you aren't going to kiss?"

"We sure won't," I countered immediately without batting an eye. I don't know why...well, okay...I felt like teasing him a little. It would spark his spirit, which was better than wallowing in self-pity and whining about nausea.

Mia merely raised an eyebrow. "Is that so?"

Oh, yeah! It's not like we kissed! Oh, fuck! What was wrong with me today? How could I forget?

"Argh!" Robbie said soulfully and I chuckled as he buried his face in the pillow. "I feel sick again..." he mumbled suddenly and Mia jumped up.

"Do you have to throw up?' she asked and I rolled my eyes because she was panicking and overreacting. She lifted the boy into her shaky arms even though he was fine to walk by himself...

"I believe so," he announced and she ran with him into the bathroom. I felt sorry for him, especially when I heard him cough and choke... And still, I didn't move. Instead, I glanced around the dimly lit room while they were gone.

It was quite tiny, but for a children's home it was probably quite luxurious to have a private haven. Under the window was a small table made of light, partially splintered wood. The chair in front of it looked as if it would break at any moment and above the desk hung a few pictures, most featuring boxing gloves or two drawn stick figures beating each other up. For such a little guy, I thought he drew quite well... In addition to the work area in the corner, there was a wardrobe — without little bear knobs... On the wall above the bed hung a giant poster of Ukrainian boxers, who I knew personally because they sponsored the gym.

The wall was plastered with friendly yellow wallpaper that, unfortunately, was already quite faded and flaking in many places.

Mia came back with Robbie, whose face had a bit more color, but he seemed weaker than before.

As soon as she put him to bed, covered him, and sat next to it, his big eyes closed and he promptly fell asleep. Mia continued stroking his bright thin child hair and I realized it was exactly what he needed. Her touch. To know she would not disappear again, to know that even though he was dreaming, someone he could rely on was there in his little world, no matter what time. To know someone who would drop everything at a moments' notice when he needed that person, regardless of where that person was or what they were doing.

I could tell by her gestures and facial expressions Mia loved the child unconditionally. It was exactly the way she looked and touched me too. So why the betrayal? Back then, did she truly not want to be with me any longer? Was she capable of getting rid of me in such a vile way? Could she do something like that to Robbie? No! Definitely not because she loved him...

For real...with all her heart.

"Do you love me?" As soon as I uttered the words, I wanted to take them back...but it was too late. Mia's head whipped around. Calmly, I returned her look while on the inside the fiercest battle of a lifetime raged. An all-decisive battle or had I already lost? *Won?* Depending on...

"I love you more than life itself, Tristan," she replied, feigning calmness. However, her eyes betrayed that she felt like I did.

Robbie turned on his side and sighed blissfully. He pulled Mia's hand along so that she had to bend over him and held it tightly against his little chest like a stuffed animal.

Gently, she smiled down at him before looking up at me ›again. I stared back — mesmerized by those caramel colored depths...

"So, why did you do it then?" I whispered. The question plagued me for years until I arrived at the conclusion that the *why* didn't matter. What mattered was the fact *that* it had happened. Her eyes took on a suspicious glint, which I didn't like one bit, but I would still insist on an answer. I could see she had a guilty conscience, felt remorse, regret...but had no intention in redeeming herself.

"I was a trap. My father set me up." She sounded quiet and calm, voice trembling minimally, like she had prepared herself for this conversation about a million times.

"How?' She swallowed hard and tried to sit up somewhat, but Robbie grumbled restlessly and she froze.

"He threatened to put you in jail and destroy your career if I did not testify against you... The statement was supposed to be his leverage...and I stupidly believed him..."

I laughed humorlessly because if it was actually the truth, then yes, that was precisely what happened...

"Tell me, how was he supposed to make sure I went to jail? Did he have evidence against me," I asked.

She squared her chin in response to my caustic tone. "He had evidence that pointed to you. He had an ally..."

Is that so?" My brow shot up.

"Yes." Mia looked me squarely in the eyes.

"Who."

Now one of Mia's eyebrows raised in such an obvious way that a verbal response was no longer required. Immediately, I knew who she was talking about. EVA!

Promptly, I started to laugh.

The woman who had played my alibi girlfriend and who had always been Mia's pussy rival, may act like a complete lunatic but, compared to Mia, *would* not be able to do such... Besides, what evidence did she supposedly have against me? She had always been too clueless as well as stupid.

"Forget it!" I had to laugh and when Robbie rolled over

I abruptly stopped. "Now you've given yourself away! Tell that fairy tale to someone else!"

"But it is the truth!" she said defensively and a few octaves too high. Robbie groaned.

"You know what, Mia Marena?" I snarled contemptuously. "I'm in no mood for your bullshit!" I forced myself to talk softer and stood up. Mia stared at me, shocked. She probably didn't expect me to react so harshly to her lie. "Eight years ago, for whatever fucking reason, you had enough of me...and I don't get why you are now going through all the trouble to dish out such fucked up crap!"

I ran a hand through my hair as I walked to the door.

"Tristan, no!" In the next moment, she hugged me from behind. I had no idea how she had managed to catch me so quickly, but her arms wrapped tightly around my stomach. Her face pressed between my shoulder blades. My shirt was soaking wet and she shivered all over, but still kept a tight grip on me. Frantically.

With my hand already on the knob, I stopped and stared straight ahead at the door.

"Let go of me," I demanded silently.

"Never!" she immediately swore and tightened her grip on me.

"What more do you want from me, Mia?" I hissed between clenched teeth and almost crushed the doorknob in my fist.

"You!" I rolled my eyes hearing her sobbing reply. *Why*

did I even ask?

"Why would you want me the way I am now?"

"I've always wanted you! No matter which you!"

Unnerved, I huffed because we simply weren't making progress.

"Okay, so be it. I'm not good enough for you." Somehow, I had to keep her at bay, dammit! All of it was already way too intimate.

Dangerously so!

Now, she snorted wryly and rubbed her nose across my back, where she deeply inhaled my scent.

"I know I hurt you. Look, not everything happened the way you pieced it together over the years... If only you had a little more confidence in us...then...you would have seen it. But I can understand what happened; I even fell for it... No woman has ever given you a reason to trust her, but you can trust me! I've learned from my mistakes," she suddenly whispered. "I know you are purposefully keeping me at a distance, Tristan, but you will not succeed! Never!

FUCK! How was it the little slut knew me so well?

"Don't you realize it was fate that brought us back together again? Can't you see we still have the same feelings for each other we had eight years ago? They won't stop simply because you want them to! Don't you realize what we could give each other? Why make it difficult on ourselves? How many times in recent weeks have I tried to get rid of you? How many times did you send me away? And yet, here we are, together again!"

"All I know right now is that you should stop ruining my shirt with your salt water..." And with that, I removed my hand from the doorknob...hung my head and gnashed my teeth. When she was right, she was right — dammit...

"I need you... *Please...*" she whispered hoarsely and I sighed resignedly... As usual, I had no chance when she acted that way... *Oh, damn old tactics...*

"Yes, okay." I waved her off and only then did she let go of me and without saying a word but clearly relieved, she went back to Robbie's bed. She smiled at me and self-consciously wiped the tears away as I sat back down in the rocking chair and watched how she stroked the little boy.

"Thank you, Tristan," she said and I leaned toward her, supporting myself with my hands on the mattress on either side of her ass so I was again oh-too-close to her and her scent.

"Don't thank me yet. I demand retribution, Miss Angel," I murmured. She bit her lip hard and drew my attention back to her damn cherry things again.

"Stop. Chewing. Your. Lip!" I hissed and she responded with a silent "Oh!" that released her lower lip from her teeth.

"Good girl." I patted her cheek, leaned back, and let my gaze travel around the room once more and dryly noted, "Quite a fucked up place." Naturally, Mia was immediately defensive.

"We have no money to renovate."

"Honestly?" Too bad for the little guy...

"Yes." She looked away from me to Robbie, who was still sleeping peacefully. "The house needs a lot work. Windows and doors need to be insulated, the heating system needs a complete overhaul, and everything could use a fresh coat of paint and new flooring. We are actually in ruins. And we are no longer receiving state funds; this home belongs to Sister Carmen. She founded it with four other nuns, all of whom have already passed on... She is broke and struggling every month to pay the bills. I don't think she can keep this place open much longer..."

"Then what?" I asked because I didn't like the thought of it.

Mia shrugged. "Then all of us lose our jobs and I'll probably never see Robbie again..." Her pain did not escape me, although she suppressed it immediately because she was a fighter. Always to the extreme — which was typical for Mia when she loved something.

"We are organizing an Oktoberfest with a beer tent to raise money. It was the older children's idea..." Crap, she was so attractive when her eyes shined full of hope.

"Oktoberfest? With beer? Lederhosen and dirndls?" I inquired quite excitedly with a raised eyebrow — I had dirndls on my mind.

Mia laughed softly. "Yes, with dirndl and lederhosen, but with lemonade."

"Crap!" I pumped the air with one fist, which she accompanied with a slight chuckle before chewing on her lip again — brooding.

"We still have no idea how we'll manage it in two weeks because, as usual, we lack funds and equipment, but we have no choice since the advertising is sponsored and we've already distributed it. So, it will happen... No matter how... We need every penny the visitors are willing to part with."

"It'll work out." I winked at her and before she could reply, I voiced my next question. "What exactly did you have in mind?"

"Well..." now she was all fired up. Typical! When she cared about something, she grew passionate.

Oh, yesss...

"We'll definitely have bratwursts and pretzels, that is a must. Then we want to set up a few booths where the kids can throw at cans, paint each other's faces, bow and arrow shooting, handcrafts, and a booth selling hand-made pottery, an egg-spoon race or sack races, a petting zoo would be nice... and something for the kids to roughhouse on because they like it so much ..."

"A boxing ring..." I added, grinning and her eyes widened.

"YES!" She clapped her hands and grinned at me euphorically, which made me laugh because she was too cute...

"Will you help us?" Now she even clung to my sleeve and lightly tugged on it. And then there were her joyful wide eyes. How was I supposed to resist her, seeing her like that? How was I supposed to *even* resist her? I sighed resignedly when I realized I would never be able to do it.

"Yessss..." I said reluctantly.

"YESSSSSSSSSSSSSS!" she screamed so loud she woke up Robbie. Mia quickly went to the bathroom with him while I used the time to go outside for a smoke and stare at the moon.

***

By the time I was back upstairs, Mia had fallen asleep lying next to the boy in his tiny bed. She was spooning him with one arm wrapped over his hip. Her lips were pulled into a slight smile. He smiled just as sweetly. Both looked completely relaxed, obviously comfortable with each other... My heart knotted up. Robbie embodied part of the future that we had always envisioned for us but had never achieved. It was as if he had existed all these years as a part of us both... It was crazy, but that was what I felt when I looked at him — as if he actually was a part of me and the link that would somehow always bond Mia and me together. A small descendant of my being, who had and would save the space the universe had chosen for me next to her side for as long as it took for me to be ready again to command it. But he did not move into the background now to just disappear...not at all...

I caught myself picturing them as *my* family.

They would sleep in my home, in their beds, in my secluded wood cabin with the knowledge that I was watching over them so nothing would ever happen to them.

As I sat there smiling down on them, I was well aware I would never be alone again.

In the life that Mia and I had imagined eons ago, it would have been possible. It had represented reality — our future. But in the last few years, I lost faith in our imaginary life, probably due to my own doing because ultimately, one alone was responsible for how one turned out. Thanks to Mia, I found my way again. As always, she brought out the good in me because she was always the only one who saw something positive in me no matter how nasty I behaved. She always believed in good for that was simply the way she was. A human being always projects onto others...

And so, I caught myself as I bent over her and just one damn time, carefully and gently pressed my lips against her smooth forehead.

Somehow, I could no longer suppress feeling they were really mine... That strange – albeit utopian – certainty was steadily increasing in me the longer I looked at it...

During that night as I watched over her as she slept, I took Robbie to throw up so Mia could continue resting and when he eventually fell back asleep on my lap, it happened... I stepped out of the darkness and back into the light because no one else would do it for me. Suddenly, I was facing the 18-year-old grinning prick I once was.

And Mia Angel belonged to old Tristan like the fucker.

She was his girl. She was everything that made life worth living, everything he ever needed in order to know who he was, where he stood, and where he was supposed to go. And it felt unusually great to embrace the feelings that had been always dormant within him. That younger, carefree, playful side — the side no person should ever lose.

I probably never stood a chance because you cannot go against your nature without breaking at some point — I was on the rebound.

But first, I still had to learn to make peace with the past. I was still a little resistant to completely letting go. For that, I saw too many inconsistencies that threatened my insight. Mia and I had to expel our demons if we ever wanted to make headway. And we would, a fact I was irrevocably certain of.

I accepted all of that in those minutes, which possibly made me into a new/old person, although I never made the mistake to think further about the event.

In fact, only one thing mattered: Mia Angel was here with me after eight damn years and still embodied everything I needed.

We had already wasted far too much time with banalities as if we had eons to live instead of just a short crappy life.

One that I wanted to spend with her...

... and would.

Note of Thanks

My dear lovers... I hope this ending leaves you in a more relaxed state than the previous ones! You can thank Anke. I was fine to leave it as another cliffhanger, but she said I would have to worry for my life and since I like my life, I've given you (hopefully) a beautiful ending... J That way, one thing is certain: The deserved happy ending for Tristan Wrangler and Mia Angel... After all, according to Tristan, only a few inconsistencies had to be resolved (Francesco, Leo! *devilish grin) Besides, Vivi and the rest of the Wrangler clan also have to learn of Mia's appearance and especially of Robbie! (My hero!) Will he get what every kid deserves? A loving family? Oh, man... I almost want to let you in on it already. However, the answer will have to wait.

Now, almost a one year is behind us. I never imagined the consequences before I published *The Unholy Books of Tristan Wrangler – Book 1.* So I became more engaged when I set the last point on *My Girl*! I have been struggling with this series! You have no idea how greatly a story can be misunderstood providing one wants to... But it was worth it! And luckily, I have brave comrades who have always been there for me when I was down... This book would not be what it is without Babels. For CS, the first time we worked together was four years ago and it is still an important part of my private life and my personal muse to this day. The stories that live in her head are awesome! Tristan and Mia are also her children!

Time and again, Anke...and Peter, the A.P.P. Verlag (my lion family)... Thank you!

Belle... my editor... I have known you for so long and it never gets boring J Certainly not! I've never met such a conscientious person like you. Yes, you're a smart ass, but almost no one I know, knows as much as you do! You are a fucking genius! Thank you for that!

Thanks also to Emma and her cell phone! (You know what I mean! I love you guys!)

And thanks to Caro without whom I might have deleted everything just before the release from sheer excitement and said, "I'm sorry, but Tristan was simply too hot and the laptop burned up." Of course, also thanks to all beta readers!

And a big fat thank you to my translators, who put their whole heart into this series and translated it so beautifully that my eyes regularly watered and thank you for taking care of the poor souls of this world. I wish there were more people like you! <3

I have met so many wonderful people without whom I would not be where, or better said, I would not be who I am now. They have helped me a great deal, taught me so much, and especially shown me that distance, appearance, and age, play no role when it comes to friendship. Obviously, there were also setbacks where people took their masks off and showed me their true faces, tried to hurt me. But that too, is probably part of one's development... In the end, it only encouraged me to do what I do!

I have laughed and cried, won and lost. I have gotten excited about unjustified criticism and have delighted /suffered/celebrated at review readings. I have fully enjoyed talking to you on Facebook... Each individual message has made me happy and I often read your incredible words to my husband with tears in my eyes. My highlight was and always will be feeling your passion and I know you have grown fond of one part of my soul as much as I have.

That is the greatest compliment for an author!

And I thank you for it!

Yours, Don Both

About Don Both

Don Both, aka Bethy Zimmermann is 30 years old. Her parents are from Prague in the Czech Republic. At the age of 12, her class held a short story contest where she discovered her true great love — writing. During her schooling and vocational training as a nanny, she wrote throughout the day and drew comics at the same time. At first, she created animal stories, family stories, fantasy stories ... As she grew older, her novels and male protagonists became hotter and hotter and she discovered her other great love: eroticism.

In 2010, she took the big step and went public with her novels. Through her cheeky, provocative, and extraordinary writing style, she quickly gained an enthusiastic fan base. At the time, the young woman won several competitions and prizes — for example, "Best Fanfiction Author" and "Best Erotic Story".

At the time, her husband's health was declining and the company where she worked as a baker's assistant went bankrupt. Practically overnight, the small family became Hartz 4 recipients (Welfare, unemployment program). In dire straits, the desperate mother discovered Amazon Self-publishing and with their last money published "The unholy Book of Tristan Wrangler". It was a smash hit. What every author dreams about. It has become a bestseller that has since grown into one of the most widely read eBooks on the German market.

Since then, she and her two best friends founded A.P.P. Verlag (publisher), which includes more than 30 successful authors. In the meantime, she became acquainted with the media. Several newspapers wrote articles and she was on television.

Privately, the curvy dynamic woman is committed to animal welfare and the fight against body shaming, while trying every day to do something good. She loves yoga and resides with her cats, her super sweet German Shepherd dog, husband, and son in a small Bavarian town.

Already published by Don Both:

The Unholy Books of Tristan Wrangler, Book 1
My Girl